Stephanie
LAURENS.

The Taming of
Ryder Cavanaugh

piatkus

PIATKUS

First published in the US in 2013 by Avon Books,
An imprint of HarperCollins Publishers, New York
First published in Great Britain in 2013 by Piatkus
by arrangement with Avon

A CIP catalogue record for this book
is available from the British Library.

ISBN 978-0-7499-5875-6

Printed and bound by CPI Group (UK) Ltd, Croydon, CR0 4YY

Papers used by Piatkus are from well-managed forests
and other responsible sources.

MIX
Paper from
responsible sources
FSC® C104740
www.fsc.org

Piatkus
An imprint of
Little, Brown Book Group
100 Victoria Embankment
London EC4Y 0DY

An Hachette UK Company
www.hachette.co.uk

www.piatkus.co.uk

Acknowledgments

Dreaming up just the right title for a pair of books, especially when working in a long-running series, isn't anywhere near as straightforward as one might think. There are numerous variables that have to be considered, including length and implication of words used, as well as simple reader appeal. Our team came up blank for the title of Henrietta Cynster's story, the preceding work, first in the Cynster Sisters Duo, so we turned to readers for suggestions for that book—and recognizing that some brilliant person might come up with a matched pair of titles, we also asked for title suggestions for this book, Mary Cynster's story, the second of the Duo pair. For both books, we listed our team's best suggestion plus the best four suggestions submitted by readers for all readers to vote on—and thus were both books titled: Henrietta's tale became *And Then She Fell,* courtesy of one reader's fabulous suggestion, and by reader acclaim Mary's tale was titled *The Taming of Ryder Cavanaugh,* which was my working title. But I wanted to give a special mention to Lisa Gunn, of Parkdale, Victoria, Australia, who suggested the title that was a close runner-up, and to thank all my readers who participated and made the Cynster Sisters Title Challenge such a blast!

This book is dedicated to each and every one of you. Enjoy!

The Cynster Family Tree

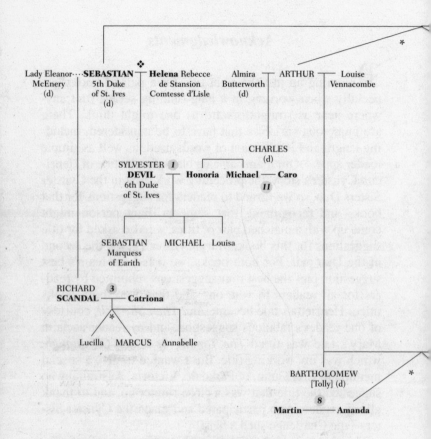

Lady Eleanor···**SEBASTIAN** ⎯ **Helena** Rebecce   Almira ⎯ ARTHUR ⎯ Louise
McEnery   5th Duke   de Stansion   Butterworth   Vennacombe
(d)   of St. Ives   Comtesse d'Lisle (d)
                (d)

CHARLES
(d)

SYLVESTER *1*
DEVIL ⎯ **Honoria** Michael ⎯ **Caro**
6th Duke   *11*
of St. Ives

SEBASTIAN   MICHAEL Louisa
Marquess
of Earith

RICHARD *3*
SCANDAL ⎯ **Catriona**
        *

Lucilla MARCUS Annabelle

BARTHOLOMEW
[Tolly] (d)

8
Martin ⎯ **Amanda**

MALE Cynsters in capitals   * denotes twins
CHILDREN BORN AFTER 1825 NOT SHOWN

THE CYNSTER NOVELS

1. Devil's Bride   *4. A Rogue's Proposal*   *7. All About Passion*
2. A Rake's Vow   *5. A Secret Love*   *8. On a Wild Night*
3. Scandal's Bride   *6. All About Love*   *9. On a Wicked Dawn*
                                                     10. The Perfect Lover

❖Cynster Special—*The Promise in a Kiss*

CBA#1—Casebook of Barnaby Adair #1—*Where the Heart Leads*

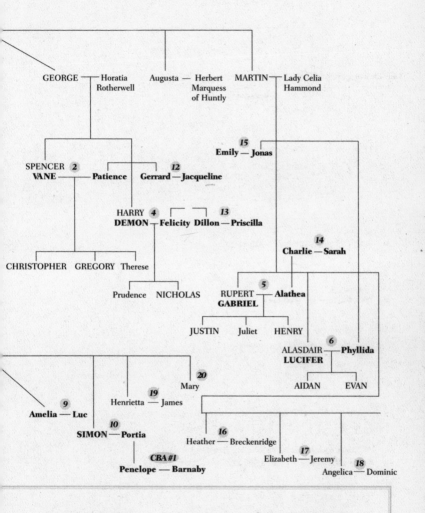

GEORGE — Horatia Rotherwell Augusta — Herbert Marquess of Huntly MARTIN — Lady Celia Hammond

15 Emily — Jonas

SPENCER **2** VANE — **Patience** **12** Gerrard — Jacqueline

HARRY **4** DEMON — Felicity Dillon **13** — Priscilla

Charlie **14** — Sarah

CHRISTOPHER GREGORY Therese

Prudence NICHOLAS

RUPERT **5** GABRIEL — **Alathea**

JUSTIN Juliet HENRY

ALASDAIR **6** LUCIFER — **Phyllida**

AIDAN EVAN

20 Mary

9 Amelia — Luc

Henrietta **19** — James

SIMON **10** — Portia

Heather **16** — Breckenridge

Elizabeth **17** — Jeremy

Angelica **18** — Dominic

CBA #1 Penelope — Barnaby

The Taming of
Ryder Cavanaugh

Chapter One

"He's the one you've set your sights on?"

Mary Alice Cynster jumped a foot into the air—or so it felt. As her jarred senses reestablished contact with terra firma, fury seared through her. Swinging around, she glared—at her irritating, infuriating, utterly irrepressible nemesis. Quite why Ryder Cavanaugh had elected himself to the role she had no idea, but since a brief encounter at her sister Henrietta's engagement ball two nights ago he'd been dogging her heels, assiduously transforming himself into a hideously distracting pest.

Before them, the Felsham House ballroom was awash with the crème de la crème of the ton, the silks and satins of ladies' gowns bright splashes of color against the black of gentlemen's evening coats. Coiffed heads gleamed, jewels glittered, and hundreds of well-modulated voices rose in polite cacophony.

She'd retreated into the shadows beneath the minstrels' gallery the better to consider her target. She'd been so absorbed studying him that she hadn't noticed Ryder drawing near; despite his size, he moved smoothly and silently. As usual, his impeccable, severely styled evening clothes only served to emphasize the fluid strength harnessed within his long, muscled frame. With one broad, elegantly clad shoulder negligently propped against the wall alongside her, he regarded her with his customary, hooded, lazy lion gaze.

Others were often fooled by Ryder's amiable, gentle giant, lackadaisical air; she never had been. Behind those brilliant hazel eyes lurked a mind as incisive, decisive, and ruthlessly capable as her own.

Yet despite the deflective glamour of his normally impenetrable languid sophistication, from his tone and the fact his lids had briefly risen, his eyes momentarily widening, identifying the object of her interest—by surreptitiously looking over her shoulder—had genuinely surprised him.

Uttering a mental *damn!*—he was the very last person she would have chosen to share that information with—she fixed her gaze, basilisk-like, on his green and gold eyes. "Go. Away."

Predictably, the order had no effect; she might as well have saved her breath. Ryder—correctly styled the fifth Marquess of Raventhorne, a title he'd inherited on his father's death six years before—was widely acknowledged as a law unto himself. There were few gentlemen society's grandes dames recognized as such—noblemen with sufficient personal power that it was deemed wiser to allow them to stalk through the ton's ballrooms, drawing rooms, and dining rooms without let or hindrance, as long as they abided by society's rules, at least well enough to pass. It was one of those unvoiced social accommodations.

Even as she held her ground—and her glare—Mary was well aware of all the aspects of Ryder's personal power.

At such close quarters, it was impossible not to be.

As if contemplating a curious, potentially succulent morsel, he looked down at her; as she was not only the youngest of the current generation of Cynster girls but also the shortest, and he stood well over six feet tall, that degree of down should have been intimidating, yet she'd never felt intimidated by him. Distracted, thrown off-balance, even mentally tripped to the point of feeling she was somehow falling, yes, but threatened in even the smallest way, no. Then again, she'd known him in passing for as long as she could remember; their families were among the oldest in the ton, and so *knew* each other in the way such families did.

His lushly lashed hazel eyes had remained unwaveringly fixed on her face, on her eyes. "You can't seriously imagine Rand will be a suitable husband for you."

She tipped up her chin, but looking down her nose at him was beyond even her. "I should think it patently obvious that *that* is a determination I will make for myself."

"Don't bother. You won't suit."

"Indeed?" She hesitated, but if anyone would know his half brother's aspirations, Ryder would. She arched her brows and infused sufficient disbelieving hauteur into her tone to, she hoped, tempt him to share. "And why is that?"

While he considered obliging and she waited, she wondered if perhaps denying having any particular interest in Randolph—Lord Randolph Cavanaugh, one of Ryder's half brothers and the nearest to him in age—might have been the wiser course . . . but when at Henrietta and James's engagement ball she'd summarily dismissed Ryder, declining an invitation most ladies of the ton, young, middle-aged, or ancient, would kill to receive, she'd unintentionally piqued his curiosity, and just like any feline he'd been, albeit apparently idly, stalking her ever since.

Even though tonight was only the second evening since the engagement ball, Ryder was more than intelligent enough to have divined her purpose. So no, there really was no point attempting to mislead him on that score—he would only grow more diabolical.

As his lips gently curved and he drew breath to speak, she fully expected him to be diabolical anyway.

"Permit me to list the ways." His voice was so deep that it was a rumbling purr. "First, allow me to point out that, as the last unmarried Cynster female of your generation, you are regarded as a matrimonial prize."

She frowned. "That's the last thing I need, but"—she searched his eyes—"I don't see why I should be considered so. I'm the youngest, and while admittedly my dowry is nothing to be sneezed at, I'm certainly not a diamond-of-the-first-water or a major heiress." As, apparently, she had to put up with him, she saw no reason not to pick his well-connected and well-informed brain.

Inclining his head, Ryder bit his tongue against the impulse to inform her that while she was correct in stating that she did not qualify as a diamond-of-the-first-water, that failure stemmed more from an excess of personality than any lack of beauty; she was more than attractive enough—vibrantly and vividly attractive enough—to turn male heads and engage male imaginations, something he'd grown exceedingly aware of over the few days during which he'd been shadowing her, driven by curiosity, pricked pride, and some less identifiable fascination. "You have, however, missed the critical point. *You* are the last chance for any of the major families to ally themselves with the Cynsters in this generation. It'll be a decade or more before your cousins' children, the next generation, come on the marriage mart. Consequently, no matter what you might wish, you are, indeed, a prize in that regard. And, of course, Rand will inherit neither title nor estate." Unlike him. His eyes locked on hers, he dismissively arched his brows. "Ask any of the grandes dames and they'll tell you the same. Everyone expects you to marry well."

She made a sound suspiciously like a snort. A smile tugged at his lips; he understood the sentiment.

But then she shook her head. "No. If that were the case, I would have been besieged."

"Not yet." He saw no reason not to share the news. "But next Season you will be. You're only twenty-two, and this year there's Henrietta's engagement and her upcoming wedding—major distractions for your family. Matrimonially speaking, no one is looking at you at the moment." Only him. And he was now intent on stealing a march on all his potential competitors.

Her lips—rosebud pink and unexpectedly lush in such a youthful face—firmed. "Be that as it may, that's all about what others think, while in the matter of whom I wed, it's what *I* think that counts." Her expression grew even more belligerent. "And in all other respects—"

"Rand will not suit. He's six years younger than I am, only two years older than you." As he stated those facts, he realized what one of the reasons she'd chosen Rand as her potential husband was. "And in case it's escaped your notice—although I'd wager a significant sum it hasn't—while at twenty-four a gentleman might be mature in body, he's rarely mature in mind." The smile he allowed to curve his lips was entirely genuine. "Give Rand time and, trust me, he'll be just like me."

Which was precisely the transformation Mary intended to ensure did not occur. Turning away, she resumed her scrutiny of the gentleman in question; he was standing in a group toward the middle of the long ballroom. "In my estimation, Randolph will be the perfect husband for me."

Aside from all else, Randolph was a significantly *milder* version of Ryder; if she married Randolph, she was perfectly certain she would be able to influence him to the point of ensuring that he did not evolve into a nobleman anywhere near as lethally dangerous to the entire female sex as Ryder was. Indeed, marrying Randolph could be viewed as doing her gender a signal service; the female half of the population definitely did not need another Ryder. In addition to his physical impact, he was utterly unmanageable.

Fixing her gaze on Randolph, she reviewed his attractions. Unlike Ryder's golden-brown mane, Randolph's hair was dark brown, more like his mother Lavinia's brown locks. While Ryder wore his hair slightly longer so that it fell in intriguingly tousled, windswept locks—a potent inducement to women to run their fingers through the unruly mass—Randolph's hair was cut in a fashionable crop, neither long nor short, similar to many men present.

Randolph's shoulders were broad, although not as strikingly broad as Ryder's, and his frame was long and tended more to the lean than Ryder's did, but then Ryder was taller by several inches, so the impressive breadth of his chest was in proportion. Randolph was entirely in proportion, too—just on a more mundane, less godlike scale.

That, Mary inwardly admitted, more or less summed up the difference between the half brothers. Not just between Ryder and Randolph, but also Randolph's younger brothers, Christopher—Kit—and Godfrey. Ryder was the only child from his father's first marriage; Randolph, Kit, and Godfrey were the sons of the late marquess's second wife, Lavinia. There was a sister, too—Eustacia, known as Stacie. Mary knew them all socially, but not well; she had yet to learn all she wished given she intended to marry into the family.

She was impatient to get on, to move forward with her campaign to convince Randolph to offer for her hand. She'd spent the earlier months of this Season determinedly examining all the potential gentlemen; once she'd realized Randolph matched her requirements perfectly, she'd turned her attention to poking and prodding her older sister Henrietta into wearing the necklace a Scottish deity known as The Lady had gifted to the Cynster sisters. The Lady was connected to the family via Catriona, the wife of Mary's cousin Richard. Catriona was a principal, and apparently well-favored, priestess of the deity. Through Catriona, The Lady had decreed that successive Cynster female cousins should wear the necklace to assist them in finding their true heroes. As a group, they'd long ago defined their "one true hero" as the man who would sweep them off their feet into love and wedded bliss. Although initially all had been skeptical of the necklace's power, it had wrought its magic, first for Heather, then Eliza, then Angelica, and even though she'd persisted in not believing in it at all, most recently for Henrietta.

The necklace of amethyst beads and gold links from which a tapered rose quartz pendant hung had been passed on to Mary; it now circled her neck, the crystal pendant warm between her breasts.

And she believed—with all her heart and considerable will *believed*—that it would work for her.

But to help matters along, she'd already done her homework, studied the field, and identified Randolph Cavanaugh as her one—the perfect husband for her. All she really needed the necklace to do was to confirm her choice.

She'd received the necklace two nights ago, just before Henrietta's engagement ball; Henrietta had clasped it about Mary's throat and she'd been wearing it ever since. The previous evening had been the first opportunity she'd had to speak with Randolph while wearing the necklace; they'd both attended Lady Cornwallis's soiree, but while she'd spent more than half an hour in the same circle as Randolph, chatting and conversing, she, at least, had sensed . . . nothing specific.

She wasn't sure what she'd expected, but from all she'd absorbed from her cousins and Henrietta the necklace didn't actively *do* anything. It was more in the nature of a catalyst; wearing it would ensure her true hero appeared before her, but she couldn't count on more help than that. Couldn't count on any definite sign.

So she was going to have to spend more time with Randolph. If he was indeed her true hero, her undisputed one, then . . . something should happen. Something should ignite.

She shifted, casting her gaze wider, evaluating the ways of approaching him. "How best to do it?" she whispered.

Instantly, she was aware of Ryder leaning closer, trying to catch her words. She ruthlessly stifled the impulse—the nearly overwhelming urge—to glance his way; he was now so close that if she did she would almost certainly find herself staring into his mesmerizing green and gold eyes, with his wicked lips and sinful smile only inches away. . . .

She could feel him as a warmth, a temptingly seductive sensation, all down her right side. Alluring, sensual, wickedly so, his presence held an indefinable promise that effortlessly attracted the female of the species; she'd long been of the opinion he'd been born with that particular brand of sensual charm oozing from his pores.

It wasn't that she didn't feel the effect, didn't recognize the tug for what it was, didn't react, but rather that she'd realized long ago that permitting her reaction to any male to show—whatever that reaction was—left him in charge, not her.

She'd long ago decided to forever remain in charge, most especially of herself.

With all the handsome and innately domineering males in her family, she'd had a lifetime of lessons on how such men behaved, how they reacted to signs of susceptibility on a lady's part, and what those telltale signs were.

She'd worked to eradicate them from her repertoire of instinctive reactions.

So while she felt Ryder's attraction as intensely as any lady, she gave him no reason to think he'd made any impression on her at all.

It wasn't his attention she wanted but Randolph's, and tonight she was determined to get it. She'd donned a new cornflower blue silk gown, which matched her eyes and also brought out the deep purple-blue of the amethyst beads.

Randolph. She focused on him. But while she could fix her gaze on him easily enough, the rest of her senses were slow to follow suit.

Damn Ryder. With him so close, no matter how she hid it, her wayward senses remained much more interested in him than in Randolph. Sensually speaking, while handsome, well-built, and in all physical respects highly attractive, Randolph nevertheless paled into insignificance when compared to his older half brother. There was not a woman in the ton—or out of it—who would not cede Ryder his own pedestal in the Hall of Superbly Handsome, Outrageously Attractive Men.

But handsome was as handsome did, and, put simply, Ryder was *too* handsome, more, too attractive on all levels and in all ways, for his own or anyone else's good.

Especially not for hers. She held no illusions regarding her own strength; Ryder possessed a will stronger than hers. She would never be able to manage him; no woman ever would.

Randolph, on the other hand, was entirely within her scope; he would suit her very well.

"At the risk of having you bite off my head," Ryder murmured from beside her, "just how do you envision convincing Rand that you are the lady for him?"

Ryder could hear movement in the gallery above their heads; with any luck, the musicians had arrived and would soon be putting bow to string. All he had to do to further his present cause was to keep Mary with him until they did.

Slowly she turned her head, just enough to bend on him what she no doubt imagined was a blackly discouraging gaze. She had a lot to learn; he would have been more discouraged if she'd smiled sweetly. Her resistance lured him as little else might; to one with an appetite as jaded as his, novelty was enthralling. However, in keeping with his aim to delay her departure from his side, he said nothing more but waited for her response with the infinite patience of the experienced hunter he was.

Her darkling gaze converted to a black frown. "I cannot imagine why that should be any concern of yours."

He opened his eyes wide. "I would have thought that was obvious—Rand is my younger brother, after all."

"Half brother." Tipping up her nose, she looked across the room at Rand again. "Admittedly, he's nothing like you, but I can't see why you should imagine he needs his older brother to shield him from such as I."

His lips twitched. "Impertinent chit." But she'd hit the nail very much on the head; she'd set her sights on his innocent younger brother and he did, indeed, feel protective. A lady like her would scare the breeches off Rand, at least at his current age.

That Ryder's protective impulses were presently aligned with his personal agenda was pure luck. Or, as most often occurred with him, a helpful twist of fate.

Eyes still on Rand, Mary lifted one delicate shoulder. "I am as I am, and what I am can hardly be construed as any threat to Randolph."

"That depends very much on one's point of view."

She shot him another dagger glance, but before she could speak, a raucous screech from above was promptly followed by the teasing lilt of the introduction to a waltz.

Perfect.

Before she had time to react, let alone escape, Ryder stepped out of the shadow of the overhang into the bright lights of Lady Felsham's crystal chandeliers and swept Mary a bow he made damn sure was magnificent. Extending his hand, he met her widening eyes. "Permit me to beg the honor of this dance."

Her gaze grew a touch wild and—yes—faintly horrified. He was watching intently so knew when she realized what would happen when he had her in his arms; she wouldn't be able to smother her response to him—the instinctive, innate response he knew, simply knew, she'd been suppressing.

Her gaze fell to his hand, then rose to his eyes. "No."

He smiled. Intently. "I'm sure you can see the sense in not causing a scene and focusing the attention of every last grande dame present on us. After all"—he arched one brow—"what possible excuse could you have for refusing to dance with me?"

Her eyes, locked with his, slowly narrowed. Her lips, those luscious lips he'd started to fantasize about, firmed, then compressed to a thin line. A second more and she nodded.

Once. "All right." She raised her hand, reached out—but froze with an inch separating her fingers and his palm.

Resisting the impulse to grab, to seize, he recaptured her gaze and arched a brow.

Indomitable will glimmered like steel in her blue eyes. "One dance. And then you'll take me to join Randolph's circle."

He didn't hesitate. "Done." Fingers closing around hers, he drew her nearer and turned toward the middle of the room, to where guests were drawing back, clearing a space for the dancers.

As he led Mary forward, his lips spontaneously curved. From the way she moved, light on her feet and almost eager by his side, he knew she thought she'd won, or at least had gained equal ground from the exchange.

But she was fencing with a master. He'd forgotten more than she would ever know about this particular game; he was entirely content to fall in with her plans.

But first came his price—the waltz. The first of many, regardless of her present inclination.

Reaching the dance floor, he turned and smoothly drew her into his arms, unsurprised when she stepped forward fluidly, raising one small hand to his shoulder, without a heartbeat's hesitation letting him settle the fingers of her other hand within his clasp, but rather than rising to his face, her gaze went to his right, to where Randolph had elected to remain chatting with his cronies.

Almost as if, despite being in his arms, her mind was elsewhere. . . .

He set his hand to the delicate planes of her back—and *yes,* there it was. The telltale quiver of reaction that shivered through her, no matter that she fought to damp it down.

Lips curving in anticipatory delight, he stepped out and swept her into the dance, and reveled in her instant, impossible-to-conceal response. The way her eyes flared as her gaze snapped to his face. The way her luscious lips parted just a fraction, the way her breath hitched.

From that instant on, her attention was his.

He didn't intend to ever let it go, let it wander.

Capturing her blue eyes, the color of cornflowers under a stormy sky, he whirled her down the floor, focusing on the swoop and sway, the sweeping dance of their senses, feeding the power, ruthlessly heightening the intensity of their effortless, near perfect grace.

If he was an expert on the dance floor, she was a svelte goddess. She matched him—not intentionally but instinctively stepping up to his mark.

Even while, her gaze locked with his, she held fast, denying any and all susceptibility.

Pure challenge.

Him to her, and her to him.

Like an invisible gauntlet, as they swirled around the floor they tossed intent and defiance back and forth between them, relying not on words but on the sheer power of what both of them could say with their eyes, communicate with their gazes.

All any observer would see was a couple absorbed with the dance, locked in each other's eyes.

No one else could see the tussle—the elemental battle—they waged.

A private war that, he suspected, would very soon advance to a siege.

His inner predator delighted, encouraged and enticed. He hadn't made any conscious decision; that wasn't how he operated. He'd long ago learned that, for him, success in life most frequently came through following his instincts.

That was what he was doing now—his instincts had led him to Mary Cynster, and now he was intent on capturing her.

She would be his, and he knew that outcome would be right. The right outcome to lead him forward, to getting what he wanted and needed from his life.

To making his life into what he wanted it to be.

And that was all he needed to know.

That, and that the battle was his to win. No matter her dismissiveness, his innate talents hadn't failed him. She might not want him now, but she would.

Mary could barely breathe. Her lungs felt tight, constricted, and then Ryder's lips slowly curved, and the intent in his gaze grew only more heated. More definite, more acute, more pronounced.

She couldn't pretend she didn't understand. She didn't waste time attempting to do so; he, damn him, had seen through her shields, if not from the first, then certainly in the moment when she'd glanced at Randolph and had temporarily forgotten that the far larger danger, in every conceivable way, had been standing directly before her.

That instant when Ryder's hand, large and so strong, had touched her silk-clad back—

She cut off the thought, the memory; that alone was enough to make her shiver. Again. And she didn't need to throw the lion whirling her down the floor any further bait.

What she did need to do was to regain control. If she'd learned anything tonight it was that Ryder—for whatever incomprehensible reason—had taken it into his head to hunt her, and he was one of the few within the ton with sufficient wit, talent, and skill to manage her. To inveigle and steer and, most irritating of all to admit, manipulate her—witness this waltz. Just the thought of being managed by anyone made her set her teeth, metaphorically dig in her heels and refuse . . . but she knew very well that, in this case, the course of wisdom was not to fight but to flee.

Wise ladies never took on more than they could handle— and she couldn't handle Ryder. No lady could.

Worse, an instant's consideration was enough to confirm that there was no sphere in her world in which he wouldn't dominate; he was, she judged, as adept at twisting the social conventions to his advantage as she.

So yes, she needed to run—to put as much space between them as possible and keep him at a distance, at least until he gave up the chase and turned to more willing prey.

Assuming, of course, that he was merely amusing himself in his customary way . . .

A worrying thought intruded, worming its way into her brain. There was no denying that she—young, unmarried, of extremely good family—didn't in any way match the specifics of his customary partners in dalliance . . .

She allowed the frown in her mind to manifest in her eyes. The fraught silence they'd maintained—a silence full of pressure and weight, and the tense clash of their characters, of two dominant personalities neither of whom would yield—still held.

Without thinking further, she broke it. "Why are you doing this?" She was perfectly certain she didn't need to be more specific.

A second ticked past, then he arched one tawny brow. "Why do you think?"

"If I knew, I wouldn't ask—and in your case, I wouldn't presume to know your mind."

His lips quirked, then, apparently reluctantly, curved in an appreciative smile. "Very wise."

She opened her mouth to pursue her point—and he drew her closer.

Close enough that the warmth of his body reached her through their clothes; close enough that she—all of her—was abruptly submerged in a sea of sensation, in the blatant physicality of being surrounded by him, by a male body so much larger and harder, heavier and more muscled, infinitely more powerful than hers.

Alien, so different, and yet so viscerally attractive.

Her lungs seized. Her thoughts scrambled. Her wits whirled faster than her feet.

As he whisked her through the turn—one unexpectedly constrained by the press of couples around them—she lost all ability to breathe. She couldn't even mentally blame him when he urged her closer still, the arm at her back tensing and tucking her protectively against him for that fraction of a second at the point of the curve, his hard thigh parting hers as he swirled them around . . .

And then they were free, out of the melee, and she fought to get her lungs working again.

The instant she did . . . "Ryder—"

The music slowed, then ceased. Lips curving, he quirked a brow at her, but very correctly released her and bowed.

Compressing her lips, she curtsied, then let him raise her.

Before she could speak and try to get an answer—any answer—from him, he raised his head, scanning the guests. "Now—where's Rand?" Ryder glanced down at her, a question—utterly mild and almost innocent—in his eyes. "If you're still keen to have me pave your way?"

She stared into his hazel eyes and didn't know what to think. She was suspicious—of course she was—but . . . she inclined her head. "Yes, please."

His eyes on hers, he waited, then arched a brow. "And . . . ?"

She knew what he wanted but let the moment stretch before yielding. "Thank you for the waltz."

He smiled—and that really wasn't fair. His smile was utterly heart-stopping. With a flourish, he offered his arm. As she placed her hand on his sleeve, he dipped his head to hers and softly murmured, "It was entirely my pleasure."

The undiluted sensuality in his tone sent another frisson of awareness streaking down her spine. Fighting the impulse to meet his eyes, she raised her head, breathed in, and looked around. "There's Randolph over there."

Without meeting Ryder's eyes, she tipped her head to where his half brother stood in a group of other guests, both male and female.

Ryder hesitated for only a second, then, as he'd agreed, escorted her to Randolph's side.

After insinuating Mary into Rand's circle at his brother's side—and earning a suspicious glance from his intended for his pains—Ryder exchanged a few polite words, then retreated. Although he knew all the males—all friends of Rand's—and was distantly acquainted with the young ladies in the group, he was sufficiently older to qualify as of a different generation; other than the young ladies' unwarranted interest in him, there was little real connection either way.

Idly drifting toward the refreshment room, he reviewed the evening's advances and owned himself satisfied with what he'd achieved. Having decided to marry sooner rather than later—later being when the grandes dames decided to take a hand in scripting his life—he'd thought to take advantage of having to attend Henrietta Cynster and James Glossup's engagement ball to further his aim. His eye had alighted on Mary, and instantly appreciating her potential he'd attempted to waylay her with nothing more definite than assessment in mind, only to be summarily dismissed.

That, of course, had been startling enough to focus him more definitely on her, which had resulted in him overhearing her admit that she was embarking on a search for "her hero"—the gentleman she intended to wed. She'd declared she'd already identified the lucky man, but until this evening he hadn't known which gentleman she'd singled out.

Learning that it was Rand she'd set her blue eyes on might have made him pause and step back, allowing his brother to make his own decision, except he knew very well that Rand had no interest in marrying yet—he was only twenty-four. The only reason he attended events such as this was because his mother, Lavinia, Ryder's stepmother, was trying her hand at matchmaking, and Rand was still of an age when he would rather acquiesce to his mother's insistence than face the alternative confrontation. Regardless, Mary and Rand would be a match made in hell, at least for Rand; Mary was far too . . . independent. Willfully strong. Single-minded, ruthless, and manipulative.

She would tie poor Rand in knots, then set him dancing to her tune.

She would, of course, try to do the same with Ryder, but not only was he more than a match for her, he was also quite looking forward to that battle. That tussle.

That *challenge*.

He knew himself well enough to admit that the prospect held significant appeal, along with the related fact that unlike most young ladies or even those more mature, Mary met his eyes constantly. When they conversed, she concentrated on their interaction, person to person, her and him, and as with all she did, her focus was absolute. Her attention didn't waver, nor was she readily distracted. When they spoke, her attention was all his.

His inner self had a great deal in common with the beast he was most frequently compared with; Mary's particular brand of focused attention was like a long stroke to his leonine ego and made his inner lion purr.

Reaching the refreshment table, he lifted a glass of brandy from a tray, sipped, then turned and, over the heads, surveyed her ladyship's guests. He let his gaze linger on Rand and Mary. They stood side by side, both listening, Rand avidly, Mary with barely restrained impatience, to one of Rand's friends, who, from his gestures, appeared to be relating some story involving riding.

Even from this distance, Ryder could see that while Rand was absorbed, Mary was disengaged. Well on the way to growing bored.

Which was precisely why he'd left her there, beside Rand, surrounded by the younger set and therefore bereft of stimulating interaction of any stripe. Or, specifically, any interaction that would engage her. All the better as contrast to the waltz immediately before.

Even better, Rand and his friends would find her a trifle

overwhelming and would treat her warily—which, more likely than not, would exasperate her.

Smiling, Ryder sipped again; Lady Felsham had provided a decently palatable brandy for her guests.

A stir alongside had him glancing down—into his step-mother's painted face. Brown-haired, dark-eyed, with the remnants of the beauty of her earlier years still visible in her face, now in her midforties and growing sadly dumpy, Lavinia, Marchioness of Raventhorne, had little to do with him—as little as he could manage. Moving with calculated slowness, he inclined his head. "Lavinia."

She flicked an irritated gaze up and down his figure, her gaze lingering on the large diamond he wore in his cravat; it had been his father's and was part of the family jewels, none of which she'd been permitted to appropriate after his father's death.

Alongside Lavinia, one of her bosom-bows, Lady Carmody, smiled obsequiously and bobbed a curtsy, to which he responded with an abbreviated bow. He'd long ago learned that implacable, icy civility worked most effectively in keeping Lavinia and her cronies at a distance.

"I have to say I'm surprised to discover you here." Lavinia fixed her slightly protuberant eyes on his face, as if searching for some hint of his agenda in his features.

"Really?" Meeting her eyes, Ryder slowly arched his brows. "I thought you knew this is my usual hunting ground. At present, I'm lacking succor, so decided to cast my eye over the herd."

Lavinia blushed. "Really, Ryder! There's no need to be explicit." She waved with exaggerated hauteur. "I'm sure I don't care where you search for your paramours."

Lady Carmody chuckled. When Lavinia and Ryder looked at her, she explained, "Well, Lavinia, the poor boy needs must find lovers somewhere, and I'm sure you would rather he find them here, in this crowd, than at some theater, or so I would think."

Ryder had never previously had reason to like Lady Carmody, but in return for that comment he stepped in to deflect Lavinia's burgeoning ire, about to break in a wave over her ladyship. "I spoke with Rand a little while ago. He's in that group over there." Ryder paused to allow Lavinia to follow the direction of his nod and locate her firstborn. "As to anyone's presence here . . . am I to take it that the interest that brings Rand here is similar to mine?"

Lavinia literally swelled with indignation. "Don't be silly!" But she continued to examine the group. "Unlike you, Randolph has no interest in dalliance. He's very correctly looking for the right lady with whom to settle down and continue the Cavanaugh line." Lavinia glanced at Ryder. "Someone needs to—it's what your father would have wanted."

Which was undeniably true, but it had been Ryder his father had asked for a promise to marry and continue the line. But rather than inform Lavinia of that, Ryder seized on the contemptuous dismissal in her tone to murmur, "And on that note I believe I'll take my leave." He inclined his head. "Lavinia. Lady Carmody."

Lavinia barely acknowledged him, but Lady Carmody shot him a conspiratorial grin.

Turning away, he set down the brandy glass and moved into the crowd.

Ryder was barely out of earshot when Lavinia gripped Lady Carmody's sleeve. "Look!" Lavinia breathed. "I hardly dared hope, but it appears my oh-so-delicate scheme has borne fruit."

Lady Carmody followed Lavinia's rapt gaze. "Well, well." After a moment of studying the group in which Randolph stood, her ladyship continued, "I have to admit, dear, that I really didn't believe that anyone could influence a chit like Mary Cynster, but there, indeed, she is, chatting quite determinedly to your Randolph."

"Yes!" Lavinia drank in the sight. "I told you—one just has to understand that suggesting anything to the likes of

Miss Cynster requires an excessively delicate touch. I've never once spoken to the girl myself, and I made sure none of the messages I seeded said anything specific about Randolph—the entire thrust was to very gently raise her awareness of him." Hauling in a deeply satisfied breath, Lavinia straightened. "And, clearly, my strategy has worked!" She glanced at Lady Carmody and beamed. "Now, I believe, we can leave nature to take its course. Randolph is no fool, and Miss Cynster will quickly discover she will find no better gentleman in the ton."

"Hmm." Lady Carmody was still studying the pair in question. "I assume that you've . . . ah, *seeded* the thought that Mary Cynster is the last Cynster girl unwed, and therefore the last chance for any family to secure a connection with her family, into your dear son's head?"

"Of course!" Lavinia linked her arm in Lady Carmody's. "But very gently, you see. Gentlemen of that age are so prickly about taking advice from their mamas, after all. But trust me." With a last glance across the ballroom at Randolph and Mary, Lavinia turned her friend to stroll in the opposite direction. "My seeds are well planted, and all looks set to bloom as it should." Raising her head, Lavinia smiled. "Which, I must say, I find *immensely* gratifying. I can't wait to inform Ryder once the engagement is made."

Well, darling, how was your evening?"

Mary glanced at her mother, Louise, seated next to her in the family's town carriage as it rolled sedately over the cobbles, taking them home. "Useful." She grimaced. "But, sadly, nothing more."

Louise smiled, her face lit by a street flare. Reaching out, she patted Mary's wrist. "Don't be in such a rush, darling. Your hero will come for you in good time."

Mary smothered a humph. Glancing down through the gloom, she considered the necklace, specifically the rose quartz pendant that lay nestled between her breasts. Stupid thing. She'd stood beside Randolph for over half an hour and once again . . . nothing. No real connection of any sort, and all he and his friends had wanted to talk about was horses!

There'd been a dearth of frissons of delicious expectation, and an absolute absence of any tightening of her nerves.

And certainly nothing even remotely like the sensations she'd experienced during that exquisite waltz with Ryder.

But she wasn't so stupid as to imagine that Ryder—he who could so effortlessly evoke said sensations—was her one. He couldn't possibly be; no female deity would ever pair a lady such as she, who valued being in charge so highly, with a nobleman who, beneath his lazy lion pelt, was nothing less than a lordly dictator.

And that Ryder did incite such feelings in her was neither here nor there; he elicited the same feelings in at least half the female population, if not more.

It was simply his way, his gift as it were, an intrinsic part of him he didn't even have to think to use.

"Incidentally, I was speaking with your aunts about the final arrangements for the wedding. Amazingly, everything seems to be falling into place perfectly, sufficiently so that the others and I have decided that a few days of peace in the country would be an excellent tonic to set us up to weather the stresses of the big day." Head back on the squabs, Louise continued, "We've decided to seize this moment of relative calm, so we'll be leaving for Somersham tomorrow and will return three days later. Just enough time to refresh ourselves."

Turning her head, Louise studied Mary. "You are, of course, welcome to come, but it is the height of the Season and your married sisters and sister-in-law are in town, so if you wish to stay . . . ?"

Mary frowned. She hadn't got anywhere with Randolph yet. She wasn't ready to even contemplate that she might be wrong and he might not be her one—perhaps she needed to spend time with him alone, or at least not in a group. "I'd rather stay." She shifted to face Louise. "And Amanda and Amelia, and Portia, too, attend all the balls I would wish to go to."

Louise nodded. "I'll send all three notes when we reach home. Provided they're willing to act as chaperons, I see no reason you can't remain and attend all the balls on our calendar."

"Good." Facing forward again, Mary turned her mind to evaluating the sort of situations into which she could draw Randolph Cavanaugh in order to reveal his herolike nature. His true nature with respect to her.

Chapter Two

Have a nice rest and don't worry about anything!" Mary hugged her mother, then stood back so her older sisters, Amanda and Amelia, could sweep in and plant fond pecks on Louise's cheeks.

"Never fear." Stepping back, Amanda cast an affectionate glance at Mary. "We'll keep her in line."

Louise laughed and patted both twins' shoulders. "I know I can rely on you both—and on Portia, too."

On cue, Portia stepped forward to hug Louise, then Henrietta, who had been in the library with her fiancé, James Glossup, wrestling with the question of where those of his more country-based family who were coming up to town for their wedding should be housed, came hurrying into the front hall, James in tow.

"Good-bye, Mama! Papa!" Henrietta bussed Louise's cheek, then turned to their father, Arthur, standing beside his wife, to repeat the process. "Have a lovely, restful time."

Arthur kissed Henrietta back, then released her. He and his brothers had elected to seize the opportunity to join their ladies for a few days of country peace—and shooting; while they'd waited for Louise to don her coat, the other girls had farewelled him.

It was an hour after breakfast, and Amanda, Amelia, Simon, and Portia had arrived to see Louise and Arthur off, and to ease any concerns they might have; with the whole family gathered in London to celebrate the upcoming wedding, everyone was eager to do their part.

Looking at his son, Simon, Portia's husband, who, smiling benevolently, was standing to one side of the hall, James, his best friend, alongside him, Arthur rumbled, "You're the effective man of the house, my boy—make sure you keep this gaggle in line."

Simon laughed.

So did everyone else.

"I'm sure everything will run perfectly smoothly," Amanda stated in her best haughty-matron voice. "And, after all, you'll only be gone for three days."

"Don't be anxious." Amelia squeezed Louise's hand. "Just enjoy the rest—you and the others have earned it."

Hudson, the butler, swung open the door and the jingle of harness reached them. Louise glanced outside. "Excellent— the carriage is here." Turning back to her brood, she swept them with a mother's eye. "Now be good and take care—in whatever manner those injunctions apply." Turning to Arthur, she smiled into his blue eyes, then let him twine her arm with his.

"Come along," Arthur said, then dramatically lowered his voice. "I think it's safe to leave them to it."

Louise laughed and allowed him to lead her down the steps.

The rest of the family followed them outside, gathering on the narrow porch to wave them away.

Once the carriage had turned the corner, Simon and Portia took their leave, Henrietta and James returned to the library and their delicate task, and Amanda, Amelia, and Mary retreated to the front hall to decide on their social arrangements.

"I can't go with you tonight." Amanda grimaced. "A rather dull dinner with some relatives of Martin's—it's been organized forever. But if you want to take a turn in the Park this afternoon, I could pick you up at four o'clock."

Mary nodded. "Yes, all right. It looks like it's going to

be a splendid day. But"—she looked hopefully at Amelia—
"what about the Castlemaine House ball this evening?"

Geraldine Carmody had been standing beside Mary in
Randolph's circle last night, and had moved on with Mary
when she'd quit the group; Geraldine had mentioned that
she'd heard Randolph and his friends say that they would be
attending Lady Castlemaine's event.

"Oh, I can chaperon you for that," Amelia said. "Portia,
too. We'll both be attending."

"Excellent!" Mary beamed. She and Amelia agreed that
it would be best for her to take the family's town carriage to
the ball and meet Amelia and Portia, both of whom would
be traveling to the event in their own carriages, in the Castlemaine House foyer.

"Just in case," Amelia said, pulling on her gloves. She and
Portia had small children, so emergency summonses were
always a possibility.

With all arranged to their mutual satisfaction, the twins
departed to walk to their own homes, leaving Mary somewhat at a loss. She debated joining Henrietta and James for
all of two seconds, but decided it was best to leave them to
work through the hurdles by themselves—if she joined in,
she would take over. She usually did.

And others usually let her.

Because it was easier that way.

She was very good at organizing, especially anything to
do with people, but Henrietta needed the experience of dealing with James's family more than Mary did.

Feeling rather virtuous for turning her back on the chance
to interrupt and take charge—the activity would at least
have kept her occupied—she drifted down the corridor to
the back parlor. Walking in, she shut the door, then continued her idle drift to stand before the windows.

Crossing her arms, she looked out over the rear garden
and waited for the wispy thought that had been nagging at
her all morning to grow more solid.

Eventually, it did.

"Ah." It was, she had to admit, a pertinent point. "Why on earth was Ryder there?" At the Felsham ball last night, and at the Cornwallis soiree the previous evening.

A few more minutes' consideration and the most likely explanation coalesced in her mind. "He must be looking for his next conquest." His next short-term lover; according to all reports, Ryder was not one for lengthy liaisons. Apparently he grew bored rapidly, much to the dismay of the ladies involved.

From all she'd gathered about gentlemen like him—wolves of the ton such as her brother and cousins prior to their marriages, or in Ryder's case, a lion of the ton, but the same framework applied—their preferred source of paramours was the bored matrons of the ton, women of their own class who understood society's restrictions and the rules pertaining to such illicit affairs.

"I suppose he has to find them somewhere, and there was certainly a good selection of bored matrons at those events, but there shouldn't be quite the same crowd at Lady Castlemaine's tonight—that will be more a matchmakers' gathering—so with any luck, Ryder won't be there, and I'll be able to get a clear tilt at Randolph." Without the distraction of his overpowering older brother. "Half brother. Regardless of what Ryder thinks, Randolph's nothing like him."

Encouraged by her deductions, she reviewed the possible opportunities the Castlemaine House event might offer in terms of getting Randolph alone.

We'll be somewhere over there." Pausing on the steps leading down to Lady Castlemaine's ballroom, Portia waved toward the far end of the room, then glanced back at Mary, on the step behind her. "Come and find us if you need us."

Already engaged in quartering the room, Mary merely hmmed.

Beside Portia, Amelia flicked open her fan and plied it vigorously. "Yes, indeed! That's where we'll be. It's already so stuffy, but at least the windows at that end are open." She, too, glanced back at Mary. "You know the ropes. Don't do anything we wouldn't have done at your age, and we'll come and find you when we're ready to leave."

Having located Randolph, once again standing in a circle composed of his male friends and several young ladies, Mary nodded. "Yes. All right."

She followed Amelia and Portia down the steps, then turned in the opposite direction and plunged into the crowd. Nearing Randolph's group, she paused and looked around. Spotting another young lady eyeing the same group, she smiled and glided over, introduced herself, and after a short exchange sufficient to establish their common backgrounds and their common cause, she and the young lady—a Miss Melchett—linked arms and strolled over to join the conversation.

By exploiting the angle of their approach, Mary ensured that, as the circle obligingly expanded to accommodate them, she fetched up by Randolph's side.

Her immediate objective achieved, she waited patiently for George Richards to complete the story he'd been telling—yet another tale of the hunt and horses. Immediately he'd received the expected accolades from his friends, along with rather weaker applause from the young ladies, Mary fixed her gaze on Colette Markham, directly across the circle and, if Mary was any judge, with her eye on Randolph's friend Grayson Manners, and inquired, "Has anyone seen the new play at the Theatre Royal?"

Colette met Mary's eyes and leapt in to remark, "I had heard it was the best theatrical event of this Season." She turned to Grayson, beside her. "Have you seen it, Mr. Manners?"

As luck would have it, Grayson had. Under Colette's and Mary's encouraging tutelage he was induced to give a detailed description of the play. Immediately he concluded, Miss Melchett chimed in with her experience of the competing offering at the Haymarket.

Mary glanced at Randolph, caught his eye, and smiled. Under cover of the others' conversation, she murmured, "Are you fond of the theater, Lord Randolph?"

"Ah . . . well." Randolph's eyes widened fractionally. "I'm not sure I've had enough experience of it to judge—well, most of my plays have been viewed from the pit, so it's not quite the same thing, is it? I daresay, in a few years, I'll grow quite partial to it—the more formal play-going, I mean."

Mary kept her smile in place. "But what of the plays themselves? Do you prefer Shakespeare or the work of more recent playwrights?"

Randolph's eyes widened even more. "Ah . . ."

From across the ballroom, Lavinia, Marchioness of Raventhorne, watched her son conversing semiprivately with Mary Cynster, and smiled approvingly.

Seeing that smile, Lady Eccles, beside whom Lavinia was presently standing, followed Lavinia's gaze, then her ladyship arched her brows. "Well, my dear—that *is* a development."

"Indeed." Lavinia glanced at Lady Eccles's face, noted her ladyship's suitably impressed expression. "It's really very gratifying. They spent time together last evening, and clearly all is progressing favorably. They make quite a couple, do they not?"

"And, not to put too fine a point on it, such an alliance will greatly aid your Randolph." Lady Eccles glanced inquiringly at Lavinia. "I don't suppose you had any hand in bringing the two together?"

Lavinia chuckled. "I might admit to a very small prod here, an almost imperceptible push there. But it's been more in the way of a word in the right ear at the right time, just so they don't miss the opportunity that clearly lies before their feet. You know young people—they never do see their own best interests clearly."

"Indeed not. I've had words on that subject with my own sons often enough." Lady Eccles gathered her shawl. "But as loath as I am to drag you away, my dear, I do have to get on. I promised Elvira I would look in on her soiree." Lady Eccles glanced again across the ballroom. "Are you coming, or do you wish to remain and ensure all continues as you would wish?"

"No . . . no." Reluctantly, Lavinia dragged her gaze from her son. She'd come to the ball in Lady Eccles's carriage. "I'm sure they'll manage perfectly well without any intervention from me—and I, too, promised Elvira I would make an appearance."

"Right then." Lady Eccles turned toward the ballroom steps. "Let's be off."

After one last, quietly delighted glance at the tableau across the ballroom, Lavinia followed.

Mary, meanwhile, had struck the first serious hurdle along her path to wedded bliss. Namely Randolph's—and his friends'—lack of conversational depth. She was an excellent horsewoman, loved riding, and was reasonably fond of horses as well, but there was more to life than horse races, curricle races, and the hunt. After Miss Melchett's exposition of the play at the Haymarket, George Richards had reseized the conversational reins and rather bluntly drawn Randolph from their discussion of playwrights to ask him about some mare who had won the last race at Newmarket two weeks before.

Randolph had replied to George's query with far greater alacrity—and detail—than he had to her own. Randolph had then swung the conversation to the latest sale at Tattersalls.

With the air of one driven beyond bearing, Miss Fotheringay had spoken up the instant Randolph and Julius Gatling had finished exchanging views on the nags sold and the sums paid. "Has anyone visited Kew Gardens recently? The new conservatory is particularly fine."

Despite the obvious desperation and consequent weakness of the gambit, Mary, Miss Melchett, and Colette did their level best to keep the conversation on plants, herbs, and anything other than horses.

Mary had a strong suspicion that Julius knew precisely what he was doing when he seized on the mention of fever-few to swing the conversation back to the poultice his stable-man recommended for a bruised hock.

Jaw setting, Mary glanced around the circle. Exasperated desperation—or was it desperate exasperation?—shone in the other young ladies' eyes. Were all young men really this . . . young?

This immature?

Randolph, she felt sure, was not—could not be so—but thus far she'd only interacted with him in the presence of his cronies. Clearly, she needed to separate him from his pack.

As if in answer to her need, the strains of the first waltz of the evening floated out over the room. Brightening, she turned expectantly to Randolph, only to see a positively hunted expression flash across his face. He looked across the circle, to where Colette had turned, as expectantly as Mary, and was waiting for Grayson to ask her to dance.

Grayson looked at Randolph, then glanced at George, for all the world as if none of them had ever waltzed before, which was nonsense.

Looking back at Randolph, Mary saw his features briefly shift, signaling to his friends: *If we must, we must.*

But before she could do more than blink, Randolph smiled and bowed. "If you would grant me the honor of this dance, Miss Cynster?"

If his bow was a poor imitation of Ryder's, and his voice held no subtly suggestive undertones, at least he'd asked. Mary smiled and extended her hand. "Thank you, Lord Randolph. I would like to dance."

Taking her hand, Randolph smiled. "Please—just Randolph."

Telling herself that it was unrealistic to expect to feel any flash of awareness from his perfectly correct holding of her hand, Mary allowed him to lead her to the floor. She stepped into his arms, eager anticipation bubbling in her veins.

It would happen now. Whatever needed to spark would surely come alive as they waltzed.

Taking her in his arms, Randolph stepped out and whirled them into the circling throng. He was a creditable dancer, but she'd expected nothing less.

Yet as they revolved down the room, sedately twirling, entirely within the constraints of the strictest mores, she realized she had, in fact, expected more, but that was Ryder's doing. She had to stop comparing Randolph to his godlike older brother.

Just thinking of Ryder was enough to bring to life her all-too-vivid memories of the exceedingly intense waltz they'd shared the night before . . . she'd finally got what she'd wanted—Randolph, more or less alone—and courtesy of Ryder, her mind was wandering.

Determinedly, she refocused on Randolph's face—a face of nice features, not yet as strong or as distinguished as they one day would be. "It's already May—do you have any special expectations of this Season?" When he looked surprised, then somewhat at a loss, she elaborated, "Any goal you would like to achieve before summer arrives and we all quit the capital?"

"Ah . . . well, I had hoped to find a new pair for my curricle—"

"*Beyond* horses."

His eyes widened at her tone, but he kept his gaze fixed above her head, using the need to steer them through the revolving crowd as an excuse not to meet her eyes.

Ryder had barely glanced anywhere else throughout the waltz they'd shared.

"Actually . . . no." Randolph cleared his throat, and finally met her gaze. "I know . . . realize that some see my attendance, and that of the others, at events like this as indi-

cating some . . . specific interest—one beyond horses." He
drew breath, briefly glanced up as they negotiated a turn,
then looked back at her and faintly grimaced. "The truth is
we come purely to please our mothers, and the hostesses,
and the grandes dames. Well"—a roguish grin surfaced,
a charming twinkle briefly lighting his eyes—"that, and
to provide dance partners for young ladies such as you, of
course."

Mary studied his face, that twinkle, his grin. Was there
hope? But then she replayed his words, his weak attempt at
gallantry . . . and couldn't quite convince herself there was.

This wasn't right. Or something was wrong.

She quashed an impatient urge to haul the rose quartz
pendant from its nest between her breasts and look at the
damn thing—hold it up between them and see if anything
happened.

Before she could think of her next conversational thrust,
the music wound down and the waltz was at an end. But due
to the dance, she and Randolph now stood at the other end of
the room, and she realized the open windows Amelia had al-
luded to were in fact French doors, propped open and giving
access to a paved terrace.

As she rose from her curtsy, Mary noted several couples
strolling in the moonlight.

"That's your sister over there, isn't it?" Randolph nodded
toward Amelia, seated on a chaise nearby. "Do you wish to
head back with me, or . . . ?"

"Actually . . ." With one hand, Mary lightly fanned her
face. "I wonder if we might stroll on the terrace for a few
minutes and get some air. It's rather stuffy in here, don't you
think?"

Stuffy, and increasingly noisy and crowded; to anyone the
terrace would appear an oasis.

Randolph looked past her, through the French doors, but
made no move to fall in with her suggestion. "I, ah . . . I
really don't think . . ."

She smothered the impulse to frown and swung toward the French doors. "There are others out there—it's perfectly acceptable." She took one step, *willing* him to join her.

"Yes, but . . ." He teetered, literally teetered, then pulled back. Stepped back—away from her and the terrace. He met her gaze as, amazed, she looked back at him. "They're all couples—older than us."

Baffled, she glanced again at those ambling on the terrace, drenched in moonlight and clearly visible through the long windows. "They're not that much older."

"But they're . . . *courting*." He said the last word as if it was one not uttered in polite company.

Mary stared at him. She couldn't believe this was happening. She couldn't count the number of times gentlemen—admittedly not quite as young as Randolph—had attempted to inveigle her out of ballrooms onto shadowy terraces.

Now she'd engineered such an interlude in a perfectly acceptable way, and offered it up to Randolph—her hero—and he was balking?

No—*worse*—he was backing away!

"I, er . . ." Randolph gestured over his shoulder, up the ballroom. "I should get back or they'll send the cavalry . . . well, you know what I mean."

She was, indeed, starting to see the light. Randolph and his ilk were *frightened* of . . . young ladies like her.

Young ladies seeking a husband.

"Ah . . ." As if realizing that just leaving her standing there after she'd voiced a wish to stroll on the terrace probably wasn't the gentlemanly thing to do, Randolph halted his backward drift but, if anything, looked even more hunted. "I suppose . . . if you really want to—need to—get some air, then . . ."

For a fleeting instant, hope bloomed.

Randolph raised his gaze and looked around. "Perhaps we can find someone to walk with you."

Mary dragged in a breath. Held it. Spoke through her teeth. "Randolph—"

"Aha!" Randolph's eyes lit. "Just the person!" His heartfelt "Thank God" didn't need to be said; his expression relaxed as he looked past her. "Miss Cynster's feeling faint—she needs some air."

Mary's eyes widened as her suddenly jangling senses informed her just who had materialized behind her left shoulder.

"Indeed?" rumbled a deep drawl she recognized only too well. "Perhaps I can be of assistance?"

Turning her head, she looked up, up, into Ryder's handsome face. She met his eyes, read the amusement therein, and hung on to her temper. "Good evening, Ryder."

"Mary."

His eyes, a crystal medley of intense greens and browns, held her gaze . . . and as had happened the previous evening he seemed to effortlessly snare her senses so that the rest of the world fell away. . . .

Abruptly blinking free of his spell, she tartly stated, "Randolph and I were—"

She glanced at Randolph, only to discover him already gone; all she could see was the back of his head as he cleaved his way through the increasingly dense crowd, hurrying up the ballroom to the safety of his friends.

Ryder murmured, "I did warn you."

She was still staring after Rand, but he heard a distinct humph.

He allowed her a moment to stew on her failure. Despite his focus on her, on his pursuit of her, he'd arrived at Castle-maine House late, as gentlemen of his ilk normally would; he had no wish to alert anyone to his novel direction. As with Lavinia the previous night, if he adhered to his normal practices, all would assume, or could easily be led to believe, that he was merely looking for his next lover.

Rather than his wife.

Given he now knew that he could play on Mary's senses, that she was susceptible and, even more enticing, wanted to play at resisting, one part of him had been eager to re-engage with her, yet he'd recognized the wisdom of a strategic delay; as he hadn't been present when she'd arrived, he'd run no risk of being tempted to monopolize her from the instant she'd appeared.

That would have alerted too many observers, at least to the point of raising questions he would rather never surfaced.

If the grandes dames got the slightest glimpse of his true intent . . . well, given his eye had settled on Mary, the grandes dames most likely wouldn't interfere, but his primary motivation for embarking on his search for a bride at the unexpectedly young, at least for such as him, age of thirty had been to remain free to choose and pursue the lady of his choice without the entire female half of the ton insisting on assisting him with that choice.

In society's collective mind, at thirty he was yet too young to have accepted the need to marry and sire an heir, but after a few more years, every grande dame would have turned her lorgnettes on him; he'd seen the value in undertaking a preemptive covert mission, so to speak.

Given his promise to his father, he was slated to marry anyway; giving up a few years of his bachelor existence—an existence that had grown rather wearying of late—seemed a small price to pay for the freedom of making his own choice, of directing his own hunt.

Especially for the position of his marchioness, a person he regarded as critical to his future.

To the future he was determined to have.

Attuned to Mary as he now was—as his quarry, she was the cynosure of his senses—he knew when she reached the point of turning away from Rand and moving on. Physically, at least.

Her face was a study in disillusioned disappointment.

"Come on." He offered his arm. "You probably genuinely could do with some air now."

She humphed, but in disgruntled resignation rather than

disagreement, and consented to lay her hand on his sleeve. Even that light touch he felt to his marrow.

"Actually," she said, as he turned her to the French doors, "I truly did want to stroll outside. It's quite cloying in here."

"No fan?" He held aside the filmy curtains and angled her through the door onto the flags.

She shook her head. "Too bothersome."

He'd noticed she had little affinity for the usual frills and furbelows; she carried a reticule, but even that was more practical than fanciful.

Resisting an urge to close his hand over hers, he steered her slowly along the terrace, adjusting his stride to hers. Trying to imagine just where she thought she was in her pursuit of his half brother.

Typically, he didn't have to imagine too hard—she told him.

"This simply isn't *right*." Eyes on the flags ahead of them, lips set in a mutinous line, with her free hand she waved at the terrace around them. "Why the devil couldn't Randolph escort me for this stroll out here?"

He heaved a histrionic sigh. "Put simply, because you're too much for him. A dish too rich for his blood."

She cast him a narrow-eyed look. "You don't seem to find me so."

He smiled; the notion was nonsensical. "Of course not."

"But if you don't—if you can interact with me—why can't he?"

"At the risk of repeating myself, I'm thirty and he's twenty-four. In the ages of man, that's a significant difference."

"Would you have scurried off like he did when you were twenty-four?"

He gave the matter due thought. "Truth be told, I'm not sure I remember what I was like at twenty-four, but . . . probably not."

She humphed more definitely; she could infuse a wealth of emotion into the simple sound.

Rand, he suspected, had managed to get fairly seriously in her bad books, but she couldn't really blame his brother. She seemed to have no appreciation of her own strength—of the sheer power of her personality, something she projected without any mitigating screens.

That was one of the things he found attractive—that lack of screens or veils—but men like Rand, regardless of age, would run; in fact Rand had merely demonstrated that he had a functioning sense of self-preservation.

They reached the end of the terrace. Lifting her hand from his sleeve, Mary executed a crisp about-face. "Right, then. I suppose I'd better get back to it."

She set off for the French doors, striding along a great deal more purposefully.

Left standing, bemused, by the balustrade, he swung around and with a few quick strides caught up with her. "Back to what?"

"Back to finding some way to speak with your brother—half brother—in private."

"Ah—I see." They reached the French doors and he held back the gauze curtains so she could march through unimpeded.

As he followed her back into the fray of the ballroom, he debated whether he should allow her to chase Rand, and possibly mark his brother for life, or . . .

He glanced at the dais on which the musicians sat—just as they started to play. "Mary."

Halting, she glanced back at him, her expression clearly stating that she didn't appreciate the delay in her headlong quest. "Yes?"

"Come and dance." He didn't make the mistake of asking but simply caught her hand, drew her the two paces necessary to gain the clearing floor, and swirled her into his arms and directly into the dance.

He hadn't given her time to resist. Once they were traveling smoothly amid the swirling couples, he glanced at her face and was skewered by twin daggers of intense blue; with her eyes narrowed to shards, her gaze was beyond sharp.

He smiled at her.

Her eyes flared. She hauled in a huge breath—causing her breasts to swell beneath her silk bodice, an interesting and rather arresting sight.

One that made him realize that, surprisingly for him, despite being unrelentingly focused on her, he hadn't really paid that much attention to her physical attributes. It had been her character, her emotions and actions that had captured his attention, and were still what most entranced him, but there was no denying that her figure was alluring, too.

He refocused on her eyes and found them spitting sparks.

"That was . . . was . . ." She was lost for words and appeared staggered by the fact.

"Insupportable?" he offered. "The biggest piece of impertinence you've ever been subjected to?"

"Yes! *Exactly*." Eyes—could blue burn?—locked with his, she drew in another fulminating breath. "And if you recognize *that*—"

"You needed deflecting."

"What?"

"There's absolutely no point in you tearing after Rand. You'll only scare him further and send him fleeing into the night." He smiled lazily down at her, knowing full well just how that would affect her. "Much better you sharpen your talons on me—I can take it."

She blinked at him; she hesitated—clearly battling the impulse—but then surrendered and asked, "Why talons?"

"Eagle. Think emperor." He held her gaze. "You're just a touch imperious, you know."

She snorted and looked away. After a moment—a moment in which he sensed through his hold on her, through the tension in her lithe frame, that the soothing sway of the dance had finally reached her—she muttered, "You can talk."

"Indeed. I can." He drew her a fraction closer as they eased into a turn. "Like recognizes like, as they say."

The rest of the waltz passed without incident, verbal or otherwise.

He wondered if she had any idea how clearly the fact that she was plotting and planning showed in her face.

At the end of the dance, he very properly released her, bowed, then raised her from her curtsy—and waited to see what next she would do.

"Thank you for the waltz." She glanced around. "If you'll excuse me?"

He let her turn away before inquiring, "Wither away, flower?"

Both inquiry and epithet earned him a darkling look. "The withdrawing room, if you must know."

He inclined his head. "I'll see you later."

As she resumed her march through the crowd, he heard her mutter, "Not if I can help it."

His grin was fueled equally by anticipation and delight.

Mary did, indeed, make for the withdrawing room; it was the only place she could think of where she could be sure of gaining a few minutes of assured privacy in which to think.

Thinking while circling the floor in Ryder's arms had proved impossible; no matter how valiantly she'd concentrated, her senses had constantly suborned her thoughts, seducing them with a type of scintillating delight, leading to unhelpful considerations such as how much more *ensnared* by the dance she was when she waltzed with Ryder, and conversely how ho-hum the experience had been with Randolph.

Such thoughts were irrelevant; Ryder was infinitely more experienced than Randolph, which was a huge point in *Randolph's* favor. Sitting before a mirror, she pretended to tidy her perfectly tidy dark curls and determinedly wrenched her mind from its sensual dallying and refocused instead on her most immediate goal: Gaining more time alone with

Randolph—preferably in a setting where he would be at ease—while simultaneously avoiding Ryder.

Of those connected aims, avoiding Ryder was the most important; regardless of what she might openly acknowledge, much less wish, he truly did distract her to the point of forgetting what she was about.

She dallied in the withdrawing room long enough, she judged, for him to have grown bored and, hopefully, been distracted by someone else. Finally emerging and returning along the corridor to the ballroom, she stepped through the archway, paused to glance around—and felt long fingers close about her elbow.

Before she could protest, Ryder said, "There's a discussion raging over there about that book, *The Yellowplush Papers*, by that fellow Thackeray. I thought you might find it of interest."

Which, of course, diverted her instantly. Allowing Ryder to lead her to a large group that included some of the more erudite personages in the ton, she told herself it was merely a pause in her campaign—and a worthwhile one at that. She'd heard of the work, a fictional memoir, and had been intrigued.

She and Ryder were welcomed into the circle with murmured greetings and polite nods, although the principal interlocutors, Lord Henessey and the Honorable Carlton Fitzsmythe, barely paused in their verbal exchange to acknowledge them.

The debate, centering on the value of such works as a mirror for society, shifted back and forth, but, to her ears at least, seemed to have no real starting point, much less any sense of end.

After a time, Ryder murmured, "It seems that it's the fact that the work purports to be this Mr. Charles J. Yellowplush's memoirs that's exciting most interest."

"Indeed," Mary murmured back. "But it's fiction—invented, made up—so I cannot, I confess, quite see the point in such high feelings."

She glanced up and met Ryder's eyes, and saw her own native cynicism reflected in the sharp hazel.

"Shall we move on?" he asked.

She nodded.

Which he took as permission to wind her arm in his and, excusing them with a few murmured words, lead her from the group into the still considerable crowd. "Thackeray—is he the same Thackeray who writes literary reviews for the *Times*?"

"I believe so." She tried to hold back the words, but . . . glancing up at him, she asked, "Do you read literary reviews, then?"

Eyes scanning the crowd, he shrugged offhandedly. "On occasion."

Which was something of a revelation; she found herself wondering if Randolph—and promptly cut off the thought. As Ryder himself had pointed out, six years of maturity lay between him and Randolph; comparisons weren't appropriate.

Only . . .

She shook aside the distraction—and, yes, just strolling a ballroom beside Ryder qualified as a distraction—and once again doggedly brought her mind to bear on her campaign.

Glancing down at her, Ryder read her expression, and immediately raised his head and searched for a fresh diversion. "Ah—we've been summoned."

Mary frowned and looked about, but with the crowd so dense she couldn't see far. "Who by?"

"An old aunt of mine—well, I call her aunt. But I'm sure she's seen you, too, so we'll have to grit our teeth and bear it." Without giving her a chance to argue, he tacked through the crowd, making for the chaise in one corner of the room on which he'd spotted his father's cousin, Lady Maude Folliwell. She had terrible eyesight and could barely see ten feet in front of her, but she always liked to speak with him, and he had no compunction whatever in using her in pursuit of his current aim; aside from all else, were she to be informed of that aim, Maude would not just approve but applaud.

Mary found herself facing a type of lady she recognized well, but Lady Maude had nothing on her own late aunt Clara. Lady Maude's conversation was still entirely rational and easy to follow, but noting the thickness of the glass in the lorgnettes her ladyship deployed, Mary had to wonder how Lady Maude had spotted them from quite halfway across the room. Regardless, she smiled sweetly, allowed Ryder to introduce her, and answered Lady Maude's questions about her family.

"I didn't notice your mother or your aunts here, my dear." Lady Maude trained her magnified gaze along the wall against which most of the older ladies were seated in chairs and on chaises.

"My parents and my aunts and uncles have retreated to the country for a few days."

"Ah, yes—no doubt girding their loins for your sister's wedding. Quite a lovely surprise, and I know the Glossups are thrilled. Do please convey my felicitations to the happy couple."

Mary accepted the charge, and Lady Maude turned her lorgnettes on Ryder. Mary expected to hear the usual exhortations ladies of Maude's age normally leveled at gentlemen of Ryder's, but instead it appeared that Lady Maude was extremely fond of Ryder and, even though from her somewhat pointed comments it was clear her ladyship was in no way blind, she thoroughly approved of her younger relative, at least in general terms.

As Ryder responded with equal fondness and the exchange veered deeper into family concerns, Mary saw her chance and promptly moved to seize it; intending to quietly step back and with a polite curtsy to her ladyship slip away into the crowd—leaving Ryder stuck while she escaped to find Randolph—she started to ease back, only to discover that Ryder was, yet again, ahead of her.

Not that he paused in his exchange with Lady Maude, or gave the slightest sign that he knew what she was about.

But the long fingers he'd had the nerve to crook into her silk skirts curled and tightened, effectively anchoring her to his side.

He kept the hand trapping her skirts at the back of his thigh, out of Lady Maude's sight, and with the crowd so tight-packed, it was unlikely anyone behind them would notice. . . .

Mary had to swallow the growl of sheer frustration that bubbled in her throat and continue to smile sweetly.

But she was now more determined than ever to pursue Randolph; one way or another, she *would* win through.

Her chance came immediately they'd taken leave of Lady Maude. As they turned back into the crowd, Lady Heskett and Lady Argyle, elegantly fashionable matrons of similar age to Ryder, pounced simultaneously—one from either side.

"Darling, I haven't seen you in an age!" Lady Heskett swooped in, all but physically dislodging Mary from Ryder's side.

Entirely willing to be dislodged, Mary slipped her hand from Ryder's sleeve and gave way.

"Raventhorne." Lady Argyle's voice was a touch shriller and held a distinctly possessive note as she brazenly claimed Ryder's other arm. "Where have you been hiding, my lord?"

For an instant, Ryder was fully occupied.

With a grin, Mary stepped back, whirled, and fled.

Plunging into the crowd, she tacked this way and that like a fox dodging hounds, then doubled back and took refuge near the archway leading to the withdrawing room.

She scanned the heads but saw no evidence of Ryder's golden mane. She exhaled in relief. "Good. Now to find Randolph."

Keeping a wary eye out for prowling lions, she edged around the ballroom. Predictably, Randolph's circle was more or less where it had been before. She was about to step clear of the surrounding crowd and approach Randolph and his cronies once more when she saw Ryder lounging against the wall nearby, free of encumbering ladies and apparently idly chatting with another gentleman, but in reality watching and waiting.

She drew back, but the movement caught Ryder's eye.

What followed was a sophisticated game of cat and mouse. Somewhat to her surprise, Ryder wasn't merely intent on keeping her from Randolph; he pursued her as she twisted and turned, trying to lose him in the crowd. . . .

He was tall enough to easily keep track of her.

All too soon he was closing in, and a peculiar frisson of panic—delicious and expectant—flashed through her.

She gave herself no time to dwell on the strangeness of the feeling. There was only one way she could see of escaping. She hurried back to the archway into the corridor; pausing beneath the arch, she glanced back—and saw Ryder only yards away. Three people away.

His gaze locked with hers.

What she saw in his eyes made her lungs seize.

One part of her mind thought that was ridiculous, but the rest was wholly focused on one thing: Escaping.

Exactly what she was escaping, much less why, she didn't know. She just had to do it.

On a breathless gasp, she swung away and plunged down the corridor, but instead of going into the withdrawing room, she rushed past and on. The long corridor ran the length of the ballroom and at the end turned a corner; whisking around it, she came to the door she'd known from previous visits was there. Dragging in a breath, calming her thudding heart, she raised her head; straightening, drawing her usual mantle of self-control firmly about her, she opened the door and stepped onto the terrace.

It was, she judged, the last place Ryder would think of looking for her. There was really no reason she would return there, especially alone.

Silently closing the door, she paused in the spill of shadow provided by the walls and surveyed the five couples strolling the expanse; being alone—strolling alone—would attract attention.

In her present position, she wasn't visible to the ballroom's occupants, but if she walked forward, she would be seen. And a single figure was odd enough to attract notice, even from those absorbed in conversation in the ballroom.

Let alone the couples strolling the terrace; at least three knew her, and would undoubtedly seek to gather her in and escort her back into the ballroom . . . where Ryder would be waiting.

She glanced to her left. A set of steep stone steps, helpfully shrouded in shadow, led down to a paved garden path. Holding still in the gloom, she waited, then seized a moment when the strolling couples were otherwise occupied and unlikely to spot her, and slipped silently down the steps, onto the path, and whisked around the corner of the house.

Ahead of her lay the rectangle of garden that faced the private rooms of the big house, and tucked into the opposite corner beyond an expanse of lawn stood a small pillared folly; constructed of white marble, it glimmered faintly in the moonlight. When the weather was fine, Lady Castlemaine often used the lawn for her afternoon teas, but there was no direct access from the ballroom, and at night the area was unlighted.

No one would be in the folly at present; she could sit in the quiet darkness for a while, long enough to calm her stupidly thudding heart and get her mind working again. She had no idea why Ryder's pursuit—his suddenly intent focus on her—had affected her to this degree, but she needed to settle her nerves, reclaim her senses, regain complete control of her mind, and then devise a workable plan to get the time she needed with Randolph to . . . properly assess if he was, indeed, her hero.

That she now doubted her earlier certainty irked. She'd been so *sure* . . . and on one hand, she still was. Logically, and by every measurable criterion, Lord Randolph Cavanaugh was the perfect husband for her—he *should be* her hero.

Walking slowly past the lawn, she turned onto the narrower path that led to the folly; it wended through the wide flower beds, small bushes and flowering plants nodding on either side, their colors washed out by the moonlight, but their scents still discernible on the night breeze. Gradually, her odd panic subsided; slowly pacing, her gaze on the path ahead, she felt her temper stir as the reality of what had just transpired coalesced in her mind.

She'd been forced out of the ballroom—her field of action—by Ryder. By an interfering, high-handed, wholly arrogant despot; no matter how much amiability he used to cloak his true nature, that was what Ryder assuredly was.

And tonight he'd trumped her.

Her—she who was always in charge. More, he'd done it in an arena she considered hers. Hers to organize and arrange to her liking.

Eyes narrowing, she raised her skirts and marched up the three steps into the deeper shadows of the folly, her temper escalating to a steady boil.

Even though there was no one to see, she set her lips in a mutinous line.

Halting at the top of the steps, she let her skirts fall.

Her senses flared.

Awareness washed over her and she froze.

Silence.

Every instinct she possessed continued to scream that a dangerous predator was close. Too close.

She blinked twice. Barely daring to breathe, as her eyes adjusted to the denser darkness inside the folly, she slowly turned to her left . . .

He was sitting on the bench that circled the structure, at his languid, feline ease. Watching her. Intent. Unmoving.

Head back, shoulders resting against a column, his arms relaxed, hands on his thighs, one ankle resting on the other knee, his pose emphasized just how large, powerful, and lethally attractive he was. In this setting, there was no escaping the obvious extrapolation—how very dangerous he could be to any woman foolish enough to stray too close.

That said . . . head tilting, she consulted her no-longer-panicking instincts and confirmed that she harbored not the slightest lick of true fear, not even trepidation. Not of him.

Anger, and a certain respect, both fueled by an increasing appreciation of what he could do to her plans, to her determined progress down her chosen path, of the degree of distraction he could create, of how masterfully he could play on her senses . . . those she had to own to.

That he would be an implacable opponent, and an even worse enemy, she had not the slightest doubt.

And he'd made it perfectly clear that he was disinclined to view her pursuit of his younger brother favorably.

Yet . . . she eyed him, studied him—and accepted that protectiveness of Randolph would propel Ryder only so far.

Not this far.

"How did you get here ahead of me?"

A flick of long fingers indicated the house. "The garden hall at the other end of that corridor. Its outer door opens directly onto the path over there."

She glanced at the door in question. Looking back at him, she frowned. "How did you know I'd come here?"

A moment passed before he replied, "You forget that a gentleman of my ilk is expected to know all the potential places for dalliance in all the major houses—and all the ways to reach them."

"But you couldn't have known I would come out here."

Another pause, then, "Clearly, I'm starting to learn how you think—well enough to predict how you'll behave."

That was not at all reassuring. Much less calming; her heart was no longer thudding, but it had yet to return to its usual unremarkable rhythm. Regardless, it was past time she made a stand. "Why are you pursuing me?" She spread her arms. "Even out here."

His eyes well adjusted to the poor light, Ryder studied her features and debated telling her.

He hadn't risen when she'd arrived, which, if she'd been paying greater attention, might have triggered her suspicions as to his motives. As it was, his claiming of a privilege normally reserved for close personal relationships didn't seem to have registered with her . . . or rather, she'd accepted the point, conceded it, without real thought.

All of which was good; another step closer successfully claimed.

He also hadn't risen because, in this setting, with the pair of them alone in the dark of the night in a relatively confined space, if he stood he would sexually overwhelm her. It would be all but impossible not to, and while one part of him was intrigued by the prospect and eager to see how it would play out, his more rational side knew she wasn't yet ready for that.

He also didn't think he was yet ready to answer her question. Not unless he had to. His gaze on the dark pools of her eyes, he arched a brow. "Why do you imagine I am?"

The answer would at least tell him how far along the path of realization she'd traveled.

She tipped up her chin—in conscious defiance or unconscious hauteur, or both. "I believe that you're bored but thus far have failed to discover fresh prey to your usual taste, and then for some reason I caught your eye at Henrietta and James's engagement ball, and for some even less fathomable reason you find me entertaining, and now that you've uncovered my interest in Randolph, you've decided to amuse yourself by not just getting in my way but diverting me."

Both voice and tone had gained in confidence as she spoke. Now she looked directly at him; even through the shadows he could feel her challenging glare. "Am I right?"

He held her gaze. "All you've said is undeniably true."

It just wasn't the whole truth.

"Ha!" She swung away and paced—two steps across the marble floor, then back again—then she halted and, increasingly militant, confronted him anew. "So *why*?" Again she spread her arms in appeal. "Tell me why—*exactly* why—you're so set on disrupting my bid for Randolph's attention."

"I've already told you—Rand is not the man for you." *I am.* But she would need to come to that realization on her own. In her own time, in her own way. He understood strong characters—like her, like him; they didn't accept others interfering in their lives, and in personal matters didn't readily accept the assessments of others as correct. Neither he nor she would be led. It wasn't a matter of trust, but more one of inviolable self-determination. In that respect, he understood her well, so would give her time—understood the value of giving her time—to reach the right conclusion on her own.

She stared at him for a long moment, then, "*Aargh!*" The sound resonated with feminine frustration. "It's not up to *you* to decree that!"

"In the circumstances, I believe it is."

"But it's *not*. Ryder—"

On a silent sigh, he uncrossed his legs and stood. It was the only way to bring this interlude to an end. His innate sense of time was informing him that the ball was winding down; he needed to get her back into the ballroom before she was missed.

And he wasn't prepared to open his mouth and inform her of his intentions. The challenge—the one she presented him with—was to win her without declaring his hand. If he baldly told her he wished to marry her . . . he wasn't a coxcomb, but no one in the ton would disagree that he was a beyond-excellent catch. If he told her, and she then decided to accept him, he might never know what her feelings toward him truly were—might never know why she'd agreed. At present he had no notion of what she felt for him—whether she felt anything at all beyond irritation and exasperation, whether she might ever feel for him something beyond the transitory desire he knew he could evoke.

But even worse, what if he told her of his intentions and she jibbed?

No—better, much wiser, and a lot safer to soften her up first.

Speaking of which . . . straightening to his full height, he took the half step required to bring them close—close enough that she had to tip her head back to look up at him, leaving him towering over her.

He could have used the position to intimidate, but standing this close to her, intimidation was far from his mind.

It wasn't in hers, either; she gazed up at him, the silvery blush of moonlight washing over her cheeks, her expression holding a certain semiblankness he recognized all too well.

She was in no way immune to him, to his sensual aura.

To the allure he was a past master at wielding.

The moment shivered with illicit potential. With his gaze, he traced the delicate curve of her cheek and jaw; his fingertips tingled. Because he could, returning his gaze to her eyes, he raised a hand and, with the pad of one finger, traced the tempting alabaster curve.

He watched her eyes flare, heard the hitch in her already shallow breathing. And wished the light was sufficient for him to see more, to be able to read her awakening desire.

Her lips, rosy and ripe, parted. Softened in instinctive, reactive invitation.

He could kiss her now—could commence her seduction here, in this moment.

Temptation whispered, more potent than he'd expected. His mouth all but watered with the urge to take hers.

But he wasn't ranked among the ton's greatest lovers because he didn't understand what seduction truly was.

Seduction wasn't about tempting a lady to surrender to her lover's desire.

It was all about inducing her to surrender to her own.

She had to want him.

She had to come to him.

And she would.

To him, for him, with her especially, it had to be that way.

He needed her to want him every bit as much as he was starting to realize he might come to desire her.

Drawing breath, he mentally stepped back from the brink he'd brought them to.

Lowering his hand, he closed his fingers about her elbow. "Come." Gently, he turned her to the steps. "I'll escort you back inside."

She drew in a sharp, slightly shaky breath, considered him for an instant—no doubt debating whether to protest his caress . . . or leave it lying unacknowledged between them. He wasn't surprised when she chose the latter option. Eyes narrowing, she nevertheless allowed him to steady her down the steps, then he released her and, head rising, she fell in beside him.

They walked back toward the house.

"Via the terrace," he murmured, waving her that way.

She obliged and headed back the way she'd come, but a few steps on asked, "Why?"

He took two more paces before replying, "If we were seen coming out of the garden hall, there would be talk—it's an obvious place for an assignation and sufficiently illicit to arouse the imaginations of the gossipmongers, regardless of your age."

She mulled that over, then observed, "But you escorting me in from the terrace won't raise eyebrows?"

"No. Not at all." He glanced at her, met her eyes. Eventually replied, "That's one benefit of a reputation such as mine. Unless we do something too jarringly blatant—leaving the garden hall together, for instance—then given my well-known predilections, anyone seeing me escorting you in, entirely mundanely via the terrace, will simply assume that I've obliged in escorting you outside for some air—as, indeed, I did earlier. Nothing in the least gossip-worthy."

Rounding the corner of the house, they climbed the steps to the terrace and saw two couples heading for the French doors. They brought up the rear.

When Mary halted to allow him to draw back the gauzy curtain, he reached around her, but paused with his arm blocking her progress, the curtain a translucent screen between them and the occupants of the ballroom.

She shot him a questioning glance.

He caught it, trapped her gaze. Lowering his head, his voice soft, his tone conversational but private, said, "So, you see, no one would ever imagine that I might seduce you." He held her widening eyes. "You're too young, too innocent." His let his lips curve. "And entirely too marriageable. Very definitely not my style of lover."

She stared into his eyes, then her gaze traveled over his face, fastened on his lips, lingered for an instant, then she sniffed, faced forward, and, when he drew back the curtain, walked calmly into the ballroom.

He followed, his gaze on her slender back. And omitted to add that he was, however, increasingly sure she was his style of wife.

Chapter Three

I had no idea we'd have to race off to Wiltshire, and Simon and Portia are keen to go, too—mostly to take the children out of London, to give them a break from town." Across the breakfast table, Henrietta looked at Mary. "But that will leave you at home all alone."

"Only alone in the sense that none of the family will be in residence." Mary waved at Hudson, standing by the sideboard. "I'll have the staff all round while here, and Amanda and Martin and Amelia and Luc are just a few streets away."

"Still . . ." Henrietta sighed. "I wouldn't go, but James must, and it really would be better if I got some idea of the situation at Whitestone Hall *before* I arrive as the new lady of the manor."

"It's too good an opportunity to pass up," Mary assured her. She took a bite of her toast, chewed, then said, "I truly can't see why you're so anxious. Mama and Papa will be back the day after tomorrow. Amanda is going to accompany me to Lady Hopetoun's musicale this evening, and Amelia will do duty at Lady Bracewell's tomorrow night, and then Mama will be back and all will roll on as usual. There's absolutely no reason you shouldn't go, and Simon and Portia, too."

Henrietta studied Mary's face. "Well, if you're sure." Henrietta held up a hand. "And yes, I can see that you are—it was a rhetorical statement."

Mary grinned. "So when do you leave?"

"Within the hour." Henrietta glanced at the clock. "Oh, blast!" She picked up her teacup and drained it, then tossed her napkin on the table and rose. "I have to hurry." She met Mary's eyes. "Be good and take care."

Mary laughed and waved her off. "Just go!"

Henrietta whirled and went.

Left to her own amusements, Mary took her time savoring her tea, then ate a second slice of toast and jam.

While she considered just where her plan to find her hero currently stood.

Her instinctive reaction to Ryder's interference was to redouble her efforts and even more adamantly forge ahead on her predetermined path, to cling even more tenaciously to her direction. But she was growing too old to react thus blindly to opposition; she hoped she was growing wise enough to acknowledge that sometimes she might not be entirely correct in her assumptions.

And, in truth, it wasn't Ryder's behavior the previous night that was leading her to question her until-now unwavering certainty but Randolph's. He'd all but pushed her into Ryder's arms and run away.

Definitely not hero-worthy behavior.

The more she dwelled on that moment, the less amused she was.

Setting down her teacup, she looked down at her chest—at the necklace visible above the scooped neckline of her pale blue morning gown. The rose quartz pendant dangling between her breasts wasn't visible, but she could feel it, sense its weight.

If, now you're wearing the necklace, you don't feel something special for this mystery gentleman of yours, if he doesn't sweep you off your feet, or get under your skin to the point you simply can't shrug him off, then please, promise me you'll listen to The Lady's advice.

Her cousin Angelica's words, uttered at Henrietta and

James's engagement ball—the first evening she'd worn the necklace. Of all her cousins, Angelica, also the youngest of one branch of the family, was most like Mary in temperament; everyone acknowledged that. The necklace had worked for Angelica, and Mary still believed it would work for her.

But with Randolph she'd felt nothing beyond exasperation arising out of frustrated expectations.

That didn't necessarily mean that Randolph was not her one true hero, but he certainly wasn't now, and, it seemed, might not attain that status for years. . . .

One hand rising to trace the necklace, she whispered, "I'm not going to wait years, and that with no guarantee." After several moments of thinking, of absentmindedly tapping a fingernail against one of the amethyst beads, she grimaced and lowered her hand. "I have to accept that Randolph might not be my hero. I can use tonight's musicale—at which Ryder will definitely not appear, thank God—to test Randolph one last time, and then, if, as seems likely, he fails to meet my standards, I will start to look about me for my true hero."

Who was proving damnably reticent over coming forward and presenting himself.

If he doesn't sweep you off your feet, or get under your skin to the point you simply can't shrug him off . . .

The latter description might have applied to Ryder, who, now she thought of it, was the first gentleman she'd actually interacted with after Henrietta had clasped the necklace about her throat, but last night he had, directly and openly, confirmed her supposition as to why he was pursuing her, and no great stretch was required to imagine that he might, indeed, feel protective of Randolph to the extent of acting as he had. Ryder was the head of his house, his family as old as the Cynsters, and she understood the protective impulses that accrued to that station; he would without a second thought act to protect any he considered in his care. Like his younger half brother.

So there was no reason to imagine Ryder might be her hero—and many, many reasons to be certain he was not.

Not least the fact that they were so much alike in character and temperament, the principal differences, aside from their genders, being that he was older, infinitely more experienced, and consequently stronger.

She wrinkled her nose. No, the truth was he was *inherently* stronger; she wouldn't allow herself to be so foolish as to not recognize and acknowledge that. But for a lady who intended to be in charge of her own life, Ryder was assuredly the antithesis of her hero.

Which meant the damn man hadn't yet made an appearance.

With one last, faintly bothered glance at the necklace, she set aside her napkin, rose, and headed for the breakfast parlor door.

At least tonight she could be assured of not having to deal with the distraction, the sensual discombobulation, of Ryder's interference. Musicales such as Lady Hopetoun's were the province of the matchmakers, their charges, and young gentlemen of good family of an age to marry, and as such were events at which gentlemen of Ryder's proclivities never appeared; tonight, she would have a clear field.

Tonight, she would make up her mind, one way or another, on the subject of Lord Randolph Cavanaugh.

Mary followed her oldest sister into Lady Hopetoun's music room. While Amanda, Countess of Dexter, swept forward, touching fingers and cheeks and merging with her own circle of acquaintances, Mary hung back just inside the door and looked around.

They'd been delayed by Amanda needing to check on her youngest, who had developed a cough, which, thankfully, was subsiding. Now an old hand at motherhood, Amanda had declared herself satisfied, enough at least to travel to

Hill Street and the musicale, yet as a precaution Amanda had sent Mary on in their parents' town carriage, which had ferried Mary to Dexter House in Park Lane, and had followed in the Dexter carriage, just in case.

So all the other guests should be in attendance by now. Indeed, the members of the chamber ensemble who were to perform that evening were tuning up their instruments, and while the majority of guests still mingled and chatted in knots in the clear space closer to the door, others had already moved down the room to the velvet-upholstered chairs arranged in serried ranks before the dais.

Randolph. Where was he?

Mary scanned the heads once, then, frowning slightly, strolled to the room's side to search more closely—

"They're not here."

She congratulated herself on not jumping. Barely turning her head, she cast Ryder a brief glance as he prowled up to stand beside her. After a second's consideration, along the lines of whether she wished to cut off her nose to spite her face, she surrendered and asked, "They who?" Tall as he was, he could search those present more effectively than she could.

"Rand and his set."

She blinked. "All of them?"

"I think they took fright."

Fright. There was that word again. Nevertheless, she asked, "Fright over what?" Resigned, she turned to face Ryder.

His customary lazy lion expression in place, he met her gaze, then arched a brow. "Everyone knows this sort of event, especially when held at this time of year, has only one real aim—and that aim has nothing to do with music."

She didn't dispute that; it was why she'd come. But . . . "Randolph and the others attended the ball last night. And he told me they—all of them—attended such events, events like this, to keep peace with their mothers, the hostesses, and the grandes dames."

"Admitted that, did he?" Ryder's grin turned proud. "There's hope for him yet."

She shot him a discouraging look. "In your terms, perhaps. But accepting Randolph's statement as true, which I do, why aren't he and his friends attending tonight?" She glanced swiftly, but comprehensively, around. "I'm sure their mothers would have wished them to. Just look at all the young ladies and their mamas and sponsors—and there's a good showing of other younger-than-you gentlemen, too."

"Most of whom, if you look more closely, are a year or so younger than Rand and his set."

She had noticed that. As, frowning slightly, she considered the guests again, Ryder continued, answering the question that was forming in her mind, "I suspect that last night Rand and his cronies reached the point of actually looking into the chasm yawning at their feet."

"And them not being here is them stepping back?" She glanced at Ryder.

His lips twisted lightly, not so much mockingly as in understanding, both of his brother and her, too. "I believe you would be correct in interpreting their absence as a declaration of sorts."

Somewhat to her surprise, she felt nothing more than resigned acceptance. "Well, in one sense that's made my way forward clearer." She met his eyes, slightly narrowed hers in warning. "As much as it pains me to acknowledge your prescience, clearly your brother is not the gentleman for me."

Ryder fought to keep his smile within bounds. "So glad we have that established."

"Yes, well." Swinging to face the room, Mary stated, "So now I must move on."

Ryder blinked and promptly moved with her as she matched action to her words. "Ah . . . where to, exactly?"

"To further assess the gentlemen of the ton to discover the right gentleman for me, of course."

"I . . . see." He trailed her to a row of chairs halfway down the room, then followed on her heels down the row until she drew in her skirts, swung around and sat, then he claimed the chair alongside hers.

As the musicians played a brief introductory piece, effectively summoning the guests to their seats, she cast him a sidelong glance. "Still keeping an eye on me?"

He held her gaze for an instant, then, as the bulk of the guests settled and conversations abated, he smiled, leaned back, and, still holding her gaze, murmured, "In a manner of speaking."

She humphed and pointedly gave her attention to the musicians.

Across the room, sinking onto a chair alongside Lavinia, Lady Carmody frowned. Under cover of the swelling music, she leaned closer to Lavinia and tugged her sleeve. "I say! What is your stepson doing here? And why is *he* conversing with Mary Cynster?" Lady Carmody glanced around. "And where is Lord Randolph?"

Lavinia, now also studying the surprising pair across and further down the room, as were a great many other ladies, replied without turning her head; the strain in her voice suggested that she was speaking through clenched teeth while struggling not to scream. "All excellent questions. To none of which I have an answer."

After a moment, Lavinia swung her gaze forward, then ducked her head and hissed to Lady Carmody, "I *told* Randolph to be here!"

"Yes, well." Lady Carmody tried for a placating tone. "Boys will be boys, I suppose."

Lavinia faced the dais, but the music had no power to hold her; her attention slid, again and again, to her stepson's tawny head, to his broad shoulders, to the way both shifted as, time and again, he and Mary Cynster exchanged comments. "The last thing I need," she gritted out, so low that only Lady Carmody could hear, "is for Ryder to turn the silly chit's head."

Lady Carmody considered, then opined, "I seriously doubt even he could turn Miss Cynster from her chosen path, and really, he can't be serious about seducing her, can he? Quite aside from him knowing better—that he can't without causing a massive scandal—she's not at all his type."

Lavinia frowned. "That's true." She cast another glance at her infernal stepson. "But why is he here?"

Lady Carmody shrugged and settled to enjoy the music. "Perhaps he's simply bored and happens to like music."

Continuing to frown, Lavinia made no reply.

Presumably he's bored and just happens to like music— and he's comfortable with me and, moreover, knows I'm not imagining snaring him. Mary settled on that as the most likely reason behind Ryder remaining by her side. Indeed, that reasoning made her inwardly smile. *He feels safe with me.*

The notion of one of the ton's most dangerous gentlemen hiding behind her skirts was one to relish.

As the recital continued, she found herself not only enjoying the music but discussing it as well—having a sensible and intelligent conversation covering such topics as the combination of instruments best able to render each piece, the selection of works, the acoustics of the room, and that the increasing temperature would doubtless soon necessitate a retuning session—with Ryder.

While she knew enough to match his interest on most aspects, the retuning was something she'd never understood, but in that he was proved correct.

The more they chatted, the more she relaxed—and the more she enjoyed.

Ryder seemed intent on nothing more than appreciating the music and sharing the moment with her in a totally unexceptionable way. During the intermission, they wandered into the refreshment salon, still talking—animatedly arguing the merits of a horn section over additional woodwinds— then, when summoned, returned to the music room and resumed their seats for the second and longer part of the performance.

So absorbed in the moment was she—so anchored in the web created by the combination of the unexpectedly stimulating interaction with Ryder and the truly quite excellent music—that it was only toward the very end of the performance that the covertly inquisitive glances directed Ryder's way from all corners of the room truly registered.

But once they had . . . she inwardly blinked, wondering, then realized what was causing the older ladies—the few grandes dames present and the older matrons especially—to cast such intrigued and penetrating glances his way.

Why was he there? More specifically, why had he come in the first place, and why had he remained?

She'd assumed he'd come to protect Randolph from her, and once he'd confirmed that Randolph wasn't there, had followed her to her chair and sat beside her because he'd wanted to listen to the performance and hadn't wanted to be bothered interacting with anyone else.

For a gentleman of his ilk to be interested in music, as he demonstrably was, wasn't unheard of, yet previously that interest had never to her knowledge been sufficient to move him to attend an event such as this. From the interrogatory glances leveled at him, no other lady had seen him—lion that he was—at such an event before, either.

A tingling sensation feathered across her nape and slid over the back of her shoulders.

As Ryder himself had pointed out, this type of event held at this time of the Season was expressly designed to promote further connection between those contemplating matrimony, witness the large number of young couples scattered about the room interacting under the watchful eye of chaperons. Consequently, the appearance of a gentleman of Ryder's status at such an event would be interpreted as a declaration that he was hunting—not for a paramour but for a bride.

The music swelled to a crescendo. Her lungs slowly seized.

Barely moving her head, she glanced at Ryder. Gracefully relaxed alongside her, he was fully absorbed in the music.

Fleetingly, she studied his face—the sculpted lines, the undeniable male beauty that in no way disguised the strength and potent power behind the façade—then looked forward again and drew a tight breath.

Nowhere near deep enough to steady her suddenly giddy head.

He was there, and had stayed, for the music.

What else?

The nervous flutter in her chest, in her stomach, was patently ridiculous. There was, she sternly lectured herself, no reason for such a reaction; it wasn't as if he'd done anything to make her feel . . .

He was there, by her side, large as life.

She mentally shook aside the ludicrous notion that, courtesy of the other ladies' visual speculation, had inserted itself into her brain.

Grimly determined to conceal her sudden and quite nonsensical susceptibility, she forced herself to listen to the last of the last sonata; when it ended, she applauded as earnestly as anyone else, smiling delightedly as with the rest of the audience she rose to her feet to deliver a standing ovation.

As the applause faded, Lady Hopetoun thanked the players, then everyone clapped once more. As the final round died, everyone turned to find their parties.

Keeping her delighted smile fixed on her face, she glibly took her leave of Ryder, very correctly thanking him for his company, then, faster than she ever had before, made her way to the safety of her chaperon's side.

His shoulders propped against the last column of the Hopetoun House porch, Ryder hung back in the gloom and listened to the exchange between Mary and Amanda. The pair had walked out of the front door, crossed the porch, and halted on the steps leading down to the street. Other guests streamed past them, leaving in twos and threes, all equally oblivious of him standing silently in the shadows out of their immediate line of sight.

Mary shook out her silk shawl, then resettled it over her largely bare shoulders. "We've got both carriages here—there's no need for you to follow me to Upper Brook Street. I'll have John Coachman and our footman—I'll be perfectly safe."

"Yes, well." Amanda checked her shawl and reticule. "I suppose that's true, and it isn't any great distance from here to there."

"And Park Lane is even closer." Mary leaned over and bussed Amanda's cheek. "Thank you for coming and watching over me—I know you wouldn't have attended otherwise. And don't worry about Ryder—as I said, he was just interested in the music. I certainly don't expect to find him dancing attendance on me."

"Hmm . . . perhaps, but remember what *I* said. He's a deep one. Don't underestimate him."

Shrouded in shadow, Ryder grinned.

The sisters parted, going down the steps to where their respective carriages waited. He watched as they were handed up by their footmen, then the doors were shut, and first Amanda's carriage, followed by the carriage carrying Mary, pulled out into the stream of fashionable coaches rumbling slowly westward.

Once Mary's carriage had disappeared around the bend in Hill Street, Ryder set his hat on his head and, cane swinging in one hand, emerged from the shadows; joining the still steady stream of departing guests, he descended to the pavement and, with polite nods to this lady and that, walked off along the street.

He rarely used a carriage in Mayfair; his long strides ate the distances easily enough, and the relative silence of the night, punctuated though it was by the familiar rattle of passing coaches, was nevertheless soothing. Certainly after an evening spent with others, in the usual cacophony of social events.

Turning north up the less frequented Hayes Mews, as the night enveloped him in its dark and its peace, he strode along easily, neither hurrying nor idling. He didn't direct his mind to any particular track but allowed it to wander over the last hours, observing and noting as it would.

The impulse that had moved him to wait on the porch until he saw Mary safely on her way home was . . . interesting. He'd never felt such a compulsion before, not even with those ladies with whom he'd shared a bed. Presumably it was an expression, a natural enough one, of how he saw Mary, an upshot of the role in which he'd cast her.

Brows faintly rising, he considered the matter but saw nothing to be alarmed at; he was who and what he was, and as he now viewed her as his marchioness, such impulses were to be expected.

Also intriguing was the sudden awareness that had swamped her right at the end of the evening. Until then she'd been conversing freely, without thought or restraining consideration, but she'd suddenly become aware—he assumed because of the myriad speculative glances thrown his way by other ladies—that his presence by her side required explanation.

He'd wondered what she would make of it. In her exchange with Amanda, she'd stated her conclusion plainly enough, but . . . did she truly believe he'd remained by her side solely because of his—admittedly genuine—enjoyment of the music?

Reaching the end of Hayes Mews, he turned left into Farm Street. Smiling to himself and swinging his cane, he crossed the cobbled street and walked on to the opening of the alley that was his habitual shortcut to his home in Mount Street when returning from the southern section of Mayfair.

At this time of night, even in this bastion of the haut ton

most law-abiding citizens would avoid the narrow alleys, but he strolled on without concern; not only did his size deter most would-be assailants but should they nevertheless make a try for him, the rapier concealed in his cane provided a more potent discouragement.

He knew how to use it, and no one his size survived Eton without learning all there was to know about fisticuffs, and even more to the point, outright brawling.

In truth, there was little he feared in life, not as pertained to his physical person. There was little that might effectively threaten him, not physically, but he'd come to understand that there were other threats in life, many potentially more damaging, holding much greater risk of true loss than anything on the physical plane.

Those threats were not ones he was constitutionally comfortable debating, not even with himself, but they largely arose from the issues that, having attained the age of thirty, he'd decided it was time to address.

Before they turned and bit him.

The alley narrowed for the last ten yards, the gap between the walls only just sufficient to allow him to walk freely through. Emerging from the dimness into the more affluent and commensurately well-lit ambiance of Mount Street, he turned left, walked several yards, then angled across the cobbles to the opposite pavement, stepping onto it a few paces short of the steps leading up to his own front door.

He let himself in with his latchkey. Stepping over the threshold into the lamp-lit splendor of the foyer, he was unsurprised to see his butler, Pemberly, come striding forward from the nether regions, eager to take his hat and cane. Pemberly had been butler to his father, and like the housekeeper, Mrs. Perkins, and several other members of his staff, had been constants in Ryder's life.

"Welcome home, my lord. I trust the evening went well?"

"Yes, indeed." Ryder dutifully surrendered hat and cane. "If anything, better than I'd hoped." He'd gone to Lady

Hopetoun's assuming Rand would be present; Rand's absence and Mary's consequent acceptance that Rand was not her future husband had simplified matters, without any effort from Ryder effectively clearing his path, and the subsequent time interacting with Mary had advanced his campaign further than he'd anticipated.

So what next?

"Will you be going out again, my lord?" Pemberly inquired.

To another ball, to a club or hell, or to some lady's bed . . . Ryder shook his head. "No. You can lock up." He started toward the corridor that led deeper into the huge house. "I'll be in the library for a while, then I'll be going up to bed."

"Very good, my lord. I'll tell Collier."

Ryder nodded. Collier had been his father's valet but had been too young to retire on his father's death. Although Ryder didn't need anyone's help to dress, much less undress, and he didn't actually like having anyone so personally close, he permitted Collier's ministrations; the man had been devoted to his father, and especially helpful through the old man's last days. Ryder's current push was to insist that everyone in the household replace the outmoded label "valet" with the more modern "gentleman's gentleman." Thus far, it had proved a battle, but it was one he was determined to win.

Reaching the library, he went in. Closing the door, he paused, letting the comforting, welcoming atmosphere of the room—the one he spent most time in and, courtesy of all the hours the pair of them had spent there, also most associated with his father—embrace him, then, with a sigh, one of pleased satisfaction more than anything else, he strolled to the massive fireplace midway down the long room.

Floor-to-ceiling bookshelves packed with leather-bound tomes covered every wall, broken only by the twin doors, the fireplace, and the three long windows facing it. With the long velvet curtains drawn tight against the night, the only light came from a lamp left burning on a low table beside one of the twin sofas angled before the hearth, and the leaping flames from a small but cheery fire burning in the grate. The resulting pulsing, golden glow gleamed fitfully off the polished wood, gently winked from the gold lettering on the books' spines, and softly caressed the dark brown leather of the sofas and chairs set about the room.

Ignoring the large desk at the far end of the room, Ryder paused beside the fireplace. From the end of the marble mantelpiece, he lifted a stack of cards—all the invitations he'd received for the coming days.

As was his habit, he removed that evening's cards from the top of the pile and tossed them into the flames. Separating out the invitations for the following evening, he returned the rest to the top of the mantelpiece, then walked to the lighted lamp. Fanning the cards for tomorrow night's events in one hand, he studied them in the lamplight.

This evening, Mary had started to question his motives, had started to wonder. Even if she managed to convince herself that he'd remained at Lady Hopetoun's for the music, that conviction wouldn't last long. If he was any judge of such things, and he was, then the time was fast approaching when she would confront him over his intentions, and he and she would have the matter out.

Anticipation welled. His lips curved.

When, exactly, that discussion would take place wasn't something he could dictate, yet he was certain he could leave initiating said discussion—one he and she had to have—to her. She would raise the matter when she was ready, which was fine by him; he wouldn't have to trouble himself over trying to guess when she reached that point—he felt confident he could rely on her to tell him.

Lips curving more definitely, he considered the events the haut ton was slated to enjoy the following evening.

As matters stood, he didn't need to do anything beyond religiously appearing at Mary's side at whichever evening events she attended. All he needed to do to advance his campaign to the next stage was to be there, and she would do the rest—would create for him the perfect opportunity to make his intentions crystal clear.

Selecting one ivory card from the seven in his hand, he reread the inscription and nodded. "This one." Tapping the card on his thumb, he murmured, "That's where she'll be tomorrow night. At Lady Bracewell's ball."

Chapter Four

What, by all that's holy, is Ryder up to?

The next morning, over her tea and toast, Mary pondered that question with steadily mounting aggravation.

For what seemed the umpteenth time, she replayed their conversations over the past three evenings; she'd asked him, twice, what he was about, and on both occasions . . . he hadn't exactly answered.

But when he'd challenged her to tell him what she thought his motives were, and she'd laid them out in neat and concise order, he'd agreed she was correct—yet he'd spent the previous evening by her side at a venue where a gentleman of his age should not have appeared unless matrimonially inclined. Although she could have excused his being there on the grounds of protecting Randolph from her, why, once he'd realized Randolph wasn't there, which he had known even before she'd arrived, had Ryder stayed?

For the music?

Was his desire to hear a perfectly fine but hardly famous chamber ensemble play entirely familiar compositions that strong?

Or had he remained for some other reason?

Mary glanced at the empty chair at the foot of the table, the one her mother normally occupied. If Louise had been there, Mary would have sought her counsel; her mother, she felt confident, would have been able to unravel the complexities of Ryder's motives in short order.

"They'll be back tomorrow morning, miss."

Glancing up, realizing she'd been staring rather longingly at the empty chair, Mary summoned a smile for Hudson. "Yes, I know. They'll be home before I know it."

"Is there anything the staff might do for you, miss—in the interim, as it were?"

"No, no." She waved Hudson to set down the teapot he'd brought in, then lifted it and poured herself a fresh cup. "I just need some advice that Mama will surely be able to provide, but there's no rush." Flashing another reassuring smile at Hudson, she concluded, "Tomorrow will be time enough."

With a bow, Hudson left to ferry her used dishes to the kitchen.

Mary leaned back in her chair and sipped. Unbidden, her memory of the previous night's conversation with Ryder rolled through her mind . . . she blinked. Teacup suspended in midair, she sat up, replayed the critical passages again, then thought back to the night before and checked . . .

She frowned, an anxiety she'd been avoiding defining coalescing, then escalating.

Given they'd been conversing frequently of late, she could understand, considering his social standing relative to hers and their long acquaintance, that he might have dispensed with calling her "Miss Cynster." But last night, and even the evening before, other than when he'd wanted to attract her attention . . .

He hadn't called her anything at all.

He'd spoken to her—and she'd responded—as if . . . they already had some sort of understanding. . . .

"No!" The denial was weak; she repeated it, increasingly strongly. "No. And *no!*" Lips firming, setting down her teacup, she shook her head. "It *can't* be so—I won't have it so!" Ryder was not, could not possibly be, her hero—not he who was universally acknowledged as the most unmanageable nobleman in the ton.

As she was determined to remain forever in charge of her life—and therefore that of her husband—ergo, Ryder was not the man for her.

But what if he'd decided that she was the lady for him?

The question echoed through her mind as she stared unseeing across the table.

"What the devil am I to do if he has?"

By the time she glided beside Amelia into Lady Bracewell's ballroom that evening, Mary was confident she'd got herself back on track.

Her track—the one leading to her hero, he who would sweep her off her feet and into wedded bliss.

All she had to do was hunt him down. The necklace and The Lady would take care of the rest.

She'd restarted her campaign by accompanying Penelope, Portia's sister, on an excursion to the park late that morning. They'd taken little Oliver, Penelope's firstborn, for an outing in the mild sunshine. While strolling beside Penelope, Mary had surveyed the gentlemen driving their curricles or strolling the lawns, but none had caught her eye. None had drawn her attention, let alone fixed it.

If Penelope hadn't been Penelope, Mary might have broached the subject of Ryder, but Penelope was more conversant with the behavior of gentlemen millennia old, or if not that, then criminally inclined; any insights she might have to offer would necessarily be questionable.

Mary didn't need more uncertainty, especially not with respect to Ryder.

From the park, she'd joined Amanda at Dexter House, and they'd driven to Lady Holland's for lunch, but that had been an all-female affair. And while the drive there and back had given her ample opportunity to consult her oldest sister on the matter of a botheringly persistent marquess, she had, somewhat to her own surprise, balked at raising the subject.

She'd told herself it was because she was trying her damnedest to forget the man. To oust him from her mind.

Much easier declared than done.

In Amelia's wake, gowned in watered blue silk, with neckline and sleeves trimmed with cornflower blue ribbon, with her customary confidence she greeted Lady Bracewell, then joined Amelia to descend to the ballroom floor—and to her irritation discovered herself prey to the most peculiar case of jangling nerves.

She needed to keep her mind on her task, needed to mingle freely and assess any and all potential gentlemen, especially those she'd had highest on her list before she'd settled on Randolph Cavanaugh.

Of course, all her previous assessments had been made without benefit of the necklace, so perhaps a gentleman who had not before registered as highly as Randolph might appear more attractive when viewed through The Lady's prism.

Walking down the white marble steps, casting her eye over the guests, she was conscious of an ever-tightening tension, an expectation she didn't want to come true yet couldn't quite convince herself wouldn't, but she couldn't see Ryder's mane of tawny golden-brown anywhere in the room.

She looked down as they negotiated the last few steps. She didn't *want* Ryder to be there, didn't want him to vie for her attention, to steal away her senses by insisting on a waltz; God knew she would even admit that she wasn't strong enough, experienced enough, to deny him. And then where would she be?

Caught up in his distracting net again, just as she had been at Castlemaine House.

But, she reminded herself as she gained the ballroom floor, raised her head, and looked out at the sea of guests, there was no longer any reason he should pursue her, not here, not tonight, not ever again.

"Good evening, Amelia."

Mary whipped her head around and smothered a curse. She narrowed her eyes on Ryder, who had stepped out from the lee of the curving steps, which was why she hadn't spotted him, and was bowing over Amelia's hand.

"Ryder." Amelia returned his smile, then glanced at Mary. "I believe you and Mary are acquainted."

Ryder smiled at her; she told herself it was fanciful to imagine his smile looked hungry. "Indeed."

Recalling that Amelia hadn't realized who she had spent most of the Castlemaine ball avoiding, and didn't know who she'd spent the previous evening being charmed by, Mary clung to her sophistication and gave Ryder a smile of her own, one weighty with warning. "Yes, we've met."

Ryder held her gaze for an instant, then looked at Amelia. "Lady Croxton said she was waiting for you. She's in a circle over there." He waved toward a distant corner of the room.

"Ah—thank you." Amelia peered in that direction, then glanced at Mary. "So you know where I'll be. Ryder." With a nod to him, Amelia departed; sliding between shoulders, she disappeared into the crowd.

Mary transferred her gaze to Ryder's eyes; she didn't need to take in the rest of his magnificence—as usual, he was the epitome of the elegant, sophisticated, superficially civilized nobleman. Lips firming, she stated, "I am determined to look over other candidates for my hand. Now I've struck Randolph from that list, you have no reason to dog my steps."

He held her challenging gaze for several heartbeats, then his lips eased into a curve that was not exactly a smile. "Possibly. We'll see."

She frowned at him. "What sort of answer is that?"

He arched his brows in his customary languid fashion. "All the answer you're likely to get."

She smothered a frustrated growl; he was toying with her again. "Ryder, please—go away."

He appeared to give the plea serious thought. She was almost starting to hope when, his eyes still on hers, he shook his head. "I'm really not sure I can oblige."

She blinked; what was she to make of *that*? "Well . . ." She couldn't dismiss him if he refused to go. Lips compressing, she narrowed her eyes on his. "Very well, but if you must hover close, at least do me the courtesy of not getting in my way."

Waiting for no reply, she pivoted and determinedly plunged into the crowd.

Ryder grinned and, at least at first, let her lead the way.

Five minutes later, he was no longer so amused. "You can't possibly imagine that either Rigby or Cantwell figure as suitable candidates for your hand. Your family—your cousins at least—would be appalled."

Mary shot him a sideways glance. "Why?"

He met her gaze. "Debts." Among less mentionable short-comings.

"Oh." She looked faintly crestfallen. After a moment of considering the pair in question—they were standing with a group of their peers, bucks and bloods of the ton all—she asked, "Are you sure?"

"Very. Rigby's close to point non-plus, and Cantwell's acres are mortgaged to the hilt." He hesitated, then added, "That's not exactly *common* knowledge, but it is widely known."

She humphed and turned away. "There should be some list—the grandes dames could keep it. The Marriageable Gentlemen register."

"I thought that was the admittance list of Almack's."

She inclined her head. "Those unmarried gentlemen admitted to Almack's would presumably qualify, but in my case I'm more interested in the unmarried but marriageable gentlemen who would require wild horses to drag them over Almack's threshold."

Gentlemen like him.

But he kept his lips shut and ambled at her heels. Better, tonight, to let her run, to let her assess whoever she pleased so he could point out their weaknesses as candidates for her hand. If they didn't have any . . . well, most gentlemen, at least, were far more awake to the implication of Ryder Cavanaugh, Marquess of Raventhorne, consistently looming by Mary Cynster's side.

He knew where he ranked in the list of eligible males; there were few who would bother trying to compete against him. And of that small number, all of whom were at least acquaintances, if not friends, none—even if prompted by the sport of it—were likely to tempt fate by making a bid for Mary's hand.

She was the sort of termagant most of them would run from.

Indeed, he wasn't at all sure why he wasn't of similar mind.

Yet he wasn't, and she undeniably held the power to surprise him, and, even more importantly, she made him laugh, albeit inwardly.

She was in full flight in pursuit of George Cruikshank, having managed to capture him on his own, when the introduction to the first waltz floated over the room.

George lifted his gaze to Ryder's in mute appeal; a mild and gentle soul, George looked like a captured rabbit, all but quivering with the urge to flee.

Before Ryder could intercede and claim Mary's hand—as he'd fully intended to do anyway—she brazenly laid said hand on George's arm and smiled sweetly at him. "Dare I be so bold, sir, but I do love to waltz."

"Aah . . ." George looked terrified. "Ah . . . gamy leg."

Mary blinked. "Oh?" She looked down at George's until then perfectly stable pins.

George gripped one thigh and grimaced weakly. "Don't like to carry a cane, you know—too vain, I suppose you might say. But it really won't hold me through a waltz, 'fraid to say."

"Oh." Her gaze still on George's legs, Mary all but visibly deflated.

Before she could throw George into paroxysms of lies by asking for details of his invented injury, Ryder closed his fingers about her elbow—and hid his smile when she jumped just a fraction. "Come and dance with me, and let's leave poor George to his pain."

Mary glanced up at him; for a moment her cornflower blue gaze was unfocused—as if she was absorbed with other things—then she blinked and focused properly on him. "Oh, all right." She glanced back at George and inclined her head. "Thank you for the conversation, sir. I hope your leg improves."

His smile firmly suppressed, Ryder nodded to George; the degree of heartfelt thanks George managed to infuse into his wordless reply threatened Ryder's composure, but he'd already realized that Mary had no notion of how much she rattled the meeker gentlemen of the ton.

Leading her to the floor, he turned her into his arms. "Not George, I fear."

"Clearly not." Frowning, Mary allowed Ryder to sweep her into the dance. And fought valiantly to keep her mind on her self-appointed task.

Within two revolutions, two powerful sweeping turns, her mind had wandered to the puzzling question of why waltzing with Ryder felt so good, so right, so fitting, so . . . perfect. Yes, he was beyond expert, but he was so much taller and larger than she that she would have imagined she would feel overwhelmed, yet instead she felt . . . protected. Not caged—the effect was too ephemeral for that—but certainly shielded from any touch, any contact with anyone else.

While waltzing, she and he formed a unit, an entity disassociated from everyone else.

Waltzing with him was like whirling freely within a fragile, essentially intangible construct, their revolutions powered by his harnessed strength, their senses and awareness given over to it, true, but not so much in surrender as in indulgence.

They'd gone down the long room once and were heading up it again when her mind caught up with reality, and she realized she'd relaxed and was delighting in the dance, and smiling easily—freely and sincerely—up at him.

And he was smiling, lazily, but with a certain satisfaction glinting in his hazel eyes, down at her.

She debated telling him that she was inclined to believe she shouldn't waltz with him again; he was spoiling her for all other men. But on the other hand, perhaps she should take all she experienced with him as a guide, as a standard, so to speak; surely, when she finally found her true hero, waltzing with him would trump even this.

This golden, delightful, deliciously scintillating experience.

Of course, given this was Ryder—who needed no further encouragement and even less any further challenges—she kept her lips shut and simply enjoyed the rest of the dance.

When it ended, she thanked him with sincere gratitude, then fastened her eye on the Honorable Warwick Hadfield, who had been waltzing with his cousin, Miss Manners, and had halted nearby.

Warwick had been on her original list, and in all the ways society counted was possibly more eligible as a suitor for her than Randolph had been. Warwick's father was Viscount Moorfield, and Warwick would inherit the significant Moorfield estates. Not that she or her family would care, but as Ryder had pointed out, society did have its expectations.

Now she was wearing the necklace, she should reconsider Warwick.

Effecting a meeting wasn't difficult; most guests were circulating from group to group. But while in response to her encouragements Warwick spoke intelligently and was

charming enough, she felt nothing. Simply nothing. Warwick, too, appeared unaffected by her; indeed, she judged he
was more honestly smitten by his lovely cousin.

Crossing Warwick off her list, she doggedly moved on.
Ryder remained by her side, more or less her escort through
the crowd—and as said crowd was growing ever more dense,
she was grateful for his broad shoulders and the imposing
presence that miraculously caused the way to open up before
them. To give· him his due, although he made comments,
most were general, entertaining, and not in the least carping;
he was wise enough not to comment adversely on her choice
of gentlemen to assess, not unless he had pertinent and helpful facts to impart.

Even then, he didn't directly interfere.

At least not until she—somewhat in desperation, truth
be told—paused in her peregrination around the ballroom
to join a circle that included several budding rakes and one
well-born roué.

Although included in the budding rakes category, Jasper
Helforth and Joselin Filliwell were, she judged, redeemable,
and both were immensely eligible in all other respects. They
were, therefore, worthy of assessment.

She actually enjoyed conversing with the pair, although
she noted both younger men took care to include Ryder in the
banter. Yet she still felt no spark, no ruffling of her senses,
nothing that registered sufficiently, for example, to draw her
senses' attention from Ryder. Whenever she consulted them,
her senses were always first and foremost focused on him,
rather than on her prospective suitors; she'd started to use
that as a barometer of the potential of other men.

If Ryder was determined to stick by her side, he might as
well be useful.

She had no idea what he was deriving from the exercise
beyond the amusement he made no real effort to hide, but
other than insisting on remaining by her side he did nothing
to restrain her in continuing her quest as she chose.

The musicians struck up another waltz, and Joselin Filliwell smiled and solicited her hand. She bestowed it upon him with alacrity; from their discussions he seemed closer to her ideal than Jasper or any other she'd thus far assessed.

Joselin waltzed commendably well.

She tried, she truly tried to capture the same elusive magic she felt when revolving in Ryder's arms, but . . .

Pasting a smile on her face and stifling an inner sigh, she allowed Joselin to escort her back to the group at the end of the entirely uneventful dance.

When they rejoined the group, it had changed composition. Jasper had not returned, but two other younger gentlemen, distant prospects both, had joined the circle, along with Cassie Michaels and Rosalind Phillips. With Ryder now on her other side, Mary spent the next twenty minutes chatting with the recent additions; it was clear to her, if not to the gentlemen, that both Cassie and Rosalind had goals similar to hers. But while pleasant and generally innocuous, the younger men could not hold her interest. They were . . . simply too immature.

She was about to turn to Ryder and suggest they move on when the musicians set bow to string in the introduction to another waltz.

"Miss Cynster—I would be delighted if you would grant me the honor of this waltz."

The languid drawl drew Mary's eyes to the gentleman further around the circle. A touch older than the other men in the group, Claude Legarde had the reputation of a roué-in-the-making. He was fastidiously, yet somehow overly, dressed, with frills at his collar and cuffs; a cloying scent of cloves and myrrh hung about his person.

Mary didn't want to dance with him; she didn't have to think—her skin crawled at the very idea.

But how to decline without giving offense when she'd clearly been prepared to dance with others? Legarde was well known for his acid tongue.

"I'm desolated to have to inform you, Legarde, that Miss Cynster promised this waltz to me." Ryder's drawl was every bit as languid as Legarde's, but somehow significantly less challengeable.

Mary felt such relief that she would have happily kissed Ryder; ridiculous, really, but she hadn't wanted to even touch Legarde. When Ryder turned to her, she smiled and readily surrendered her hand. "Thank you—I hadn't forgotten."

His smile was all appreciation, on several levels. "I didn't imagine you had."

With a vague nod to the group, one she echoed, he turned her toward the floor.

As she moved away, she caught a last glimpse of Legarde's face. The smug, almost delighted look in his eyes made her frown, but she kept the expression from her face as Ryder led her onto the floor.

But why had Legarde looked like that, reacted like that? As if he'd seen something, learned something, secret—even illicit. Something no one else knew.

But then Ryder swung her into his arms and stepped fluidly into the swirl of the dance, and she put Legarde and his reactions from her mind and gave herself up to the moment.

After several revolutions, she marshaled her wits enough to say, "Thank you for rescuing me. Mr. Legarde is definitely not on my list."

"Thank God for that." Ryder looked into her eyes, watched her lips curve in a confident smile, and used her words and tone, and that assured smile, to further placate his natural impulses, more intense where she was concerned than he'd expected, at least, not yet. But she somehow had, more or less from the first, connected directly with that primitive, instinctual side of him, and if anything that connection had only deepened over their recent meetings.

It had grown more distinct, more defined, on learning her purpose in attending this ball.

Still, he'd weathered the challenge thus far. The challenge of letting her run without pouncing and seizing and making off with her. Thus far, he felt, he could congratulate himself on his performance.

The waltz was uneventful; he kept it that way. No need to press his advantage just yet. Better to let her realize—as she eventually would—that no other gentleman could match her as he did, without the distraction of the sensual connection he knew would come to be. That connection was there, as yet nascent but potentially powerful, his to call upon when he wished, but she, he sensed, would be more swayed, and better convinced, by her own logic.

He was confident enough in his character, and in his prowess, to let her chart her own course. It would lead her to him in the end.

At the completion of the dance, both of them were smiling and in complete accord. She allowed him to steer her to a group of ladies and gentlemen closer to his age. He knew them all and introduced her; to his mind she could use a little contrast the better to compare him to the puppies she'd been assessing.

Lady Paynesville, a long-ago lover, turned to him with a smile. "My lord, my brother asked me, were I to see you, to inquire whether you're inclined to come north to Scotland for the hunting this summer?"

Looking into Juliet's eyes, Ryder understood perfectly that game wasn't the only thing that would be on offer should he elect to accept her—and her brother's—invitation. But it was just such interludes—enjoyable but essentially meaningless, with no long-term benefit—that he'd started to find wearisome; his hunter's instincts had decreed they were no longer worth his time. "Thank John for me, but I'm not yet sure what I might be doing this summer."

Juliet took the refusal in good heart. "Ah, well." She smiled and her gaze traveled past him to Mary. "One never does know, I suppose."

Ryder smiled, too, and followed Juliet's gaze—and immediately had to suppress a frown. A scowl. An irritated growl.

While he'd been distracted—for only a few minutes—another gentleman had joined the circle, insinuating himself on Mary's other side.

And that gentleman—assuming one used the term loosely—was Jack Francome. Handsome, debonair, and outwardly as easygoing as Ryder himself, courtesy of his excellent birth, Francome had the entree throughout the ton and was accepted in most drawing rooms, but he'd long been known as a man of dubious character and distinctly shady morals. He'd gambled away his patrimony before he'd reached the age of twenty-five and had subsequently been living off a succession of well-born mistresses.

Although his usual targets were widows rather older than Mary, Francome wasn't the sort to balk at seducing a young innocent in pursuit of a fortune.

That said, he had to be desperate to try for a Cynster.

Francome knew all the ways; he'd engaged Mary so that she'd turned slightly, and he and she were now speaking semiprivately despite still being within the circle. Looming as close as he dared, Ryder eavesdropped on their exchanges, but Francome was toeing the line, carefully avoiding any subject or suggestion that might trigger Mary's suspicions.

Then the damned musicians started playing again.

Mary raised her head, confirmed that it was to be another waltz, then angled an encouraging look at the intriguing Mr. Francome. She had met him before, but only in passing at some ball or other; she hadn't previously had occasion to converse with him, and he was certainly more interesting than the younger gentlemen she'd assessed.

Perhaps she needed to widen her net?

Francome smiled; his brown eyes danced invitingly. "I would ask you to waltz, Miss Cynster, but it's become such a crush I wonder if, instead, you would prefer to take a stroll on the terrace?"

They were standing mere yards from a pair of French doors left open to a paved and balustered expanse and the balmy summer night beyond. Glancing at the couples already strolling in the moonlight, Mary was seized with a sudden yearning for fresh air. "Thank you. I would." She looked eagerly at Francome, and gallantly he offered his arm. She reached out to lay her hand on his sleeve—

A large male hand closed over hers, preventing the contact.

Surprised—indeed, shocked—she looked up at Ryder. The last she'd seen he'd been speaking to the lady on his other side. Her weak "What are you doing?" was drowned out by his forceful and deadly "I think not."

She stared at him; he wasn't speaking to her but to Francome. Ryder's face was harder than she'd ever seen it; carved granite would have been softer. As for his eyes, they were locked on Francome's face.

If looks could kill . . .

Suddenly breathless, she looked at Francome. He was staring at Ryder.

As she watched, Francome paled, swallowed, then, lowering his arm, rather more quietly and with a great deal less of his until then charming bonhomie, said, "I didn't realize . . ."

With something of an effort, Francome wrenched his gaze from Ryder's and looked at her, then his eyes narrowed. "But perhaps—"

"Think again." Ryder's voice remained hard, his tone laden with menace—enough to have Francome immediately look back at him.

After a second's pause, Ryder went on, "Most especially think about how lucky you are that I am not one of her cousins."

Francome searched Ryder's face, his eyes. "You wouldn't . . ."

Looking from one to the other, Mary glanced at Ryder as,

his features easing not at all, he said, "How much are you willing to wager on that?"

She gritted her teeth; there was nothing like being treated like a bone by two dogs to send her temper soaring. She drew in a huge breath. "Ryder—"

Francome spoke over her. "If you'll excuse me, Miss Cynster, I believe I've been summoned elsewhere."

She blinked. "I . . . see."

With a brief bow, not meeting her eyes but, as he straightened, exchanging a much longer glance with Ryder, Francome turned and took himself off, rapidly disappearing into the crowd.

Mary watched him go, then rounded on Ryder—and caught a glimpse of the faces of the others in their circle.

Everyone had heard, or at least seen, the exchange, even though they were pretending they hadn't, but what struck her forcibly was the lack of surprise.

Their acceptance of Ryder's actions . . . like a kaleidoscope, phrases, looks, fragments of memory shifted and swung, realigned—and fell into place.

And she suddenly saw what had been happening.

Over the last three nights, in front of her unsuspecting eyes.

Raising those now opened eyes to Ryder's face, she stared at him. He looked blandly back at her; even as she watched, his expression eased the last little way back into his customary affable mien.

Nothing like it had been a few seconds before.

His gaze lowered to her hand, which he still held in a firm, but not crushing, grip. Slowly, as if he had to force his long fingers to uncurl, he eased his hold and released her.

It was that even more than the preceding exhibition that verified her new understanding—and set a match to her temper.

Narrowing her eyes, rather than lowering the hand he'd released, she grabbed his sleeve, locked her fingers tight.

Yanked his arm down between them, then smiled as sweetly and as vaguely as she could manage at the others in the group. "If you'll excuse us, we're going to stroll."

From the corner of her eye, she saw one of Ryder's brows arch. She shot him a glare. As she dragged him away, she hissed, "Outside!"

He sighed. "Very well, but let's at least be civil about this." Twisting his arm gently, he broke her hold, caught her hand, and tucked it in the crook of his elbow. "Come along then, before you faint. Or have a seizure."

She was, she decided, ready to throttle him.

But she played along and let him steer her onto the terrace. Stepping outside, they both looked around; both saw the empty space at the far end of the long terrace and without further consultation headed that way.

She would have stormed along, but, his hand closing over hers on his sleeve, he held her to an ambling stroll—one that would attract no attention.

Her temper was steaming, well past boiling and ready to explode. She recognized what had been happening now, that he'd been casting an invisible net of possessive protectiveness about her, a broader and more nuanced version of the protectiveness she'd felt when they'd waltzed. Other men could sense it; no doubt some ladies were experienced enough with men of his ilk to detect it, too.

In some primitive way, it marked her as his.

Protectiveness she could understand; she knew the type of man he was, knew that for men such as he protectiveness was a deeply ingrained trait. Which was why the protectiveness she'd sensed when they'd waltzed hadn't set off any alarms.

But possessiveness . . . oh, no. In men like him, for ladies like her, that was not an emotion she would allow.

The spot they were making for was out of clear sight of those in the ballroom but not the many couples strolling the flags; as they neared it and slowed, she slipped her hand from the warmth of Ryder's arm and whisked around to place her back to the balustrade, facing him. With him standing before her, she was effectively screened from all interested onlookers, while she doubted anyone could read anything from his back.

Understanding his role as a screen, he halted directly before her, a foot or so away.

The instant he did, she narrowed her eyes to shards and pointed a finger at his nose. "I asked you before—twice— what you thought you were about dogging my every step through the ballrooms, and it did not escape my notice that on both occasions you didn't actually answer." She paused only to draw breath before continuing in the same force-ful, excessively clipped tone, her gaze locked, gimlet-eyed, with his, "After that little episode in the ballroom just now, I want to make one point absolutely clear—I am not yours!"

She'd expected some response. When seconds ticked by and he continued to stand before her, unmoving and immov-able, she frowned. "What? Cat got your tongue?"

"No. I'm trying to decide how to tell you you're mistaken."

Drawing in a portentous breath, holding his gaze, she crisply stated, "I am not mistaken."

"Permit me to disagree."

"No! You cannot disagree!" Good God, no, he couldn't. Not him of all men . . . she suddenly felt giddy. "This can't be happening."

All he did was open his eyes wider, as if she was still amusing him.

"Arrgh!" She poked her still raised finger into his chest. It was like stabbing rock. "Answer me this then, properly this time. What the devil do you think you're about?" She flung her arms wide. "What on earth do you think to gain with this peculiar campaign of yours?"

"You. As my bride. As my marchioness." Ryder was only too ready to drop all pretense. Aside from all else, she'd seen too much in his fraught exchange with Francome; there was no point in further dissembling.

Arms slowly lowering, she stared at him, utterly shocked. Then, very slowly, as if only just reteaching herself how to, she shook her head. "No. That is not going to happen."

He sighed, the sound clearly conveying his lack of faith in her assessment, then asked in the tone of one humoring another, "And why is that?"

"Because I don't want to marry you."

"So you say at this point—which merely means I'll have to exert myself to change your mind."

She stared up at him for several moments, then, in a tone to mirror his, asked almost conversationally, "Do you know how many people have tried to change my mind about something and given up in abject defeat?"

"I had heard. Your reputation precedes you."

Tilting her head, she studied him, then asked, "If you know so much about me, about my character, why do you want to marry me?"

And that was the truly critical question. The one he couldn't answer, for the simple reason he wasn't sure of the truth himself. Dropping his gaze, he adjusted one sleeve. "Because, contrary to your current belief, we will suit very well, you and I." Raising his eyes to hers, he went on, "There's no reason I can see for you to resist, but I feel honor-bound to point out that resistance, in this case, isn't likely to discourage me." He held her gaze. "I already know you too well."

That got her tipping her nose in the air. "You understand nothing about me if you believe considerations of that nature are likely to sway me."

He could have argued the point, but instead grasped the chance to ask, "What is important to you then?"

"Independence. Being in charge—of my own life, certainly, but also those about me. The freedom to act as I choose without forever having to gain a husband's consent."

The answers had come so instantly that, given the fervor

in her tone and the defiant tilt of her chin, he could not doubt those aspects were critical to her.

Her gaze locked with his. "And you should bear in mind that, regardless of what you might try to tell me, I know your kind. You're a despot—a genial, amiable, caring one maybe, but a despot all the same."

He couldn't argue that, yet . . . holding her gaze, he studied her, considered, then more softly said, "Has it never occurred to you that even despots might be willing to . . . shall we say, find ways to accommodate a lady, a specific, independent, strong-willed, intelligent, and willful lady, who they want as their bride?"

The thought . . . Mary suddenly felt like Randolph and his friends must have, abruptly staring down into a chasm that had unexpectedly opened at their feet. Searching Ryder's hazel eyes, something very like vertigo sent her thoughts, all her previous certainties, spinning . . . "I . . ."

"Don't know what to say?" He lightly shrugged. "At this point, you don't have to say anything."

A general movement of couples back into the ballroom had them both glancing along the terrace; it appeared the ball was winding down.

"We should go in." She inwardly acknowledged a craven desire to bring this astonishing conversation to an end—before she did something truly silly, like ask him what accommodations—

No. That way lay temptation of a kind she wasn't yet prepared to face.

She knew what he was, and he hadn't sought to deny it. Not that denial would have done any good . . .

Instead, he'd offered her something she'd never imagined might exist, a novel option, a chance to seize something she hadn't known could ever be there to be grasped.

She drew in a breath. Temptation, indeed, and he was intelligent enough, insightful enough, to have guessed how much it would appeal to her.

Which only made him even more dangerous—to her, to her future, to her peace of mind.

He'd been studying the thinning crowd through the windows; with a nod, he stepped back and offered his arm. "Sadly, yes. We can't remain here any longer."

Ryder had spotted a shocked face through the window—a face whose owner he would have wished hadn't been in the ballroom at all, much less that she'd seen what she had, little though that had been.

He didn't need Lavinia leaping to any conclusions about him and his current direction. Especially not conclusions that were correct.

Mary placed her hand lightly on his arm and fell in beside him as, with passable savoir faire, they strolled back along the terrace.

As they neared the doors into the ballroom, she glanced up at him. Waited until he met her eyes to declare, "I am not going to allow you to seduce me."

A reckless challenge. He was curious as to how she thought she might stop him, but all he said was, "Just don't try to avoid me—trust me, that won't work." He wouldn't allow it.

She studied his eyes for a moment more, as if hearing, and reluctantly accepting as true, the words he hadn't said, then she sniffed and elevated her nose.

Content enough, he handed her over the threshold, and at her direction escorted her to where Amelia was rising from a chaise, shaking out her skirts and gathering her shawl, preparing to depart.

Leaving Mary with her sister, he didn't dally but quickly left the ballroom; better that any interested observers thought nothing specific had come of that interlude on the terrace, and that he was heading off supremely unconcerned as to Mary's passage home.

Allowing his protective instincts to show at this point would, he felt certain, be counterproductive. And she was safe enough with Amelia.

From the corner by the terrace windows, Lavinia watched her stepson quit the ballroom—and presumably Bracewell House—without a backward glance. Eyes narrowing, she swung around and focused on Mary Cynster. "I don't *believe* it! How *dare* that dastardly knave try to poach the young lady I've selected for Randolph?"

Alongside Lavinia, Claude Potherby, an old friend and Lavinia's escort that evening, was engaged in shaking out and refolding his lace handkerchief. "Now, now, my sweet. There's really no reason to get so het-up. As you haven't informed your stepson of your plans for dear Randolph and so can hardly accuse Raventhorne of intentionally interfering, perhaps you should view his interest in the young lady as confirmation of your astuteness in choosing her for your son."

Lavinia scowled at Potherby. "Don't be absurd. I don't care what Ryder thinks."

Potherby glanced at Mary, presently walking beside Amelia toward the ballroom steps. "Regardless, from all I can see your stepson's agency met with little success. The young lady does not appear enamored."

"Mary Cynster has too much sense to tangle with Ryder. He's too much a hedonist for any sane lady's taste." Lavinia waved dismissively, then rearranged her shawl, preparing to join the stream of departing guests. Potherby gallantly offered his arm. Lavinia took it, then leaned closer to whisper, "But you're right. There's no reason I need to worry about Ryder. It won't be he who fronts an altar soon, at least not with Mary Cynster by his side."

Potherby's smile was both wry and cynical. "Of course not, my dear. Perish the thought. Your plans will doubtless succeed wonderfully. How could they not?"

As she had with Amanda at Hopetoun House, Mary parted from Amelia on Lady Bracewell's steps and climbed into her parents' town carriage. As the footman, Peter, shut the door, she lowered the window, leaned out, and waved to Amelia as her sister, about to be handed into the Calverton carriage further along the line of carriages drawn up at the curb, looked back to check on her.

Satisfied, Amelia waved back, then climbed up.

Closing the window, Mary sat back; a second later, the carriage jerked, then started to roll slowly along the cobbles. Bracewell House was in Berkley Street, just south of Berkley Square. Given it was the height of the Season, countless balls, parties, soirees, and dinners had been held that evening in Mayfair; judging by the chaos of carriages surrounding the square, many events had finished at much the same hour.

Accustomed to such delays, Mary sank back into the comfort of fine leather and welcomed the darkness and relative coolness. The carriage rocked and managed the turn onto the south side of Berkley Square, only to immediately halt again. Glancing through the window, Mary glimpsed the Calverton carriage pull free of a snarl of carriages and roll at a decent clip up the west side of the square; Amelia, at least, was well on her way home.

Alone and with no real distraction, Mary embraced the moment, drew in a deeper breath, and, finally, let her thoughts free. From the moment she'd stepped back into the ballroom she'd kept them and her reactions contained, restrained, suppressed; she hadn't wanted to alert Amelia or anyone else to the sudden and cataclysmic uncertainty that now ruled her.

Ryder had just changed the rules of her world, in the process shaking her to her foundation; she needed to deal with the ramifications, the questions of where she was now, and where she truly should aim to go, and that sooner rather than later.

Drawing in another breath, she let it out slowly, waiting for the whirl of her thoughts to subside. No matter what

Ryder thought or did, she remained in charge of her own life—the decisions that would define her future were still hers to make.

Gradually, her customary self-confidence returned. Growing calmer, she turned her mind to her new situation, to the new landscape Ryder had created between them.

Recalling all the details, visual as well as verbal, she revisited and reexamined all they'd said on the terrace—and all they hadn't. He'd stated his intentions, baldly and unequivocally, and although he hadn't underscored the point, he wasn't about to accept any dismissal.

But the possibility he'd raised . . . oh, what a dizzingly tempting prospect. A prospect made even more enticing by him being him, the man, the nobleman he was.

To have a man of his stature, his character, his traits, make an offer like that—to change whatever he needed to change to accommodate her in his life . . .

"Well!" She blew out a breath. "At the very least, that's impressive."

And oh-so-tempting, especially to her. Not just because she was a Cynster but because of the well-nigh irresistible challenge of taming a man like Ryder Cavanaugh.

He'd agreed to allow her to at least make the attempt.

Whether she succeeded or not was a different matter.

"But I'm getting ahead of myself," she murmured to the shadows. "If I discount his obvious personality defects and calmly assess him on the usual criteria as a possible candidate for my hand, would he make my list?"

It didn't take long to decide that in the affirmative; Ryder's title, family, wealth, estates, social standing—all were the pinnacle of what a lady such as she, the youngest daughter of a major house, might think to claim.

"Society and the grandes dames would definitely approve." She thought, then added, "But I don't really care about them. And the family will agree with whoever pleases me, so what do I truly want?"

Would filling the position of the Marchioness of Raventhorne please her? Satisfy her?

Be to her liking?

"That's not so easy to answer." She glanced out of the carriage window, but they were still on the south side of Berkley Square. Deciding it was nice to be able to think aloud
without risking anyone overhearing, she continued her ru-
minations.

"Being Ryder's wife. That's the issue here. Whether as his
wife I'll be able to be as I wish to be . . ."

She grimaced into the dark. "And although that's not at all
easy to decide, deciding one way or another is not something
I'm going to be able to avoid. I'm going to have to accept him
or refuse him . . . and refusing him is going to be a battle,
because he won't accept that readily." Denying Ryder would
demand a degree of strength and a wealth of conviction. "A
lot of certainty, which at present I'm not sure I have."

Could she trust in what he'd said? "I'm sure he meant
every word—that he would *try* to find ways to accommodate my wishes—but what if he fails? He might be willing
enough to attempt it, but will he actually be able to"—she
gestured in the dark—"make the necessary adjustments?"
Even if he wanted to, could the lion change?

No matter how she viewed it, accepting his proposal
would be a massive risk—for her. Not for him.

"If I accept him, regardless of how matters play out, he
will have got what he wants."

Her. As his bride. She frowned. "Why has he settled
on me?"

A highly pertinent question, but he'd told her at least one
reason. She was the last Cynster girl unwed; given his age,
for him she was the only possible chance of forming an alliance with her family.

Added to that, she had to admit that, somewhat to her surprise, they rubbed along fairly well together. Their similar
backgrounds made it easy for her to stand alongside him

socially, and her far-more-extensive-than-was-customary acquaintance with and experience of men like him—namely all the men in her family—was also undoubtedly a boon in terms of her understanding him.

And, to some extent, making allowances for certain behavior that other ladies might find trying.

It wasn't that she wouldn't find the same traits annoying but more that she would understand that, in some situations, he wouldn't be able to help himself. "For instance, with Francome."

She dwelled on all she'd sensed in the incident, then shook aside the distraction. "Where was I? Ah, yes. He clearly finds me amusing, and I have to admit he's more than passably entertaining, and he can certainly waltz. As for the rest . . ." The way he made her feel, the effect he had on her that she habitually ignored, given she'd never been able to suppress it.

"Hmm . . . I'd wager Grandmama's pearls that he has the same effect on every woman with functioning senses, so I don't think I can deduce anything from that."

The carriage had been inching forward; now it rocked and canted on its springs as the coachman turned the horses north along the west side of the square. Gradually, the carriage's speed increased to a steady walking pace.

Refocusing on the dimly lit seat opposite, Mary replayed her thoughts. By all the customary social and familial measures, she and Ryder were well suited. "But none of that says anything about love."

And that was her biggest question, her stumbling block, her highest hurdle. Not by any stretch of the imagination could she believe that Ryder was in love with her. Not now. But the big question was: Could he be?

If she gave him—them—the chance, could he fall in love with her, and she with him?

Could he, Ryder Cavanaugh, Marquess of Raventhorne,

possibly be her true hero, the man who would sweep her off her feet and into wedded bliss?

She gnawed on the question as the carriage gradually picked up pace. As the coachman slowed the horses to negotiate the entry to Davies Street, Mary reached up, found the necklace about her throat, and drew the rose quartz pendant from between her breasts.

In the faint light cast by a streetlamp, she studied the pendant, turning it between her fingers. She'd thought it would be so easy. That finding her one, her true hero, would simply be a matter of wearing the necklace, and he would promptly present himself and bow before her. . . .

She blinked, her mind reeling back to the night she'd first worn the necklace. The first gentleman she'd had any real interaction with . . . had been Ryder.

She'd dismissed him, walked around him and away.

If he gets under your skin to the point you simply can't shrug him off . . .

Angelica's description of how her hero might appear to her.

Under such a definition, Ryder qualified.

She stared at the rose quartz pendant, then, lips tightening, tucked it back under her bodice. She believed in the powers of The Lady's talisman—she truly did—but she hadn't expected her quest for love and her true hero to require her to court the sort of risks that walking into the den of an acknowledged lion of the ton would entail.

Sitting back as the carriage rolled around the corner into Mount Street, she grimaced. "I suppose it comes down to whether or not I'm convinced that there's no other true hero out there for me—that Ryder is truly my one."

Sudden movement outside the carriage had her glancing out. As if her use of his name had conjured him, Ryder stepped out of the mouth of an alley just ahead . . .

No, not stepped—reeled.

As the carriage drew level, she watched as he staggered, slowly pivoted, then collapsed facedown on the pavement.

He might have been drunk, but she knew he hadn't been, that he couldn't be.

Leaping to her feet, she thumped her fist on the trapdoor in the ceiling. "John! Stop! *Stop!*"

Chapter Five

She leapt out of the carriage while it was still rocking. Her heart in her mouth, she raced back along the pavement. The shouts from John and Peter for her to wait seemed distant, far away.

Even before she reached Ryder, she knew something was terribly, horribly wrong.

Blood glinted, fresh, ruby red, by his side.

She fell on her knees beside him. "Oh, God!" One glance at his face confirmed he was unconscious. An unsheathed rapier, the blade stained with blood, lay weakly clasped in one hand.

Frantic, she tried to push him onto his back, to find where he was wounded. There was too much blood . . . but he was too heavy for her to shift.

Peter reached her. She didn't even glance up. "Quickly! Help me!"

With Peter's assistance, she managed to heave Ryder onto his back.

An ugly gash on his left side, near his waist, was steadily pumping blood.

Her heart stopped. "No." She pressed a hand over the wound, then as blood immediately seeped through her fingers, she slapped her other hand over the first, trying desperately to staunch the flow.

Glancing up and about, she realized Peter had circled

around; he stepped cautiously into the alley. He came out almost immediately, his face ashen. "Two ruffians in there, miss. Reckon as they're dead. Must've set on him." Dragging in a breath, he nodded at Ryder. "Gave a good account of hisself, but they'd already stuck him."

"Yes, well, don't just stand there!" When Peter did just that, looking mournful, she snapped, "He's not dead yet!"

The warmth flooding under her hands assured her that was true, but for how long? "For God's *sake*!" Wild panic gripped her. Looking around, she saw John Coachman, who had had to brake the coach and find some urchin to hold his horses, running toward them. "Thank heaven." She raised her voice. "John—it's the Marquess of Raventhorne. He's been badly wounded, but his house is just there." Without taking her hands from Ryder's side—was it her imagination, or was the steady stream slowing, and was that good or bad?—she hauled in a breath, swallowed her fear, and nodded to the houses on the opposite side of the street. "It's the one with the iron railings—go and summon his staff immediately!"

"Yes, miss!" Skidding to a halt, John turned and raced across the street.

Despite the traffic about Berkley Square, and a conglomeration of carriages some way down the street, there was no traffic passing along that stretch just then. Mary didn't know whether to be thankful for the lack of distraction or annoyed not to have had more help.

She looked down and attempted to take stock. The closest source of light was the streetlamp several yards beyond Ryder's feet. She couldn't see well enough to be sure the gash she was pressing on was his only wound. "Peter, can you see any other cut? Is he bleeding from anywhere else?"

"Not that I can see, miss." Peter had retrieved Ryder's hat and his cane—the empty outer sheath of the rapier—from the alley. Coming to stand opposite her again, he shifted, clearly nervous. "Is there anything else you want me to do, miss?"

Her mind seemed to be operating on two levels simultaneously. One was a tumult of emotions; the other was surprisingly clear. Just as well; this was no time for panic—Ryder couldn't afford it. Holding her emotions at bay, she clung to what needed to be done—to what she was good at. Taking charge. "Yes. Go across the road and tell his lordship's people that he's unconscious and they'll need a door, or a gate, or a stretcher of some sort to move him. And they must send for his physician immediately."

"Ah—I don't think I should leave you—"

"There's no one about. Just go!" She used the tone of voice with which few argued.

Peter wasn't proof against it; he ducked his head and went.

She refused to think about how much blood lay on the pavement beside Ryder, let alone had soaked into his clothes and was turning sticky around her hands. As she registered the cloying warmth about her fingers, instinct shrieked at her to draw her hands away; ruthlessly she quashed it. Her senses drew in; her gaze locked on the rise and fall of Ryder's chest, she followed the rhythm until it became her own heartbeat. . . .

His heart was higher than where she was pressing; she could sense the faint thump through her fingers.

Dragging in a ragged breath, she raised her gaze to his face, that unbelievably beautiful sculpted face, now pale in the moonlight and so still, devoid of its customary animation— the glint in his hazel eyes, the inherently wicked curve of his chiseled lips, the languidly suggestive arch of his brows.

Something in her chest shifted; her vision blurred. "Don't you *dare* die on me, Ryder," she whispered, fierce and low. "Not now."

Ryder sensed hard pavement beneath him. He felt cold all over, chilled; he wasn't sure he could actually feel much of his body. Everything seemed far away.

But he sensed warmth beside him. He would have liked to get closer.

He remembered getting stabbed, and wondered why fate, who had never been fickle to him before, had suddenly deserted him.

He tried to lift his lids—and was surprised when they rose a fraction.

An angel with lustrous dark hair was leaning over him. His vision swam into focus and he recognized Mary. Not an angel then, but for him even better.

Her normal skin tone was alabaster, but she looked even paler. Her brows were drawn. She looked worried, anxious . . .

Why? His lips were oddly dry, his tongue leaden. "What . . . ?" More breath than speech.

She looked at him, startled, but she didn't move her arms, her hands. Then her expression grew fierce and her blue eyes burned. "Stay with me!"

He blinked—would have told her he had no intention of doing anything else, but then his lids wouldn't rise again, and everything grew dim, and he tumbled into the waiting darkness.

Mary stared at Ryder's face, willing him to open his eyes again, to give her that much hope, but his features had slackened; he was unconscious again.

A clatter of feet, a rush of people, and she was surrounded by a bevy of men all exuding unbridled concern but with no idea what to do, and she was forced to focus and organize them. "No, I'm not stepping back. I can't take my hands away, not yet." She glanced around. "Good—there's enough of you. One at his head, one at each shoulder, one at each hip, and one man to lift his feet. The other three of you can slide that door under him when the rest of us ease him up."

They shuffled, and under her continued direction, acting in concert they managed to ease Ryder onto the door, then six of them lifted the panel while Ryder's butler—he'd introduced himself as Pemberly—helped Mary to her feet so she didn't have to shift her hands.

But the pressure she'd exerted necessarily eased a trifle before she could press down again; blood welled, but much less, and more sluggishly.

Sending up a swift prayer, she grimly nodded and they started off, John and Peter holding back the traffic so they could ferry their burden across the cobbled street and up the steps into Raventhorne House.

As, slowly and awkwardly, they negotiated the steep steps, Mary said, "He regained consciousness just before and spoke—it was only one word, but . . ." She paused to steady her voice. "He's not dead yet."

Whether she was speaking to reassure them or herself she didn't know, but the butler audibly drew in a breath; quickening his pace, he crossed the narrow porch to hold open the double doors. As he did, he spoke to others within, "He's still alive."

"Oh, thank *heaven*!"

Crossing the threshold, Mary realized the feminine exclamation hadn't come from any female member of Ryder's family but from a woman she took to be his housekeeper.

The staff were all gathered, all trapped by concern and an eager, almost desperate desire to help, but with no notion of what needed to be done. Mary didn't hesitate—this was no time for social niceties, and if she was treading on some lady's toes by assuming command, then that lady ought to have been there to take charge. "Pemberly—some names, please. We need to get his lordship upstairs."

Snapped into action by the whip of her voice, Pemberly shut the double doors and introduced the housekeeper, Mrs. Perkins, and a man Mary took to be Ryder's gentleman's gentleman, Collier.

"Good. Mrs. Perkins, perhaps you might go up and ensure his lordship's bed is ready to receive him, but please don't start any fire in his room, not until the doctor has seen him."

"Yes, miss." Eyes round, Mrs. Perkins curtsied and hurried for the stairs.

Mary turned her sights on Collier; the man was all but dithering in his helplessness. "Fetch scissors to cut his lordship out of his clothes—we won't be able to ease him out of them. And round up bandages and a basin. You might also take charge of his lordship's swordstick." She glanced around. "My footman has it."

Collier gulped in a breath and straightened. "I'll find it, miss. And the rest."

Keeping her hands pressed to Ryder's side, she turned to Pemberly. "Have you sent for his lordship's physician?"

"Yes, miss. A boy's already gone."

"Excellent." Mary eyed the long first flight of stairs. "In that case, let's take his lordship to his room."

"Indeed, miss . . ." Pemberly tried to catch her eye.

"Cynster. Miss Mary Cynster." Shuffling alongside the door-cum-stretcher bearing Ryder's still form, Mary cautioned the men, "Very carefully, now. No need to rush."

Taking due note of her tone, the six burly men—footmen and grooms—climbed the stairs one slow step at a time.

Mary largely lost track of the following hour. With a great deal of organizing, they managed to lift Ryder off the door and onto the wide expanse of his bed without her shifting her hands; she ended up perched on her knees alongside him, keeping steady pressure on his wound. Collier and Mrs. Perkins worked around her to strip the clothes from Ryder's upper body, then Mrs. Perkins washed the worst of the blood from his too-pale skin.

Her gaze drawn to the wide expanse of his chest, the broad, heavy muscles garlanded with crisp golden brown hair, the skin, more olive than her own, smooth and taut over the sculpted hardness, Mary found herself fascinated, but in a distant, detached way.

Some currently submerged part of her noted the immense weight of his shoulder bones, the heavy muscles of his upper arms, the impressive width of his chest that tapered down past his lower ribs and ridged abdomen to his waist, and then further to his still narrower hips. Her hands were pressed to his side, just a touch above his waist. Theoretically, she supposed, her palms were—shockingly—pressed to his skin, but the blood between nullified any true tactile contact.

The first time she'd seen him half naked shouldn't have been like this.

The first time she had her hands, skin to skin, on his torso, she would have hoped to feel more than the sticky slickness of blood.

She registered the oddity of the thoughts but didn't have time to dwell on them.

"There now, miss." Mrs. Perkins ducked her head to catch Mary's gaze. "I think it's time we had a closer look at that wound. There doesn't seem to be much more coming from it."

Seeing that the housekeeper was holding a clean, damp cloth in her hand, Mary drew breath, nodded, and slowly—ready to slap them back if need be—she peeled first one, then the other hand from the wound.

Collier appeared beside her with damp rags; without shifting her gaze from the wound, she let him wipe her hands. Revealed, the tear in Ryder's skin was less than two inches long, a stab wound obviously deeper than it was wide.

Eyes locked on it, breathing suspended, they watched, waited, but no more blood flowed from the gash.

"Shall I wash it, miss?" Mrs. Perkins brandished her cloth.

"No." Frowning, Mary turned as Collier brought a bowl of water for her to wash her hands. "I think we should wait for the doctor." She looked at Pemberly, who had observed all from the foot of the bed. "How long will he be, do you think?"

"Dr. Sanderson's rooms are in Harley Street, miss, so he should be here soon."

Mary glanced at the bloody patch marring Ryder's otherwise perfect form; to her it looked obscene. "In that case,

I suggest we place a pad of clean cloth over the wound—gauze first, if you have it—and then lightly bind it in place." She glanced at Ryder's face. "Just in case he regains consciousness and moves."

Between them, they managed it, then she and Mrs. Perkins withdrew, allowing Collier, with Pemberly's help, to divest Ryder of the rest of his clothes.

When Mary returned, the room was softly lit by shaded lamps. Ryder lay still, the covers drawn to his neck, his golden-brown hair bright against the pristine ivory of the pillows. But beneath his mane, his face was shockingly pallid, his lips faintly blue, his features leached of all animation.

He might have been an effigy except his chest discernibly rose and fell, his breathing shallow, but still regular.

Pemberly had left, going downstairs to wait for the doctor. Mrs. Perkins had departed, carrying all the bloodied rags away.

Collier remained, sitting quietly in a corner, his hands between his knees, his gaze fixed on the figure in the bed.

Inwardly acknowledging her dashed hopes that Ryder might have regained consciousness, Mary fetched a straight-backed chair from the side of the room. Collier started to rise to help her, but she waved him to remain where he was, then set the chair beside the bed, sat, and, like Collier, prepared to keep vigil. Leaning her elbows on the side of the high mattress, she folded her hands and fixed her gaze on Ryder's face.

Now the first rush of activity was past and they'd done all they could to that point, she took a moment to reach for calm, to reconnect with the wider present.

After a few minutes, she murmured, "Collier—am I correct in assuming there's no lady of the house?"

"Yes, miss." Collier shifted on his chair. "Meaning to say there isn't." After an instant's hesitation, he went on, "The marchioness and his lordship don't get on. He bought her a house in Chapel Street, and she lives there."

"His half sister, Lady Eustacia?"

"Lives with her mama."

"His half brothers?"

"Lord Randolph and Lord Christopher have separate lodgings, and Lord Godfrey still lives in Chapel Street."

After a moment, Collier cleared his throat and carefully, somewhat diffidently, said, "I suppose, if you thought it necessary, we could send for Lord Randolph."

Ryder's heir. If she had Randolph summoned now . . .

Quite aside from the likelihood that Randolph would still be out on the town and wouldn't return to his lodgings until dawn, sending for Randolph—who could in no way assist with Ryder's survival—would be like taking the first step in acknowledging . . . something she wasn't prepared to give credence to at all.

She drew in a breath, held it until she was sure her voice wouldn't waver and her tone would be as authoritative as she wished. "As his lordship's not about to die, I doubt summoning Lord Randolph will help at this point."

Collier eased out the breath he'd been holding. "Indeed, miss. And when it comes to one helping the other, it's usually the other way about."

Lips lifting cynically—she could well imagine that— Mary settled on the chair.

After several minutes, Collier asked, "Will you stay, miss?" As if to excuse what was clearly a request rather than a question, he hurriedly added, "Yours was the last face he saw. Might be helpful if you're here when he wakes."

It was as good an excuse as any. She inclined her head. "Yes, I'll stay. At least until the doctor arrives and gives his verdict."

She would stay until she was convinced beyond doubt that Ryder would survive. She didn't need to think, to consult any part of her rational mind to know that was her decision, and one from which she would not be moved.

Just the thought of him dying . . .

Quite how she imagined her presence might prevent Death from taking him wasn't the issue; if she left and he died, she would never forgive herself.

Sounds in the corridor had her glancing around. She hadn't truly noticed the room itself—until then she'd registered little beyond Ryder—but in instinctively surveying it in light of what she assumed was the doctor's imminent arrival, she wasn't surprised to discover that, while the overall decor was unquestionably masculine, it was equally undeniably sumptuous.

The velvet hangings draping the massive four-poster bed, with its elegantly turned oak posts and restrainedly carved headboard, were heavy and plush, in a shade of old gold that complemented the rich patina of the oak, both of the bed and the tallboys and chests arranged about the room. On either side of the bed, long windows were presently screened by curtains of the same gold velvet; the same fabric had been used to upholster the two straight-backed chairs and two oak-framed wing chairs.

A silk counterpane in a tapestry of golds was spread over the bed; the ivory sheets and pillowcases were of the finest linen, stark in their simplicity, yet in perfect counterpoint to the richness, the haven of sensual lushness, within which they lay.

The door opened; Mary turned her head and watched as a man—a gentleman by his dress, long, lean, with an angular face and kind, if weary, brown eyes—strode in. The black bag he carried confirmed he was the doctor. What name had Pemberly given?

The man's eyes had instantly fixed on Ryder, so silent and still in the big bed; his steps slowing, he paused at the foot of the bed—almost as if expecting Ryder to open his eyes and make some joke—then he appeared to shake free of whatever held him and, frowning, walked swiftly around the bed to the side opposite Mary.

Setting his black bag on the bed, he met her eyes.

"Good . . . ah, I believe it's morning. I'm David Sanderson. And you are?"

"Mary Cynster." She'd been correct in her judgment; physician he might be, but Sanderson was also a gentleman. "I saw Ryder collapse on the street outside. I went to his aid and had my people summon his."

Sanderson blinked. Several times. But all he said was, "I see."

He reached for the coverlet. Mary rose and helped him turn the covers down to Ryder's waist.

Taking Ryder's wrist between his fingers, Sanderson closed his eyes. After a moment, he murmured, "His pulse is steady, but weak." He opened his eyes.

Mary pointed to the pad they'd bound over Ryder's wound. "He was stabbed there. He lost a huge amount of blood."

Sanderson humphed. Reaching up, he raised one of Ryder's lids, examined his eye. "Has he been out to it since you found him?"

"He regained consciousness for a short time—very briefly—while we were still outside."

Sanderson glanced at her. "Did he speak?"

She nodded. "To me."

"And he knew you?"

She went to nod, then hesitated, replaying the short exchange in her mind. She grimaced. "I believe so, but he didn't say enough for me to be sure."

"But he interacted—he reacted to something you said?"

She forced herself to say, "I think so, but I can't be certain."

Sanderson was busy untying their makeshift bandage; he shot her a curious look. "All right." As he lifted the pad, then eased the gauze away, he murmured, "It doesn't matter that he's unconscious now—it's probably for the best if he lost a lot of blood." He paused, then went on, "And judging by the coolness of his flesh and his pallor, he's lost far more than I'd like."

Frowning, Mary said, "I would have thought, as his doctor, you'd rather he didn't lose any blood at all."

Finally lifting the gauze away, Sanderson gave a short laugh. "I've known Ryder since Eton. Trust me, his losing blood was a common enough occurrence." Looking down at the wound, Sanderson sobered. A moment passed, then, lips thinning, he said, "He usually had the sense never to lose this much."

Bending close, Sanderson very gently probed the wound, then he glanced at Collier. "I'm going to need hot water to clean this. Have them boil it now, and bring it here in the kettle in which it boiled, along with a metal basin and a smaller bowl, metal if you have one, porcelain if you haven't."

Collier had risen when the doctor had entered and had silently hovered, waiting for such orders. He nodded crisply. "Yes, sir. Right away."

Pemberly had followed the doctor in, closing the door and standing with his back to it; he now opened it for Collier, then closed it again.

Mary kept her gaze on Sanderson, who had gone back to examining the wound. After a moment more, unable to help herself, she asked, "How bad is it?"

Pausing in his probing, Sanderson glanced up at her. "I'm not yet sure. How exactly did this happen, do you know?"

"As far as we can tell, he was set on in the alley"—she waved in the direction of the street—"while walking home. All we know is that two ruffians are there, dead now, and Ryder had his rapier in his hand when he fell."

"Two dead?" Sanderson glanced at Pemberly.

"Indeed, sir," Pemberly intoned.

"They're still out there?"

Pemberly looked faintly offended to have been asked. "I would presume so, sir."

Lips compressing, Sanderson straightened, his gaze fixed on Pemberly as he clearly weighed . . . something; Mary realized what when he spoke. "I suggest we get both bodies in—your master will want to find out who attacked him when he wakes and can think."

"Ah." Pemberly looked struck. Slowly, he nodded. "Indeed, sir. I take your point. I'll send some footmen to retrieve the corpses and—"

"I don't want to know, Pemberly."

A faint smile touched Pemberly's lips. "Naturally not, sir. The disappearance of any bodies from an alley is in no way connected with you."

Sanderson's lips twisted wryly. "Just so." Bending again, he returned to his examination as Pemberly quietly let himself out.

Mary considered Sanderson's dark head. "As I understand it, you just took quite a risk."

Without looking up, Sanderson shrugged. "In the matter of taking risks, Ryder's taken more than his fair share for me." With a sigh, he straightened.

Catching sight of Mary's openly inquisitive look, he pointed at Ryder. "Eldest son of a marquess—a viscount as he then was." He pointed at himself. "Youngest son of an entirely undistinguished family attending Eton on a scholarship." His gaze returning to Ryder, Sanderson more quietly said, "I was the brains. He was the brawn. That worked for us both, surprisingly well."

Mary glanced at Sanderson, then looked back at Ryder. Sanderson wasn't giving either of them sufficient credit. Although distinctly on the long, tall, and lean side, Sanderson did not appear weak in the least, and everyone knew that the life of a doctor was physically demanding. As for Ryder, he used his obvious brawn to deflect attention from his intelligence; she, at least, had never been fooled.

While she'd been looking at Ryder, Sanderson had been studying her. When she looked up and caught his gaze, he drew a deep breath, then said, "Rather than ask you what the hell you're doing here, in Ryder's house, by his bed . . ."

Again she got the impression Sanderson fought some inner battle with his scruples—and, as before, his common sense won. "I will instead inquire whether you can stand the sight of blood without fainting."

Mary held his gaze. "When Ryder was carried in here, my palms were where that wad of gauze and cloth was. My hands were coated in his blood. It had clotted between my fingers and was horribly sticky." She paused, then added, "If you must know, it didn't occur to me to even feel queasy."

Sanderson grinned. "Good. Very good, as it happens." His grin swiftly faded as he looked again at the wound in Ryder's side. "I'm going to need another pair of steady hands for what I think I must do."

Mary tried to read Sanderson's expression; he looked worried, but determined. "You don't seem all that certain about what you intend to do."

He briefly met her eyes. Again he swiftly debated, then said, "It's like this. Ryder has the constitution of an ox and the heart of a lion. With an injury like this, the former is a great help, but the latter . . . might not be such a boon."

She frowned. "How so?"

"His heart would have been beating hard in the alley—in reaction to being attacked, in anger and in defense, in fighting for his life. And his heart is very strong. That's why he lost so much blood so quickly." Sanderson glanced at her and this time held her gaze. "Frankly, if you hadn't reached him and done what you did—pressed your hands there and kept them there—he would almost certainly have died, have bled out, within minutes."

She took a moment to absorb that, then let her frown deepen. "But he didn't die, so—"

"He didn't die because the pressure from your hands slowed the blood enough for the worst internal cuts to clot." Sanderson glanced down at Ryder. "That's good—but until I see what it was that was cut, and whether it requires sewing to stay closed permanently or not, we won't know if, when he wakes and moves, some bad cut won't open up again. If I sew him up without checking and some major internal cut opens again, he could very easily bleed to death before he or anyone else realizes what's happening."

"Because the bleeding will then be on the inside?"

"Exactly." Sanderson glanced at the corridor; multiple pairs of footsteps were heading their way. He looked at her again, again caught her eyes. "Washing away the clotted blood enough to see what was cut carries its own dangers—he might start bleeding heavily again. But I can't risk not checking, and if you're willing to help me by holding the wound open—I'll show you how—then I'll have a better chance of doing the job without starting a fresh round of bleeding." He glanced at Ryder's face. "Which, truth be told, he really can't afford."

"Of course I'll help." Mary added for good measure, "I wasn't about to leave him to your tender mercies, anyway."

Sanderson smiled; the expression lifted the weariness from his face, revealing a rakishly handsome man beneath. "Looks like Ryder has at least the two of us on his side."

As the door opened to admit Mrs. Perkins, Pemberly, and Collier, between them bearing two steaming kettles and an assortment of metal basins, bowls, and a pile of clean cloths, Mary murmured, "If it counts in any way, from all I can see he has everyone in this house on his side."

Sanderson dipped his head in acknowledgment, then set about organizing his surgery.

Mary had never assisted in any medical procedure before. It was painstaking, back-breaking work. In addition to her, all three of Ryder's staff remained in the room throughout, holding lamps as required, replenishing hot water, handing Sanderson fresh cloths.

Eventually Sanderson, his bent head blocking Mary's view of the wound, murmured, "He always had the devil's own luck." He briefly shifted to glance up at Mary, then went back to his task. "I'd hardly dared hope, but the only cut I can see is to his liver, and while that's more than enough to account for all the blood he lost, it will heal and take care of itself—I don't need to disturb it by trying to stitch it."

Mary had no idea how to interpret that. "Does that mean he'll be all right once he wakes?"

"As not one of the major vessels has even been nicked, then . . . yes." Slowly Sanderson straightened, eyes closing as he eased his back, which had to be aching even more than Mary's. Opening his eyes, he met her gaze and smiled faintly, albeit tiredly. "Once I sew him back up, the skin and inner layers will eventually seal, and that will be it—at least as far as more bleeding goes. *However,*" he continued, sobering significantly, "before we get too relieved, let me hasten to add that he still has to survive the shock of losing so much blood."

Mary narrowed her eyes. "What does that mean? Specifically, what does that mean for someone with the constitution of an ox?"

"It means," Sanderson said, bending to dab again, "that I sew him up, and then we wait. *If* he wakes, we can proceed from there with more confidence, but whether he wakes . . . I regret to inform you that that is still in question."

The relief in the room abruptly faded.

Sanderson finished his inspection, cleansed the wound's surrounds, then plied his needle. Mary watched, quite literally unable not to.

At last all was done, the wound rebandaged and the covers tucked around Ryder again. While washing his hands, Sanderson gave orders for the fire to be lit and the room to be allowed to warm. "But not to the point of being a hothouse. Just normal, reasonable warmth." He glanced at the assembled staff. "Do not allow him to overheat. That won't help."

"Yes, Doctor," the three chorused.

Finally, Sanderson returned to the bed. He checked Ryder's pulse, then looked across the bed at Mary, once again seated in the straight-backed chair on the bed's other side. "His heartbeat's still steady, but barely the right side of thready, much too weak. His pulse is unusually slow. I wish I could give us all better hope, but the truth is it's still touch and go." He drew a tight breath, then said, "I expect we'll know by morning, when he wakes."

Her gaze on Ryder's face, Mary nodded, understanding that Sanderson meant *if* he wakes. Without looking up, she said, "I'll stay. Until he wakes."

If Ryder was going to die, she couldn't let him die alone.

Sanderson studied her silently for several moments; she could feel his gaze but didn't meet it, then from the corner of her eye she saw him incline his head. "I have an accouchement to attend—the boy has already come to call me. I'll return as soon as I can, but that will most likely be late morning. Regardless, if there's any change for the worse, send word—I'll leave my direction with Pemberly."

She nodded in farewell. Thanking Sanderson wasn't her place, and more, thanking him would be an insult to the devotion he so clearly felt toward Ryder.

With murmurs to the others, Sanderson left.

His mention of the wider world had reminded Mary that it was still there; John and Peter would be waiting downstairs, and Hudson and the staff in Upper Brook Street would soon start worrying about where they all were. Looking up, she said, "Pemberly—if you would fetch paper, pen, and ink, I should like to write a note for my coachman to take to my home."

"Of course, miss. Right away."

Before Pemberly could depart, Collier volunteered, "His lordship's traveling writing case is in the dressing room next door, miss—if that would do?"

"Thank you—that would be perfect."

By the time Collier fetched the writing case and laid it on the bed before her, she'd realized she had two notes to write. One to Hudson, to relieve any anxiety as to her safety, and a second to her parents, to be handed to them the instant they crossed the threshold that morning, in case she had not by then returned home.

Both notes were straightforward and to the point, the first simply telling Hudson that all was well and not to worry, the second explaining her absence in more detail and asking her parents to come to Ryder's house as soon as they could.

Their arrival would lend her all the countenance she required and, if Ryder had not yet woken, the support she suspected she would need.

Mrs. Perkins fussed about the room, tidying things away, then, with a last look at the bed, she left. Still keeping station by the door, in hushed tones Pemberly discussed keeping watch with Collier.

Mary folded the note to her parents, wrote their names and the instructions for delivery on the outside, then enclosed that note inside her missive to Hudson, and inscribed the resulting package with his name.

Waving the packet to dry the ink, she turned to Pemberly. "Please give this to John, my coachman, and tell him he and Peter are to return to Upper Brook Street and deliver it to Hudson, my parents' butler."

Accepting the packet, Pemberly bowed. "At once, miss." Straightening, he waited while Collier cleared the traveling writing case away, then said, "If there's anything we can do for you, miss—anything at all—please let us know."

Collier softly added his agreement.

Finding a faint smile, Mary trained it on the pair; their gratitude for her help, for her rescue of Ryder and even more for her staying and holding them together, shone plainly in their faces. "Thank you. Should I need anything, I'll ring—or ask Collier." She had no doubt the little man intended to remain at least figuratively by his master's side.

Pemberly cleared his throat. "Ah . . . in light of Doctor Sanderson's verdict, do you think we should send for Lord Randolph, miss?"

Mary considered, then shook her head. "Not at this point." Swiveling so that she was once again gazing at Ryder, she forced herself to say, "If his lordship hasn't woken by mid-morning, perhaps then."

Openly relieved, Pemberly bowed and departed, taking her note to pass on to John Coachman. Collier straightened the covers, then retreated to the chair in the corner.

Silence gradually sank, enfolding the room in a hush tinged with expectation, broken only by the very faint sound of Ryder's breathing. The scent of antiseptic hung in the still air. The small fire had already reduced to glowing coals, the room warm, but, as instructed, not too much so.

Softly exhaling, trying to ease the grim tension locking her muscles, Mary settled on the chair to wait. To hope, and pray, and see.

Her gaze fixed on Ryder's still face, she allowed her mind to open, to broaden the scope she'd held so tightly focused over the last hours.

It was long after midnight; glancing fleetingly at the clock on the mantelpiece, she saw that it was, indeed, past two o'clock.

She was well aware of the impropriety of her remaining by Ryder's bed—in his house, in his bedroom, with him present. But he was unconscious, and Collier was there, and . . . she really didn't care what society thought. Her parents, her family, would understand; they wouldn't expect her to do anything else.

Anything but wait, and keep vigil, in case Ryder died.

Someone had to bear witness to the passing of a life such as his. He was the head of a house much like her own, ancient, wealthy, endowed with title, estates, and proud heritage.

All of that was unquestionably true; she could use it as an excuse, but she was quite clear in her own mind that such considerations weren't what was holding her there.

Binding her, above all else anchoring her there.

She couldn't let him die alone purely because of him being him.

Because of the sort of man he was, the fascinating male he'd allowed her to glimpse over the past several nights.

Because he'd revealed to her the true magic in a waltz.

Because of the challenge he'd so arrogantly, forcefully, and with calculated enticement laid at her feet mere hours ago.

Because he might be her one.

And she hadn't yet given him a chance to convince her.

Hadn't yet had a chance to decide if he truly was.

She wanted to be there when he awoke, to tell him he could have his chance—that she was prepared to explore the possibility.

But she wouldn't be able to tell him anything if he didn't wake.

Her entire future, the one she'd longed for and had finally set out so determinedly to secure—them having the deity-ordained future they might have been fated to have—rested on Ryder's innate strength, on his ability to recover from a wound that had already come within a whisker of being fatal.

So she sat by his bed and willed him to keep breathing, to keep on living as the night hours rolled on.

And sometime in the dark watches of the night, she vowed to The Lady that if he survived, if come the morning he woke and looked at her with his glinting hazel eyes, she would, indeed, give him the chance he'd asked for—the chance to convince her that he was "her one."

Chapter Six

Ryder drifted in and out of consciousness, or was it sleep? Some part of his mind wondered if he could tell the difference.

Relevant yet not very important thoughts like that wreathed through his mind and trapped his wits, distracting him. Leading him astray, away from more critical observations.

Such as Mary, and what she was doing there, seated by his bed, and what that meant.

Stay with me!

He could still hear her words echoing in his head, even through the dimness shrouding his recent past. Could still hear her voice make that demand—her command.

But it appeared she'd ensured the outcome she'd desired by staying with him . . . which, given their setting, seemed wrong.

Not as things should be.

But he wasn't going to complain. Her presence soothed him, literally comforted on some level he didn't truly comprehend.

Sometime later, the pain in his side reminded him of what had happened, of the pair of thugs he'd left dead in the alley. The ambush had been well planned; they'd waited, hidden, at either end of the stretch where the alley, his habitual route home from the south, narrowed. Absorbed with thoughts of

Mary and the question of what next, he'd stridden past one of the pair—who must have been concealed in a doorway—then the other had come charging toward him from the Mount Street end, and before he'd had time to realize the danger, the other man had sneaked up behind him and under cover of his partner's charge had stabbed him.

If he'd been of average height, he'd be dead.

Instead . . . he was so damn weak, weaker than he could remember ever being, even as a sickly child. He couldn't summon the strength to move a muscle, not even to lift his lids properly and look about. The best he could manage was to catch a glimpse through his lashes, and even that only for a few seconds.

He must have drifted off, but when he swam up to the world again, he didn't bother trying to open his eyes but concentrated on his wound. . . .

By taking a fractionally deeper breath, he could sense the constriction of a bandage around his waist. So Sanderson must have come and gone at some point. A fleeting flare of possessiveness gave him the strength to force his lashes up—but Mary was still there.

Despite the hour—it had to be very late—she was awake. She was staring at him, in the low light unable to discern that he was awake and studying her; he would have smiled, but even that was presently beyond him.

Her expression remained serious, concerned; one hand at her bodice, she was—absentmindedly, it seemed—fingering whatever it was that hung from the end of the curious old necklace she wore.

The sight reassured him; the weight of her gaze soothed him.

His lashes lowered and he sank back into the deeps.

Accepting as inevitable that she would eventually nod off, Mary had exchanged the straight-backed chair for one of the wing chairs, and had persuaded Collier to do the same by pointing out that either of them falling asleep and consequently off their chairs wouldn't help anyone.

So when she woke, she was curled in the wing chair, her legs tucked beneath her skirts, one hand beneath her cheek. Opening her eyes, even before she moved her head she looked over at the bed—and fell into Ryder's hazel eyes.

She blinked, looked again—saw the sharp mind she'd grown accustomed to glimpsing behind the medley of bright greens and golds looking back at her, his expression as usual lazily amused—and felt inexpressible relief swamp her. "You're awake! *Thank God!*"

Uncurling her legs, she stretched, then straightened.

Ryder's lips curved, his expression wry. "I'm not sure God had all that much to do with it—if I'm remembering correctly, it's you I have to thank."

"Well, yes." Pushing out of the chair, she nodded. "That, too." She wasn't foolish enough to refuse any advantage he might hand her.

The soft snoring that had been emanating from the corner of the room abruptly broke off in a series of snorty snuffles. Ignoring Collier, walking to the head of the bed, she leaned across and placed her palm on Ryder's forehead.

The rose quartz pendant swung free of her bodice.

Raising the fingers of the hand lying on his chest, Ryder caught it. "So that's what it is." He turned the hexagonally cut crystal between his fingers. "I glimpsed you clutching it during the night and wondered what it was." Fingers stroking the long, flat surfaces, he frowned faintly. "Odd—it seems quite hot."

Considering where it had been resting, Mary wasn't surprised. "Yes, well." Tugging the pendant from his fingers—he allowed it to slip free without hindrance— she gripped it and, ignoring his interested gaze, tucked it back between her breasts, registering as she did that it was, indeed, very warm. "It seems to hold heat."

Drawing her hand from his forehead, she stepped back. He quirked his brows questioningly.

"You're warm, but I don't think you have a fever."

"Given how cold I felt last night, feeling warm again is exceedingly welcome." Still weak as a newborn kitten, Ryder barely managed a vague wave down his body. "I take it Sanderson was summoned."

"Yes. He came and checked your wound, then sewed you up." Mary hesitated, her eyes on his, then more quietly added, "He said if you woke up, all should be well."

So until she'd woken and discovered him awake, she hadn't known . . . if she'd wake to a living man or a corpse.

"Thank you for staying." If he could have moved his arm, he would have taken her hand and kissed it. "If I could bow, I would. As it is, I'm not up to even nodding, but you may take my abject gratitude as read."

Concern reappeared in her cornflower blue eyes. "How weak are you?"

He told himself admitting the truth wouldn't hurt—not to her. "Extremely."

"You lost a horrendous amount of blood, so that's probably not surprising." Her frown grew more definite. "Sanderson said he'd be back as soon as he delivered some lady of her baby, but until then I don't even know if we should feed you."

"At the moment, I'm not sure I can even swallow—not food, anyway."

"Perhaps we can try some water, and if you can manage that I'm sure Mrs. Perkins will have some broth prepared." Mary glanced at the mantelpiece clock, blinked, then stared. "Good Lord! It's eleven o'clock already!"

Collier chose that moment to snort himself awake. He looked across the room—and came out of his chair on a highly unprofessional cry of delight. Immediately recollecting himself, he bowed and apologized profusely, although his beaming smile didn't dim in the least. He concluded with, "I'm just so relieved to see you awake, my lord."

"And compos mentis," Mary dryly observed. She met Ryder's eyes as he glanced up at her. "You appear to be in full possession of your faculties."

He grinned; facial expressions, at least, were within his ambit. "You'll be pleased to know that my mind is unimpaired."

"Can I do anything for you, my lord? Can I fetch anything?" Collier fussed eagerly at the foot of the bed.

"Water," Mary answered. She pointed at the pitcher on the table beside the bed. "Fresh water would be preferable."

"Yes, of course." Collier swooped on the pitcher and bore it off, delighted to have something to do.

"And let the others know I'm back from the dead," Ryder called after him, "and tell Pemberly to send Sanderson up as soon as he appears."

"Yes, my lord!' Collier left with a spring in his step.

Ryder inwardly shook his head. "You'd never think he'd spent all night asleep in a chair."

Looking up, he found Mary regarding him steadily. "They're all very devoted to you."

He managed the hint of a shrug. "They've been with me, as they say, boy and man." But now Collier had gone, he could ask some of the questions banking up in his brain. "The two who attacked me—I left them in the alley."

"Sanderson realized you'd want to investigate when you woke, and told Pemberly to take in the bodies and store them somewhere."

"Good man." Now for the trickier question. "What arrangements—"

The sound of the front doorbell pealing reached them; Collier had left the door ajar.

"Ah! That will be my parents." Mary started for the door; glancing back she said, "They've been away for the last few days and were due home this morning. I sent them a note explaining where I was and why, and asked them to come as soon as they could and"—reaching the door, she gestured—"lend me countenance, so to speak."

She whisked through the door even as, lids rising fully, he called, "No, wait!"

When she didn't reappear, he swore, mostly at the weakness that prevented him from going after her and stopping her from doing something no lady ever should, namely rushing down the stairs of a single gentleman's abode without being certain who was about to be admitted through the door.

Feeling drained by even that degree of exertion, falling back against his pillows, he mentally grimaced. "Pemberly will reach the door first. He'll see her and order her back." He tried to imagine it but couldn't see anyone—much less his loyal, devoted, and in the current circumstances no doubt immensely grateful staff—ordering Mary to do anything. At least, not successfully.

But there was nothing he could do. Heaving a sigh of resignation, he sank deeper into his pillows, thinking words he'd never thought he would. "Pray God it is her parents."

Raventhorne House was every bit as large and impressive as St. Ives House, just a block north in Grosvenor Square. Mary hurried along the corridor that led to the massive gallery about the grand staircase, noting with approval the trappings of luxury she'd been too distracted to notice during the night. Thick Oriental carpets in jewel tones muffled her footsteps; the walls were richly paneled in dark wood and hung with paintings large and small in ornate gilded frames. The well of the front hall was lit by a circular skylight high above. Reaching the gallery, she glanced over the wooden balustrade and saw Pemberly pacing in stately fashion across the black-and-white tiles, heading for the tall front doors.

She would be glad to see her parents, her mother especially; a smile blooming, she grabbed up her skirts and hurried even faster to the head of the stairs.

As she started down, Pemberly opened the door. "Yes?"

"Good morning, Pemberly. We are here to see my stepson."

Mary froze. Teetering on a tread just below the half-landing, she stared, increasingly aghast as the Marchioness of Raventhorne ignored Pemberly's valiant attempt to deny her and with an irritated "Do stand aside, man!" pushed past him into the front hall.

Followed by two middle-aged ladies who, heads high, expressions set, reticules determinedly clasped before them, marched inside in the marchioness's wake.

All three ladies instantly saw Mary. They slowed, then halted.

Their mouths fell open, expressions turning slack with astounded astonishment as they registered who she was . . . and where she was . . .

Breaking free of the shock, Mary swung around and hared back up the stairs.

Heedless of decorum, she raced around the gallery and down the corridor to Ryder's room.

Flinging open the door, she burst in—startling Collier, at least, who had just finished helping Ryder, now semi-decently clad in a nightshirt, sip from a glass of water—then she whirled and shut the door.

She stared at it for a second, then rushed to the bed. "Ryder—"

"I take it that wasn't your parents." His expression unflustered, but instead rather cynically resigned, he arched a brow at her.

"It's your stepmother." Mary pointed to the door. "She's coming up here." As she'd fled, she'd heard an exclamation; as she'd darted into the corridor, she'd heard determined footsteps start up the stairs.

With a put-upon sigh, Ryder looked at the ceiling. "Wonderful."

"*No*—it's even worse." Mary resisted the urge to grab his arm and shake him. "She's brought Lady Jerome and Mrs. Framlingham with her!"

Ryder's gaze snapped to her face. "Ah." All lazy humor flown, he stared at her for two seconds, then barked, "Collier, help me up."

Mary would have argued but instead found herself kneeling on the bed, assisting Ryder to shift higher on his pillows. At his orders, Collier helped him raise his left arm, placing his hand behind his head. . . . She frowned. "Why are we doing this?"

"Staging."

"But why?"

"Because Lavinia is one of those to whom you never show weakness."

She didn't understand, but she trusted that he knew what he was doing; he was unquestionably more experienced in this sort of situation than she.

"Help me raise my other arm," Ryder said to Mary. "Collier—out of sight."

"Yes, my lord."

Ryder had intended, between him and Mary, to set his right arm in a similar position to his left, making it appear he was lounging back with his hands behind his head, but he was still so weak, and Mary struggled to push the nearly dead weight of his arm higher—and then he caught the sounds of many footsteps approaching, Pemberly's protests overridden by Lavinia's waspish dismissals, and readjusted. "No—leave my arm where it is along the pillows. Sit and face the door. Now!"

Mary threw him a stunned look, but then obeyed.

Leaving her, still clad in her watered silk evening gown from the night before, with her dark curls gently disarranged and becoming color in her cheeks, sitting on his bed within the curve of his arm as he lay apparently relaxed and at his ease.

At eleven o'clock in the morning.

With a last spurt of effort, he managed to shift his right hand enough to drape his fingers over the curve of her right shoulder.

Pemberly entered first, all but propelled through the doorway. "My lord! I tried . . ." He gestured helplessly at Lavinia, who, eyes lit with a conflagration of disbelief and mounting fury, swept into the room.

Lady Jerome and Mrs. Framlingham, arch-gossipmongers and two of the busiest bodies in the ton, hung back in the shadows of the corridor, apparently sensing rather better than his stepmother that barging into his bedchamber without an invitation might just be that one step too far.

Grateful that the pillows allowed him to keep his head upright, he didn't attempt to move it. "Thank you, Pemberly." His gaze on Lavinia, his tone chilling significantly, he continued, "Good morning, Lavinia—I wasn't aware I had arranged a meeting. To what do I owe this unwarranted invasion?"

Predictably Lavinia's gaze had swept over him and fixed on Mary. His stepmother goggled; her lips opened and shut several times—which he would have found amusing had the circumstances been different—but then she finally wrenched her gaze to his face and brusquely waved at Mary. "What the devil is she doing here?"

Playing to the audience peering in from the corridor, he sighed gustily in the manner of a man supremely beset by uncomprehendingly obtuse females and lightly, warningly, gripped Mary's shoulder. "If you must know, last night Miss Cynster did me the honor of accepting my offer for her hand."

Ryder slanted a fleeting, heavy-lidded glance at his bride-to-be. Via his hold on her shoulder, he'd felt the jolt his words had unsurprisingly sent through her, but although he could only see her profile, he didn't think any overt shock showed in her face; if anything she seemed to be regarding Lavinia with becoming, somewhat icy, hauteur. Returning his gaze to his stepmother, he continued in the same arrogantly cold tone, "Her presence here should therefore surprise no one, and, indeed, be of no interest to anyone. Your presence, however, has yet to be explained."

Lavinia could not have looked more stunned. It took her three attempts before she could get her tongue to function. "You . . ." Then her gaze switched to Mary and her fists clenched. "You silly chit! You could have had my Randolph . . ." Lavinia trailed off, no doubt realizing any suggestion that Mary should have preferred Randolph to Ryder was, in ton terms, ludicrous.

Somewhat to his surprise, Lavinia paled, but then hot color surged into her cheeks. Her gaze locked on Mary and her eyes narrowed. "Why, you—"

"Lavinia!" Ruthlessly, he reseized the reins; his strength wasn't going to last much longer. "You—and your friends— have burst into my home and have erupted into my private chambers without so much as a by-your-leave. I suggest you retreat. Now." He held her gaze. "Pemberly, please show her ladyship out."

"Indeed, my lord." Pemberly didn't utter the words, but "it will be my pleasure" hung in the air.

Lavinia glared at Pemberly as, with the weight of Ryder's authority behind him, the butler advanced and took her arm. With a muttered oath, she wrenched it free, cast one last, furious, yet still stunned and reeling look at the bed, then swung on her heel and marched out. Pemberly followed, closing the door behind him.

Exhausted, Ryder fell back on the pillows; his eyes closed all by themselves.

He heard Collier emerge from the dressing room.

An instant later, still beside him on the bed, Mary murmured, "Would you like to lower your left arm?"

"Please."

Between them, they eased his hand from behind his head and lowered his arm to the bed.

He hated, absolutely hated, being weak. And now, courtesy of his stepmother, he had another battle on his hands. "Collier—get out."

"Yes, my lord."

He waited until he heard the door snick shut before drawing in a deeper breath and forcing his lids up, at least enough to see.

Although still sitting on the bed, Mary had shifted to face him. The look on her face, the expression in her eyes as they rested on him, was . . . utterly inscrutable.

That surprised him; until now, he'd been able to read her reasonably well, relatively easily. It hadn't occurred to him that he might not always be able to, that she might be able to hide her thoughts, her feelings, from him.

A faint line etched between her brows, she was patently considering him . . . as if he was of a species she'd encountered before but was a specimen that broke the mold.

Regardless of what her thoughts actually were, for him there was only one way forward. "I apologize. Unreservedly." He managed to wave the fingers of his right hand. "That bore no resemblance to how I would have wished to propose to you."

Her brows arched. She hesitated, then said, "As I see it, you've now proposed, and I've accepted."

Understanding the question concealed in her words, he grimaced. "There was no other way."

When she continued to study him—when he continued to have not a clue about what was passing through her mind—he said, "If I might make an observation?"

Raising her brows, she invited him to proceed.

"I rather expected you to be hissing and spitting at me by now—at least ranting and raving a trifle." Another weak wave. "Perhaps pacing back and forth." He caught her gaze. "You know, the expected reaction."

Her lips faintly curved, but she sobered immediately. "I can't see that ranting and raving will get either of us anywhere."

He regarded her, wariness growing. "How terribly rational of you."

That elicited another fleeting grin. "As much as I might be tempted to berate you, I can't find it in me to be so *irrational* as to blame you for what just occurred. You had no choice—it wasn't as if you'd invited your stepmother and her cronies in."

He managed the tiniest inclination of his head. "Thank you. I assure you that little performance was certainly not what I meant when I stated I intended to work to change your mind."

She humphed but said nothing.

When she continued to consider him in silence to the point he was growing increasingly concerned about just what plan she was hatching, in an endeavor to tease it from her he sighed feelingly, then said, "I suppose, if I were other than I am, I would make some chivalrous declaration over finding some way of releasing you from the contract in which we've just become unintentionally snared."

Her blue eyes narrowed on his face. "But you won't, will you?"

Holding her gaze, he shook his head. "No. I had no idea I would be stabbed last night, had no idea you would come along and aid me, had no idea you would remain by my side all night, and I had no hand in bringing Lavinia and her bosom-bows down on our joint heads. And I haven't reached where I am today without learning to take advantage of every blessing Fate sends my way." He paused, then more softly said, "So no, I won't be searching for any way to undo what Fate has seen done." When she still didn't react, he went on, "So if you want to find some way out of this, you're going to have to search for it yourself."

Eyes fixed on his, all she said was, "Hmm."

If he could have flung his hands in the air, he would have. Letting his head fall completely back onto the pillows, he looked at the ceiling and baldly asked, "What the devil are you thinking?"

A half minute ticked past, then she replied, "To be perfectly honest, I'm not sure."

He frowned, then returned his gaze to her face. "You're always sure. Of everything."

"Yes." Her lips firming in clear disapproval of her unaccustomed state, she shook her head. "But not about this."

Distantly, the front doorbell pealed.

"And that," she said, "*will* be my parents." Slipping off the bed, she shook out her skirts, then glanced sharply at him. "I'll go down and explain, and seek their counsel. Then I'll come back and we can discuss where we stand. Meanwhile, you should rest. Doctor Sanderson should arrive shortly."

Ryder watched her neaten her hair and generally compose herself, then, head held high, she glided to the door and let herself out.

Once the door shut, he sank back into the pillows and swore some more. Being helpless grated beyond bearing.

By the time Mary reached the gallery, Pemberly had admitted her parents into the front hall. Hurrying down the stairs, she couldn't remember ever being so glad to see them. "Mama! Papa!"

Louise and Arthur turned toward her. Louise smiled. "There you are, dear."

Although both her parents took in her appearance—not something they could miss—they welcomed her with encouraging smiles and open arms. She returned their hugs with feeling.

"My dear." Louise drew away, her expression sobering. "How is Ryder?"

"Recovering, thank goodness. But I fear we've had a complication of a different sort."

"Oh? How so?" Arthur's expression had turned serious.

Mary glanced at Pemberly. "Pemberly, is there somewhere . . . ?"

Pemberly immediately indicated a door and strode to open it. "The drawing room, miss."

"Thank you." Mary led the way in. The room was large, long, and fashionably furnished, but more with an eye to masculine comfort and style. The chairs were well padded, upholstered in green leather, and the sofas matched. After an instant's pause to get her bearings, she led her parents to the sofa facing the massive fireplace; it was flanked by two large wing chairs, and a low table sat in the center of the arrangement.

"Should I bring in a tea tray, miss?" Pemberly inquired.

"Oh—yes, thank you." Mary sent him a grateful look. "That would be welcome." Knowing her parents, they'd read her letter immediately they'd reached home and had come on to Mount Street directly. And she could certainly do with a cup of tea; she'd slept through breakfast.

Pemberly bowed. "At once, miss."

Noting the exchange, Louise briefly met Arthur's eyes, then at Mary's wave, they both sat on the sofa and gave her their undivided attention.

Sinking into one of the wing chairs, Mary faced them. "First, I should tell you that Ryder has been . . . well, pursuing me, if you know what I mean, since he and I crossed paths at Henrietta and James's engagement ball."

"Pursuing you?" Arthur bristled.

"Hush, dear." Louise patted his thigh. "You know very well what she means."

"Exactly." Mary gave thanks for her mother's insight—as she so often did. "In just that way—perfectly acceptable, with not so much as a toe over any line. He's been at all the balls I've attended recently, and two nights ago, he appeared at Lady Hopetoun's musicale and stayed by my side throughout."

Louise sucked in a breath. "Good heavens! So he's in earnest, and not backward in declaring his interest."

Mary bit back words to the effect that Ryder wouldn't know how to be "backward" about anything, and nodded. "Indeed. But until then I'd thought he was just . . . well, amusing himself because he was bored—or later, because he realized I was interested in his half brother Randolph, and Ryder didn't approve. Well, he didn't approve, but he wasn't just pursuing me to distract me from Randolph, as I'd supposed."

Arthur nodded. "Had his eye on you himself. Never thought Ryder was slow."

"Yes, well, when, in the wake of the musicale and his subsequent behavior, I suspected that and taxed him with it, he . . ." She paused, recalling the exchange on Lady Bracewell's terrace. "He was entirely forthright in declaring that he wanted me as his marchioness."

Louise smiled. "My dear, that's delightful news—yet why do I fear I'm about to hear a 'but'?"

Arthur looked puzzled. "No buts about it—what answer did you give him?"

Mary met Arthur's eyes, a shade lighter than her own. "I pointed out that he was an unmanageable despot, and that as I prefer to be in charge of my own life, in my opinion he and I would not suit."

She glanced at her mother, only to see a delighted grin break across Louise's face.

Louise tried to rein it in but failed. "Oh, darling—if you truly wished to discourage the likes of Ryder, that was definitely *not* the right answer."

"Well," Arthur opined, "I don't see why she would want to discourage Ryder anyway, but that's a fair enough observation—so what did he say, heh?"

Looking into Arthur's eager eyes, then glancing at Louise

and seeing her mother's rather deeper understanding, Mary drew breath and said, "Aside from vowing to succeed in changing my mind, he insisted we would suit—and he suggested he was willing to find ways to accommodate my . . . requirements."

Even Louise looked taken aback at that, but in a wholly approving way. "So . . . what did you say?"

Mary grimaced. "I didn't know what to say, and then we had to go inside—we'd been on the terrace."

"So you left it at that?" Arthur said.

She nodded. "That was how we parted at Lady Bracewell's ball last night. And then, on my way home in the carriage . . ."

Crisply and concisely, she related the events of the previous night.

Pemberly appeared with a well-stocked tea tray; he set it on the low table, then withdrew. Mary paused to pour and hand around the cups; she sipped, then continued her recitation.

Both Arthur and Louise were thoroughly shocked by Ryder's so-close brush with death, and entirely supportive of her actions.

"I should certainly hope you did everything you could—rest assured, my dear, no one will censure you for that," Louise said. "Especially as there's no one living here but Ryder himself. In the circumstances, even waiting for the doctor was the right thing to do."

"Yes, well, that's not quite all." Mary wondered how to explain and decided she would simply have to take the bull by the horns. "Even after that, as you've realized, I stayed. I simply couldn't bring myself to leave him—not when we didn't know if he would live or die."

"Entirely understandable," Arthur gruffly said.

"Indeed." Louise nodded. "Besides, quite aside from any finer feelings on your part, if you'd left and he'd died . . . well, you know the sort of questions a man of his station dying alone can raise."

"And anyway, you knew we would be home this morning and would come and cover for you. That's why you sent us that note." Arthur set down his empty cup and eyed Mary shrewdly. "So what's got you in a flap, heh?"

She'd hoped she hadn't been that transparent, but . . . "Collier, Ryder's gentleman's gentleman, remained with me in Ryder's room throughout the night. But both Collier and I eventually fell asleep, and we didn't wake up until"—she glanced at the clock gracing the massive mantelpiece—"about an hour ago. That was when we realized Ryder had woken, and although he's extremely weak, he's as well as he could be given the circumstances." She paused, drained her cup, and set it on its saucer. "That's when the doorbell rang, and I thought it was you and came rushing down . . ." She met her mother's gaze. "Only it wasn't you but Ryder's stepmother, and she'd brought Lady Jerome and Mrs. Framlingham with her."

Louise frowned. "How very odd to be sure. Why on earth would Lavinia have brought those two with her to call on Ryder?"

Mary blinked. Until then, that question hadn't occurred to her, but Louise was right; it was odd. After a moment, she shrugged. "For whatever reason, she did—and all three ladies saw me on the stairs." Setting her cup and saucer on the table, she waved at her ball gown. "Dressed like this. Hurrying down Ryder's stairs at eleven in the morning."

Her gaze on Mary's face, Louise sat back. "Oh, dear."

Arthur frowned. "Don't see what the problem is—the boy was at death's door, and his man was there, too, and the doctor will explain—"

"No, dear." Holding up a staying hand, Louise shook her head. "You forget. This is Ryder Cavanaugh we're talking about. No amount of physical impairment will serve as excuse." She met Arthur's eyes. "Trust me, he would have to be dead—*pronounced* dead—for the ton to accept such a tale. And even then there would be gossip."

Arthur bristled. "But the doctor—"

"Is a close friend of Ryder's from his Eton days." Mary shook her head. "Mama's right—no amount of explaining would have sufficed, and to give the devil his due, Ryder instantly understood that."

Louise tipped her head, regarding Mary quizzically. "So what happened?"

Mary dragged in a breath. "I raced back to Ryder to warn him, and even though he could barely move he insisted we set our stage, concealing his injury as revealing it would do no good, and instead making it appear that we'd been . . . well, doing exactly what those three ladies would think anyway—then when they burst into his room—"

"They didn't!" Louise looked scandalized.

Mary nodded grimly. "They most certainly did—or at least his stepmother did. The other two hovered in the corridor."

"And then?" Arthur growled.

Giddiness threatened; Mary hauled in another breath. "Then Ryder declared that he'd offered for my hand the previous night, and that I'd accepted, and that therefore my presence in his house, in his room, sitting beside him on his bed, should be of no particular interest to anyone."

"Well!" Louise stared at her.

Frowning, Arthur stared at her, too, but more in the sense of puzzling something out.

A short silence ensued, then Mary shrugged. "I had to go along with it, of course."

Louise blinked.

Arthur stirred. "Let's see if I've got this straight. Last evening, Ryder informed you he wants you as his marchioness. You discussed the matter but left it unresolved. And then because of a succession of events, during which neither of you behaved other than you ought, this morning you and he wind up engaged."

Mary considered, then nodded. "That sums it up nicely."

Shaking his head admiringly, Arthur muttered, "I'd heard the boy has the devil's own luck."

Mary bit her tongue. Her father was a Cynster male; she really couldn't have expected anything else.

Several seconds ticked by, then her mother, who had been studying her, leaned forward and laid a hand over hers, currently tightly clasped in her lap. Looking into her eyes, Louise asked, "How do you feel about this?"

Meeting her mother's gaze, Mary searched for the right words among her whirling thoughts . . . in the end, the truth was all she had. "I don't know." She glanced at Arthur, then looked back at Louise. "When I stepped onto Lady Bracewell's terrace before we spoke, I thought I did, but now?" Slowly, she shook her head. "Now, I simply don't know."

And she didn't understand how that had come to be—didn't comprehend how or why her emotions had risen up as they had, with sufficient strength and unruliness to derail her will and divert her from her rational, logical, self-determined path.

She'd known where she'd wanted to go—and yet she'd ended up here, for all intents and purposes engaged to Ryder Cavanaugh.

The very last man she would have chosen as her husband.

Yet over the past days, her emotions—normally so quiescent and amenable, forever subservient to her will—had been . . . growing. Swelling, rising, in a burgeoning tide of nascent turmoil.

From irritation, through being charmed, through the sensual magic, the allure of waltzing in a way she never had before, to her acute reaction to Ryder's possessiveness, entirely understandable yet never provoked to such a degree by anyone else, all capped by her response—so complex and unexpected—when he'd declared his intentions, further complicated by his unnervingly astute offer of accommodation, all immediately trumped by the indescribable horror of finding him dying.

Yet nothing to that point had prepared her for the avalanche of feelings that had all but buried her at the thought of losing him. Of no longer having him in her life.

Ever since Ryder had pushed his way into her life, she'd felt so much.

And her certainty—the certainty that until now had formed the bedrock of her life—had shattered.

She'd thought she'd understood herself, that she'd known what she wanted, known wither she was heading, and even why—and she'd been wrong.

Adrift. No, worse. She was being drawn inexorably down a path she hadn't intended taking, and she had no real idea of where it led.

Oh, Mama—what am I to do? If she'd been a weaker sort of young lady, she might have uttered the words.

After holding her gaze for several heartbeats, Louise patted her hand and answered as if she had. "In that case, my dear, you will simply have to go forward and learn the answer. And knowing you, I have every confidence you'll meet the challenge."

Arthur looked from one to the other, then shook his head. "I won't pretend I understood any of that, but it sounds as if it's time Ryder and I had a chat."

As if summoned by the words, Pemberly knocked and entered. "If you would, my lord, my lady, the marquess requests a few minutes of your time. As he is presently unable to come to you, his lordship asks your indulgence in stepping upstairs to his room."

"Excellent!" Arthur rose. "Perfect timing."

Dismissing Pemberly, Mary led the way up the stairs and down the corridor to Ryder's room. The staff had already accorded her the status of lady of the house, and if, as it seemed, she was to take up the position permanently, she saw no reason to take a backward step. Had Ryder been in her shoes, she was sure he wouldn't have.

Reaching his door, she tapped. Hearing his "Come," she opened the door and led her parents inside.

Washed, shaved, his hair brushed until it gleamed, Ryder, although still deathly pale, was now garbed in a shirt, cravat, and a burgundy velvet smoking jacket; despite having to sit propped up by pillows, now freshly plumped, with the coverlet of golden silk straightened over his long legs, he still managed to project the aura of a king holding court.

His gaze swept her, then moved on to her parents. He inclined his head. "My apologies for not greeting you appropriately Lord Arthur, Lady Cynster, but I assume Mary has explained my recent injury." With a small wave, Ryder indicated her mother should take the chair beside the bed.

Louise moved to do so. "Thank you. And yes, Mary has explained the situation." She glanced at Mary as she sat. "Quite thoroughly, I believe."

At a signal from Ryder, Collier slipped from the room.

As the door clicked shut, Ryder looked at Lord Arthur, who had strolled to take station behind his wife's chair. "I regret, my lord, that the circumstances of this meeting are not as I would have wished. However, I confess it was my intention that such a meeting would take place, albeit in a more conventional way and at a somewhat later date. Be that as it may, the matter we must discuss is straightforward, and I believe you already comprehend the reasons why I must speak now. Consequently, I wish to apply for leave to address your daughter, Mary, to ask if she will do me the honor of becoming my wife."

From under his bushy eyebrows, Arthur studied him for several seconds, then humphed. "Very prettily said." He glanced down at his wife. "What say you, my dear?"

Louise, too, had been assessing Ryder. At her husband's question, she glanced at Mary, who had shifted to stand on the other side of the bed the better to follow the exchange. After several moments of studying her daughter, Louise looked at Ryder, met his eyes, then nodded. "Yes. I believe granting such leave will be in everyone's best interests."

Her faint emphasis on "everyone's" gave Ryder an instant's pause. He knew the Cynster ladies by repute and, as far as possible, had steered clear of them. But from those of his peers who circled within their orbit, he'd learned enough to view them with healthy respect.

He inclined his head to both Mary's parents. "Thank you."

Turning his head to meet Mary's gaze, he held out his hand, making every endeavor to mask the effort that cost him.

She hesitated for only a heartbeat, then walked forward and laid her hand in his—and gently bore his hand down until his arm rested on the covers and he no longer had to expend strength to support it.

Closing his fingers around hers, looking into her lovely eyes, he fought to screen the sudden surge of primitive possessiveness that flashed through him, but he was fairly certain he failed.

Yet she held his gaze steadily; despite what, standing so close with her gaze trapped in his, he suspected she could see, he sensed not the slightest tremor in the fingers trapped in his.

The traditional, conventional words were there, on his tongue; he'd rehearsed them while dressing. Yet he left them unsaid. Between her and him . . . he wanted more. "Clearly this is not as I would have had it, but, as you know, it is what I wanted, what I intended at some point to ask of you. But Fate has intervened and brought us to this moment without allowing us the customary time to get to know each another. To understand each other. So in what is, after all, one of the most important decisions in life, you and I have to, are being forced to, take each other on trust. And so we must. In return for the trust I hope you will accord me, I vow that I will place my trust in you—that I will work with you to make our future life, the one we will share, all that it might be." He paused, then, his gaze unwaveringly fixed on the cornflower blue of her eyes, drew breath, and said, "So what say you, Mary—will you take my hand and go forward by my side, as my marchioness, as my wife, and make our life, create from our shared life, all we wish?"

Mary was trapped in his eyes, but not lost, not overwhelmed; she could see his intent, clear and unshielded, could discern the powerful drive behind it, even if she couldn't as yet guess from whence it sprang. He wanted her as his wife; he had from the first. She knew beyond question that he meant every word, those of today, and of the days past—all he'd ever offered her on this subject. "Yes." She heard herself say the word, recognized and acknowledged that it came from somewhere deeper than her rational mind. Accepting that, she nodded, more to herself than him, and affirmed, "Yes, I will be your marchioness. Yes, I will be your wife."

His lips, those wicked, sinful, compelling lips, slowly curved. Even though his muscles shook, he tried to raise her hand; smoothly, she lifted it, allowing him, helping him, to carry it to his lips.

His eyes, sharply intelligent, glinting with subtly screened desire, held hers as he set the seal on their pact and pressed a kiss to her fingers.

Possession was stamped on his features.

She read the confirmation that shone in his eyes.

Mine. You're mine.

This is an unmitigated *disaster*!" Lavinia, Marchioness of Raventhorne, raged before the fireplace in her boudoir.

The only other occupant, Claude Potherby, sat at his fashionable ease in the wing chair angled to the hearth and watched Lavinia pace. He was too wise in her ways to say anything just yet. Inured by long acquaintance to her histrionics, he left her to rail unimpeded. In days past, he would have been styled her cicisbeo, a longtime confidant, although in his case never a lover. Once, it was true, he had aspired to the more intimate connection, but that had been long ago—before Lavinia had turned from him to so eagerly throw herself into an arranged marriage and the marchioness's shoes she still wore.

Yet to his cynical surprise, his devotion had proved both durable and persistent; despite being taken for granted for more decades than he cared to count, he was still there, still listening to Lavinia's ravings—still quietly amused by her unending, ceaseless quest for self-advancement.

"I tell you it's insupportable!" Eyes flashing, fists clenched at her sides, she whirled to face him. "How *dare* that wanton seduce Ryder?"

Claude blinked. "Ah . . . was that the same wanton you wanted for dear Randolph? Mary Cynster?"

Lavinia huffed. "Yes—her! To have landed herself in Ryder's bed—and then—"

"You know, my sweet, I fail to follow . . . well, several points in your thesis. For instance, everything we, and indeed all the ton, know of Mary Cynster strongly suggests that she is highly unlikely to use seduction as a means to secure her future. As the last Cynster girl of this generation unwed, she has no reason even to expend effort—every eligible gentleman would shortly have been lining up to offer for her hand."

Before Lavinia could interrupt, Claude continued, "And while I admit your stepson has never been backward in seducing ladies, he's never preyed on young ladies, much less any of Miss Cynster's caliber." Intrigued by the little Lavinia had thus far let fall, Claude fixed her with an innocently inquiring look. "Are you sure, my dear, that what you and your friends saw wasn't something rather different? That you didn't leap to a conclusion that wasn't, in fact, correct?"

Lavinia scowled and kicked her skirts about. "I don't see

how else one *could* interpret what we saw. She was sitting on his damned bed, still in her ball gown, and *he* was looking like a cat who'd supped well."

Claude frowned. "Actually, another point that escapes me is why you and your bosom-bows called on Ryder at all."

Lavinia avoided his gaze. After another round of pacing, she all but spat, "If you must know, after Ryder appeared at Lady Hopetoun's musicale and spent the whole evening by Mary's side, I realized that he must have decided to look for a bride, and, of course, he isn't stupid, so he was looking at Mary—"

"Ah." Claude nodded. "I see it now. You wanted Mary for Randolph, so you and your friends . . ." He blinked, then trained a mock-disbelieving look on Lavina. "The three of you went to Ryder's house to offer to help him find a suitable bride?"

"Why not?" Lavinia gestured to herself. "I am his step-mother. I'm the current marchioness. If anyone would know what the position entails, and which young ladies might best fill it, it's me. And Joyce Jerome and Kate Framlingham both know all the young ladies on the marriage mart."

"Let me guess." Claude's voice dripped cynicism. "If Ryder had proved amenable, you and your friends would have tied him up in pursuing unsuitable young ladies for years."

"Well," Lavinia said, "there's really no reason he has to wed at all. Randolph soon will, and after Ryder, he, and then his son can carry the title. My dear departed husband would, I'm sure, have been entirely content with that. Randolph is, after all, as much his son as Ryder."

"Oh, dear." Claude fought very hard to keep his lips straight.

Lavinia frowned at him. "What?"

"Well, my dear, if we *do* entertain the possibility that Mary Cynster was at Ryder's house for some other reason entirely . . ." Sitting back so he could better watch Lavinia,

Claude went on, "Then it's possible that your . . . ah, well-intentioned attempt to interfere in Ryder's life might just have landed him with Mary Cynster as his wife."

Lavinia stared at Claude for several seconds, then, fists clenching, arms rigid by her sides, she gritted her teeth, tipped back her head, and screamed.

Chapter Seven

"You look like hell." Ryder peered at David Sanderson as the later adjusted the wick on the lamp beside the bed.

David's gaze swept his face. "I take it no one's offered you a mirror."

"I have an excuse. What happened to you?"

"Difficult first delivery. It ended well, but it was touch and go there for a while."

"I've just decided that I don't want to know. Childbirth." Despite his prevailing lack of strength, Ryder managed a shudder. "The one topic guaranteed to make grown men weak—and I'm weak enough as it is."

David humphed. "I want to take a look at that wound."

Ryder tried to turn down the covers, but David rapped his wrist. "Just lie still and let me do it. Unless I miss my guess, you'll be somewhat weaker than a kitten."

Ryder sighed and obediently desisted. "If it were a matter of arm wrestling, the kitten would win."

David grunted. He inspected the bandage, then raised the pad covering the wound itself. "Amazing."

"Yes, I know."

That elicited a bark of laughter. "Well, let's see how amazing." His gaze rising to Ryder's face, David gently palpated around the wound. When Ryder sucked in a breath, he asked, "Pain?"

Ryder considered, then replied, "Not lancing. More a solid ache."

"Better when I take my hands away?"

"Fading rapidly."

"Mostly bruising, then. Understandable. I had to poke around to make sure nothing vital was nicked."

"Again, I'm sure I don't need to know." Ryder forced himself to lie still and let David cover him up again. "I'm alive—oh, and incidentally, I'm also now engaged to be married."

Straightening, David looked down at him, then his surprise gave way to a frown. "Not that young lady who was here—Miss Cynster?"

Ryder grinned. "The very one." He proceeded to tell David what had happened.

At the end of the tale, David studied him, then arched his brows. "So is this good or bad?"

Feeling like a cat with a bowl of cream promised and certain in the offing, Ryder beamed. "It's *excellent*."

Laughing, David shook his head. "I have never encountered anyone with luck to match yours." He paused, then more soberly said, "You do realize you came within a whisker of dying? That if it hadn't been for Miss Cynster acting as decisively and effectively as she did, I would have been attending your funeral, and not your sickbed?"

Growing serious himself, Ryder nodded. "So I gathered. But she did, and I didn't, so tell me—how long before I'm up and about, and can . . . er, enjoy my good fortune."

David pulled a face at him. "Were it any other man, I'd say a few weeks at least, but knowing you and your powers of recuperation, I'd recommend eating whatever and however much you wish, and in a few days you should be downstairs—going up and down will help rebuild your strength—but as for enjoying your Miss Cynster, for God's sake, not within a week."

Ryder grimaced. "I think we can be sure it won't be that soon."

"What? Losing your touch?"

"Not this side of hell. But she's a Cynster, and she's to be my marchioness, so our relationship will progress very much by the book."

In pursuit of that aim, the next morning, feeling significantly improved, Ryder sat in the chair beside his bed and wrote several formal notes, which he subsequently dispatched to various houses around Mayfair.

Mary arrived shortly after and bullied him into getting back in bed. As she promised to spoon-feed him the restorative chicken broth Cook had prepared for him, he acquiesced. He couldn't recall ever having any female other than a nurse fuss over him before; he decided that, in small doses, he rather enjoyed it.

But he drew the line at her feeding him the rest of the five courses Collier ferried up; when she realized he was fully capable of wielding knife and fork, she narrowed her eyes at him, then allowed Pemberly to serve her her meal at a small table he set up beside the bed.

After the meal, he grew drowsy, much like a well-fed cat. She watched his lids droop; when she thought he was asleep, she approached the bed, stood staring down at him for a long while, then bent and dropped a kiss, light as thistledown, on his forehead and left.

He felt like he'd been branded. Pleasurably so.

He dozed, read, and dozed again through the afternoon, then Mary returned to share an early evening meal with him. She brought news of the first reactions of the ton to the inevitable rumors of their engagement, then he and she discussed the notice he would, eventually, send to the *Gazette* after he and her father had dealt with the matter of the settlements.

Everything, he was determined, would be done correctly.

She left while he was still awake, so he didn't receive another tantalizing kiss.

The next day, as David had predicted, Ryder conquered the stairs in time to meet with Lord Arthur and their mutual man-of-business, Heathcote Montague, to negotiate and finalize the settlements. When Lord Arthur departed, Montague remained to discuss various aspects of Ryder's changing circumstances. After Montague left, Ryder remained downstairs; he was looking forward to sharing luncheon with his betrothed, who had sent word via her father that she would arrive in time for the meal.

Had his household not already known of their pending relationship, Mary's reaction on finding him downstairs would have made the connection plain; rushing into the dining room and seeing him standing by the head of the table, she strode down the room, skirts swishing, her gaze raking him from head to toe, then returning to his face. "What by all that's holy—or even unholy—are you doing downstairs?"

He smiled and pulled out the chair beside his. "Waiting to have luncheon with you." He wasn't game to try a full bow yet, but he gracefully waved. "Your seat, my dear."

Halting, she narrowed her eyes at him—a habit he was growing quite fond of. "You," she stated, "are a terrible patient."

He arched his brows and looked from her to the chair.

On a muted sound of frustration, she swept her skirts in and sat.

Allowing a footman to settle her chair, he moved to his own. "I'm surprised David—Sanderson—didn't mention that I tend to recover from injuries fairly rapidly."

"He did mention something about you having the constitution of an ox." She smiled briefly up at Pemberly as he shook out her napkin, then, more sharply, looked back at Ryder. "The good doctor, however, didn't say anything about you having the brain of a mule."

Ryder laughed. The footman smiled. Even Pemberly had trouble maintaining his usual imperturbable demeanor.

Ryder held up a hand in a fencer's gesture of surrender. "Pax. I promise I'll resist overtaxing myself." When she met his eyes, a distrustful look in hers, he held her gaze and more quietly said, "You can't seriously imagine I don't want to recover as fast as I possibly can."

She was passably good at comprehending his meaning, even when he spoke obliquely. A soft flush of delicious color rose in her cheeks, but she didn't look away. Instead, somewhat to his surprise, she held his gaze for just an instant too long for the action to be anything other than a challenge, then she glanced at the platters Pemberly was laying before them. "Just as long as you agree not to push too hard."

Leaving him to wonder how she intended him to interpret that, she directed Pemberly as to which delicacies to place on her plate.

After the meal, they repaired to the library. While she acquainted herself with the room, ambling down its length admiring the artworks and examining the leather-bound tomes, he sat at his desk and dealt with the most urgent of his neglected correspondence.

As the afternoon wore on, he debated gently suggesting she leave, but he couldn't quite make up his mind to do it. Consequently, when the front doorbell pealed at three o'clock, she was there to greet her cousins—and their wives—as Pemberly ushered the six into the library.

Ryder had invited the gentlemen—Devil Cynster, Duke of St. Ives and the head of the Cynster family, plus Vane and Gabriel Cynster, the three being Mary's oldest male cousins—but wasn't surprised that their ladies had elected to accompany them. Rising from his desk, he strolled up the room, aware that Mary, who had been examining books in the corner behind his desk, had shaken off her astonishment, directed one of her narrow-eyed looks squarely between his shoulder blades, and was now swiftly walking forward to join the company.

Reaching Honoria, Duchess of St. Ives, Ryder smiled, took the hand she offered, and was about to bow when Mary hit him on the arm with one small fist.

"No!" she told him, when, surprised, he glanced at her. Then she looked at her cousins' wives and explained, "He's been stabbed. He shouldn't even try to bow."

"Ah." Honoria recovered first and pressed his fingers. When he looked at her, she smiled, richly entertained. "In that case, you're excused."

Mary made the introductions; although he knew the men, and had recently met the ladies at Henrietta and James's engagement ball, he was nevertheless grateful to have the names repeated.

As he'd expected, they'd all heard the news. All offered their congratulations, which he and Mary accepted with due grace. Waving them to the chairs and sofas angled about the fireplace, he added, "Lord Arthur and I signed the settlements this morning. The official announcement will appear in the *Gazette* tomorrow."

Devil sat on a straight-backed chair alongside the chaise on which his duchess had settled, and regarded Ryder with a direct and rather penetrating gaze. "But I'm sure you didn't invite us here simply to share that information."

Sinking into an armchair facing them all, Ryder inclined his head. "Indeed." Briefly, he looked at the others. "I invited you here to explain that the attack in which I sustained my recent wound wasn't, as no doubt the wider ton believes, a random act of opportunistic thievery that went sadly awry."

Several moments of silence ensued while his guests—and Mary, who, seated on the nearer end of the sofa, turned a stunned face to him—digested that.

"I had wondered," Vane eventually said, "why any thief in his right mind would accost you."

"No matter how dark the alley," Gabriel said, "they had to have been able to see your size."

Ryder nodded. "And I was openly carrying a swordstick. Any of the miscreants who frequent this area know well enough to be wary, even if they can't be sure it is, indeed, anything more than a cane."

"But the two who attacked you—it was two?" Devil asked. When Ryder nodded, Devil continued, "They weren't so aware."

"No. They weren't. But they did know my customary route home from the south—I almost always walk if I attend an event in Mayfair."

"As do we all." Vane leaned forward. "But are you saying they were lying in wait?"

"Not just lying in wait but in the perfect position to best ambush me—along a short stretch, no more than ten yards, where the alley to the south narrows so much I can only just pass freely through."

Gabriel grimaced. "The one place where you would be most vulnerable."

"What you're saying"—Devil's green eyes had narrowed—"is that you were specifically targeted. By whom?"

Ryder inclined his head. "And that is a question to which I have no answer."

"Your two attackers?"

"Sadly, dead. I . . . ah, slew them before I realized I might need to question them as to who'd hired them. However, I had a private investigator examine the bodies before having them carted off to the police, and he's searched, but other than confirming that the pair were killers-for-hire more normally employed around the docks, and that they and their services had been solicited by an unknown man of indeterminate years and character, the investigator got no further. His inquiries have met a dead end."

"So," Gabriel said, "the question is: Who would want you dead?"

Ryder lightly shrugged. "As to that, I have no idea."

A short silence was broken by Vane's wife, Patience. "I

hesitate to mention it, but I suspect there are several gentle-men of the ton who would happily see you if not dead, then severely wounded."

Ryder managed to convert his grin to a grimace. "Actu-ally, no. Not that many, if any. I fear that, at least in that regard, my reputation has been somewhat exaggerated."

Honoria humphed. When Ryder met her eyes, she stated, "That I find very hard to believe. However, I can think of one instance that might prove relevant. Lady Fitzhugh."

He stared at Honoria, then slowly shook his head. "I don't think I've even met Lady Fitzhugh."

Honoria nodded. "I didn't think so—she's not at all your type. A more highly strung female I've yet to meet. However, I know for a fact that she has used a supposed liaison with you to goad her husband into fits of jealousy—and Fitzhugh, one must remember, is a red-haired Scotsman with a temper to match."

"I've heard him railing about you myself," Alathea, Ga-briel's wife, said. "He was all but apoplectic."

"True," Gabriel said, "but in all fairness to Fitzhugh, if he was disposed to come after you, he would be more likely to do it in person."

"I wouldn't be so sure of that," Devil said. "I heard a tale last night that last week he'd been frothing in fury over some new jibe by his wife, and the next day he packed her up and hied north to that castle of his in the Highlands." Devil met Ryder's eyes. "While I hesitate to voice the possibility, I could imagine Fitzhugh being so consumed by rage that, in lieu of being able to deal with you himself, he had two thugs hired to exact his vengeance."

Ryder looked his disgust. "But I don't even know the woman."

"Sadly, Fitzhugh doesn't know that." Vane met Ryder's eyes. "But one way or another, we can take care of that. And if it was Fitzhugh behind the attack, it's unlikely there'll be another."

Ryder inclined his head. "True." He glanced at Mary. "Tea?"

Mary blinked, then nodded and rose. "I'll ring."

Pemberly and the kitchen had the tea tray waiting; he carried it in and at Mary's direction set it on the low table before the sofa.

Mary glanced questioningly at Honoria.

Honoria smiled. "The position will soon be yours. You pour."

Mary did. Gabriel helped hand around the cups, and the conversation shifted into a more social vein.

Mary knew that her cousins' wives were eager to ask questions, questions they couldn't ask while Ryder and their husbands were hovering.

Eventually, however, Gabriel drifted up the long room, drawn to examine the ancient globe that sat in the corner by Ryder's desk. Ryder ambled in Gabriel's wake, then Vane and Devil followed.

Leaving the men to their low-voiced conversation, the ladies shifted closer.

"I take it," Honoria said, opening proceedings, "that you're happy with the situation?"

Mary considered. "I . . ." Lips firming, she nodded. "Yes. I am."

"That sounded surprisingly equivocal for you." Patience studied her over the rim of her cup.

"It was very unexpected." Mary frowned. "But as Mama said, I can and surely will meet the challenge."

"Well," Alathea said, her gaze traveling up the room to Ryder's broad back, "Ryder Cavanaugh is certainly challenge enough, even for you."

"You do realize," Patience said, "that you will be expected to bring him to his knees?"

Alathea chuckled. "Indeed. You will have to exact from him the full price for marrying a Cynster—he absolutely must declare his love for you."

Patience nodded. "And from such as him, it will have to be in words, with no roundaboutation."

Mary considered, then said, "I don't think roundaboutation will be a problem, not with Ryder. But as for the rest—well, that's my challenge, isn't it?"

The others softly laughed and agreed.

"But what happened with this necklace you've all set such store by?" Honoria asked.

Mary glanced down, then hauled the pendant from between her breasts and realized it wasn't overly warm.

She thought back to all the times it had been . . . slowly, she blinked. "I think," she murmured, "that the necklace worked exactly as it should have."

The other three ladies studied her face, then Honoria said, "In that case, I believe we can have faith that all is exactly as it should be."

At the far end of the room, Gabriel turned to Ryder. "I can see you have doubts that it was Fitzhugh behind the attack. I wondered if there was anything in your finances, any investments or estates matters or even recent acquisitions"—Gabriel nodded at the antique globe—"that might in any way have precipitated the incident."

Ryder grimaced. "Not that I'm aware of. We haven't made any acquisitions of that type for years—most of the art and antiquities date from my father or grandfather—and as for the estate and finances in general, mine are handled by Montague, as are yours." Ryder glanced at Devil, now leaning against the desk beside him. "So how likely is that as a cause?"

"Not likely at all." Vane met Ryder's eyes. "So now we're out of earshot of the ladies, tell us why you really got us here."

Ryder fleetingly grinned. "I did, indeed, have another purpose. The attack was specific, targeted, and very nearly did for me—if the knife had struck a few inches higher, I would have died. And now there's Mary. If in the near future anything should happen to me—"

"We would, of course, step in and take care of Mary." Devil met Ryder's eyes. "Is that what you wanted to hear?"

Ryder nodded. "Randolph, my brother—half brother, to be exact—is my heir, but he's too young to adequately protect her. And I would prefer Mary is never . . . I hesitate to say 'left at my stepmother Lavinia's mercy.' While I don't imagine Lavinia would do anything truly heinous, she is capable of behaving atrociously and is highly antipathetic toward me, and I fully expect that to extend to Mary."

Devil nodded decisively. "If anything should happen to you, we'll make sure Mary is taken back into the Cynster fold."

Ryder inclined his head. "Thank you."

"So your stepmother doesn't like you." Gabriel caught Ryder's gaze. "Could she have been behind the attack?"

Ryder considered, then grimaced. "I really can't see it. Lavinia is all melodrama and sweeping accusations. She's one of those women who always feels put upon, or let down, or done badly by, but while she will rant, rail, and even rage, I can't imagine her ever actually *doing* anything about me— she never has. Aside from all else, if she removed me, who would she blame for all the disappointments in her life? And as for hiring men to kill me, I seriously doubt she'd have the faintest idea how."

"In that case"—Devil straightened from the desk and turned toward the ladies—"Fitzhugh remains the most likely suspect. I'll see if there's any way to get word to him that there's nothing to his wife's assertions. Failing that, perhaps we can arrange to get word should he return to the capital."

Ryder strolled with the others toward the assembled ladies—and for the first time ever, one of them was his.

Fifteen minutes later, ignoring the look Mary cast him that stated very clearly she thought he should remain in the library conserving his strength while she did the honors,

Ryder walked out to the front hall to farewell his Cynster guests. The ladies went ahead while Vane and Gabriel followed, leaving Devil and Ryder strolling more slowly in the rear.

Grasping the moment of relative privacy, Ryder murmured, "I'm rather surprised you've all taken this so . . . *amicably,* shall we say? I was anticipating a somewhat more hostile reception."

His gaze fixed on those ahead, Devil fleetingly grinned—a flash of white teeth in his harsh-featured face. "Ah, but you are who, and what, you are, and given we know Mary rather better than you, we can appreciate just how much you deserve her."

Ryder blinked. "That doesn't sound comforting."

"It wasn't meant to." Devil's grin returned. "Let's just say all the Cynster males are distinctly grateful to you for volunteering to take her off our hands—the headache of dealing with her is now officially yours."

Ryder pondered that, and the light it cast on his soon to be formally betrothed, but when, turning from waving her relatives off, allowing Pemberly to shut the front door, she immediately glided to his side, exasperated anxiety in her blue eyes, he smiled and decided that her challenge was one he was looking forward to meeting.

"You must be flagging," she nagged.

Immediately seeing the possibilities, he reached a hand to the top of the hall table, as if bracing his weight, and lightly shrugged. "Perhaps a little."

She made a disgusted sound. "Men—you're all alike. Would it actually hurt to admit you're in less than tip-top condition?"

Keeping his expression bland, he pointed to the hall stand. "Perhaps if I had my cane?"

She fetched it. "You should be using it all the time—at least until you're back to full strength."

Leaning on the cane, he took an awkward shuffling step.

Making another of her disapproving sounds, she swooped closer. "Here—let me help." Grabbing his free arm, she draped it over her slender shoulders.

Ryder smothered a triumphant grin. Because he was so much taller—the top of her head barely reached his shoulder—the only way she could assist him was to brace his body with hers. Which she promptly did.

"Thank you," he murmured. Letting her press as close as she wished, he allowed her to steer him across the hall and on down the corridor.

The feel of her against him—the svelte but definite curves pressing against the side of his chest, her feminine warmth seeping temptingly through the layers of fabric separating their skins, the pressure of her small hands on his chest and back—stirred him to an uncomfortable degree, but as they made their slow way back into the library, he decided this much nearness was worth every second of the resulting discomfort.

Especially as it gave him the chance, once they'd reached the middle of the library and Pemberly had shut the door behind them, to halt, shake loose the light hold she had on his arm, and slide it around her—and then he was holding her.

Wide cornflower-blue eyes stared up at him, her wits—if he was any judge—momentarily suspended. He seized the moment to indulge his senses, but the instant her lips started to firm and her eyes started to narrow, he said, "I haven't yet thanked you for saving my life."

Her eyes stopped narrowing, but the expression in them declared she didn't intend to allow him the upper hand. "I'm still considering what I should claim as my reward."

"Indeed. You must tell me when you've decided. For now, however, I thought I should start paying my dues . . . like this." Eyes locked with hers, leaving his cane resting against his thigh, he raised his hand, tipped up her chin, and slowly, giving her plenty of time to anticipate the moment, lowered his head and, very gently, kissed her.

The first touch of his lips on hers . . .

Mary felt a shivery tremor slide deep, to her marrow. A tantalizingly delicate caress—more promise than substance, more lure than bait; he supped while she savored, and promptly wanted more.

Both of them wanted more. Without direction, she parted her lips, thrilled to her core when he angled his head and immediately accepted her invitation.

His lips firmed on hers, pressure and heat, veiled hunger and even more heavily screened desire—both were there. She unfurled and reached for him; even though all she did was lean more definitely into the kiss, that's what it felt like, a physical unfolding and stretching.

A coming alive in a wholly novel way.

She felt no surprise that it was he who made her feel so; he was an expert in this sphere, after all.

His arms, both now, slid around her and gently tightened, gathering her to him. She shifted closer yet, tilting her face to his in clear demand.

She sensed his satisfaction.

Then his tongue traced her lips, then plunged between.

And she stopped thinking.

Ryder teetered on an edge he hadn't walked in years, an instinctive compulsion to dive deep and plunder almost overwhelming the sensual tactician who knew the best strategy was slow and steady.

Slow so he could savor, could draw every last iota of significance from, and invest every possible nuance back into, the exchange—the first kiss they'd shared. The first of many, true, but this was one to embed in their memories—hers, most certainly, but in this instance his as well.

And steady as a rock so she wouldn't take fright; virgins were like unbroken fillies—they had to be gentled to a man's touch, to his tasting, eventually to his taking. His claiming.

But she clearly had no notion of the way things should,

for her own sake, be; as reining his baser self well back, he traced the inner contours of her luscious mouth, tasted tea and the honey biscuits she'd nibbled, and gloried in the promise of latent passion the hunter in him sensed dwelled beneath her innocence, she boldly and brazenly stepped fully into him.

The contact seared him, frazzled his control.

And the kiss tumbled headlong into the heated and wanton.

Into a sudden rage of giddy passion and unscripted delight.

Not so slow. Nowhere near steady.

His head shouldn't have been whirling; his senses should have been far too jaded to fall so easily to the glory and the wonder.

She drank him in; he couldn't get enough of her.

Sirenlike, she lured him in, on . . .

The pealing of the front doorbell jerked them back to the present.

As one they broke from the kiss. Stunned, he gazed down at her . . . and saw a smile—one of discovery tinged with wonder—curve her slightly swollen lips, then spread to her eyes, making them shine. . . .

The sound of approaching footsteps and familiar voices dragged his attention to the door. "My half siblings," he murmured.

"Ah."

He released her and she stepped back. He grabbed his cane before it fell, and together they turned to the door.

It swung open, propelled by a vision in fashionably frothy apple-green muslin.

"Ryder! My God! Are you all right? We only just heard!" Stacie raced across the room.

The sight of Mary standing beside him brought his half sister to a skidding halt, stopping her from flinging herself into his arms—which, in light of his injury, was just as well.

"Oh!" Eyes riveted on Mary, Stacie searched for and found a polite smile. "Hello."

From Stacie's tone and the questioning glance she slid him, Ryder deduced she, at least, hadn't heard about his engagement. "This is Miss Cynster." Turning to Mary, he said, "Mary—allow me to present my half sister, Lady Eustacia, known to all as Stacie."

Mary calmly smiled. "Yes, I know. We've met. Good afternoon, Stacie."

Unsurprisingly wide-eyed, Stacie politely nodded and touched fingers. "Mary." Glancing at Ryder, then around, confirming the room was otherwise empty, devoid of lurking chaperons, Stacie asked, "What's going on?"

As at that moment Rand, Kit, and Godfrey—Ryder's three half brothers—reached them, he managed to avoid answering, having to deal instead with a barrage of exclamations and questions.

"What the deuce?" Rand said. "Why didn't you tell us you were attacked?" He bowed to Mary. "Miss Cynster—a pleasure . . ." Noticing what Stacie had, Rand frowned.

"How bad is it?" Godfrey asked, then promptly answered with the obvious, "Well, clearly not that bad." He dipped his head to Mary. "Miss Cynster."

The most observant of the four, Christopher—Kit—had halted a yard away, looking from Ryder to Mary and back again. Eventually meeting Ryder's eyes, he raised both brows. "Thought you were at death's door, and instead . . ." Fluidly bowing to Mary, he said, "Your servant, Miss Cynster." Then he looked back at Ryder. "Well, for heaven's sake, tell us—what the devil's going on?"

Ryder held up a hand. "First, from whom did you hear I was attacked?"

Rand looked sheepish. "I bumped into David on the street a few hours ago—literally. He was dead on his feet. Don't blame him—he was half asleep and mumbled something about you recovering well. After that, of course, I browbeat him into telling me what the deuce you were recovering from. He made me promise not to tell anyone, but"—Rand glanced at his siblings—"obviously he didn't mean this lot."

Ryder had his doubts about that, but . . . "Very well. Let's sit down like civilized people and I'll tell you all."

"But where are you hurt?" Stacie took his arm as if to assist him to a chair.

Ryder didn't budge. "My side, which means I'm perfectly able to walk."

Stacie met his eyes, then wrinkled her nose at him. "Then do—to a chair."

Ryder chuckled and did, but he elected to sit beside Mary on the chaise. The others all subsided into the various chairs, all fixing demandingly inquisitive gazes on his face. Inwardly sighing, he gave them a severely edited version of events—which naturally led to all four expressing their heartfelt thanks to Mary.

She accepted the accolades with serene calm and the observation "It was the least I could do."

"Yes, well." Ryder took back the conversational reins. "That's not my only news. Miss Cynster has done me the honor of accepting my offer for her hand, and will therefore soon be your sister-in-law."

"Really?" Stacie sat up, eyes widening, totally distracted from his injury. "There's to be a wedding?"

Rand leapt in to offer his congratulations, and the others followed suit. There could be little doubt of either their sincerity or their enthusiasm; Ryder sat back and watched Mary laugh, then more freely interact with the four.

And felt an unacknowledged little weight lift from his shoulders.

He'd always stood as protector for the four; for him, for his peace of mind, it was essential that his wife see them in the same light, acknowledging as he did their right to his attention. He would never put them above her, yet equally he would never refuse them whatever aid and succor they required.

It was Stacie who asked, "I take it Mama doesn't know—about either the attack or your betrothal?"

"Not about the attack—and if you please, do keep that to yourselves. There's no point bruiting such a piece of information abroad." He'd given them the most likely explanation for the attack, that some cuckolded—or supposedly cuckolded—husband had thought to remove him from competition for some lady's favors. "But as to our betrothal, of that Lavinia is already aware, and as for the wider ton, the notice will appear in the *Gazette* tomorrow."

"Oh. But then I haven't really seen Mama for the last two days—I've been out with friends." Stacie turned pensive. "I wonder what invitations I have that will serve to keep me out of the house tomorrow?"

Kit laughed and teased her over not wanting to face their mother; Stacie countered that he and Rand didn't live under the same roof, so did not have the same pressing need as she and Godfrey to take evasive action.

Rand groaned. "I'll have to, I'm sure." He glanced at Ryder. "She'll want to haul me over the coals for not getting leg-shackled myself."

"You and me, both," Kit replied. "Godfrey, at least, is too young—you'll escape the repercussions, pup."

Ryder caught the faintly puzzled glance Mary threw him and almost imperceptibly nodded, indicating that he would explain later.

Predictably, Stacie had questions about everything—about when they'd first met, why they'd decided they would suit, and when he'd proposed—and, of course, how; while his brothers did not have quite the same focus, they were curious, too, but Mary proved as nimble as he in skirting those issues they did not wish to air. She then turned the questioning back on his siblings, exploiting her soon-to-be position to learn more about them.

Somewhat to Ryder's surprise, his half sister and half brothers responded readily to her interrogation and were soon treating her with the same openness they accorded him. As the comments, quips, and questions swirled, and Mary—closer to his half siblings' ages than he—all but became one of them, he smiled and relaxed, too.

His immediate family—this family—had never been stable, had never had the firm foundation and solidity of the Cynsters, an unshakeable base he suspected Mary and her cousins took for granted; they'd never known anything else.

Such rock-solid cohesion, based on loyalty and devotion and unquestioned trust, was something he'd yearned for from his earliest years. As he'd grown, that yearning had grown with him, melding into and coloring his view of his ideal future.

He'd known he could never have that sort of family—could never build his own Cavanaugh version of it—without the right wife. Without a wife who innately understood all that family could and should mean. Who understood how, at base, such a family worked.

Mary possessed that inherent understanding.

Even though she'd picked up the oddity and strain of his relationship with Lavinia, and had realized, he was sure, that it impacted on his half siblings, too, she'd already reached out to the four, was already—before his very eyes—making the sort of interconnections he'd hoped she would.

As the minutes rolled by and those burgeoning connections only deepened and grew stronger, as the laughter—more laughter than this house had heard in many a long year—rolled through the room, he wished it didn't have to end so soon. Turning to Rand, under cover of one of Kit's tall tales, he asked, "I'm not going out, so will be dining early. Can you stay?"

"Yes—of course." Rand glanced at Mary, then looked at Ryder.

He nodded, and when Kit concluded his tale, Ryder put the notion of a shared early dinner—"a family dinner"—to a vote. His other half siblings instantly agreed.

Ryder turned to Mary. "We would count ourselves honored if you would stay and dine with us." Capturing her hand, he raised it to his lips, his eyes on hers brushed a kiss to her fingertips. "Please do."

Muted catcalls came from Kit and Godfrey.

Mary ignored them and smiled into his eyes. "Thank you. I would be delighted to join you"—she glanced at the others—"and the rest of your family."

Ryder grinned. "Excellent." Retaining his hold on her hand, he glanced at Rand. "Ring for Pemberly, Rand—" He broke off as the front doorbell rang again. He arched his brows. "Now who?"

Along with the others, Mary looked toward the door.

Pemberly entered to announce, "Mr. and Mrs. Simon Cynster, Miss Henrietta Cynster, and Mr. James Glossup, my lord."

Mary rose with the others; she stood beside Ryder as her brother, sister, sister-in-law, and soon-to-be brother-in-law walked in. Stepping forward, she greeted them and made the introductions.

Congratulations and the inevitable quips flowed once again. For several minutes as the two groups merged, greetings and comments, exclamations and explanations wrapped the company in a pleasant hubbub.

Eventually leaving Simon and James chatting with Ryder and his half siblings, Mary turned to Portia and Henrietta.

Henrietta said, "Mama wasn't sure what you were planning for the evening. As we'd just returned and heard your news, we offered to come and either bring you home with us, or else take home word of your plans."

"I see." Mary hesitated, then looked up as Ryder joined them. "Henrietta was just asking about my plans for the evening. How large is your dining table?"

Ryder smiled, all lazy lion, down at her. "The big one seats forty-eight, but as we're only ten, we can use the family dining room."

Mary looked back at Henrietta, then at Portia. "Have you any plans yourself for tonight? Or can you stay and join all of us here for an early dinner?"

Portia glanced at Henrietta, then looked back at Mary. "As we weren't sure when we'd be back . . ." Glancing at Ryder, she explained, "We'd gone to Wiltshire to deal with some matter at James's estate—I've already cried off all events for tonight, so for myself I would be delighted to stay. And I'm sure Simon will be, too."

"You can count on me and James." Henrietta looked across at the others and grinned. "It will be like having our own impromptu engagement dinner."

Ryder's smile deepened. "Excellent." He looked down at Mary. "If you would ring for Pemberly, my dear?"

Meeting his eyes, seeing very clearly how happy he was with the direction in which she'd steered events, she inclined her head. "Of course."

Chapter Eight

The following morning, Mary sat in the window seat in the back parlor of her parents' house and studied the formal notice of her betrothal that had appeared in that day's *Gazette*.

While one part of her mind remained faintly stunned that this was where her quest for her hero had landed her, the greater part was . . . already relishing the challenge.

Absentmindedly toying with the rose quartz pendant, she read the notice again. Her eyes dwelled on Ryder's full name: Ryder Montgomery Sinclair Cavanaugh. His middle names, she had not a doubt, would be past marchionesses' family names; when combined with Cavanaugh, his name was redolent of the power and majesty of England's nobility.

Challenge. It was there, staring her in the face, impossible for any to deny—not that anyone would; Ryder's character was known the length and breadth of the ton.

But this particular challenge, the one he had with his customary arrogance laid at her feet, was hers alone to meet. No other lady would ever have the chance of being his chosen marchioness. Of being able to deal with him, to treat with him, with that specific advantage.

Fate might have cut short their courting, but she was now where she was, the notice in the *Gazette* made her position irrevocable, and forward was her only possible direction.

Which meant she needed to learn more, much more, about

Ryder—and in short order. She might never be able to control him, yet regardless she needed to start looking deeper, focusing more on him, on what was important to him, on what drove him.

He'd enjoyed the previous evening—they all had—but he in particular, albeit it subtly, had encouraged and facilitated; she'd sensed he'd been deeply content with how the evening had gone. It had been after nine o'clock before, noting a certain tension about his eyes and guessing his strength was flagging, she had, also subtly, called an end to the gathering. Everyone had departed in a rowdy group, all delighted with their new connections; Mary had left with Henrietta and James but had made sure to alert Pemberly and Collier to ensure they stood ready to help their master up the great stairs to his bed.

At least he wasn't of that nonsensical type of male who wouldn't let those close to him physically assist him.

Lips curving, she refocused on the announcement. She'd enjoyed her first taste of being his marchioness and knew he'd appreciated and approved of her skills.

It was a minor success, but it had been a start. Indeed, the events of yesterday had given her significant insights into her husband-to-be's life, and left her with questions she needed to further explore.

She was mentally listing said questions—what the situation between him and his stepmother truly was topped the list—when the door opened and Henrietta walked in.

"There you are." Seeing the *Gazette* in Mary's hands, Henrietta grinned. "Still amazed at your fate?"

Mary swiveled to face her sister as Henrietta tugged an armchair closer and sat. "You have to admit that, given my requirements regarding my hero, Ryder isn't a candidate anyone would have nominated."

Tipping her head, Henrietta regarded her. "Actually . . . I would have to disagree. Quite aside from what I observed last night, I know Mama's pleased. She thinks he's perfect for you and you and he will do very well together, and I gather the others—Honoria, Patience, and Alathea, as well as the grandes dames, Aunt Helena, Aunt Horatia, and Lady Osbaldestone included—all think the match well nigh perfect on all sides."

"Hmm." Mary had been curious as to how others would see it. "Still, he's rather . . . I suppose one might say 'more than I bargained for.'"

Henrietta's smile flashed. "Possibly, but he does seem utterly intent on sweeping you off your feet and into marriage."

"Indeed. But it's the 'love and wedded bliss' part of our equation I'm unsure about."

"Ah, but that's why you're perfect for him."

Mary frowned. "That's what I don't understand—why *is* everyone so sure of that?"

For half a minute, Henrietta regarded her as if wondering if she was jesting or not, then, as if puzzled herself, said, "You know—well, I know you know because we all often tell you so—that you're the bossiest female ever to walk the ton's ballroom floors."

Still puzzled, Mary returned Henrietta's gaze steadily. "Of course I know that. Quite aside from all your complaints, it's not as if I don't behave so deliberately."

"Exactly!" Henrietta sat back with a wave. "There you are then." When Mary continued to look blank, Henrietta spread her arms. "Don't you see? On the list of gentlemen of the ton who need to be bossed, Ryder Cavanaugh ranks supreme—indeed, well out of range of any others. More than any other, he's the one who needs a lady like you—one with the right nature to counter his—to take him in hand."

"Ah." Suddenly, Mary saw it. "*That's* why the grandes dames are so thrilled."

The look Henrietta cast her clearly said, *Well, of course!*

The sound of footsteps in the corridor preceded the opening of the door. Louise walked in, saw them, and smiled. "Perfect. I need to speak with you both."

Closing the door, Louise crossed the parlor and sank onto the cushions alongside Mary. "We have the flowers for the wedding to finalize today, but before we head off on that errand, we need to discuss when to hold yours and Ryder's engagement dinner and ball."

Mary blinked. "I have to admit I hadn't yet thought of it."

Louise nodded. "Indeed, but in this case, this household has to juggle your engagement event with Henrietta's wedding."

"Oh, but"—Mary glanced at Henrietta—"the wedding takes precedence, surely?" She looked at Louise. "Can't we leave any engagement ball until after the wedding?"

"We *could*," Louise allowed, "but it would have to be at least a week after, and then we run into the question of when your wedding would be held." She waved her hands. "It's become something of a logistical nightmare, what with all those of the family who have traveled to town for Henrietta's wedding, and who would feel compelled to remain for an extended time if we put off your engagement ball, and so pushed back your wedding, too." Louise grimaced and met Henrietta's, then Mary's, eyes. "We—the ladies of the family—all gathered at Horatia's yesterday and discussed the subject at length. It was agreed that if you and Ryder are amenable, then the most felicitous timing for all would be to hold your engagement ball and dinner *before* Henrietta's wedding, with your wedding following a week or so after Henrietta's." Louise paused, then added, "Unless, of course, you and Ryder were content to put back your wedding until September or so."

Both Henrietta and Louise looked inquiringly at Mary. Considering the prospect, she pulled a face. "While I can see some benefits in a longer engagement"—such as giving her time to learn how to better deal with Ryder before she let him put his ring on her finger—"I can't imagine either he or I will be . . . comfortable with waiting until September."

"Indeed." Louise nodded. "That was the consensus of feeling yesterday—and really, no one could see any great sense in delaying formally acknowledging your engagement." Louise nodded at the paper Mary still held. "Especially as the announcement has already been made. It's taken people by surprise, and although that's neither here nor there, compounding surprise by delaying a formal engagement ball was something we all saw as simply unnecessary. And making you and Ryder wait until September to marry seemed equally senseless. So!" Louise drew breath and faced Mary. "What do you think, and how do you think Ryder will see it?"

"I don't know—as I said, I hadn't thought of it, so we haven't discussed the subject at all." Lips firming, Mary looked at Henrietta, then met Louise's gaze. "But clearly he and I need to do so. When, exactly, were you thinking of holding our engagement ball?"

"With the wedding six days away, the latest we could manage it is four nights from now."

"And our wedding?"

"It was suggested, from our Cynster point of view, that a week after Henrietta's would be the earliest date that would suit, but that's more flexible, of course. We need to consult more definitely with Ryder and his family on that."

Mary nodded. "Very well—I'll suggest that. Our engagement ball four nights from now, and our wedding a week after Henrietta's."

"Good!" Louise rose. "Now, we really should be on our way to Covent Garden. The florist suggested we visit her shop and see the blooms for ourselves, just to make sure we're happy with the flowers we've chosen."

Henrietta rose with alacrity, but Mary was slower coming to her feet. When Henrietta arched a brow at her, Mary grimaced. "I was going to come with you, but four nights from now isn't all that much time." She met her mother's eyes. "I suspect my morning will be better spent determining Ryder's thoughts on the timing of our engagement ball and our wedding."

That the Marchioness of Raventhorne had elected to breakfast at the small table before the fire in her boudoir in company with Claude Potherby, who had called to keep her company, was the only thing that saved her Sèvres tea service from certain destruction.

Perusing Lavinia's copy of the *Gazette,* Claude glanced at her, then folded back the paper to reveal the Announcements section and held it out to her. "Here—you'd better read this."

Setting down her teacup, Lavinia accepted the news sheet and focused on the print.

"Argh!" She shot to her feet, overturning her delicate hoop-back chair, which smashed on the polished boards.

She stared at the paper. *"Damn* it! Why didn't they stop it?"

Claude smothered a sigh. "My apologies, but I thought it better you see that now, rather than hear about it later—in public—but, after all, you knew it was coming." He frowned. "And they who? Who would want to even try to put a stop to it?" Other than her, but Claude knew Lavinia's wishes were neither here nor there, at least not with regard to her stepson.

"Bah!" Lavinia flung the sheet into the fireplace.

The flames flared and consumed the thin paper. Claude didn't care; he'd already read all the news it had contained.

Tightly folding her arms, Lavinia fell to pacing. "I'd thought the Cynsters would decide that Ryder was no fit husband for their darling." She flung out an arm. "He's a known seducer!"

Of bored matrons only too ready to be seduced. Claude thought the words but knew better than to utter them. Instead, he drawled, "I believe you should take this as a sign that Mary Cynster is not the lady for your Randolph."

Lavinia snorted. "Clearly." Still pacing, breakfast forgotten, she started to chew one fingernail. "I'll have to find someone even better for Randolph—a young lady of impeccable background with an even bigger dowry—and with all speed."

Lucky Randolph. Content that he'd discharged the duty of a friend and circumvented any public display of unseemly temper on Lavinia's part, Claude raised his cup, shut his ears to her mutterings, and gave himself over to savoring the really quite excellent coffee Lavinia's cook produced.

Half an hour after seeing her mother and Henrietta off to Covent Garden, Mary walked into Ryder's library unannounced. Seated behind his desk, he'd glanced up at the sound of the door opening. Seeing her, he smiled, the gesture carrying open appreciation of her statement in not permitting Pemberly to usher her in.

"Good morning, Mary." Ryder's deep, sonorous tone resonated through her. Rising, his gaze traveling from the top of her head to her feet, then somewhat more slowly returning to her face, he came forward to meet her. "I trust you slept well?"

"I did, thank you. But what about you?" Suppressing all awareness of his hungry lion gaze, of the sheer physicality of him, heightened now they were again alone, halting before the chaise she pointed to his side. "What about your wound?"

Waving her to sit, with only the slightest check he sank into the armchair beside the chaise. "Sanderson called this morning and examined his handiwork. Both he and I are in agreement that all is healing well."

"Good. Given what we need to discuss, that's just as well." When he raised his brows, she continued, "The dates for our engagement ball and, subsequently, our wedding."

He stared at her for an instant, then said, "Ah—I see. Henrietta and James's wedding is . . . when? Six days from now?"

She was pleased he saw the difficulty. "Precisely." Setting her reticule beside her, she drew off her gloves. "According to the collective wisdom of the ladies of my family, we have two choices—sooner, or later." Briskly, she outlined the arguments; Pemberly arrived with the tea tray as she concluded, "So that's why they've suggested four nights from now for a formal dinner and engagement ball, with our wedding to follow Henrietta and James's, but with at least a week between."

She paused to pour. When they both sat back, cups in hand, she sipped, then asked, "So what do you think?"

His heavy-lidded hazel gaze was resting on her, yet she got the impression he wasn't truly seeing her but was considering, juggling options and outcomes . . . then he refocused on her.

"I'm in complete agreement with the argument that, having announced our betrothal, regardless of the proximity of Henrietta and James's wedding, society will expect some formal acknowledgment of said betrothal by both our families." He sipped, then went on, "More, that our engagement surprised most observers also argues for a sooner rather than later acknowledgment, simply to quash any potential speculation on our families' attitudes to the match, no matter that there aren't any adverse views." He grimaced lightly. "You know what the ton is like."

She inclined her head. "Indeed." She was pleasantly surprised that his grasp of society's foibles was so acute.

"So," he went on, "although a formal dinner and engagement ball four nights from now would, in the general way of things, rank as somewhat precipitous, it would nevertheless suit our purposes best—and, of course, the imminent wedding gives us a solid excuse."

"Agreed. So that's the timing of the dinner and engagement ball decided—it will be held at St. Ives House." She sipped, over the rim of her cup met his gaze. "In recent times, all the family's engagement balls have been held there."

He nodded in acceptance.

Lowering the cup, she went on, "There's one point I didn't discuss with Mama—I couldn't while Henrietta was with us.

However . . ." She met his eyes, held his gaze for an instant, then simply said, "In social importance, your engagement to me rates significantly above James's marriage to Henrietta, but I don't want our engagement ball to"—she waved—"outshine Henrietta's wedding."

Ryder slowly blinked; seeing opportunity beckon, he asked, "Is there any reason it should?" Leaning forward to set down his cup, he went on, "In light of the nearness of the wedding, if you and your parents are agreeable I see no reason our betrothal dinner can't be restricted to our families—principal cousins, but no connections—and the ball could be similarly restricted to the more important connections and acquaintances." He raised his eyes to hers, arched a brow.

She smiled, plainly delighted. "Thank you—and the correct term isn't 'restricted.' It's 'select.' "

Grinning faintly, he sat back. "My apologies—our engagement ball will be a highly select affair." He studied her, read the clear approval in her face, watched her drain her cup, lean forward and set it on the tray, then sit back. "One thing." He waited until she raised her gaze to his. "Our wedding. It must be an event befitting the alliance of two of the oldest, most powerful and wealthy families in the ton."

Brows slowly arching, she held his gaze for several moments, then said, "I have nothing against your suggestion—but is there some reason . . . ?"

He shrugged lightly. "Other than my appreciation of the benefits of applying the right degree of pomp in certain circumstances . . . not really." For himself, he didn't truly care, but for her . . . he wanted their wedding to be an event to remember, and in ton terms that meant a major production. Her comment about not wanting to outshine Henrietta had been a sacrifice on her part; she hadn't intended him to see that, but he hadn't been fooled. Mary was a lady who thrived on big events, and in the matter of their wedding he saw no reason to shortchange her.

Indeed, he saw multiple reasons to ensure their wedding was as big an event as she might wish, but he wasn't about to articulate any of them, not to her.

When she continued to regard him with a not-so-faint degree of skepticism, he gave her another reason, one he was fairly certain she would accept. "Aside from all else, a very large wedding will ensure no one even vaguely imagines either family is less than thrilled with our union."

Slowly, she nodded, her eyes on his. "Speaking of which . . . yesterday, when your half siblings were here, I gained the distinct impression that there's some . . . strain, shall we say, between them and their mother over you. And therefore over me."

"I should warn you about that." Regally, she waved to him to proceed. He took a moment to gather his thoughts, only to realize . . . he grimaced and sank back in the chair. "In order to properly explain, sufficiently to adequately prepare you for what you might, at some point, find yourself facing with Lavinia, I suspect I need to go back to how and why she became my father's second wife."

Mary considered him, then shifted into a more comfortable position on the chaise. "You perceive me all ears."

He smiled, then, levity fading, commenced, "Believe it or not, I was a sickly babe. Then my mother died of a fever when I was three, and I caught it, too, and nearly died. The doctor was astonished that I survived. Subsequently, any ailment of any sort in the vicinity and I caught it. I was deemed at death's door more times than my poor father could count. After a few years, the medical men all agreed that it was highly unlikely I would survive to adulthood. My father had been devoted to my mother, and throughout his life he remained devoted to me, but he knew his duty. He wasn't getting any younger and he had to have an heir, so he married again—and he chose Lavinia. Aside from her unexceptionable birth and background, her principal attractions, my father later informed me, were her willingness to marry a man twenty years her senior, and to bear him several children. Rand was born in short order, then Kit, then a few years later, Stacie, and then Godfrey.

"At that point Lavinia and my father reached an accommodation, and their marriage became one in name only. Both lived their separate lives, and from all I ever saw the arrangement proved satisfactory." Ryder paused, then, lips curving cynically, continued, "For my father, myself, and my half siblings, all rolled on relatively peaceably. We all got along and there were no real tensions—to the others I was their older brother, and to me they were my younger brothers and sister. But for Lavinia it transpired there was one fly in her ointment—namely, me." Ryder met Mary's gaze. "She'd been led to believe I would die, but I didn't."

Mary's eyes widened. "She wished—wishes—you dead?"

He quickly shook his head. "No—it never was that, has never been quite like that. As I explained to your cousins, while Lavinia would be happy to see me dead, she's never shown any inclination to act to make that happen. It's more that she'd expected Rand to inherit, for *her* son to become Viscount Sidwell, as I was, and later step into my father's shoes as Marquess of Raventhorne, and my continued existence means something she'd assumed would ultimately come her way out of marrying my father isn't being delivered. In a convoluted way, she views my not dying as something akin to a breach of promise."

"Ah." Mary nodded. "I see." Then she frowned. "What about Randolph? How does he feel about your continued health?"

Ryder smiled. "Rand has absolutely no aspirations to be marquess. Oh, he would step up if he had to, but he has no ambition to take on the responsibility—as you might have noticed from his congratulations yesterday."

She nodded. "I would have sworn he was sincere—I would have been surprised if you'd told me he had eyes on the title."

"He doesn't, and Kit is even less enthralled by the prospect. As for Godfrey, I doubt it's ever occurred to him to imagine himself the marquess—and he'd be horrified if he did." Ryder paused, then went on, "But, of course, the four of them are very aware of Lavinia's . . . shall we say continuing frustration with me, with my being alive. And, naturally enough, as they and I are close, and they're devoted to me—as you correctly divined yesterday—it leaves them feeling exceedingly awkward when Lavinia and I are forced to interact. When she and I are in the same room, in the others' presence, for any length of time."

"I can't imagine you ever being so gauche as to insult your stepmother. Not even in private."

"You're correct—I don't. Oh, I might think the words, but as a general rule I treat her with the chilliest civility—I've learned from long experience that that serves best. And although she is occasionally indiscreet, even, if we're alone, insulting, Lavinia has a very fine notion of her position as marchioness, and as her standing derives from the title I hold, she's not going to do anything to diminish the Marquess of Raventhorne in society's eyes."

Mary nodded, appreciating the point. "So she's caught in a cleft stick of sorts and can't curse you in a ballroom."

"Or over a dinner table, but in order to spare both our nerves, I try to avoid her. Given our respective circles, that's usually easy enough."

"I can't see why she's *still* so frustrated." Mary studied him; regardless of his injury, he exuded palpable physical strength, and with his color back to normal the last thing he appeared was weak. "It must have become apparent long ago that, whatever ailed you as a child, you've grown out of it. No one would imagine you're likely to readily succumb now."

Ryder pulled a face. "Well, yes and no. My sickliness had receded by the time I reached ten, enough for me to go to Eton. But my exploits there, and later at Oxford, and even

when I first came on the town would have encouraged Lavinia to believe she would hear of my death any day. I'm
quite sure she, as well as my father, *were* told that by various
masters and others over those years."

He glanced at Mary. "I was wild to a fault—a hellion,
a hell-raiser. Having been told for so long that I couldn't
expect to live, that I wouldn't see my majority, I . . . grasped
every second of life I could. I *wrung* from every second all
the life I could. From childhood scrapes, the inevitable falls,
and consequent injuries, to schoolboy fights and pranks
of all the most dangerous kinds, to horse racing, phaeton
racing, hunting—in all truth there was every reason for Lavinia to believe that where illness hadn't done the deed, I,
myself, would accomplish it."

He paused, then smiled faintly and went on, "Actually, it
was Sanderson, when he returned from his medical training
in Edinburgh, who finally convinced me that the only way I
wouldn't die of old age was if some self-inflicted injury did
for me first."

"Remind me to thank the good doctor when next I see him."

"Indeed. However, as had happened through my earlier
years, whenever I grew out of one area of danger, another
always seemed to loom, at least in Lavinia's eyes." Ryder
met Mary's gaze. "She's told me, more than once, that she
fully expects to hear of my death at the hands of some cuckolded husband."

Coolly sober, Mary arched her brows. "As very nearly occurred."

"True. If she only knew . . . but, even then, you turned up
to save me."

Mary met his eyes, held his gaze for an instant, then in a
tone of discovery stated, "That's why you've kept the attack
so secret."

Trapped in her eyes, he hesitated for too long for an effective denial. He shrugged. "There's no reason to encourage
her to believe she has cause to resent you."

"Because I helped you cheat death?"

"Because you helped me avoid the one thing that would have delivered to her her ultimate desire—seeing Rand in my shoes. That's what her focus is—it's purely incidental that I have to die for it to happen."

After a moment, Mary said, "Your poor brother must feel . . . quite set upon."

"Sometimes, yes. He bears with it—she is his mother, after all. He knows I know and understand his feelings, and the others do, too, but it is, indeed, hardest on him. I, at least, can avoid her—he can't."

"Is that—her antipathy to you—why she doesn't live here?"

Ryder hesitated, then admitted, "I bought her the other house . . . not just because of that." After a moment, he went on, "At Raventhorne, she lives in the Dower House, with her own staff. Here in town, she lives in a house in Chapel Street, again with her own staff—for the same reason. After my father's death, she . . . I suppose you might say tried to usurp me. Tried to take over the Abbey, and also this house—both are kept fully staffed. When the staff at the Abbey, and later here, too, refused to accept her orders on matters that properly needed my consent, she attempted to dismiss them." He met Mary's gaze. "These are all people from families that have served the Cavanaughs for generations. In the end, Lavinia became so heedlessly disruptive, I had to banish her from the house. All my houses, actually."

Mary reviewed all he'd told her—and why he had; protectiveness was, indeed, one of his major motivating forces. She glanced at the clock—and was shocked to see the time. "Heavens!" She grabbed her reticule. "I really must go—I'm due at a luncheon at my aunt Celia's."

Ryder rose to his feet as she stood.

Turning to the door, she started tugging on her gloves. "Is there anything else I should know about your stepmother and your relationship with her, or with your half siblings?"

Falling in beside her, he went to shake his head, then stopped. "Perhaps one other thing."

Glancing up at his face, she arched her brows invitingly.

Shifting his gaze to the floor, he walked several paces alongside her before saying, "On his deathbed, when I was sitting alone with my father, he asked me to promise I would marry well and continue the line. By that point, he had grown to distrust Lavinia, and he . . ."

When he didn't continue, she filled in, "He didn't want her blood in the main line?"

His lips twisted. "Yes. Exactly."

Connecting the facts . . . she opened her eyes wide. "And that, I suppose, explains why you were in the ballrooms at all, enough to bump into me and realize I was pursuing Randolph." Reaching the door, she paused and faced him, waiting for him to open it.

Halting, he looked down at her, searched her eyes, her face, then, voice low, said, "It's exceedingly tempting to leave you believing that, but in the interests of complete honesty, I was hunting you—specifically you—for days before I realized it was Randolph you had misguidedly set your sights upon."

She tried to keep her eyes from narrowing on his. "Why?" He seemed disposed to answering her questions, and that one ranked at the top of her list.

Without moving, he said, "For the same reasons I gave you on Lady Bracewell's terrace."

And just like that she was back on that moonlit terrace with him, standing close enough for her senses to riot, to be overwhelmingly aware of him, of all he was, all that, beneath the fashionable clothes and civilized manners, he had the potential to be . . .

Temptation whispered over and through her. She knew she shouldn't, yet still she said, "Remind me."

Challenge, deliberate and clear, rang in the words.

He heard it; one tawny brow faintly arched. "Because I believe we will suit." His green and gold gaze grew sharper, more intent. "Very well. In many if not all ways." His voice deepened to a mesmerizing purr. "And because I want you. And for me . . . that's enough."

Hunger, desire, passion—all were there, unscreened, in his eyes. Mesmerized in truth, she moistened her lips, found breath enough to evenly state, "Words such as those are not terribly compelling."

His lips curved; he inclined his head slightly. "As you find it so . . . perhaps we might try actions."

Then she was in his arms and his lips were on hers, and she inwardly exulted.

She hadn't even admitted it to herself, but this was what she'd wanted—the most important thing she'd come there that morning to further explore.

Letting her reticule dangle from her wrist, she spread both gloved hands, fingers wide, on his chest. The fine fabric of his coat met her leather-sheathed palms and fingertips, but beneath lay him, solid and hard and immensely intriguing.

Fascinating. Her senses flared, then raced, reaching and searching, absorbing every last little insight they could.

She'd yielded her mouth from the first; as her senses reeled, overwhelmed by all there was to take in, she grew increasingly aware of his slow, typically lazy—unbelievably possessive—claiming of her lips, her mouth, her tongue.

As if he were branding her in some subtle, addictive way; even as she followed his lead and started to copy and return his undeniably expert caresses, some inkling of just how potent was their allure was blossoming in her brain—

Enough. Ryder artfully drew back and broke the kiss. Holding her easily within one arm, he studied her delicately flushed face, drew satisfaction from the vestige of sensual haze clouding her eyes. "So have I convinced you of my proposition?"

She blinked, twice, faintly frowned. "What proposition is that?"

He couldn't entirely hide his triumph. "That we will

suit—exceptionally well. In many if not all ways." Even though he wasn't holding her tight, she had to be able to feel the tangible evidence—proof, if she wished it—of the truth of his statement that he wanted her.

If the sudden consciousness that flooded her expression, the awareness that flared in her eyes, was any guide, she wasn't likely to question that point again.

But then her gaze, the cornflower blue a fraction more intense, steadied, and she gave a small nod—whether to him or herself he wasn't sure. "Perhaps. You might be right."

She eased back and, faintly surprised, he let her go; even though he didn't like losing her warmth, much less the tantalizingly light touch of her hands on his chest, he reminded himself, his instincts, that there would be plenty of time for more, later.

That it was wiser not to push for more yet. Strategy, tactics; better she come to him.

As she just had.

He watched her step back, shake her skirts straight, take her reticule in one hand, and felt a definite spike of satisfaction; not only had he met her immediate challenge more than adequately but his strategy of how best to deal with her was also bearing fruit. If he played his sensual cards correctly, she would come to him, and then he would have her without having to admit to anything more binding than desire.

Desire, passion, lust—all emotions he was entirely willing to own to. Especially with her.

When, ready to leave, she glanced at him, he opened the door, waved her through, then strolled beside her down the corridor to the front hall. "Do you have a carriage waiting?"

"Yes." She glanced at him. "I often use my parents' second town carriage."

He nodded and made a mental note to buy her her own carriage.

Reaching the front door, he went to open it but paused with his hand on the knob. He caught her eye. "One last point—the date of our wedding. Unless you specifically wish to delay it, I believe it will be in our best interests to tie the knot as soon as practicable."

Returning his gaze, she didn't pretend not to understand; for a twenty-two-year-old lady of quality, she was refreshingly short on guile.

Although faint color again rose in her cheeks, after an instant's pause she nodded crisply. "Yes, I agree. That being the case, I believe we'll be meeting at St. George's a week after Henrietta and James."

Looking down, she resettled her gloves.

Amused, he swung open the door and managed an abbreviated bow.

She slanted him a glance, then inclined her head. "Good day . . . my lord."

He smiled back, making no attempt to conceal his appreciation. "Good day, my lady."

Still smiling, he watched her walk down the steps to where her footman waited to open the door to a small black town carriage. He'd suppressed a very real impulse to ask which events she would be attending that evening. He was still too sore to attempt standing for long; he had to be content with remaining where he was and watching her drive away.

Two evenings later, having surrendered to her mother's insistence that she attend Lady Percival's ball, Mary accepted that she'd lost all patience with her current social role, given over as it was to adequately responding to the constant stream of congratulations and not-so-subtle queries the announcement in the *Gazette* had spawned.

She hadn't expected being feted would prove such a chore.

Standing by the side of Lady Percival's ballroom, alongside the chaise on which Louise sat chatting to several other matrons, close enough to intervene if necessary, Mary continued to smile and accept the proffered felicitations—some less than sincere—with passable grace, pointing out that she and Ryder had in fact been acquainted for more than a decade . . . she wished she'd stayed at home.

Which was shockingly unlike her. Being a bossy soul meant she needed people to steer and direct . . . indeed, she knew the people she wanted to steer and direct, but none were present, not even Stacie. More to the point, being the focus for so many others, she couldn't march off and find something to amuse her; she had to stay in one place and provide amusement for everyone else.

She was debating how soon she could nudge her mother toward the door when the crowd to her left parted and Ryder appeared.

He was carrying his cane but otherwise appeared his usual, rakishly eye-catching self, perfectly groomed, his golden-brown hair gleaming, his linen and cravat precise and pristine, the latter arranged in an intricate fall, the ivory at throat and cuff in stark contrast to the midnight black of his elegantly cut evening coat and trousers, and his subdued black-and-gold checkered waistcoat.

Meeting her eyes, he smiled his lazy lion smile—no one observing it could doubt the sexual possessiveness with which he viewed her—and made straight for her.

The few still between them melted out of his way; the pair of matrons who had been about to approach her, their charges in tow, fell back in a tittering flutter.

She barely heard them. Something in her chest leapt; interest and more geysered. As if she'd been a desert, parched and dry, renewed engagement flowed like revivifying rain down her veins, yet . . .

As he neared, concern for him welled. She opened her mouth to upbraid him for having left the comfort and protection of his house, but before she could speak, he swooped. Even though he didn't actually surround her, she felt as if he somehow had, as if she was enfolded within his protection; capturing her hand, he bowed—only she was close enough to register that the gesture lacked his customary fluidity—but as he straightened, both the expression in his eyes as they trapped hers and the tension inherent in all his movements carried a clear, if unvoiced, warning.

Eyes locking with hers, he carried her hand to his lips and brushed a lingering kiss over the backs of her fingers, and she battled to suppress a shiver.

Apparently oblivious—although she doubted he was—he murmured, in that sinfully deep voice he reserved for such moments, "My dear delight, I hoped I'd find you here. I fear I grew bored, and nothing would do but to seek your company."

Ryder held Mary's gaze, watched her blink, saw sudden awareness of where they were flare in her eyes, along with the understanding that quite half of her ladyship's guests were now surreptitiously watching them and she couldn't—shouldn't—give him the piece of her mind currently hovering on the tip of her tongue. He'd elected to carry his cane, a necessary precaution, but as he wasn't at the moment leaning on it, there was no reason for anyone to imagine he was recovering from any near-fatal wound rather than nursing a twisted ankle.

Then her awareness refocused on him and she smiled. "I'm delighted you did." The quality of her smile assured him she was sincerely happy to see him.

Which led him to ask, *sotto voce,* "Has it been that bad?"

Her smile escalated by several degrees. "Worse," she whispered as, beaming smile in place, she turned to the two matrons now even more eager to engage.

He dutifully stood beside her and played second fiddle to her lead; it was, after all, what he'd come there to do—to support her in whatever way he could. Hiding in the peace and quiet of his library while leaving her to face the social barrage alone hadn't appealed on a number of counts; given his wound no longer troubled him unless he twisted and his strength had returned enough to risk the time on his feet, he'd sent a footman to inquire of her parents' butler as to where she might be found, and had followed her there.

Despite his intentions, within ten minutes his lazy smile had grown somewhat forced. Slanting a glance at Mary, he seized a second between congratulatory exchanges to murmur, "How the devil can you swallow such syrup?"

Glancing up, she arched a brow. "With more than a grain of salt?"

"Ouch." He had to desist while they chatted with the next couple waiting to offer their felicitations and archly marvel at how he and she had managed to reach an understanding without any of the gossipmongers, let alone the grandes dames, realizing they had formed an attachment. Which reduced him to all but whining as the pair withdrew, "Do we have to do much more of this?"

She cast a swift glance at her mother; earlier Ryder had seized a moment to pay his respects. "Perhaps"—glancing around, confirming there were no others immediately about to pounce, she gripped his arm—"we might stroll."

"Excellent idea." Closing his hand over hers, anchoring it on his sleeve, he immediately stepped out. "Perhaps if we're ambulatory we won't be such easy targets."

He glanced down at her—and discovered she was studying him, her eyes faintly narrowed.

"I didn't expect you to turn up here. Are you sure you're strong enough to weather this?"

He grinned. "Quite." He felt a trifle guilty over the pleasure he derived from the concern filling her eyes. He held up a hand, palm out. "I swear I won't overtax myself. There—will that do?"

She made a huffing sound. "I suppose it will have to, but I warn you I expect to enjoy my engagement waltz, and I won't be able to if I have to hold you up through half of it."

He laughed. When she arched a haughty brow at him, he waved. "The image was just a little too much."

She pinched his arm. "You know what I mean."

Chapter Nine

Three evenings later, Mary sat beside Ryder at the middle of one long side of the massive table in the formal dining room of St. Ives House and, buoyed on a wave of exuberant happiness, surrounded by her family and his, listened as her father, from his place closer to the head of the table, proposed a toast to "the baby of our family in her generation, and the gentleman she will wed."

With smiles, supportive cheers, and much tinkling of glasses and thumping of the table, everyone raised their glasses high and called in unison, "To Mary and Ryder!" then enthusiastically drank to their health.

Mary couldn't stop beaming; she was finally here, perhaps not, in the circumstances, at the very end of her quest, but well and truly on her way. This, in effect, was the point of no return; she was now committed beyond recall, and had her ultimate goal front and center in her sights.

She could barely contain her impatience to get on—to press ahead, to take the next step, whatever that might be, toward bringing Ryder, metaphorically speaking, to his knees.

As the noise subsided and everyone returned to their conversations, he caught her eye. "Happy?"

They'd conversed enough over recent days for her to know he meant the question literally and specifically; she reined in her enthusiasm enough to actually consider, then, meeting

Still chuckling, he patted her hand. "Never fear—I swear you'll have an engagement waltz to remember."

"Very well." She tipped up her chin. "Just as long as you don't forget."

He resisted the impulse to assure her he wouldn't, not now she'd made such a point of it, and instead devoted his energies and talents to the twin tasks of steering them clear of those trying to catch up with them through the crowd, wanting to wish them well while simultaneously trying their hand at extracting more details of their unexpected romance, and amusing her, which in turn amused him.

Although Fate had determined that they would wed without benefit of any real wooing, he saw no reason not to claim the days until their wedding to give her what he could of the moments her saving his life had denied her.

They strolled and talked, teased and laughed, and occasionally stopped to chat with others.

Somewhat unexpectedly, he enjoyed the hours— principally because he knew she did, too. He'd known she was direct, that she didn't often bother with guile, but the openness she displayed in interacting with him was something he was growing to treasure.

They reached the end of the evening in pleasant accord. After handing Louise, then Mary, into their carriage, Ryder waved them off, then climbed into his own, smiling to himself as he sank back in the leather-cushioned dimness. Mary had, of course, demanded to be told how he intended returning to his home; that he'd brought his carriage had earned him an approving, if somewhat imperious, look.

As the carriage rolled along, he realized he was still smiling—for no specific reason that he could discern.

his gaze, nodded. "I can't think of any part of the evening thus far that might have gone better."

He smiled, not his lazy-lion smile but an expression several degrees more personal, and for a moment amid the madness there was just the two of them—a second of privacy within the swirling chaos.

Then Luc, Amelia's husband, seated a few places to Ryder's right, called to him and he turned to respond, and Marcus, Mary's cousin Richard's son, seated to her left, posed a question, and she turned to answer.

Nearly seventeen, Marcus, dark-haired and blue-eyed like his father, together with his twin, Lucilla, had traveled down from Scotland with their parents for Henrietta's nuptials. Being able to attend Mary's engagement ball and wedding, too, was an added bonus in Lucilla's and her parents' eyes, but Mary wasn't so sure Marcus saw dallying in the capital in the same light.

Yet even as she chatted with her younger relative about the sights he'd seen thus far in town, her attention remained in some way linked to, attuned to, the man on her other side.

He who would shortly be her husband.

They'd spent the days and evenings since he'd joined her at Lady Percival's ball and had so definitely claimed the position by her side largely in each other's company. Until the following morning in the park when he'd arrived in his carriage to stroll the lawns beside her, she hadn't fully appreciated the degree to which he'd established his social claim on her, but the way others now treated her, ladies young and old and gentlemen, too, eventually impinged and opened her eyes.

Once she'd realized . . . she'd been ready to narrow said eyes at him the instant he stepped beyond protective into possessive, yet although he'd sailed very close to that line on several occasions, as if sensitive to her impending ire, he'd tacked away from overstepping her mark every time he'd got too close.

They'd walked in the park, had strolled the length of Bond Street, and spent countless hours in his library—talking, discussing, arguing, relating anecdotes, and, even more amazing, indulging in companionable silences. Somewhat to her surprise, she'd discovered that they shared rather more than just a liking for always being in charge. In the evenings, he'd joined her and her mother in Brook Street, without argument or complaint accompanying them to whichever events her mother had selected; once there, he had set himself to make her evenings as pleasant as he could.

This morning, he'd arrived in a closed carriage—not his phaeton because, as he'd informed her, mindful of her strictures regarding their engagement waltz he'd decided against attempting to hold his horses—and they'd been driven out to Richmond to spend the day in the peace of the park there, returning to town with only just enough time to prepare for the whirl of this event, their engagement dinner and ball.

That he was putting himself out to please her, perhaps viewing that as an avenue to ease their way into their somewhat rushed union, was neither difficult to see nor particularly surprising. What had, however, captured her attention was the simple fact that in all he had set out to do, it truly was the case that her pleasure defined his.

He enjoyed the things they did, the moments they spent together, because she did.

He measured the success of anything he caused to happen against the yardstick of whether it pleased her.

That could have been a purely superficial exercise, one dictated more by reason than feeling, more deliberate than instinctive, but for him, with her, his focus on pleasing her seemed an intrinsic part of him.

Something that sprang from somewhere deep within him.

When Marcus turned to respond to Portia, on his other side, Mary seized the moment to, from beneath her lashes, slant a glance at Ryder; she couldn't stare too hard or he would notice, but . . . seeing him in this setting, joking with

her cousins, her brother, and brother-in-laws, all of whom she knew well and of whom over the years she'd heard revealing tales aplenty from their wives, she had to wonder if, perhaps, Ryder's propensity to focus on a lady's pleasure had become an intrinsic part of him because of his lengthy reign as one of the ton's great lovers.

That was a thought to give any lady pause.

Feeling warmth rise in her cheeks, she quickly looked away before he—or anyone else—noticed.

Glancing around, she confirmed her assessment that the dinner was a resounding success; both it and the preceding gathering in the long drawing room looked set to pass off without the slightest hitch. Ryder's family were all present, including his stepmother, but, as he'd predicted, Lavinia appeared to be on her best, albeit it rather chilly, behavior, although to give her her due she was warm and encouraging to everyone except Mary and Ryder.

Making a mental note to, at some later date, see what she could do to thaw the marchioness's ice-clad spine, Mary rose along with everyone else as, under Honoria's direction, the company quit the table and moved toward the doors and the stairs up to the ballroom.

Ryder had risen and drawn back her chair; he offered his arm with a smile. Smiling back, she laid her hand on his sleeve; as they walked slowly along the table, following other couples, it registered just how familiar walking beside him, at his side, had so quickly become.

Familiar, and on some level reassuring. *Safe.*

She had never felt any physical threat from him. A sensual sparking of her nerves, definitely, but even that instinctively flaring alarm had transmuted to something more akin to . . . curiosity.

Smiling still, she glanced up at him, but he was watching those ahead. She was about to speak, to draw his attention back to her, when movement ahead and to the side drew her eye.

Lucilla, slender, almost elfin in pale green silk with her rich red hair cascading in ringlets about her face, was weaving through the crowd, her green gaze locked on Mary, her expression intent.

Mary halted and looked up as Ryder glanced at her. "I have to speak with Lucilla for a moment—in private. Why don't you go ahead? I'll join you and the others in the receiving line."

Ryder's gaze shifted to Lucilla, who had halted several paces away; smiling, he inclined his head to her, then his gaze returned to Mary's face. He briefly searched her expression, as if to confirm that she wasn't anticipating any difficulty, then he simply said, "Don't take too long."

"I won't." Drawing her hand from his sleeve, she made for Lucilla.

As she neared, Lucilla said, "I believe you have something for me."

"Indeed, I do." Grinning, Mary took Lucilla's hand. "Come on—I'm fairly certain we're supposed to do it over here."

Lucilla looked puzzled, but she allowed Mary to tow her to one side of the room, to a spot beside one of the long sideboards. "Why here?" Lucilla asked as Mary released her.

"Because this is where Angelica gave the necklace to Henrietta, and where Henrietta then gave it to me." Reaching for the clasp at her nape, Mary slipped it free. "I don't know where Heather was when she handed it to Eliza, or where Eliza was when she gave it to Angelica, but it might well have been here, too." Gathering the necklace as it slid from her throat, Mary considered it, then held it up by the clasp so that the chain of amethyst beads and gold links hung straight and the rose quartz pendant swung. "It just seems to be sensible to follow the same pattern, given we can."

Lucilla nodded and reached for the necklace, closing her hand around the links. "Thank you—and you're right. With any talisman based on belief, adhering to any tradition, no matter how minor, never hurts."

Mary released the necklace, but Lucilla didn't immediately move her hand. When the younger girl stood there, stock still, Mary looked at her face. Lucilla's gaze had grown unfocused, as if she was viewing something distant and far away.

Then Lucilla blinked, faintly frowned. After a few seconds, she looked at Mary. "Don't fall into the trap of being as blind as Simon was—and never forget that Ryder . . . isn't blind at all."

Mary frowned. "What does that mean?"

Widening her eyes, Lucilla shifted, lightly shrugged. "I can't truly say." Meeting Mary's eyes, she paused, then grimaced. "I get messages sometimes—like that—but as for their meaning, that's more . . . nebulous." She paused again, as if studying something only she could discern, then offered, "What I can say is that The Lady is pleased—that in her eyes you're exactly where you're supposed to be, marrying Ryder . . ." Lucilla blinked, then added, "Being challenged by him." She glanced at Mary. "If that makes any sense."

Mary stared at Lucilla for several seconds, then nodded. "Yes, actually, it does."

Lucilla's smile flashed. "Good. In that case"—she waved the necklace she still held in one hand—"I thank you for this. I hope it will be as efficacious north of the border as it has been for all of you down here."

"Mary?"

They turned to see Henrietta beckoning urgently from the doorway.

"You'd better run," Lucilla said.

With a grin, Mary picked up her skirts and rushed as fast as decorum would allow for the stairs, her betrothed, and their engagement ball.

Ryder was waiting at the top of the stairs; unable to hide

an appreciative smile, he offered his arm as his giddy be-trothed reached him. "I've been instructed to bring you im-mediately to the receiving line."

She rewarded him with an effervescent smile. "I'm ready—lead on!"

He laughed and they turned to cross the wide foyer. His gaze lingered on the expanse of fair skin above the neckline of her shimmering violet gown. "What happened to your necklace?" She'd been wearing a fine cameo on a purple velvet band, and that was still in place, but the necklace was gone.

"It was only mine for a time. I passed it on to Lucilla."

He remembered when he'd first seen the curious necklace about Mary's throat—at Henrietta's engagement ball. As the earliest guests, just entering the hall below, had yet to climb the stairs, he slowed and asked, "Did Henrietta pass it on to you at her engagement ball?"

Mary glanced at him more sharply. "How observant of you to notice."

He smiled one of his sleekly persuasive smiles. "So it's what?" Recalling the conversation he'd overheard between Mary and Angelica about Mary embarking on her quest to find her hero, he guessed, "A talisman of sorts?"

She regarded him for several seconds, patently debating whether to answer, and if so, how much to tell him; eventu-ally she said, "It's a gift from Catriona's Lady—The Lady—and is supposed to assist those it's given to in locating the right gentleman for them." She looked forward as they neared the ballroom doors. "It went to Heather first, then passed to Eliza, Angelica, and Henrietta in turn—and then to me." She glanced at him, clearly anticipating disbelief. "Each of us believe it worked, although I don't expect you'll credit such a superstitious tale."

Holding her gaze, conscious of the others in the receiving line just ahead, he wondered if he dared state that he knew for a fact the necklace had worked for her—it had steered her to him, after all. Instead, he smiled easily and looked ahead. "The Lady?" Swinging Mary into position in the receiving line, he lowered his head and murmured just for her, "Admittedly I've never called her that—I've always simply called her Fate."

Looking up, she met his eyes, an arrested expression in hers, but then the first of the select guests invited to their engagement ball—Lord and Lady Jersey—swept up, and all conversation, all revelations, were necessarily suspended.

For the next hour, neither Ryder nor Mary had any chance to do anything beyond greet and chat with guests, but the nature of the gathering ensured neither of them had to exert themselves—they knew everyone and everyone knew them. Despite being a ball held at the height of the London Season to celebrate an unexpected betrothal linking two of the oldest and most powerful families in the ton, the atmosphere remained relaxed and genial, lacking the heightened tensions of a larger and consequently more formal event.

For Ryder, the only less than perfect note was struck by his stepmother, but his half siblings' efforts to keep Lavinia both amused and out of his and Mary's way warmed him and made him smile. Together, he and Mary circled the room, moving smoothly from group to group, confirming that their wedding would take place in just ten days, a week after Henrietta and James's.

Then the musicians set bow to string, and the moment Ryder had been waiting for—the moment Mary had been so looking forward to—was upon them.

Smiling into her eyes, he bowed—with unrestricted grace now that Sanderson had removed his stitches and pronounced him fully healed. Straightening, he closed his fingers firmly about the hand she offered him—and felt something inside him tighten, lock. Her eyes were pools of blue-violet alight with expectation, with shimmering anticipation as he led her to the floor.

Without taking his eyes from hers, he swept her into his arms and stepped out, and took her with him, into their engagement waltz.

The music swelled and sent them swirling across the parquet floor as the crowd, smiling and delighted, fell back.

Leaving them whirling alone under the chandeliers, with crystal-fractured light glinting in their hair, in their eyes, as the world fell away and there was only them.

With his gaze locked with hers, with her eyes locked on his, they were caught and held captive by the moment.

He smiled intently, outwardly and inwardly. He'd heeded her words, had seen in them opportunity—the perfect moment in which to take the next step. To draw her closer yet, to stake his claim on her, on her senses, in a significantly more absolute way.

To move to the next stage and to capture her as his. As his bride-to-be, recognized and acknowledged not just by society, not just by their families, not just by him but by her. And not just by her rational mind but by the sensual, emotional, steely-tempered and iron-willed female every instinct he possessed assured him dwelled inside her.

That was his aim—to capture that fey creature—and he was highly experienced in that type of hunt.

As they whirled down the room, effortlessly revolving, his well-trained muscles without conscious direction sweeping them through the turns, as she followed his lead with even less thought, his focus never wavered. For them, for his intent and purpose, and for hers, too, they weren't dancing in Mayfair.

They were waltzing in a world of their own.

Mary sensed the difference, not just the drawing in of her senses but their heightening. The ineluctable tension. It gripped her, and him, and resonated between them.

She'd been looking forward to this moment, to the waltz and all it meant, but when she'd originally imagined her first waltz with her betrothed, she'd assumed it would signal an end. That their courtship would be done, and that this dance would be an acknowledgment of their love, a love already owned to and owned by them both.

Instead, this waltz, their waltz, was a beginning. The first step down a path she'd never imagined treading—not without the confidence of love to bolster her.

Yet here she was, and here he was, whirling her about the floor in his arms, his gaze locked with hers, his awareness meshed with hers in a way that consumed all her senses, and as Lucilla had confirmed, this was where they—he and she—were supposed to be.

For them, this was the right way, the right path, even if it was so very different from the one she'd imagined. Fitting perhaps, given he was so very different from the man she'd imagined would be hers. She'd assumed her gentleman would be an easy man to tame . . . instead, trapped in his hazel eyes, she was waltzing her engagement waltz with the ton's most untamable nobleman.

Challenge? Oh, yes.

It was there, inescapable, a subtle clash of fire in their gazes, but as they whirled again and at a distant remove she sensed others joining them on the floor, she had to wonder if he saw that challenge in the same way she did. If he recognized its basis, knew her fell intent.

Of his intent she harbored no doubt; she would have had to have been unconscious, her senses all blind, not to see, sense, feel the primal possessiveness that reached for her. To give him his due, his desire was screened by the veil of sophistication he so expertly wielded, yet immersed in the moment, so focused on him, she couldn't miss the signs. Couldn't miss the power and passion that burned undisguised in his eyes.

He'd chosen her, he wanted her, and soon she would be his in all ways. She suspected he thought that, via the burgeoning passion rising between them, he would then be able to manage her.

Still trapped in his gaze, she returned his smile with one carrying the same intent.

They would see.

As the musicians commenced the final reprise, she couldn't resist murmuring, "You should perhaps remember that we're both rather determined people, and"—tilting her head, she watched his eyes—"we're now both committed . . . to this."

To us. To what will be.

Ryder blinked; a faint frown in his mind if not on his face, he returned to reality as the music slowed. Spinning them to an elegant halt, he released her, stepped back, and bowed.

She curtsied—a fully court curtsy perfectly judged for his station.

As she'd no doubt intended, it made him smile and dissipated the lingering tension that had held them.

A tension he'd evoked, yet . . . it had been rather more than he'd expected.

He'd intended to capture her in the moment, not to himself be captured by it.

By it, by her, by what had swelled and welled between them.

That . . . had been more than he'd planned for, significantly more—and different in feel—than what he'd anticipated. Yet . . . as she'd said, they were both determined people, and they were now committed to this.

Raising her, he drew her to his side, tucked her hand in the crook of his arm, and smiled one of his usual, lazily charming smiles. "Shall we return to the fray?"

She met his eyes; hers glinted commiseratingly. "I fear we must."

They did. He had only to raise his head and others gathered around, to chat, to comment, to enthuse. As the evening rolled on, courtesy of various oblique comments, he realized that their determination and commitment had been more openly on show than he, at least, had realized.

While passing between groups, he murmured to Mary, "It seems our engagement waltz made a statement more public than I'd intended."

She blinked up at him, then glanced around. "Ah—I hadn't realized, but now you mention it, I can see it might have." She shrugged and looked up at him. "But perhaps that's for the best." Arching her brows, she faced forward. "And I can't see that it will hurt."

He wasn't so sure of that—and even less sure what her words portended, of what was going through her willful mind, but as they joined the next group of guests he reflected that, Mary being Mary, he would, most likely, soon find out.

Across the ballroom, Lavinia leaned on Claude Potherby's arm and sniffed. "Have you heard what everyone—at least all the grandes dames and the major hostesses—are saying? That after that little performance there's no question but that *those two* will be future powers in the ton?"

Claude wondered if he should lie. "Well . . . yes." He didn't consider himself at all sensitive, yet even he had seen it, the indefinable aura of will and strength that, combined, spelled power that had cloaked the betrothed pair as they'd revolved down the room in the first waltz. "But really, my sweet, not even you can deny that being here tonight is very much like viewing history in the making. Quite aside from their stations, given who they are it's difficult to view this alliance as anything but major."

Lavinia all but pouted. "Perhaps. But I would much rather have seen Randolph as her partner in that dance."

Claude forbore to point out that Randolph wouldn't agree, nor would the resulting waltz have made the same impact. With no ready way to alleviate Lavinia's mood, he murmured instead, "Don't forget, my dear, that as Ryder's step-mama you have to be delighted."

Immediately plastering back the false smile that had slipped from her lips, she dipped her head in acknowledgment and turned to greet the next couple intent on paying her their compliments and congratulating her on her stepson's excellent match.

In Claude's opinion, she bore up reasonably well, which was really all he and her children—and her stepson and his fiancée—could hope for.

It was past one o'clock, and Ryder had just walked into his dressing room, tossed his evening coat on a chair, unbuttoned his waistcoat and set his fingers to unknotting his cravat when, in the distance, he heard his front doorbell peal.

Ambling back into his bedroom and out into the corridor, he wondered who the devil it was. Hearing Pemberly's even steps, then the sound of the bolts being drawn, he halted in the corridor; continuing to unravel his cravat, he strained his ears.

Pemberly said something, then the door shut, almost drowning out the reply someone made . . . someone female.

The possibility that, having heard of his engagement, one of his previous lovers had come to call flashed through his mind. Muttering a curse, he stopped untying his cravat and strode down the corridor.

Frowning, he swung into the gallery—

Mary ran into him.

"*Oof!*"

Instinctively he wrapped his arms around her, preventing her from staggering back. Frowning still, he looked down at her. "What are you doing here?" He blinked. "Has something happened?"

She looked up at him. "No." She studied his face, then pulled back; reluctantly, he made himself let go.

Before he could say anything, she waved him back.

Increasingly puzzled, rather than comply he glanced over the balustrade and saw Pemberly, door relocked, bolts in place, retreating toward his quarters, bearing away the lamp that he'd brought to light his way.

As darkness reclaimed his front hall, Ryder looked again at Mary; she'd wound a shawl about her shoulders but otherwise was dressed as she had been at the ball. "I repeat, what are you doing here?"

One part of him knew, but his mind was madly scrambling, trying to decide if this was a good idea or a bad idea—for her, and for him.

She tipped up her chin. "Coming to see you, of course."

"You saw me, were talking to me, only half an hour ago."

She wiggled her head impatiently. "That was there. This is here."

An unarguable fact.

But they were standing in his darkened gallery, lit only by the moonlight streaming through the big skylight, and in addition to being only half dressed, he was more than half aroused; even though a foot of clear space lay between them, he could still feel the warmth of her in his arms, feel the imprint of her body against his. After the last days, after the elemental desires unexpectedly spurred by that so-much-more-than-anticipated waltz . . . he wasn't at all sure her being there was a good thing.

Certainly not if she'd come to talk.

He managed to manufacture a sigh, one laden to dripping with patronizing boredom; forcing his body to project the same emotion, he waved. "Very well. We're here. You have my attention." Through the gloom, he met her eyes. "So what is it?"

She narrowed her eyes at him; he felt the increased belligerence in her glare. "If you think I'm going to be the first female in my family to go to the altar a virgin, you're mistaken."

Shutting his eyes to hide his instant reaction, he muttered, "Did I just hear aright?"

Her small finger stabbed his chest hard. "Yes! You did."

Sensing movement he opened his eyes, but was too late; having whisked around him, she was already marching, silk skirts shushing, down the corridor to his room.

He set off in pursuit, but, slowed by not knowing which tack he actually wanted to take, he didn't catch her up before she reached his open door.

She swept through.

Halting on the threshold, deeming it unwise to follow her further, he forced himself to lounge in the doorway, one hand gripping the door frame.

Reaching the area before the foot of his bed, she whirled to face him. Spine straight, head high, she leveled a look of blatant challenge at him. "So now we're officially betrothed and our alliance has been approved by all those who count, I've come here so you can show me what your vaunted reputation is all about."

Several thudding heartbeats of silence followed.

Arm braced, fingers clenching on the doorjamb, he studied her. And fought to think, but his mind kept tripping over her words. What was he supposed to say? To do?

He was accustomed to being the hunter; when his prey turned and flung themselves at him, it understandably gave him pause. Enough to register that in this, with her, matters were clearly not destined to follow any conventional path.

When, despite the stretching silence, she didn't waver, didn't soften or back down by even a fraction, he opted to do what he usually did in circumstances beyond his ken.

He listened to his instincts.

Drawing in a breath, easing his grip on the door frame and lowering his arm, he stepped inside, turned and closed the door, then, straightening, faced her. "Far be it from me to argue."

She nodded crisply. "Excellent." Her expression intent, she glanced around, then crossed to set her silver reticule on top of a chest of drawers.

As she unwound the silk shawl from about her shoulders, still grappling with the unexpected turn of events, he asked, "How did you get here? You didn't walk?"

"Of course not." Neatly folding the scarf, Mary laid it

alongside her reticule and tried to calm her galloping heart. Her voice, at least, remained steady and assured. "I had my coachman drive me. He waited until Pemberly let me into the house, then left."

"Your coachman?"

Ryder's incredulous question came from just behind her; her heart skipped as her greedy senses reached for his heat, for the solidity and sheer maleness of his body. Whirling, she fixed her eyes on his. "Yes." Anticipating his next question, she added, "John dotes on Henrietta and me. He'll do anything we wish, and keep his mouth shut afterward."

Ryder studied her for an instant, then, lips firming, shook his head. "I'm still having trouble accepting this." When she opened her mouth, he held up a hand. "No—wait. Just answer me this. Have you truly thought this through?"

"Of course I have." She let irascibility color her tone. "It's not the sort of thing one does on a whim."

He arched his brows. "I suppose not, at least not in your case. Still—"

Slapping her palms to his chest, she stretched up and pressed her lips to his. She kissed him—took advantage of his parted lips to send her tongue on a flirtatious foray— and thrilled when he responded, when his arms closed around her and he bent his head and took possession of her mouth. . . .

For long moments, she let her wits spin, let her senses glory, but then she gathered her will and drew back—pulled back from the kiss just enough to state, "No more arguing." Her palm to his cheek, she briefly met his eyes, then fitted her lips to his again.

But after the briefest of exchanges, he drew back. "Why? Because you might lose?"

"No—because we're wasting time!" Clasping his nape, she hauled his head down, and kissed him again—even more blatantly, ever more flagrantly.

Still he held against her, against himself . . .

She remembered and stepped into him, plastered her body against his—and felt him shudder.

Felt his resistance fall—not dropped, but with deliberate intent set aside.

She inwardly exulted; he was hers.

Then his hands closed about her waist and he took control of the kiss, and there was nothing uncertain in the acts. With irresistible expertise, he filched the reins and took unfettered charge—and she ceded and followed, eager to her soul.

Ryder gave up all pretense of not doing as she wished, of not seizing with unbecoming alacrity all she so innocently offered.

That she was innocent—an innocent who had never taken a man to her bed—was, somewhat shockingly, an unexpected thrill, spurring anticipation and setting an unfamiliar edge to his hunger, yet simultaneously the knowledge was a restraint, a restraining awareness that sang in his brain.

Slow. Thorough, yes, but *slow*.

This wasn't about a single night, not just one time; whatever came of this engagement, whatever interest accrued from his performance tonight, would color their enjoyment of each other going forward.

Tonight had to be right.

The pressure might have made a less experienced man falter, but he knew he could and would meet her challenge. Indeed, he hungered for the chance—the very chance she'd just flung at his feet.

Her mouth was all honeyed delight, sweet and tempting; her lips were pliant and demanding, an intriguing contradiction. For untold minutes he savored, not just the pleasures of the kiss but the unabashedly intimate promise of the slender and soft, vibrant and vital, undeniably female body in his arms.

He could have spent longer simply relishing the prospects, but he knew her—she wasn't going to wait on his cues. If he wanted to remain in the driver's seat, he would have to actively drive. Reluctantly drawing his awareness from the kiss, from the nearly overwhelming temptation of her mouth, from the subtle spur of the increasingly assertive caress of her lips and tongue, he freed enough wit to take stock, to assess the possibilities.

The bed stood beside them, the gold silk coverlet neat and straight, the mound of pillows at its head undisturbed. Inviting. Soft light spilled from four lamps, one on each bedside table, and two on the tallboys on either side of the room. The curtains were drawn; the fire had been burning earlier but was now mere glowing coals, the room nicely warm but not overheated.

Without further thought, he eased one hand from her waist, let his palm sweep up the sleek planes of her back, over her sensitive nape; she shivered evocatively, then her lips turned demanding. More demanding. Encountering and passing over the knot in the ribbon supporting the cameo about her throat, he slid his fingers into the glorious mass of her hair, searched, found, and pulled pins, and let them rain on the floor.

He kept kissing her, holding her, anchoring her deep in the exchange, submerging her in the warmth and the heat and the slowly rising hunger, swamping her senses while he let down her hair.

When the lush, silken locks cascaded free, he inwardly delighted, but then she pulled back. Curious, he let her break the kiss, watched as she shook her head, sending her curls tumbling. Her gaze was sultry, heavy-lidded; he saw her swollen lips form an O of discovery as her gaze rose—to his hair.

As countless women had before, she leaned into him, reached up, and with open delight ran her fingers into and through his thick mane.

Unlike all those previous times, her innocently claiming caress made him shiver.

Her eyes locked on his. She searched for an instant, then

boldly pressed closer, rose up on her toes, and with his head held steady between both hands, she kissed him.

Passionately.

For unexpected, uncounted moments, his head reeled. His hands gripped her waist again, holding her up—there, flush against him . . . as his senses steadied he reminded himself that she was a novice; she hadn't kissed many men before so she didn't comprehend the effect . . .

Her questing tongue speared past his lips, tangled incitingly with his, then retreated, effortlessly hauling him and his awareness fully back into the increasingly heated kiss, into the slick pleasures of her mouth which she freely, flagrantly, like a houri, offered up for his delectation.

She was clearly a fast learner; he should have expected nothing less.

And, of course, she was impatient.

Which shouldn't have been a problem, except some part of him was, too.

Reining that suddenly insistent beast back, shoving it to the rear of his mind, reminding himself that he was in charge—that it would serve them both best if he ensured he remained so—he raised his hands, spread them over her back, searched, and found the buttons securing her gown. Perhaps slow should mean even slower, but his palms already itched, his senses already hungered to savor her skin without any barriers to mute his touch, or his sensual appreciation.

Mary was ready, oh-so-ready to plunge headfirst into this. Into this fascinating arena that, to her mind, was now hers to explore. Hers to conquer and claim.

More, there was purpose and reason at her back; she had a considerable way yet to travel to reach her ultimate goal with him, and this, she was beyond certain, was her surest route to success.

And while kissing Ryder and being kissed by him definitely ranked as a splendor all its own—the sleek sophistication disguising an infinitely more potent, almost animalistic hunger enticed and enthralled—there was so much more she wanted and needed to see, to learn . . . to experience. To convince him to demonstrate and share with her.

Tonight.

That was her immediate goal—her next step.

Dragging a portion of her wits free of the richly sensual engagement of their mouths, the alluring mutual pressure of their lips, the slick, seductive play of their tongues, took effort. Indeed, it required something of a mental wrench, but the instant she managed it she realized he was ahead of her, his fingers deftly working the tiny buttons at the back of her gown free.

Delighted to discover his intent aligned with hers, she drew her hands from his face, his hair, and fell on his partly untied cravat, blindly unraveling, then tugging—

He made a strangled sound and shifted—as if to dislodge her hold on the cravat. Amenable to leaving it for later, she let go and reached for his waistcoat instead. It was already open; she grasped the sides, hauled them wide. Her awareness abruptly shifted from his lips to the wide expanse of his linen-draped chest; senses leaping, ravenously eager to explore, she ran her hands up the waistcoat's sides to his shoulders, then gripped and pushed, trying to press the garment over his shoulders and off.

She expected him to stop undoing her gown and oblige by lowering his arms, but all he did was grunt. *Disobliging beast*. She pushed and tugged harder.

Abruptly he released her, but his hands rose rather than lowered, then he was peeling her gown off, his hot palms skimming the curves of her shoulders, pushing the silk over and down her arms—attempting to press her arms and hands down.

"*Um-mph!*" She refused to lower her hands, refused to let go of his waistcoat and her desired goal.

But he, too, refused to cede.

He tugged; she tugged. Several seconds of crazed tussling ensued, driven not so much by stubbornness as by a wish to see who would give in first—

They broke from the kiss, gasping, half laughing.

Distracted by the laughter—bubbling up through her, gleaming in his eyes—she unintentionally eased her grip.

In two swift moves, he pushed her hands and dragged the sleeves of her gown down, trapping her arms at her sides, the bodice now at her waist, leaving her breasts screened only by the translucent silk of her very fine chemise.

She hauled in a breath intending to narrow her eyes at him, but then she saw his eyes—saw the flare of hunger as his gaze fastened on her breasts. Her breath hitched; her mouth turned dry, but her tongue managed the complaint, "Not fair."

His gaze lifted, slowly, to hers. "Fair?"

His hands had closed above her elbows, preventing her from sliding her arms free. She wriggled against his hold, uncaring that the movement shifted the screening silk over her breasts—over her suddenly painfully tight nipples. "Yes—fair. Turn and turn about. Now my gown is half off"—she gestured with her chin—"you have to take off your waistcoat."

Ryder stared, but, really, he should have expected it. "Just who do you think is in charge here? No, wait—let me phrase that more pertinently. Which of us has the experience to take the lead in this?"

She narrowed her eyes. "You. But that doesn't mean—"

He picked her up, tossed her on her back on the bed, and followed her down, pinning her beneath him.

Far from being shocked into stillness, let alone quiescence, she wriggled and shifted beneath him—effectively, if momentarily, distracting him—and succeeded in freeing her arms from her sleeves.

Her hands rose, reaching for his waistcoat.

With a growl, he caught them, one in each of his, and

pressed them back to the coverlet on either side of her head. Anchored them there.

The move pressed their bodies even more firmly together.

He met her exasperated gaze with more than a degree of exasperation of his own. "Stop rushing."

She searched his face. "Why?"

A good question, and he knew there was an answer, just not one he was up to explaining at that juncture. Not when his mind, the better part of his awareness, and every last one of his slavering senses had locked—intently—on her. On her lithe body trapped beneath his, on the utterly absorbing sight of her breasts, full and taut, rising and falling so enticingly beneath the nearly sheer screen of her chemise.

He didn't realize his gaze had fallen and fastened on those alluring mounds, on the tightly furled nipples all but begging to be tasted, until, using his hold on her hands as leverage, she arched, then even more provocatively twisted and writhed beneath him.

"Stop thinking—just . . . teach me. Now."

The demand she infused into the last word had him instinctively lowering his head . . . he jerked to a halt. No. *Slow.* It had to be slow.

Raising his eyes to hers, he saw she'd realized that she'd almost succeeded. Letting go of her hands, he abruptly pushed up, off—her and the bed.

"No!" She reached for him. "Come back."

He gave her her own medicine and narrowed his eyes at her. "Will you behave and follow my directions?"

That earned him a narrow-eyed bright blue glare.

When she continued to consider him, mulishness and mayhem in her expression, he unequivocally stated, "My way."

He couldn't get his tongue to add the words "or else"— such a huge lie. Regardless of what route they took, there was no chance on earth that she would leave this room a virgin, but he wasn't about to call attention to that fact and give her even more ammunition in this already fraught battle of wills.

She gave vent to a sound of frustration and slumped back on the bed. "Oh, very well. Your way, then."

A second later, she shifted her head and looked at him. "So." She arched her brows. "What's next?"

"Next," he said, giving her the incentive of shrugging off the waistcoat she'd been so intent on ridding him of, "you can answer me this: Why now? Tonight."

It wasn't that he needed to hear the answer so much as he needed the time—to cool his blood, and hers, too, before he rejoined her on the bed.

Mary frowned and didn't immediately reply. That would involve thinking, and at that moment her mind was in a de-lightfully delicious jumble. A novel and exciting whirl of expectation, anticipation, and burgeoning wants had taken possession of her wits. Was it desire? Physical desire? If so, she was perfectly certain she'd never felt it before.

And it clearly had the power to reorder her priorities. She would have thought that lying with her gown about her waist, her breasts virtually exposed to Ryder's gaze, would have dominated her attention, but no. Her senses, her wants— her desire—were much more focused on arranging a repeat of those moments when his hard, heavy body had lain atop hers, impressing her mind, body, and senses in myriad and deliciously pleasurable ways.

Losing that—the experience of him on top of her—had nearly made her cry out. Craving his return, and how to ensure that, filled her mind . . .

He finished unwinding his cravat and tossed the long band after his discarded waistcoat, set his fingers to the buttons of his shirt, then paused and arched a brow at her. She roused herself, dragged in a breath—conscious of the way his gaze dipped to her breasts when she did—and said, "Because I want to experience this, to know and understand this before you put your ring on my finger."

He started to unbutton his shirt, paused to undo his cuffs, then resumed the deliberate freeing of the buttons fastening the shirt's placket. Coming up on her elbows, she settled to appreciate the resulting slow but steady baring of his chest.

"Why?" When she looked at him vaguely, he smiled faintly. "Do you imagine jilting me if my performance doesn't live up to your expectations?"

She met his hazel eyes, saw his complete and absolute confidence shining there, took in the utterly unshakeable masculine conviction of sexual dominance and control, and felt something inside her uncurl, unfurl, then steadily rise and spread through her.

Letting her lips slowly curve, she gracefully lay back but continued to hold his gaze. "That," she murmured, her voice as sultry as she could make it, "is for me to know, and you to guard against."

His shirt fully open, Ryder paused to look down at her. He knew she was teasing, yet he had to wonder at her brazenness even while he delighted—nay, reveled—at the prospect of meeting her challenge. Arching one brow, he murmured, "Indeed?"

He shrugged off his shirt—and hid a grin when her gaze locked on his chest and her eyes widened. Tossing the shirt aside, he bent and dispensed with his shoes and stockings, then, bare-chested, bare-footed, prowled to the bed. Flicking the first two buttons at his waist free, he put a knee on the bed, then slowly leaned over her. Planting his hands palms flat on either side of her shoulders, bracing his weight on his arms, he looked down—into frankly expectant, blatantly and flagrantly encouraging blue eyes—and couldn't stop his slow smile. "In that case"—breaking eye contact, he looked down at her breasts—"I'd better get to it, hadn't I?"

He swooped and captured her lips—in exactly the same instant that her hands touched his chest.

The contact seared him, entirely unexpectedly ripping his awareness in two, fragmenting his focus, leaving him ineffectually vacillating between savoring the lush delights of her mouth and following the tantalizing drift of her fingers over his skin, their innocent questing through the mat of crinkly hair, the careful, gentle tracing of her fingertips along the raised seam of his wound, which suddenly, unexpectedly, felt intensely erotic . . .

My way.

Angling his head, he plunged into her mouth, soft and welcoming and all his, and fought to block out the distraction of her touch. Claiming her lips and her tongue, seizing her awareness and anchoring it in the kiss, he gained some relief as her hands slowed, then stopped moving and simply rested against his heating skin.

That was still too much contact; keeping her locked in the kiss, he shifted and came down on one elbow alongside her. In response, she half turned toward him, her hands drifting higher, to his shoulders. Much better. With his free hand, he nudged hers higher still—but then she went too far and in a rush slid her hands into his hair, fingers spearing through the thick locks and clenching, clinging, holding him to the kiss as she turned the tables and kissed him so wantonly he temporarily lost track, then she compounded her conquest by arching against him.

Her barely covered breasts pressed against his chest, tempting, luring; she drew back a fraction and the silk-shrouded mounds caressed . . . and he jettisoned all thought of a carefully orchestrated campaign.

And surrendered to his instincts.

Boldly he closed his free hand about one pert breast and drank down her gasp. Sensed the searing sensation that lanced through her at his touch and considered it no more than she deserved.

Onward. He knew what he had to do, knew he could do it, but wasn't entirely sure she understood enough to allow it.

His goal was straightforward: To seduce her senses and

make her his lover in a way that left her not just eager but hungry for more.

That would keep her coming back, night after night, for however long the magic between them lasted.

He had no idea how long that would be, but he was too experienced to waste time wondering. Their compatibility, their physical liking for each other, for the pleasures of each other's bodies, would be whatever it would be.

In reality, in the long run, he knew he could influence that only superficially, but as for the depth and degree of their mutual delight, that was well within his scope.

That was what being one of the ton's greatest lovers was all about.

He sent his hand skating over her body, tracing the curves, learning them. Making her arch to his hand, making her grow hotter and more urgent as he stroked, toyed, then caressed ever more explicitly. Stripping away her gown, flinging it away, he set his hand to her bare calf; after a senses-riveting moment absorbing the glory of her silken skin, he ran his palm up the taut curve, over the sensitive hollow behind her knee, rising to glide over the hem of her chemise and on, letting the gauzy fabric evocatively shift beneath his hand, a tantalizing addition to the caress, then he cupped his hand about one luscious globe of her derriere.

Deliberately provocative, blatantly possessive, he kneaded, flagrantly claiming, then, fingers gripping her firm flesh, he urged her hips to his, molding her to him so she would feel the rigid column of his erection.

Far from shrinking back in virginal modesty, she kissed him ravenously and arched more definitely against him in instinctive invitation; the sirenlike call of her body pressing into his, the feel of firm, heated female curves and delectable hollows offered so lavishly was a potent lure, a nearly overwhelming temptation.

Then she released her grip on his hair and sent her hands

skating—grasping, tracing, and wantonly demanding—over his chest. Across, then, taking advantage of his sudden sensual distraction, down. Over the ridges of his abdomen, out to his sides, then down to his waist.

He pulled away from the kiss, let his head fall back, tried to suck in sufficient air.

His reaction delighted her. Eagerly, she shifted and pushed her hands up again, spreading her fingers, boldly tracing the heavy muscles across his chest with open appreciation and unconscious—or was it conscious?—possessiveness.

He kept his eyes closed—he didn't need to see; he could feel it all in her touch, but . . . he had to stop her.

He liked his lovers petting him, loved feeling their small hands stroke and caress, then tighten and grip as desperation overtook them, until they sank their small claws into him in surrender. Normally, he noticed, delighted, but that was all. But Mary's hands—her evocative touch—raked him with such intense sensation that she effortlessly subverted his focus from the pleasure he was giving her to the pleasure she was lavishing on him.

He drew in a too tight breath. Later, he told himself, he could lie back and thrill to her worship, but not yet. Not now. He took half a second to consult his instincts as to whether there was any other way . . . then he moved.

Capturing her questing hands, he locked them in one of his. Angling over her, pressing her back to the bed, he anchored her hands over her head.

The frown she aimed at him was more a sultry pout. "Unfair!" Her tone held a siren's charm.

He shook his head. "No—fair." His voice was beyond gravelly. "At least on this occasion." When she arched her brows, he added, "Trust me—this time we need to go more slowly."

She widened her eyes at him. "And me touching you isn't helping?"

Her eyes had darkened to violet. He considered the sight while debating . . . lips setting, he admitted, "No."

"Oh." An expression of wholly feigned innocence. "What about this, then?" She twisted and arched, sinuous and supple as, catlike, she stroked her body—legs, hips, and torso—against him.

"*Mary!*" He gritted his teeth, closed his eyes—battled to hold onto even a semblance of control.

He heard her laugh softly. "Ry-der!" she mimicked, but her voice was softer, not so much a taunt as an invitation. Then he felt her shift, a second later felt her lips lightly, delicately, evocatively brush his.

Felt her breath wash over his lips as she whispered, "I won't break, you know."

He cracked open his lids enough to look down at her.

Feeling powerful, emboldened, and very sure, Mary let her lips curve. Her gaze locking with the glinting gold of his, she murmured, "I'm impatient, I know, but you don't need to protect me, not from this, not with you. You just need to lead, just like when we waltz." She paused, then said, "So can we dance now, please?"

She sensed rather than saw him abandon his stance, sensed his dominant, arrogant, always-in-control self surrender and give way. And felt quietly, deeply thrilled; she'd had no idea their engagement would spin out in this fashion, but she'd already learned a thing or two about dealing with him, and to have the chance of simply going forward hand in hand without any hint of supremacy on either side . . . she hadn't expected to get so far—to gain so much accommodation from him—not on this, their first night.

Although she shifted first to press even closer, he released her hands and let her come into his arms. Closed them around her and bent his head as she lifted hers . . .

Their lips met—and it was in truth as if they were waltzing again, stepping out in perfect accord, meeting and matching, their entire beings, mind, body, and senses, sliding into the moment until they each revolved entirely about the other.

Desire flared, rich and hot and luscious, laced with burgeoning passion and building heat. His hands wove fire over her skin; her own hands quested, urging him on. Dark murmurs fell from his lips and wrapped about her, then he stripped away her chemise—and she gloried in the possessive flare of blatantly male passion that lit his eyes.

His hands touched, almost reverently at first, but then they firmed and caressed, possessed. Every curve, every hollow. Then he bent his head and took her nipple into his mouth and she arched and cried out.

Held tight as he licked, laved, then suckled again, sending molten delight lancing through her body to pool, heavy and turbulent, hot and demanding, at her core.

With his lips and tongue and his hot wet mouth he explored her breasts, introducing her to a stream of rich and heady delights she hadn't known existed. Until heat and fire, and steadily escalating desire, filled her. Until clawing need all but overwhelmed her.

Finally, his strong hands cradling her naked body, curving it against his, he returned to plunder her mouth. Breathless, heart racing, burning from the inside out, and with not an iota of patience left, she reached for the buttons at his waist—and he let her.

Let her open the placket fully, slide her hand within and find him—hot as forged steel, rigid as iron. She closed her hand and he pulled back from the kiss on a hiss.

He was large—much larger than she'd expected—but sliding her hand along his length, watching the hard edges in his face grow even more chiseled, she told herself it didn't matter, that he would know and show her how . . .

Biting back a curse, Ryder caught her hand and drew it from his aching erection so he could strip away his trousers.

Turning back to her, he felt her arms reach around him, urging him nearer, felt the imprint of her breasts against his chest as she pressed herself to him from chest to calves, then she tipped her head back, eyes closed as she savored . . .

As she felt.

As she absorbed the sensual impact of feeling his naked body flush against hers for the first time.

Her expression was all bliss.

Something in him shuddered.

Enough.

Easing her onto her back, parting her thighs, he slipped his hand between and touched her. Eyes on her face, drinking in her reactions, with fingers that trembled, he traced the slick folds, circled her entrance, then, as her hips lifted and her restlessness rose, and he glimpsed the intense violet of her eyes beneath her lashes, he eased one finger past her entrance, into the velvet slickness of her sheath, and stroked.

Her eyes glinted; he worked his hand and she writhed, softly panted. He pressed in, deeper still, then slid another finger in with the first, and readied her.

He'd intended giving her her first climax before entering her, but as desire flushed her skin and her need rose, and swelling urgency gripped her, she sank her nails into his forearm and, arching her hips, gasped, "Now. Please, Ryder—*now*."

Denying her was beyond him; drawing his fingers from her scalding sheath, with hands that shook, he spread her thighs wide and settled his hips between. Fitted his erection to her tight passage, then he bent his head and took her mouth in one last, searingly passionate kiss.

Determinedly clinging to control, he thrust in—just as she arched up, impaling herself.

Shocking herself into a small scream.

He drank it in, used the spur to block his awareness of the hot, slick tightness that gripped him unbelievably powerfully, used the implication to lock his muscles and hold his body still; she'd succeeded in driving him in to the hilt, and—

Beneath him, she eased, then experimentally moved. Then drew back from the kiss enough to breathe, "Show me . . . just how does this go?"

Laughing, he discovered, was also beyond him. He grated, "Like this."

He withdrew and thrust in again; after one repetition, she rose to the rhythm, caught it, matched it. Matched him as he allowed all reins to slide free and let the age-old dance take them.

Simple, straightforward, something he'd done countless times—there shouldn't have been anything in the moment powerful enough to make him lose his mind.

To lose all contact with the here and now, to become so deeply immersed in the primitive give and take that he lost himself wholly in the pounding rhythm. In the indescribably evocative sensations of her body intimately caressing his, accepting his with such unalloyed passion.

The tempo escalated, then together they raced—hearts thundering, lungs laboring, will, intent, and focus all locked unrelentingly on reaching the shining peak.

He knew nothing beyond the primal drive, the compulsive friction. His breathing harsh and ragged, blind with desperation, arms braced, head hanging as his body plundered hers, he saw, felt, tasted nothing beyond the soaring passion that rose between them, answering their call—

It swamped them, caught them, tossed, wracked, and shattered them.

Dimly, distantly, he heard her scream, felt her body arch desperately, felt her nails sink into his arms, more than anything else felt the powerful contractions of her sheath as, unraveling, she tumbled from the peak—

Bodies, senses, and wills merged, locked so inextricably with her he had no choice but to follow, a roar ripping from him as release shuddered through him.

And together they fell—through searing ecstasy into a cataclysm of blinding glory. It surged through him, filled him to overflowing, then, slowly, faded, leaving him to sink into the familiar void.

Familiar, but not the same.

Deeper, fathoms deeper.

Satiation weightier than any he'd previously known rolled over him and dragged him down.

Some indefinable time later, sufficient consciousness resurfaced to shape his first coherent thought: Was he crushing her?

Even as the question formed, his senses registered the slow, gentle touch of her fingers stroking his hair. For long moments, eyes closed, he simply savored; if he'd been the lion most likened him to, he would have purred.

He couldn't recall ever feeling this degree of postcoital glow.

He dwelled on the feeling for several smug seconds, but as his senses expanded and registered the glory of her very female body lying surrendered and thoroughly possessed beneath him, some part of him insisted he had to take his weight off her. Surrendering to the compulsion, he shifted his arms and eased up. Looking down at her face, he murmured, "Are you all right?"

She didn't open her eyes, but her lips curved in a smile that reinforced the words. "I'm de-light-fully splendid." Her hand resting on his shoulder gently squeezed. "Thank you."

The degree of triumph he felt was ridiculous. "It was entirely my pleasure."

A spurt of soft laughter escaped her. "We could go on for ages if I tried to cap that, so I won't."

"Good thinking." He started to ease back, to withdraw from the slick sheath still lightly gripping.

Her legs, which had at some point risen to grip his flanks, tightened, along with her sheath. "Must you?"

He looked back at her face; she still hadn't opened her eyes, but there was not a single tense line marring the madonna-like bliss stamped over her features. "No, but aren't I too heavy for you?"

She shook her head, dark curls whispering across his pillow. "I feel like Goldilocks. You're *just* right. I like the feel of you on me, inside me—I like the hardness and the heat."

Arguing with that . . . was impossible. With a soft grunt, he let himself back down, not entirely as he had been before, but enough to satisfy her as well as him.

Relaxing again, he settled with his head beside hers, and she resumed her gentle stroking of his hair.

Sensing that remarkably intense satiation rolling back, he mumbled, "I'll have to take you home fairly soon."

"Hmm," was all Mary said. Her boldness had gained her far more than she'd hoped. Her lips curved lightly. "Soon."

Chapter Ten

It's beyond bearing!" Lavinia swept into her boudoir. Tossing her fashionable bonnet across the room uncaring of where it landed, she rounded on Claude Potherby as he followed her in; her color high, she spread her hands in appeal. "Who will rid me of this wretched knave?"

Claude smiled. "Very dramatic, my dear. Sadly, I see no one lining up to do the deed, and if you imagine I might be moved to consider it, do please hold me excused."

"Hah!" As was Lavinia's wont when agitated, she fell to pacing back and forth before the hearth. Eyes cast down, she gnawed on a nail. "Did you see that new phaeton of his? It's the most outrageously dangerous contraption—I'm surprised the Cynsters didn't raise a fuss rather than allow their darling to be driven at such a clip about the streets."

Having joined Lavinia in the park, Claude had seen the couple of the moment tooling about the avenues. Sinking into an armchair, he inwardly sighed. "My dear, if you're entertaining any notion that Ryder might lose control of his horses, overturn his carriage, and break his neck, I fear you'll be disappointed. He's a highly regarded whip, and while I grant his horses are headstrong, he's more than capable of holding 'em."

Lavinia replied with a disgusted sniff.

After a moment, she said, as if reciting a litany, "First, he was born sickly, and everyone, even his doting father, was sure he would die. But he didn't. Then he went off to school and embarked on every dangerous exploit you might name. And he survived them all. *Then* he took up with blades and bucks and hunted and whored and raced curricles and mail-coaches and God knows what. Others died, but he never came close!" Dark eyes burning, she kicked at her skirts. "And then he came on the town, and started on his merry way seducing every second lady— you'd think at least *one* of the small army of husbands he cuckolded would have had the grace to challenge him, but did they?"

Claude converted his involuntary grin into a grimace. "My dear, you really will have to excuse them. As I understand it, Ryder has never given any gentleman cause to risk their necks—and it would be that, you know. He's a tolerably good shot from all I've heard."

"I don't *care*!" In a huff, Lavinia flung herself into the other armchair. "I just want him gone and Randolph the marquess."

Claude studied her for a moment, then quietly, soberly, said, "My dear, you really must give this up. All you said of Ryder might be correct, but if anything, that should convince you he leads a charmed life. He's not going to die, and Randolph is not going to become the marquess, and no good ever came of railing thus against Fate."

"Huh!" Lavinia sulked.

Regarding her critically, Claude quietly sighed. He really didn't know what he saw in her. Certainly he had no good explanation for why he continued to remain so devotedly by her side.

Rather like a spaniel.

He didn't see himself as a lapdog, and he doubted others did, either. The truth was . . . Lavinia had become a convenient habit. Remaining by her side allowed him to move in their mutual social circles without becoming the target his wealth would otherwise have made him, and as he'd never been interested in any other woman, the arrangement suited him. It still did. So he waited with a patience that was growing wearyingly thin for her to set aside her impractical dreams and return to real life, and him.

"You know, it's a very good thing that you insisted that our wedding be a lavish affair." Mary glanced up at Ryder, standing beside her midway down the St. Ives House ball-room; it was midafternoon, and all around them, the guests gathered to celebrate James and Henrietta's wedding mingled and conversed. "Given Henrietta and James elected to have a small wedding, and it's been more than a decade since Amelia and Amanda wed, then I'm sure if we'd opted for a small wedding, too, poor Mama would have felt quite shortchanged."

Settling his hand over hers as it rested on his sleeve—a proprietary gesture he couldn't seem to resist and one she didn't appear to notice, or did and chose to allow—Ryder smiled and, like her, considered those present. Although small by ton standards, the wedding and this subsequent breakfast had overflowed with familial warmth, genial good cheer, and the expectant joy of a new couple devoted to their joint future. Participating had left him even more certain that, on his own quest for a similar future, he was precisely where he needed to be—by Mary Cynster's side.

As Henrietta's maid of honor, Mary was wearing a gold gown, rather than her signature blue. Most of her gowns were blue—not just her ball gowns but her day gowns and walking gowns as well—in a variety of shades that either matched or made the most of her eyes.

Which, admittedly, were a striking color.

He wondered whether their children would inherit his hazel or her blue.

Which thought, unsurprisingly, led to memories of their activities two nights before.

When they'd finally stirred and left his bed, the sense that, regardless of appearances, with her he'd stepped into unfamiliar territory had only intensified. There'd been a pronounced lack of any awkwardness; their admittedly temporary parting had all gone too easily. He'd told himself it was because between them the question of whether they would meet again in a bedroom did not apply, yet . . .

Why that ease had bothered him he had no clue, but getting her safely home had been a simple matter; if her coachman was discreet, his was even more so. But he'd insisted on seeing her into the house, thus learning of the back parlor window she used to gain access.

He hadn't seen her last night, which the experienced strategist within considered just as well. No reason for her to realize that he was as eager for their second round as she had been for the first. She'd seemed in fine fettle the following morning when he'd taken her for a drive in the park, but from midday yesterday to now she'd been caught up in the whirl of the wedding; he'd used the time to catch up with business, but last night had joined James, most of the Cynster males, and several others in bidding adieu to James's bachelorhood.

It had been a merry night, one filled with more examples of the familial camaraderie the Cynsters possessed in such abundance and that he craved; he wanted to establish and nurture that same feeling between the Cavanaughs, starting from his generation. Deep in his instinctive warrior-brain, he viewed such a fundamental and emotional linking as a massive strength—one his family lacked.

Beside him, Mary stirred. Before she could direct him, he stepped out, taking her on a perambulation through the gathered guests.

She shot him a glance, but he kept his gaze fixed ahead, feigning obliviousness; he delighted in confounding her, especially when she thought to order him about.

They paused to speak with Lord and Lady Glossup,

James's parents and connections of Ryder's. The senior Glossups spent most of their time at Glossup Hall in Dorset, but they had traveled to London for the wedding. Their delight in their son's joy was transparent, and in the company of those present the reclusive pair felt little restraint in allowing their pleasure to show.

As Ryder and Mary moved on, she leaned close and confided, "Henrietta was worried that they might find the crowd difficult, but they seem quite at ease."

Ryder glanced at her. "They used to spend much more time in the ton, but as the years went by, they grew to prefer the country—Catherine, mostly, but Harold, too."

"I think Henrietta was more concerned that after the unfortunate incident involving the wife of James's older brother Henry"—Mary gestured—"Lord and Lady Glossup might find socializing more difficult, but they seem to have recovered, enough at least to do James and Henrietta proud, which is the main thing."

"Indeed." Ryder glanced over the heads at a sober gentleman standing quietly by one wall. "Although he put on a brave face for the wedding, Henry still seems . . ."

"Sad," Mary supplied. "Just that—simply sad. One can only hope he'll recover."

Ryder arched a brow at her. "You do realize he's a connection of mine? And once we wed, you will be the matriarch of the wider family. I would have thought," he went on, looking ahead, "that you might consider assisting with Henry's recovery."

From the corner of his eye, he saw Mary's smile brighten. "What a lovely idea—I hadn't realized the connection was so definite."

Ryder nodded, without compunction throwing Henry to her wolf. "Roundabout in a way, but solid." From all he'd seen, male familial camaraderie invariably involved encouraging those not leg-shackled to surrender to their fate. And if one could earn approval from one's wife along the way, all the better. "And don't forget Oswald—James's younger brother. He'll assuredly need help."

"Hmm," was all Mary said.

Simon hove out of the crowd and waylaid them. "There you are." He grinned at Mary, then addressed Ryder. "I—" Simon broke off as the Honorable Barnaby Adair joined them.

Barnaby greeted them with his customary debonair charm; Mary knew him well, and Ryder had met him on several occasions since throwing his lot in with the Cynsters.

"We," Simon resumed, "wondered if you'd got any firm word on who sent those two men to kill you?"

Ryder hadn't intended to bring up the subject, but . . . "No. St. Ives sent word that Fitzhugh had denied any knowledge, and those who heard him are inclined to believe him—and I'd have to say that would be my reading of the man, too. In the throes of a red-hot rage he might have sent men after me, but he's not the sort, once he cools down, to lie and deny."

"No matter the likely repercussions?" Barnaby asked.

Ryder considered, then slowly shook his head. "I would say that, regardless of his temper, Fitzhugh is an honorable man."

Simon wrinkled his nose. "That was Devil's view, too." He met Ryder's gaze. "So as matters stand we still have no idea who hired those men to kill you, much less why."

Mary shifted so she could see Ryder's face. His gaze flicked her way, rested on her eyes; she didn't need speech to know he would rather she wasn't exposed to the discussion, but if he thought she would excuse herself and move away—or let the three of them leave her—he could think again.

Apparently doing so, he shifted his gaze to Simon and Barnaby, and after a moment said, "My investigator pushed harder and learned that the man who hired the pair was a shady solicitor, but one working well outside his patch. The investigator paid said solicitor a visit, but only hit an even more definite dead end. The solicitor helpfully described the man who hired him to hire the pair of thugs, but the description would fit thousands of men in ton household staffs."

Barnaby frowned. "The man who hired the solicitor was a servant?"

Ryder nodded. "No livery, of course, and the solicitor thought not upper-level staff, but from the solicitor's description the man could have been anything from a footman out of uniform to a groom or stableman."

"Or he could have been someone hired to hire the solicitor, and so on." Simon shook his head. "Our chances of finding such a man amid the thousands . . ."

For a moment, no one said anything, then Barnaby stirred. He met Ryder's eyes. "Given the situation, while I would rather it wasn't so, I feel compelled to point out that you need to stay alert." Barnaby's eyes shifted very briefly to Mary, then returned to Ryder's face. "If someone went to all that trouble to hire two men to kill you, then in my experience it's unlikely that after a single failure, they'll stop. It's much more likely that they'll try again."

An instant passed; Mary looked from Ryder to Barnaby and back again. Then Ryder inclined his head. "Thank you. I'll bear that in mind."

Mary inwardly frowned. Bear what in mind? She got the distinct impression that the last part of the conversation had turned masculinely oblique.

Before she could think of how to press for clarification, Barnaby distracted her with a message from Penelope, and then an observation about his heir, young Oliver.

Simon trumped that with an anecdote about his two, also very young children. Mary had to hide a grin; it was truly amazing how fatherhood affected men like her brother, like Barnaby—and presumably, like Ryder. Something to look forward to; her grin blossomed into a smile and she shot a glance at him.

He felt it, met it; his eyes studied hers briefly, and she suspected he read her thoughts reasonably well, for he arched a brow at her.

But then the musicians started playing the wedding waltz, and the crowd eagerly drew back to give Henrietta and James the floor.

Mary watched her sister revolve in James's arms and had no trouble at all discerning the love that flowed between them. It was there for all to see, given shining life in the gaze they shared, in the way Henrietta's lips softly curved and her whole countenance glowed. Equally definite love shone in James's expression, not intent any longer but focused in that particular way that signaled to any who were sensitive to the sight that his entire life was now Henrietta's, devoted to her, committed to her and to the life they would establish and share.

With my body, I thee worship.

That was what the wedding waltz signified. They'd made the vow earlier, but this—this was the physical expression, one that brought tears to many eyes and a soft smile to the faces of all those watching.

Mary blinked, and realized she, too, was smiling, but beneath the joy for her sister and her new brother-in-law welled a determination that she, too, would have that. Precisely that.

A wedding waltz like that was what she wanted.

Simon had left to find Portia; Barnaby had gone to hunt for Penelope.

Ryder gripped Mary's elbow, bent his head, and murmured, "Time to join them."

"Indeed." Keeping her smile appropriately gentle, keeping her determination screened, she allowed him to lead her forward and turn her into his arms, and together they stepped into the swirl of family members joining the newly-weds on the floor.

Ryder was grateful for the waltz; it gave him something

with which to satisfy, however temporarily, the hungry beast prowling within. To soothe and distract that inner self from the concatenation of provocations all prodding him in one direction.

As they swirled down the floor and with her usual abandon Mary gave herself wholly to the dance, he drank in the sight—and clung to his façade of sophisticated and languidly bored lion of the ton for all he was worth.

He'd spent the last two days lusting after her with a sense of utterly blinkered need he couldn't recall feeling for any other woman, much less after he'd had her beneath him. After a first engagement, normally several days, even a week, would pass before he would feel any impulse to a repeat performance.

With his bride-to-be, he'd been plotting a repeat engagement while he'd been taking her home—and he wasn't at all sure if that was an encouraging sign, or, instead, a portent that should have him backpedaling. Fast.

Regardless, his now thoroughly focused inner self wasn't at all interested in stepping back. And Barnaby's suggestion that anyone taking another tilt at him could harm Mary, too, had only escalated his burgeoning need to have her safely under his paw.

Sleeping safely beside him. Sated and drowsy and . . . as happy as only he could make her. That was how his inner self saw things, and in that it wouldn't be moved.

He'd never felt the smallest iota of possessiveness toward any of his previous lovers; even though he excused his new-found compulsion on the grounds that she was destined to be his wife, he still felt oddly off-balance. A tad uncertain as to where their interaction was leading him; it wasn't down a path he knew.

Yet regardless of how he rationalized, whether the reason his instincts saw her as different was due to her more willful, challenging character or because said instincts already deemed her his, the impulse to seize and hold remained, and more, continued to grow; against his expectation, the waltz did nothing to allay it. Much less slake it.

The music slowed, then ended; they swirled to a halt and he bowed, she curtsied, then he raised her, tucked her hand in his arm, and they resumed their strolling.

The afternoon wore on, until, laughing and joking, the bulk of the company clattered down the stairs to see a radiant Henrietta and a proud James off on the beginning of their journey as man and wife. Rice was hurled, comments and recommendations flung, then James handed Henrietta into the waiting carriage, climbed in and shut the door, and the beaming coachman cracked his whip, and they were off, trotting smartly along the side of Grosvenor Square, and then out along Upper Brook Street.

"Wiltshire?" Ryder turned to Mary, one step higher than he on the steep front steps.

She nodded. "They'll be back in five days, in time for our wedding, but they wanted to start where they intend ending, so to speak, and that as soon as they could."

He arched his brows. "As impatient as you?"

She met his gaze. Held it for an instant, then softly said, "I seriously doubt that's possible."

The opening was there; he took it. "In that case . . . leave that window open tonight."

She stared levelly back, then shook her head. "No—you'll break my bed. I'll come to you as I did the other night."

"No." His protectiveness wouldn't allow that. But seeing haughty independence welling in her eyes, he rapidly reevaluated, then amended, "I'm not enamored of you wandering even as far as your mews alone, so let's do the reverse of what we did the other morning. I'll meet you in the garden outside the window. My carriage will be waiting to take us home."

The last word was an instinct-driven, semi-deliberate slip of the tongue; she caught it, tipped her head as she considered, but then she smiled and left it unchallenged. "All right." With a general wave, she indicated the wedding breakfast, now winding down. "After this, we'll be retiring early tonight. Meet me at eleven."

He didn't smile, just nodded. "I'll be there."

He was waiting in the shadows at the rear of the house to give her his hand as she climbed out of the window. Quietly lowering the sash and reclaiming her hand, he led her out through the night-shrouded garden, then along the street to his unmarked town carriage.

Harness jingled as he handed her up, then followed and shut the door. The night was overcast, the moon screened, leaving little risk of anyone seeing them well enough to recognize. He sat beside Mary on the leather seat; as the carriage shifted, then slowly rolled on, with the deeper shadows within closing around them, he was tempted— sorely tempted—to draw her into his arms and kiss her wit-less, to plunder her mouth and taste her passion . . . but he didn't.

Instead, anchoring her hand, still locked in his, firmly on the seat between them, he pretended to watch the houses slide past. And tried not to think about why he didn't dare surrender to the nearly overwhelming impulse.

It had been a long, *long* time since he'd questioned his control. Since he'd had any reason to doubt it. But the hunger presently crawling beneath his skin was simply too powerful to ignore; once he started kissing her . . .

Luckily, the drive to Mount Street took only a few min-utes. The instant the carriage halted, he opened the door, stepped out, and handed her down to the pavement. Shutting the door, he nodded to his coachman, Ridges, then escorted Mary up the front steps into the concealing shadows of his porch.

Pulling out his latch-key, he fitted it to the door.

"No Pemberly?"

"I've dismissed him and the rest of the staff for the night." Through the dimness, he looked down at her. "Ridges will return to drive us back to Upper Brook Street in the small hours." Opening the door, he ushered her in.

"Poor Ridges." She walked further into the shadowed hall.

Shutting the door, Ryder snorted. "Not so poor, and he's only too happy to assist."

Swinging to face him, she arched her brows. Crossing the tiles to halt before her, he added, "He knows you'll soon be his mistress."

"Ah." After a moment of studying his face, she asked, "Are they happy with the prospect then, your staff?"

He hadn't brought her there to discuss his household. "If anything, they're ecstatic." Her brows rose; a smile curved her lips. He studied the sight and found himself admitting, "They are not, however, as happy as I am." He hesitated, then, entirely against his better judgment, asked, "You know that, don't you?"

She continued to study his face, then her smile deepened. "Perhaps I do." Turning, skirts swishing, she headed for the stairs. "But then again"—pausing with one hand on the newel post, her foot on the first step, she glanced back at him—"perhaps you should remind me just how enamored you are over our prospective union."

He locked his gaze with hers; slowly, he walked across the tiles to her side. Halting there, he looked into her face, let a heartbeat pass, only then asked, "Is that a challenge?"

"I'm hoping you'll see it in that light and exert yourself accordingly."

A part of him laughed; the rest rose to her lure. Lips curving—amused, yes, but intent, too—he reached for her . . .

She bolted.

On a smothered laugh, she raced up the stairs.

He was on her heels before he'd thought.

Then he did. He let her reach the landing before looping

an arm around her waist, spinning her into him as he turned. Setting her back to the side wall, he crushed her lips with his.

And devoured.

Mary sank her hands into his hair and hung on for dear life. Let her wits spin away and opened her senses wide. Gloried, for one long instant simply drank in his passion— then she flung her heart and soul into returning it.

Fingers clenching in his hair, she kissed him back, returning every rapacious foray with her own fire. Her own need. Her own burning brand of desire. She could feel it surging inside her, undeniable, all-powerful, a heated yearning to be together, to be naked and merged and totally lost in the flames.

The compulsion built, rose higher.

Urgency raced down her veins.

Lips melding, hungry, hot, and urgent, the kiss raged back and forth, first driven by him, then by her, their tongues dueling, seeking, searching—he for supremacy, she for equal strength.

She won. He didn't.

She held her own and pressed him even harder.

Knew when he broke, when he accepted that he didn't care how, just as long as he had her—and she had him.

She only had a split second to wonder what next before he hoisted her up against him. She responded immediately, adjusting the angle of the kiss, unwilling to allow the connection to break, to allow either of them a chance to think, even for a heartbeat. Then he turned from the wall and she raised her legs and wriggled and hitched and conquered her skirts enough to grip his hips with her thighs.

He grunted, but, like her, made no move to end the ravenous engagement of their mouths; sliding his palms beneath her hips, carrying her, he started up the stairs.

Giving thanks for his strength, she left it to him to get them to his bedroom and focused her will on the kiss, on keeping them both, he and she, so deeply immersed that the flames they'd already ignited didn't wane.

She succeeded so well that, on reaching the corridor to his room, he sat her atop a wall table, clamped his hands to her face, took over the kiss, and poured fire down her veins.

On a gasp, she tipped her head back and broke the kiss— and he let her. One hand framing her jaw, angling her chin, he ducked his head and set his lips, burning, branding, to her throat. Followed the arching line down to the hollow where her pulse raced. He licked, laved, and she shuddered.

He made a sound, low and guttural, and then her bodice was loose and he was drawing it down; before she gathered her wits enough to react, he stripped bodice and chemise to her waist, and set his mouth to her bared breasts.

She cried out as he sucked one furled nipple deep; evocative and arousing, the sound echoed in the dark.

He chuckled, harsh and ragged; cupping her other breast, he kneaded and squeezed while with lips and tongue he claimed. One hand sliding to the back of her waist, holding and supporting her, he waited while she blindly freed her arms from her sleeves, then he tipped her backward until the back of her head rested against the wall and he bent to his task—apparently intending to reduce her to an utterly wanton state . . .

She was already there. Hands sunk in his hair, eyes closed, head back, she moaned, then arched, wanting more of all he lavished on her—the hot worship of his mouth on her sensitive flesh, the excruciatingly piercing sensations he sent streaking through her.

Driving passion was already a pounding thud in her veins; she wondered how much stronger it could get.

Shivered with anticipation at the certainty of finding out.

Despite the potent compulsions of desire, tonight she was more aware—more able to appreciate his sensual expertise. Previously, her senses had been swept away; tonight, they were riding the tide.

And she wanted, craved with a deep-seated need, the heat and the flames and the surging, swelling passion. More than anything else she craved the fusion they would lead to, the intense, intimate, physically powerful joining.

She'd been too distracted earlier to properly absorb every detail; tonight her senses were greedy and grasping, devouring every nuance.

Her gown and chemise lay crumpled about her waist. Standing as he was, his hips forced her knees wide; he shifted, then the hand at her breast released and stroked down. Down over her waist, pressing her clothing aside, sliding over her stomach to splay there, then his long fingers reached further, parting the curls at the apex of her thighs to push down and in.

She started, shivered, then caught her breath on a gasp as his fingers explored, caressing and parting her slick folds, then circling, lightly pressing. Delicious sensations spread under her skin. Panting, she squirmed, needing more, wanting . . .

Drawing his mouth from her breast, he softly cursed and withdrew his hand from between her thighs.

She clutched his arm. "No—"

"Wait." The gravelly order brooked no argument, but he was already hauling up her skirts, pushing them high to reach beneath. Locating her stockinged knee, he skated his hard palm over her garter and up her thigh, then boldly cupped her swollen flesh.

Reaction jolted her, the possessiveness in his touch sharp and keen.

She shivered when he pressed first one, then two fingers into her. Deep, then deeper.

On a gasp, fingers gripping his arm, clutching his skull, she arched, lifting, instinctively giving him greater access. Access he seized; his hand flexing beneath her, he pressed in and stroked, deeper, faster, ruthlessly playing on her senses.

Tension gripped her—similar yet not the same as the compulsive need of their previous time, but swelling, rising, built and driven by his intimate touch. By every deep stroke of his fingers.

Then he returned to her breasts, setting his mouth to the aching, swollen mounds, catching the tightly furled buds of her nipples between his lips, tugging, then taking them into his mouth and suckling.

Sensations cascaded, clashed and sparked, flushing beneath her skin, pulsing through her flesh. She closed her eyes, listened as her breathing grew harried and desperate. Felt the flames rage and coalesce, sinking deeper, searing and burning, then flaring ever hotter.

Tighter, harder, faster, hotter—she gasped, squirmed, yet nothing seemed to ease her escalating need, to appease the hungry emptiness yawning within.

Then he shifted his hand and his thumb found the nubbin hidden amid her slick folds, and he artfully pressed in rhythm with his increasingly forceful penetrations, with the increasingly powerful suckling at her breast—

She fractured.

Cried out and clung as her world shattered and her senses fragmented and spun.

Overcome by the cataclysm of sensation, she swayed. All strength fled; a deep, unraveling lassitude swept her.

All awareness seemed distant, remote, detached, yet she still felt, still knew. Could still follow what was happening.

Her breathing in ragged disarray, her heartbeat echoing in her ears and pulsing in the honeyed flesh between her thighs, she felt—acutely felt—the retreat of his fingers from her body. Drawing his hand from beneath her skirts, he swept her unresisting—unable to resist—off the table and into his arms, and carried her to his room.

Juggling her in his arms, Ryder opened his bedroom door, angled her inside, then heeled the door shut. Tonight, Collier had left only the two lamps on the bedside tables burning; although both were turned low, they spilled golden light over the golden bed.

A perfect shrine for beauty in aftermath.

Carrying Mary to the bed, he knelt on the mattress and laid her gently down, her head on the pillows, her sable curls a sharp contrast against the ivory. He took an instant to savor, to give thanks he'd been able to rush her on to her climax and so grasp the chance—the slim and possibly only chance—to reassert control. To regain the upper hand.

Passion beat powerfully, unrelentingly, in his veins, insistent and demanding, but this was a situation he—and that driving need within him—recognized. A familiar pause in proceedings, not a denial but a staving off, a temporary holding back that would ensure he would soon reap a deeper and even more complete satisfaction.

God, she'd been . . . the word that came to mind was potent. A drug that held the power to drive him crazed with desire, and make him ache with passion.

With a powerful drive, one he needed to rein in and manage; even after their first encounter—perhaps even more because of it—he felt an absolute need to remain in charge, of himself at least, if not her as well.

Knowing he would have only so long before she stirred, and sought to manage him and them, this, and all, he leaned over her and stripped her of gown, chemise, and stockings. Tossing the gold silk coverlet over her cooling body, accepting that if he didn't shed his clothes himself, she would be eager to assist him—and God only knew where that would end—he shrugged out of his coat and waistcoat, unknotted his cravat and dispensed with shirt, shoes, stockings, and trousers in record time.

He felt the caress of her gaze as he turned to the bed. With an openly sensual appreciation, she examined and surveyed, her lips lightly curving, her gaze warming, the blue growing more intense as he neared.

He knew well enough how women saw him; impressive was an epithet frequently applied.

Somewhat to his relief, he detected nothing more than a

certain smug, very feminine possessiveness in her face, with no hint of surprise, much less fear, clouding her violet-blue eyes.

Indeed, all he could discern was expectation, an anticipation that was more specific, more focused, than two nights before.

Her expression stated she knew what was to come and was looking forward to every second.

Already fully aroused, that expression, its implication, only made him more rigid.

Pausing beside the bed, he reached out and drew down the coverlet, and took one last instant to drink in the sight of her, rumpled and sated, limbs asprawl in sensual abandon in his bed.

Slowly, he let his gaze sweep from her small, delicate feet, over her shapely calves, dimpled knees, and sleek thighs, up over the already dampened thatch of dark curls at their apex, over the slight curve of her stomach, the indentation of her waist, gliding up over her firm, high breasts, her nipples puckering under his gaze, to her throat, her chin, to her lips, and finally to her eyes.

Mary had been waiting. She smiled, gentle yet intent, and slowly, gracefully, raised her arms and beckoned.

He blinked, but complied, letting himself down on the bed, propping on one elbow and stretching his long limbs and heavy bones alongside her.

He reached to set a hand on her stomach, but before he made contact she rolled toward him and sat up, the movement making him instinctively tip back—he realized and tried to reverse, to sit up again, but she'd already spread her hands on his chest.

Greedily.

She swiveled to hang over him, sinuously sliding her body along his until his hips lay half under hers, her stomach brushing his, her legs tangling lightly with his, his heavy erection grazing her hip; she closed her eyes for a second, breathed in as she savored, this time fully aware of the evocative feel of his naked body against hers, of his hair-dusted limbs lightly abrading her smooth, fine skin, of the ineluctable tactile contrast between his hard muscled frame covered by taut skin and her firm, silky sleekness.

He could easily have forced her back, yet as she opened her eyes, met his, then sent her hands skating, caressing and tracing, unabashedly reveling, he lay still and searched her face, trying to guess what she was about.

Thoroughly pleased with him, she smiled and obliged. "Before we reengage, I wanted to ask . . . can you—will you—go slow when I say?"

He blinked, then arched his brows in patent disbelief. "*You* want to go slow?"

"Only when I say," she quickly clarified. "And only for those moments." She held his gaze, then arched a brow back; with him, challenge was undeniably her best weapon. "For the rest . . ." She raised a shoulder. "I would prefer to go at our usual headlong pace. So much more us, don't you think?"

When he didn't reply—when she saw wary suspicion bloom behind his eyes—she laughed. "No, truly." Folding her arms, she settled on his chest, pillowing her breasts on the thick muscle, delighting in the tension that spread through him in response, and smiled into his eyes. "So what do you say?" Abrasion from the crinkly hair on his chest made her nipples ruche painfully tight; resisting the impulse to close her eyes in bliss, keeping them on his, she pressed, "Can we do it my way—just this once?"

"Once?" Ryder wasn't at all sure it would be once. Or rather, that the once wouldn't affect him—and them—forever more. His instincts, entirely uncharacteristically, were no help; on the one hand, they warned—stridently and insistently—that danger lay waiting along the path she was, sirenlike, luring him down, consequently urging caution, if not retreat, while simultaneously, those very same instincts were pushing him to give her whatever she wished. More, were insisting it was his duty to slavishly pander to her every whim.

And there really wasn't any choice. Despite awareness of the former, the latter impulse was dominant, if not paramount. Drawing in a deep breath, steeling himself against the more definite pressure of her breasts against his chest, he held her gaze. "All right. Your way. This once. So how?"

Her smile beamed like the sun. Shifting higher on his chest, eyes sparkling, expression eager, she reached for his face. "I'll tell you when." Then she bent her head, set her lips to his—and plunged them back into their fire.

Leaving him reeling, then mentally racing, trying to catch up with her—trying to exert some degree of control.

He hadn't known the flames had hovered so *very* close. Yes, he'd been brutally aroused from the moment he'd joined her on the bed, but he'd thought—had expected—that she would have cooled, that it would take time—

But no. Just one kiss, one flagrant foray into his mouth, coupled with his instinctive response, and she turned to living flame in his arms.

And there was no slowing down, no controlling the fiery passion, the conflagration of desire that raked and razed and raced through them both. That consumed them both.

Abruptly, she rolled onto her back; he didn't need her urgent tugging to follow. And then they were tussling, her hands streaking over his skin, reaching for his erection, greedy fingers searching, finding, closing, palms hungrily stroking.

Her breasts filled his hands while he filled her mouth, and she, his wanton, urged him on.

Slow? Where was her slow?

It was she who parted her thighs wide, who wriggled and writhed to get his hips just so. On a curse, he pulled back from the kiss long enough to reach between them and position the blunt head of his aching erection at her entrance.

Scalding slickness bathed the broad head. She was wetter than wet, so ready and willing, as the desperation in her clutching hands assured him.

Equally trapped in the heated desperation, lying fully and heavily atop her, prey to her every arch and writhe, he clamped both hands about her hips, plunged back into the fiery delight of her mouth, and tensed to thrust home.

She wrenched back from the kiss. Hoarsely panted, "Now. Slow now!"

Now?

"*God almighty.*" His weight on his elbows, he gritted his teeth, jaw clenched to cracking as he locked every muscle against the driving, pounding insistence that he move—that he thrust into the heated haven waiting, beckoning.

She gulped in air, managed a tiny nod. "I want to feel . . . you. There. I didn't get a chance to the first time . . ."

Her explanation wasn't helping. "I'll try," he ground out, then shut her up in the only way that ever worked.

And fought, battled, to give her what she wanted.

He eased in—a fraction. Just enough to push the head of his erection past her tight entrance.

Beneath him, he felt her quiver—not with fear but with a sensual expectation that reached to his bones and made him shudder, too.

Gave him the strength to try for another half an inch. Then pause. Then another incremental advance.

Her body tight as a bowstring, every bit as tense as he, she sighed into his mouth, then shifted her lips enough to whisper against his, "Oh. My. Lord. *Yes.*"

The quality she invested into the last word—that alone would have been worth his pain.

Accepting that, accepting that acceding to her request had indeed lavished untold pleasure on her, made it easier still to continue to penetrate her inch by slow inch.

Mary lay beneath him, utterly overwhelmed, her senses locked on the sensation of the veined rod, hot as flame and as unforgiving as forged steel, slowly, and now more steadily, pushing into her. Stretching her, filling her, in some way she didn't fully comprehend, completing her.

The moment overloaded her mind in every way, obliterating the hollow emptiness that had dwelled deep within her when he'd first laid her on the bed.

With an effort, she raised her lashes. His eyes were shut; his face appeared graven, every plane sharp-edged with desire. With reined passion. She could feel the rigid control he wielded—to give her what she'd asked for.

Lids falling, she mentally reached out and wrapped her expanding senses about them—and savored all the excruciatingly sensation-filled moment was doing to them both. They were both panting, heated breaths mingling, lips dry, but still hungry.

They were both poised, nerves tighter than drum skins, reined, teetering on that sexual brink . . .

Then with a last, small thrust, he was there. Embedded within her, filling her completely, the head of him nudging her womb, the heaviness of his sac brushing her sensitized skin.

This was what made her his, but equally it made him hers.

Lips curving as much as the overwhelming tension would allow, she whispered, "Thank you." Blindly reaching for his head, sinking her fingers into his hair, she raised her head a fraction, whispered against his lips, "Now let go," and kissed him.

Passion erupted. Held back for so long, it raged unrelenting, unforgiving. It whipped them along, harder and faster, whirling them through the age-old dance and straight into the flames and the fire.

Up, and higher, harder, and yet more furiously needy, they gasped and raced, driving for the peak, the ultimate pinnacle of intimate joy.

Their hearts thundered; their breaths came in raspy pants. Locked together, striving together, they yearned and stretched, reached and sought.

She was as caught as he, as subject to the passion they'd unleashed, yet she was aware and was with him, much more so than the first time, able to sense and feel, know and appreciate the turbulent power they'd evoked. Provoked.

Physical and ephemeral; even as they gasped and clung, she felt his hands on her, felt his awareness of her, felt how through his body he spoke to her, through hers, through her senses.

No words could breach this plane, could encompass this elemental reality.

Making love could, and did.

She tightened around him and they raced on through the searing wonder.

And in a heady rush of pounding joy they found that pinnacle, their oh-so-desired destination, without pause leapt past and on and flew.

Tension imploded. Sensation, molten and scalding, erupted and flashed outward from where they joined, flooding their veins, sinking deep into their flesh.

They shattered. She screamed; he roared.

Ecstasy speared through them, broke them, wracked them.

Caught by her own primal contractions, she felt him stiffen in her arms, felt the heat of his seed pulse deep within her.

She surrendered. Felt him do the same.

And ecstasy's benediction flooded them, a blessing so richly sensuous it brought tears to her eyes and made her cling.

To that moment, so fleeting, so precious.

Then it faded, as it always would, yet even as she let go and, with him buried deep within her, connected beyond the physical, sank into satiation's sea, she knew that it—that moment of ultimate intimate communion—would always exist, would always be there, waiting for them, forever a part of them.

Satisfied beyond measure, lips gently curved, she let bliss draw her into its embrace.

Ryder slumped on top of her, too wracked to move.

Too wrung out to think, to even care.

The danger had been there—and he'd fallen.

His last conscious thought before he surrendered was: Is this how it feels to be conquered?

There were only seven more days to their wedding—and those passed in a blur.

The morning after Henrietta's nuptials, Mary found herself plunged into preparations for her own. Ryder had brought her back to Upper Brook Street in the small hours; sated and deeply content, she'd tumbled into her own bed, but her mother roused her early—much earlier than she'd hoped—to remind her that they had a fitting for her bridal gown that morning.

As the same modiste had so recently made her gown for Henrietta's wedding, the fitting was more an opportunity for her aunts, her cousins' wives, and some of the females of the next generation to ooh and aah over the fine Flemish lace and pearls, layer upon layer of which made up the delicate bridal gown.

Lucilla and Prudence, Demon and Flick's eldest daughter, had stars in their eyes. "You look like a fairy princess," Prudence said.

Viewing herself in the modiste's cheval mirror, Mary had to agree. The gown played off her relatively small size and also her coloring. When the modiste set the fine veil in place, to Mary's surprise, her eyes looked huge. Pools of pansy-blue.

The rest of the day passed in a whirl of female family interactions. With time so short, everyone claimed a role, parts they were eager to play.

Mary met Ryder at a ball that evening; while she'd thought to join him in Mount Street later, he suggested that, with the wedding only days away, perhaps they should simply wait.

He waved languidly. "Rather than unnecessarily sneaking around."

Mary wondered, but acquiesced and let him go. For that night.

Through the next two days, she, Louise, Honoria, Patience, and Alathea, aided by all the others, repeated their tasks from the previous week, arranging for flowers, food, wine, music. The seating in the church and at the wedding breakfast. The schedule, the carriages, the additional staff to be drawn from the family's various households. Yet because this wedding was to be a massively larger affair, those tasks, while essentially the same, assumed the nature of a military campaign, one the Cynster ladies flung themselves into with unanimous alacrity. Mary's aunt Helena and Therese Osbaldestone established themselves as the final arbiters of all things, the ultimate major generals of the massed troops.

Footmen constantly ferried notes between the various houses—directions, questions, suggestions, and more.

It was a giddy time, and courtesy of several soirees and must-attend balls—it being the height of the Season—three nights passed before Mary had a chance to refocus on Ryder. On he who would be her husband.

She'd seen him every evening, had attended the soirees and balls on his arm, yet Ryder in public was a very different proposition from Ryder in private, at least for her. In public, he could and did direct their interactions, using his experience and resulting expertise to counter any too-willful move she made. In private, she could hold her own, but through those days she never had him in private for long.

From Stacie—who, everyone had agreed, should be Mary's second attendant—she heard that Ryder had immersed himself in estate matters, including preparing his several houses to receive his new marchioness. When interrogated, Stacie admitted to being asked her opinion on several issues regarding the latter, but she refused point-blank to divulge further details.

Mary decided she was willing to allow him such secrets, but that evening when he accompanied her and her mother home, and he and she were left alone to say their farewells in the front hall, she trapped his gaze and simply said, "An hour from now." Then she smiled and gave him her hand.

He held her gaze for a long moment, then took her hand, bowed, and kissed her fingertips. "As my lady wishes."

He met her at the window and took her to his home, and the hours that followed were a reckless and undeniably abandoned repetition of their last engagement. Much to her relief. Between them, all was, indeed, proceeding exactly as she wished.

After seeing her home, Ryder retreated to the rumpled wreckage of his bed, stretched out upon it, and considered the trap in which Fate had snared him. Mary was all and everything he wanted in his bride—and more; it was the more he hadn't expected to have to grapple with.

Indeed, that more, he was increasingly certain, was the price he would have to pay . . . for having all the rest. For being blessed with all the rest. Being allowed to seize and keep all the rest.

Sleep eluded him. Driven by some incomprehensible impulse, as early as was acceptable he called in Upper Brook Street and all but abducted Mary for a drive in the park. He tooled her around the Avenue and let her tell him of all the last-minute arrangements; when he returned her to her parents' home—she was due for a final fitting of her bridal gown, which, apparently, he was not allowed on pain of death to see before she walked down the aisle—her glowing smile and the light in her eyes . . . somehow soothed him.

Calmed the restless beast inside.

Returning to his house, he threw himself into his own preparations, into overseeing the final touches to the changes he'd directed be made. Then there were meetings with Montague, then later with Rand and Kit, and subsequently various entertainments with the male Cynsters, and others with his close friends, Sanderson included.

Knowing him so well, David asked how the wound had stood up. To what didn't need to be stated. Ryder informed him that his handiwork had come through with flying colors. At which everyone around the table smirked.

J've a good mind to wear black." Lavinia glowered into the mirror in her boudoir. "It would be a fitting declaration of how I view this match."

Claude Potherby sighed and folded the news sheet he'd been perusing. "Sadly, I can assure you it wouldn't be seen in that light."

"Oh?" Brows arching, Lavinia swung to face him. "How would it be seen?"

"As a revelation about you, my dear—which I really don't think is what you would wish." Claude waved languidly. "Of course, that's assuming you made it into the church, and weren't bundled out and back into your carriage by some Cynster." He paused, as if considering the image, then shook his head. "I really wouldn't risk it if I were you." He met Lavinia's eyes and smiled. "Besides, my dear, surely you'll reap a greater revenge by looking your best, and you know black doesn't suit you."

Lavinia pursed her lips, but after a moment she nodded. "Yes—you're right. I hadn't thought of it like that."

Still smiling, Claude reached for the teapot.

Henrietta's return to the capital, accompanied by a beaming James, signaled the start of the last stage, the final mad rush to the wedding.

Mary found herself swept up in a whirl of last-minute decisions—what her attendants would carry aside from their bouquets, whether she wished a diamond- or pearl-encrusted comb to anchor her veil, whether she would wear her great-grandmother's pearls. Beribboned silver horseshoes, pearls, and yes were the answers, but nothing, it seemed, could be decided without the canvassing of wider opinion. She would have expected to feel irritated, impatient of the restraint; instead, caught up in the embrace of her family and close friends, in the love that flowed from all, the clear exposition that her happiness was everyone's concern made bearing with their interference surprisingly easy.

And if she wondered at herself—at how she'd changed, of how over the last days and, indeed, weeks she'd come to more deeply appreciate her family, warts and all—the few stolen moments she shared with Ryder, quiet exchanges about the arrangements for their life to come, only sharpened that appreciation, emphasizing, as those moments did, that after the wedding she would be . . . moving on.

Leaving her family and starting a new life, one it was up to her—with Ryder—to define.

The challenge stood clear and unequivocal before her when, pleasantly exhausted, she fell into her bed to sleep through her last night as an unmarried young lady.

She woke the next morning to the bright sunshine of the day during which she would walk down the aisle as a bride, with her hero waiting before the altar to take her hand . . . she could barely contain her joy.

Tossing back the covers, she bounced to her feet; already beaming, she rang for her maid.

Chapter Eleven

For all of London, the wedding of the Most Noble Ryder Montgomery Sinclair Cavanaugh, Marquess of Raventhorne, Viscount Sidwell, Baron Axford, Lord Marshal of the Savernake, to Mary Alice Cynster on that bright early summer day in June '37 was a notable entertainment, with the carriages of the ton overflowing the streets of Mayfair and uncounted nobs and grand ladies in their finery on show for all to see. Those who were early enough to secure the prime vantage spots around St. George's, Hanover Square, and in the surrounding streets were impressed by the sheer number of the aristocracy attending; the carriages, at times almost stationary on the cobbles, continued to arrive and disgorge their well-heeled owners long after the crowd had imagined the church full.

For the haut ton, the wedding was a must-be-seen-at event, one which would almost certainly rank as the premier social spectacle of the year. While all had noted the recent alliance between the Glossups and the Cynsters, few had anticipated the much more strategically powerful union between the Cynsters and the Cavanaughs. The uniting of two such houses, both with their roots in the distant past and their present wealth and influence beyond question, transfixed the ton in a way little else could; everyone who was anyone wished to be seen to accord the marriage due respect, and, as such an occasion called for invitations to be spread to all associated in even the smallest way with either house—and as that encompassed most of the haut ton—it was no surprise to anyone that the church's galleries were packed.

For Mary, her wedding day started wonderfully and only improved. The gregariously happy breakfast with her family, including her sisters, sister-in-law, brother, and brothers-in-law, as well as all their children, was followed by the giddy scramble to get everyone dressed and to the church on time. Of course, with her mother and all the other Cynster ladies supervising, not a single thing was permitted to go wrong. As, to exuberant cheering from the dense ranks of onlookers, her father handed her down from the white-ribbon-bedecked carriage, Mary doubted her smile could ever be wider. Doubted that her heart could ever feel so full as she met her father's eyes, then let him wind her arm in his and lead her up the steps and into the church to where her attendants waited with the page boys and flower girls. Their procession formed up in good order; with stately tread, they approached the big double doors, which were swung open by Martin and Luc, both smiling and encouraging, and then the music swelled and carried them all on down the aisle—to where the man she now recognized as her true hero waited.

For Ryder . . . in the moment when, standing before the altar of St. George's, his half brothers to his right, alerted by the organist he turned and saw Mary on her father's arm, walking slowly, steadily, deliberately to him, a smile of unalloyed delight on her lips, he finally and fully appreciated how cataclysmically his life was about to change.

His heart stopped, then, as his eyes met hers, started beating again, but he would swear to a different cadence.

Beneath the filmy veil, her eyes looked huge, intensely blue, bright, alive, eager, and enthused.

Her gown shifted and swayed as she walked, a delicate, exquisite, fragilely beautiful thing . . . just like her.

Covetousness flared, but his possessiveness was tinged with an unnerving sense of gratitude.

As she slowed and came alongside, he offered his hand and Lord Arthur formally placed her hand in his. His eyes locking with hers, he closed his fingers about her slender digits, and it felt like a new beginning.

They both drew breath, and together turned to the altar.

He barely heard the minister's words, let alone the hymns. Through the hour-long service, his focus and every vestige of his awareness remained locked on Mary; all else seemed superfluous, irrelevant. Only their vows stood out in his mind; he spoke his firmly, meaning every word, feeling each resonate within him, and heard her give hers in reply, a clear, feminine echo of his own commitment, and felt his world shift, realigning, and, despite his lingering wariness, willingly let go, allowing Fate to turn the key and lock them together as husband and wife.

As the minister pronounced it done and gave them permission for their first kiss as a married couple, as he turned to Mary and she turned to him, their gazes met and held—and he saw himself in the vivid blue, saw the man she saw before her, the man she stretched up to share a sweet, delicate—for them, ridiculously chaste—kiss.

The man she'd accepted as the "true hero" for whom she'd been searching.

He surprised himself by finding a smile to match hers, that it came so easily, then he anchored her hand on his arm and they turned and faced the congregation—faced their world.

Confidence and more was theirs to claim, strength and purpose and certainty; as with all the self-assurance they both possessed, they walked up the aisle to thunderous applause, he made a conscious decision that, from that day forward, he would be the man reflected in her eyes.

Their journey in an open barouche over the short distance into Brook Street and thence to St. Ives House in Grosvenor Square was marked by cheering, catcalls, and, courtesy of his half siblings, a hail of rice and flowers from the crowds thronging the route.

The same unrestrained gaiety and a species of giddy joy infused the great crowd gathered for the wedding breakfast. The speeches and congratulations flowed like fine wine, bubbled and effervesced like champagne. The wedding waltz, when it finally came, felt like a benediction, a moment when the irrevocable power they'd both that day bowed their knee to shone through the heady whirl and touched them. For those moments, claimed them.

And then, surrounded by a crowd of their relatives, they were being ushered out of the house and down the wide steps to the carriage waiting to take them into the country, to Raventhorne Abbey, to commence their shared life.

Mary's transparent delight at the prospect mirrored his. She'd changed into a new carriage gown of violet-blue and, with her eyes shining with happiness, her rosy lips curved in unfettered joy, looked even more stunningly striking than usual.

He finally managed to hand her into the carriage, then follow and shut the door on all those cheering and calling out suggestions. Settling on the seat and looking out of the window, beaming and waving to the last, Mary said, "Everyone's so happy! More than anything else, that's made this such a wonderful day—I didn't see one less-than-joyful expression."

At last the carriage pulled away, trailing the inevitable old boots and—inventively—a spade. Hearing the racket following along the cobbles, feeling flown on the combined good cheer, Ryder smiled, met her eyes, nodded, and let the comment—generally speaking correct—pass unchallenged. He saw no reason to dim their mood by mentioning his stepmother; Lavinia had, of course, been present, but his half siblings and her friend, Potherby, had endeavored to keep her suitably restrained.

But as they'd left, Lavinia had been standing amid the crowd on the steps, and her expression had very definitely *not* been happy.

A fact that bothered him not at all. Shifting to sit on the seat beside Mary, he caught her hand, raised it to his lips, kissed it, then said, "Now we can relax, at least for the next several hours until we reach the Abbey."

Mary made a humming sound and, her fingers curling to grip his, settled beside him.

The hard line of her lips belying her otherwise neutral expression, with her hand on Claude Potherby's arm, Lavinia was swept up in the wave of guests returning to the St. Ives House ballroom when, from a little way ahead, she heard that old battle-axe, Lady Osbaldestone, opine, "I daresay there will soon be countless wagers entered in those ridiculous books the gentlemen's clubs keep as to the birthday of Ryder's heir."

"Without a doubt." It was Lady Horatia Cynster who replied. "And equally undoubtedly the favored date will be nine months from now."

Several other ladies laughed.

Lavinia's lips tightened. She narrowed her eyes, but then Claude squeezed her hand. Reminded of where they were, suppressing her emotions, she smoothed her expression and let him lead her on.

Mary waited until the carriage had left the outskirts of London before acting on the thought that had grown minute by minute more tempting ever since she'd first learned of this five and more hours' carriage journey to her new home.

Raventhorne Abbey lay beyond Hungerford; they'd arranged to leave the wedding breakfast in good time to ensure that it would still be light for her first sight of the great house. That meant they had hours of bowling along in Ryder's well-sprung traveling carriage down relatively well-made roads to endure—and she was familiar with the road as far as Reading, so felt no need to study the scenery.

The coachman had drawn up once they were out of sight of St. Ives House and removed the numerous articles attached to the carriage's rear; subsequently, they'd rolled along in comfortable peace. She and Ryder had exchanged comments and observations on their day, on the guests, on minor social matters either or both had noted; that degree of social acuity, of awareness of issues affecting others in their orbit, was a trait they shared. Information was power; they both understood that.

Eventually, however, their observations had come to an end, and they'd lapsed into companionable silence.

She hadn't traveled in this carriage before, but she was impressed by the modern design and the extra little touches of luxury, such as the brass window locks, the concealed window screens, and the superbly sumptuous dark blue leather seats.

Appreciation of the amenities, however, did not divert her for long, and by the time they passed through Hounslow and the coachman whipped up the horses to speed on over the fabled heath, she decided the moment to broach her tempting thought had arrived.

Ryder was sitting beside her, shoulders relaxed against the seat back, long legs bent at the knees, thighs splayed, at ease, one elbow propped on the windowsill. A swift glance showed he was idly watching the trees dotting the heath flash past.

The coach was now traveling at significant speed, rocking slightly on its excellent springs. Without warning she rose and used the sway of the coach to assist her in tumbling onto Ryder's lap.

He caught her, of course. He hesitated for an instant, then as she wriggled to face him, his hands gripped and he lifted her and settled her as she wished—so they were face-to-face and she could smile and lean her arms on his chest, the better to discuss her tempting thought.

Ryder looked into her brilliant eyes, took note of the luscious curve of her lips, and faintly patronizingly arched a
deliberately languid brow. He'd known something like this
was coming, but no matter that one part of him—the baser
part—was eager to fall in with whatever she had in mind, he
hadn't been about to initiate the event.

He'd yet to figure out exactly where the road she'd lured
him down was leading them, and encounters of the sort she
clearly had in mind only pulled him further down said road.
Unresisting, because resistance was futile. No, worse, impossible.

That didn't alleviate his growing wariness one iota.

At some point in the last hours it had finally become clear
to him that she *was* his fate.

She was his now, and in order to keep her he had to pay
her price.

She studied his eyes, then the tip of her tongue appeared
and swept over her lips, leaving the lower glistening, ripe
and luscious.

He inwardly groaned and tried not to too obviously react.

She must have felt something, because the gleam in her
eyes grew just a touch brighter, the curve of her lips a touch
deeper. "I thought," she murmured, her gaze falling to his
lips, "that given we have this very long and otherwise quite
boring drive to live through, we might try enlivening the
moments with an adventure."

He arched his brows higher. "An adventure."

"Hmm. One where we explore just what, for us, is possible within the confines of a traveling carriage." Her gaze
returned to his eyes. "I'm sure you've experienced this sort
of adventure before, but I haven't." She leaned closer. "So I
think you should show me."

Trapped in her pansy-blue eyes, caught—so effortlessly—in the net of her attraction, he heard himself admit,
"Actually, I've never . . . indulged in a carriage."

Those fabulous eyes flared wide. "Never? Not ever?"

He shook his head. "The opportunity never arose."

He hadn't thought it possible, but her expression brightened further, eagerness and delight infusing her features. "Even better. We can explore together, learn and discover all . . . there is to uncover." Her gaze fell to his lips, then lower, to his cravat. "Speaking of which." She reached for the folds.

He caught her hands, flattened them against his chest. "No—that's one thing I do know about such adventures. Clothes stay on."

Her eyes widened. "They do?"

He started to nod, then paused. "Well, mine do. Yours"—he lowered his gaze to her breasts—"more or less."

She considered him for a moment, then she laughed—in that register he'd realized she reserved just for him, sultry and sirenlike. To his well-honed instincts, the woman so revealed was the real her, the Mary Cynster who lived inside the bossy, pragmatic, shrewd, and domineering social shell.

The woman of immeasurable warmth and sensuality.

The female his inner lion craved.

Her eyes locked on his and he read the challenge writ in the blue.

"Very well, my lord. You take the lead and I'll follow. So." Leaning closer, she brought her luscious lips to within a whisker of his and breathed, "Lead on, and show me how."

He couldn't have resisted the lure had his life depended on it. Moving slowly, deliberately, he slid one palm up her spine, letting her feel the weight, the strength in his hand as he traced between her shoulder blades and swept higher, skimming the sensitive skin exposed at her nape, then he cupped the back of her head.

Holding her not just steady but immobile, he closed the last inch, covered her lips with his, and without so much as a by-your-leave took complete and absolute possession of her mouth.

And did as she'd asked, and went adventuring with her.

Several hours later, with Mary thoroughly sated and, by all the signs, still blissfully satisfied, lying dozing, secure and safe in his arms, Ryder realized he was smiling inanely, at nothing and for no particular reason.

Resting his jaw more definitely against her dark curls, he felt his smile turn wry.

Adventuring, she'd called it, and it most certainly had been that; she was every bit as inventive as he, and significantly more prepared, nay eager, to experiment than he'd expected any young lady of the ton to be.

She constantly gave him all he wanted, all he expected, and just a little bit more.

He certainly hadn't expected the laughter, the sheer rollicking fun that had delighted and teased and spurred them both on, nor yet the sudden spike of passion laced with yearning and sharp, unadulterated desire that had gripped them as they'd ultimately come together, when, straddling him, she'd finally sunk fully down and taken him in—and simultaneously, in the same heartbeat, they'd realized that that moment was the first of such moments for them as husband and wife.

Even less had he foreseen the incredible closeness that had followed, when she'd laid her hand against his cheek, kissed him, and together they'd stepped beyond all the boundaries, beyond all restraint, and let that sharply vibrant passion unfurl, then dictate.

He couldn't have foreseen it because he'd never felt with any other woman what he felt with her.

So much more potent, powerful, so much more complex. More layered; he couldn't come close to adequately describing all she made him feel.

He wasn't sure where that left him, much less what it meant, yet this was one road that, once having started down it, had no turns, no branches.

As hints of rosemary and lemon rose from her hair, combining with the lingering scents of their passion to wreath through his brain, soothing and placating, he accepted that going forward with her, hand in hand, was his only option.

To go forward with her, see what eventuated, and trust in them both to meet the challenges.

They arrived at Raventhorne Abbey just before the sun slipped below the western horizon. Located just north of the Savernake Forest, large tracts of the estate remained heavily wooded; the sprawling three-storied mansion only came into clear sight when the carriage left the shelter of the massive oaks lining the drive to that point. Thereafter, the view was unimpeded, the drive following the edge of the great south lawn to the graveled forecourt before the steps leading up to the impressive front door.

Ryder had experienced that first view many times, knew just how the westering sun would be gilding the pale stone, how it would glint and gleam in the leaded glass of the many windows. Regardless, normally he would have looked— would have let his gaze skate over the massive structure, the crenellated roofline, the dome of the skylight above the front hall rising behind—and felt the satisfaction of ownership, of looking upon that which most clearly defined him; today, however, another sight compelled his complete and unwavering attention.

He watched Mary's face as she set eyes on her future home—on the house that would be their principal residence, their true home—for the first time. To his disquiet, sudden panic of a sort threaded through his thoughts: What if she didn't like it?

Before he had time even to register concern over being subject to such a needy feeling, it was rendered irrelevant by the sheer delight that swept over his new wife's face.

Her expression one of avid, eager, indeed covetous interest, she leaned closer to the window the better to drink in all there was to see. Relaxing against the seat, he assured himself that all was, and would be, well.

As the carriage slowed to swing into the forecourt, he seized the moment to look out himself, an emotional as well as practical reassurance. Although parts of the great house were ancient, the façade had been renovated in the Palladian style so beloved by his grandfather's generation. The result had been worth the blunt; not even he, who saw it so often, failed to appreciate that first glimpse.

As per his orders, the entire household were turned out in their best, ranked in a long line that stretched from the middle of the forecourt all the way up the steps to the front porch, ready and waiting to welcome his marchioness.

When the coach rocked to a halt, he waited for the groom to drop down and ceremonially open the door, then he stepped out, turned, and offered his hand to Mary. Reaching out, she laid her hand in his; looking past him, she hesitated.

Understanding, he murmured, "Everything's in place. You look perfect."

Her eyes flicked to his, her lips curving in acknowledgment that he'd read her thoughts correctly; after their adventuring, he'd relaced her gown and helped her tidy her hair, but, of course, she'd wondered.

Gripping his fingers, Mary drew in a breath and allowed Ryder to help her out. She was finally there, at a point she'd always dreamt about—she was about to walk into her own home, to be welcomed by the staff who would henceforth be hers to command.

Flicking out her skirts with her free hand, she raised her head and fixed her gaze on the stately butler waiting at the head of the line.

Ryder led her forward. "My dear, permit me to present Forsythe. He's been butler here since I was in short-coats."

Despite Forsythe's efforts to rein in his smile, it broke through the instant before he bowed. "Welcome to Raventhorne Abbey, my lady." Straightening, he went on, "On behalf of the staff I bid you welcome to your new home, and tender our sincere hopes that your reign here will be a long and happy one."

Returning Forsythe's smile was easy. "Thank you, Forsythe." Mary raised her voice as she looked down the length of the line. "I'm delighted to be here, to have been chosen by your master to fill the shoes of his marchioness. I'm looking forward to working with you all." Glancing at Forsythe, she waved him forward. "If you would?"

"Thank you, ma'am." With a little nod, Forsythe moved ahead of her, pausing before each member of the household to introduce them, and in a few words outlining their position or duties within the house.

The housekeeper, Mrs. Pritchard, was a thin woman of indeterminate years, with a poker-straight back and an incipient twinkle in her gray eyes; after being greeted by her and exchanging a few words, Mary felt reasonably hopeful that their relationship—arguably the most vital to the success of her tenure as Ryder's marchioness—would prosper. If she was reading Mrs. Pritchard aright, the housekeeper was disposed to approve of any lady Ryder had chosen as his.

Very likely the housekeeper was a longtime victim of her husband's insidious charm; if so, Mary wasn't about to complain.

Collier was next in line; Mary greeted him with open pleasure. Her own maid, Aggie, stood next to Collier, beaming fit to burst; Aggie had left Upper Brook Street immediately after the wedding, driven to the Abbey in another of Ryder's coaches along with Collier and all their luggage. Although Aggie put nothing into words, from her sparkling eyes Mary could tell her maid was beyond delighted with her new post, her new household.

Following Forsythe down the line, with Ryder strolling nonchalantly behind, Mary quickly realized that she, rather than Ryder, was the absolute focus of every member of the staff's attention. Ryder, apparently, they knew well—well enough not to exhibit any nervousness of him; curious, she gauged the quality of their ease and concluded his staff had long ago learned that while the lion might roar, he wouldn't bite.

Which, given that that relaxed ease extended to even the young grooms and pot-boys, told her quite a lot about Ryder. The Ryder who lived there, away from the ton and the more rigid social demands of his position.

She looked, too, for any adverse reactions to her advent into the staff's lives. She'd assumed there would be at least one or two less than happy with her arrival—having a mistress as well as a master was a very different situation—yet all she detected was a universal curiosity and interest, the mirror of the interest she felt toward them.

Reaching the scullery maid at the end of the line, after smiling encouragingly at the young girl, Mary stepped onto the porch at the top of the steps. Turning, she said, "Thank you, Forsythe." She nodded at the housekeeper, who had followed behind Ryder. "Mrs. Pritchard." Raising her head and her voice, she smoothly continued, "And thank you all for your welcome. I hope we'll have many years of working together in this house, making sure the House of Cavanaugh prospers into the future."

An enthusiastic chorus of "Yes, my lady! Indeed, my lady! Thank you, my lady!" rolled up the steps as the assembled staff bowed and bobbed.

Mrs. Pritchard beamed. "Thank you, ma'am. Now, pending your approval, we've held dinner back until nine o'clock, thinking you might want to see your new rooms and settle in, but if you'd rather dine earlier . . . ?"

"No, no." Mary looked at Ryder, recalled the hints Stacie had let fall, and Aggie's bubbling eagerness. "I believe I would like to see my rooms first." Glancing back at Mrs. Pritchard, she nodded. "My compliments to Cook—nine o'clock will be perfect."

Ryder smiled his slow smile. "In that case, my dear, allow me to show you upstairs."

Taking his arm, she smiled and did.

Ryder hadn't expected to feel . . . whatever it was he felt. A complex mix of pride, subtle excitement, an insidious eagerness he couldn't remember experiencing since he'd been a young boy, and, beyond all else, simple happiness. He'd got what he'd wanted; Mary was his wife, and now she was here, in the house he considered his home.

Triumph had never felt so . . . fulfilling.

So filled with promise.

He led her up the wide staircase with its twin suits of armor on the landing. "Incidentally, don't think of getting rid of these—they're Forsythe's pride and joy."

She glanced at him, then halted to study the armor; after a moment, she turned and went with him up the next flight. "I think they're rather fitting. Appropriate. I take it they belonged to some ancestors?"

"So we've been told." Ryder glanced back at the armor. "Mind you, I've never been convinced. They're rather short for Cavanaughs."

She laughed. Smiling, he caught her hand and towed her around the gallery, then on down the wide north corridor. "This is the family wing. Our apartments lie across the end and on either side of the corridor, but the primary access is through the door at the end."

Reaching that door, he grasped the knob; watching her face, he set the door swinging wide. "Which leads to the marchioness's sitting room."

She looked in, and her eyes grew round. Pleasure bloomed in her face as her lips formed a soundless O of delight, then she rushed in.

Grinning, as delighted as she, he followed.

"Oh, my lord!" Pirouetting in the center of the room, Mary meant the words literally. "The colors . . . they're perfect!" A silvery blue contrasted with her signature cornflower-blue, highlighted with a stripe of dark violet; the three colors in various strengths combined in the silks covering the walls, in the fabrics of the upholstery on the twin chaises and various chairs, in turn echoed by a similar but darker version of the same leaf-pattern in the long curtains, presently looped back to allow light to stream in through the two long windows.

Between the windows sat a delicate lady's writing desk, the lamp upon it a fanciful design echoing the leaf motif. A set of crystal inkwells and fine ivory pens lay ready to be used beside a blotter framed in blue leather.

All the wooden furniture—the chests against the walls, the low table between the chaises, the frames of the chaises themselves—was of golden oak, with a patina that just begged to be touched, stroked. As she flitted about the room, trailing her fingers over this surface and that, appreciating the tactile and visual delights and the small, subtle touches like the lamp and the clock on the mantelpiece—a simple gold dial framed in delicate gold leaves—Mary registered the implication. Slowing, she turned to Ryder.

He'd closed the door but had halted before it, watching her.

"You had all this done." Statement, not a question; he had to have for the color to match so perfectly. "In just . . ." She paused to calculate. "Fifteen, sixteen days at most." She looked around, marveling. "You managed all this." Clearly he had, but she knew what that must have entailed. Not just the cost, but the organization.

He shrugged lightly and came forward. "You being you made choosing the colors easy, and as for the rest . . ." He glanced around, then looked down at her. "Your rooms at Raventhorne House are still being finished, but"—he waved to the door to his left—"all your rooms here, your bedroom and more, are ready to receive you."

She didn't need a second invitation but went straight to the door he'd indicated. There was another door in the mirror position in the opposite wall; she assumed it led to his bedroom. Opening the door to which he'd directed her, she walked through, knowing he followed, that he was watching, gauging her reaction, her response, that his satisfaction sprang from pleasing her. From knowing his gift had.

It wasn't hard to openly show her pleasure and give him that satisfaction; the bed was a large oak four-poster, solidly framed but delicately carved, the same leaf motif dominating. The fabrics and patterns from the sitting room were redeployed, but in more luxurious, sumptuous weights. The silver-blue sheets were fine satin, the coverlet a heavier, richer satin rendition of the upholstery pattern, with the embroidery on some of the mound of pillows picked out in the deeper hues.

And then there were the windows. One pair, long and narrow, looked north, but the pair flanking the bed, although equally tall, were wider. Sweeping up to one, she looked out.

"The rose garden." Ryder came to stand behind her.

It was June; the large, well-tended bushes were in full leaf, and buds were starting to unfurl, the rich pink, apricot, white, and deep red blooms splashes of color amid the dark green. Stone paths framed the beds, and an old stone fountain stood in the center of the square garden. Mary knew about roses. "Someone did an excellent job designing it." She glanced over her shoulder at Ryder. "Your stepmother?"

He shook his head. "As far as I know, Lavinia never had much interest in the gardens. According to the old head gardener—who is older than Methuselah—it was my mother and he together who made it." He hesitated, then added, "Even though she died when I was young, I still remember it was her favorite place outside. If she was in the gardens, I'd always be taken to her there. She'd be sitting on that bench at the end of the walk."

Mary noted the bench, could guess the view it would give of the house. "There's a rose garden a bit like this one at

Somersham Place—with a similar bench." She glanced up at Ryder and grinned. "Perhaps it's one of those things the principal residences of all the major families are supposed to have."

He softly snorted, then met her eyes. "More like something all the relevant ladies decided needed to be—their civilizing influence made manifest."

She chuckled and turned to the door leading to the next room; as she'd supposed, it proved to be her dressing room.

A fabulous dressing room, large and airy, with a wide dressing table set between a smaller pair of windows, and numerous chests of drawers and two armoires. Her gowns were already hanging in one, her petticoats and shawls in the other. "This," she said, slowly twirling to take in the entirety, "is more like a boudoir."

Ryder shrugged as he joined her. "Lavinia used it as such—she used to meet with her children here, rather than in the sitting room."

Detecting something more behind the comment, Mary arched a brow.

His lips twisted wryly. "So she ran no risk of my father coming in or overhearing anything she said. By tacit agreement this room was hers, and he wouldn't have intruded without an invitation."

She held his gaze. "Does it bother you that these rooms were once Lavinia's? That she replaced your mother here"— she gestured—"in the marchioness's suite?"

He didn't try to duck the question. After a moment of consideration—while staring into her eyes so she saw him look inward and actually consult his feelings—his lips slowly curved. Refocusing on her, he shook his head. "No. In fact . . . I suspect that's one reason I so enjoyed doing this— finally and completely supplanting Lavinia with you—and why I so enjoy seeing you . . . happy here."

Holding his gaze, she smiled back, equally sincere. "And I am very happy." Even more that he'd answered without reserve. Stretching up, placing a hand on his cheek to steady herself, she lightly kissed his lips.

When he didn't respond, she drew back and, openly puzzled, cocked her head in question.

His lips quirked. "Before we get distracted, there's something I want to give you."

She opened her eyes wide. "More?"

In reply he crossed to the dressing table. Her brushes and combs, her box of hair ornaments, and her jewelry box were neatly arrayed on the surface, reflected in the triple-paned mirror. Opening the narrow drawer below the center of the table, he reached in and drew out a velvet-covered box. Turning to her, he offered it. "These are for you."

Eyes locked on the box, eagerness, delight, and expectation flaring, she reached for it. Took it, opened it—and gasped. "Oh!" That was all she could manage; mere words couldn't do justice to what lay within. "It's . . . they are . . ." Fabulous, unbelievable, amazing. "*Exquisite.*"

She continued to stare at the matching necklace, bracelet, and earrings in utterly speechless delight.

Ryder drank in the sight and felt his own delight well. Reaching into the box, he eased the necklace from its bed on the white velvet. "I'll remember, next time I want to see you stunned, to offer you jewelry."

"Oh," she breathed, "but this isn't just jewelry. This is a fantasy rendered in jewels." Swinging around, presenting him with her back, she all but jigged. "Put it on. I have to see."

Her joy was infectious. His smile couldn't have got broader as he looped the delicate confection about her throat, then bent to fasten the catch. "There." He straightened.

Standing before the mirror, eagerly and excitedly viewing her reflection, with spread fingers she gently patted the necklace into place, then with her fingertips touched, lightly traced.

The complex creation of diamonds and violet-blue sapphires quivered. Each marquise-cut diamond represented a leaf or the petal of a flower, each individual diamond suspended on fine wire around the richly colored sapphires. The latter, large and vivid, formed the center of each flower, and were set in the actual links of necklace, while the diamonds trembled in a delicate, glittering, surrounding frame.

She looked up, in the mirror met his eyes. Then she whirled and flung herself into his arms.

He laughed and caught her; setting the jeweler's box aside, framing his face with her hands, she pressed her lips to his and kissed him.

He tried to kiss her, but she drew back and pressed kisses to his jaw, his cheeks, punctuating each with a "Thank you."

But eventually he recaptured her lips and took her mouth, slow and achingly complete, and she sighed, relaxed against him, and allowed it.

For long moments they communed, through the simple kiss sharing the essence of thoughts and feelings, alluding to the wants and needs that, unsurprisingly, smoldered, presently latent, but nonetheless there.

The whir and bong of a clock drew them back to earth, to the here and now of their new reality. Their now joint life.

Breaking the kiss, they yet remained as they were, locked together. She looked into his eyes, her own reflecting a deep content, as if for once she saw no reason to rush, and every reason to savor. Then her lips, lightly swollen from his kisses, curved, and she pulled back. Reluctantly, he let her go.

Her smile deepened a touch. "Come, my lord, and help me drape myself in your gifts." Turning to the dressing table, she picked up the bracelet and held it up for him to take. "And then"—she met his eyes—"we have our first dinner to attend."

His smile a mirror of hers—his content a mirror of hers—he lifted the delicate bracelet from her fingers and did as he was bid.

The dinner was, in Mary's estimation, impossible to fault. Although they were separated by the length of the table, at least it was the smaller table in the family dining room and not the formal dining room's fifty-plus-foot monstrosity, and neither she nor Ryder was so foolish as to suggest she move up the table to the place on his left, not when the staff were so obviously primed to serve her her first meal in the house with all due pomp and ceremony.

Aside from said pomp and ceremony, which was flawlessly executed, the dishes were a superb combination of light and delicious for her, and hearty and tasty for Ryder. While he endeavored to do justice to the cook's offerings, she chatted, wine goblet cradled between her hands, reminiscing about moments during the wedding ceremony and the breakfast, filling him in on scenes he might not have noticed, happenings he might not have observed.

The table could comfortably seat twelve, but she had no difficulty projecting her voice to the required degree. Ryder clearly heard, nodding, fleetingly smiling or laughing as appropriate. Mary also noted that the two footmen who stood like statues, their backs to the wall, and Forsythe, too, who waited behind Ryder's chair, were listening avidly, no doubt making mental notes so they could share with the rest of the staff later. Recognizing the likelihood, she extended her descriptions, making them more colorful; at one point, Ryder cut her a puzzled glance, but when she smiled and let her gaze wander to the footman to his right, he realized, grinned, and returned to the business of eating.

He was a large man; he ate a lot. But when the covers were finally drawn and she arched a brow at him, questioning whether he intended to indulge in a brandy in splendid isolation, he smiled, tossed his napkin on the table, rose, and came to join her as the footman drew back her chair and she came to her feet.

Taking her hand, Ryder twined her arm with his. "Come—I'll show you the drawing room."

He did. In typical country house fashion, it was a large and comfortable room, sufficiently fashionably furnished to pass muster, but here, in the country, practical comfort had a higher priority. Drifting about the room, taking note of the gentle warmth thrown by the small but cheery fire, she murmured, "It's a warm place—and I'm not talking about the temperature." Turning to Ryder, she smiled. "It's welcoming and relaxing—it feels like home."

Eyes on hers, he merely nodded. After an instant's hesitation, he asked, "Do you want to sit here?"

She glanced around the room, then looked back at him. "I know Mrs. Pritchard will show me around tomorrow on my official tour, so to speak, but perhaps you could give me a quick introduction to the rooms down here, and tell me which ones are used for what." She wanted to, was impatient to, find his place—the room he retreated to when in this house—preferably without asking him directly.

Patently content to fall in with her wishes, he showed her the morning room and the garden parlor; they spent several minutes in the formal dining room while he appeased her curiosity over those of his ancestors who looked down from the portraits on the walls. They glanced into the estate office and his study next door—too tidy, in her estimation, to be his principal den.

But at the last, he ushered her into the library, and she knew she'd discovered his particular spot. The long room was laid out similarly to the library in the London house, with packed bookshelves lining the walls, a massive stone hearth in the center of the inner wall, three long double windows set in the wall opposite the fireplace, and a heavy desk in prime position at the far end of the room.

Two long sofas and four well-padded armchairs were grouped before the fire, and nearer to hand a large round library table provided a place on which to consult the leather-bound tomes. A library ladder stood in one corner, providing access to the upper gallery that ran around all four sides of the room.

Her gaze drawn upward, she slowly turned, taking in the glory of the paintings in the panels high above.

This library, she realized, was the original the other was drawn from. Both were so similar, but this room was created on a scale several times greater and grander. Also older, and somehow more solid.

And this room was lived in; she could sense it, a subtle scent of longtime human presence that had sunk into fabric and wood. The desk, moreover, showed obvious evidence of frequent use—marks on the blotter, several pens in the tray along with a letter knife and stubs of sealing wax.

"Your father used to use this room, too, didn't he?" She looked to where Ryder had paused near the sofas. When he nodded, she asked, "When did he die? Some years ago, wasn't it?"

"Six."

No lingering effect could be so strong; it was Ryder's presence she was sensing.

Satisfied she'd discovered his den, she walked past the desk to study the books in the shelves beyond it. Lamps in the room's corners had been lit; in the soft light, the lettering on the leather spines glinted. "Philosophy," she murmured, then continued her ambling perusal.

Ryder stood and watched her for several minutes, then picked up a book he'd left by his usual chair, sat, made himself comfortable, and left her to it.

Wondered if he could.

As he'd suspected, the words on the page failed to divert his attention from her. Weren't strong enough to drag his senses from her, she who had become their cynosure.

When she paused to examine the twin suits of medieval armor standing between the windows, he murmured, "Forsythe again. They've become his hobby."

She glanced at him; even though he hadn't looked at her he felt the touch of her gaze. "Are there more of them?"

"In the attics. I gather Forsythe occasionally slips up there to oil and polish them. He's become something of an authority, I believe."

"Hmm." With that she wandered on, effortlessly leading his senses on a circuit of the room.

At the end of it, she returned to the southwest corner—books on gardening—selected a tome, then came to sit with a swish of her skirts in the armchair across from his.

Legs curled half under her, she wriggled, then settled, opened the book, and, without a single glance at him, started flicking through it.

Returning his gaze to the book in his hands, Ryder attempted to persuade his errant senses to focus on the words, and not on her.

Locating an appropriate page, Mary fixed her eyes on it but didn't read. Instead, she reviewed. Herself, her state. And his. Here they were, husband and wife, sitting comfortably in his library reading. She'd surrendered to Fate, and The Lady's dictates, and this was where they'd landed her.

Which was well enough in its way, yet she was only halfway to her ultimate goal.

She had his ring on her finger and was certain she could rely on having his strength at her back, but she'd yet to secure that one most vital thing—his love declared and acknowledged, at least between them.

That was the minimum she would, could, settle for.

So here they were. How should she move them forward?

Staring unseeing at the neat black print, she revisited all their previous private interactions; she searched and evaluated, seeking to identify the most direct and unrestrained and unrestricted means of communication, the most certain route to claiming his unfettered attention and persuading and convincing him of the value in taking that one last step.

She now knew him well enough to be sure that, with him,

persuading and convincing was the only way to go. And regardless of all else, she was going to have to demonstrate the value, the real and true purpose of love.

Which meant she would have to define exactly what that was for him and her and their future together—the shared life they would live in this house.

And this was, after all, their wedding night; what better time to start?

Closing the book in her lap, she looked at him.

Although he responded slowly, she knew that was a sham. Raising his gaze to her face, he searched her eyes, then arched a fashionably languid brow.

She was perfectly certain he hadn't forgotten it was their wedding night, either. Setting aside her book, she rose; shutting and laying aside his book, he did the same. When he stood before her, she met his eyes. "I have a request to make, my lord."

He held her gaze; she could see him trying to decide what she might ask, but eventually he surrendered. "And that is?"

"Take me to your bed."

Chapter Twelve

Ryder blinked, nearly swayed with the effort of hauling back his impulses enough to clarify, "My bed? Not yours?"

"No—yours." Brazen and bold, she tipped up her chin. "I think my room is lovely and I want to thank you properly. In your bed."

He raised his brows. "In that case . . ." He swept her up into his arms. Ignoring her gasp and her consequent laughter, he carried her to the door, juggled her enough to open it, then strode along the corridor to the front hall.

She looped her arms around his neck and, softly laughing, held tight as he carried her up the stairs two at a time. Her eagerness shone in her eyes, infused her expression, the teasing tension in her lithe frame—and effortlessly fed and incited his own.

Swinging into the gallery, intent edging his curving lips, he strode around the well of the stairs and on down the wide corridor into the north wing.

The door to the sitting room wasn't quite shut; it swung open as his arm brushed it. He angled her through the doorway, then turned right and crossed to his door. A heartbeat later it swung inward, then they were through; kicking the panel shut, he made for the bed.

He didn't even pause, just tossed her on the green and gold coverlet and followed her down.

Her breath left her on a gasp; she wriggled, squirmed, trying to gain the ascendancy, but he pinned her beneath him, grasped her wrists and anchored her hands to the bed, then swooped and covered her lips with his—and kissed her.

This was their wedding night, and she was his.

He wanted her—naked and writhing, his to pleasure until she screamed.

She, of course, had a different perspective. The instant he released her hands to attack the buttons closing the front of her gown, she speared her fingers into his hair, gripped, and then she was kissing him with a potent blend of incitement and demand sufficiently powerful to distract even him.

The kiss turned into a heated melding of mouths, of hot, slick tongues and wildly escalating hunger. Then her gown was open to her waist, but the instant he pulled back to haul the halves apart, she got her hands between them and seized his cravat.

What followed was a tussle the like of which he'd never previously participated in. Women didn't strip him; he stripped them, but his new wife clearly wasn't of a mind to play a passive role. And her hands, those grasping, gripping, eager little hands, were everywhere—streaking over him, seeking out skin, pulling and tugging, searching and finding . . .

She drove him to a state of sensual madness he hadn't known existed.

And if her gasps and smothered moans were anything to go by, he did the same to her.

Their clothes literally flew from the bed, tossed here and there in a near frenzy of focused passion. In a fleeting moment of lucidity when he fell back, chest heaving, on the bed, he wondered whether it was the definition of madness itself to permit it—this driven merging of two powerful wills, neither willing to bend, to turn from their path, but both, it appeared, able to feed off the other, to seize the advance gained by the other and force the wild, tumultuous maelstrom of their passions further and on, each striving to take the other along their chosen path, and in the end following neither.

Following instead some path between. One he, for one, had never trod.

Straddling his hips, she visually and tactilely devoured his now naked chest, her palms searing, her fingers spread, then she swept her hands down and fell on the buttons of his trousers.

Hauling in a breath, he tipped her back, rolled—only to find her rolling him even further. He only just caught himself before his momentum tipped them both off the bed. Growling in warning, he fought to get his hands on her skin, pushing up her flimsy near-translucent chemise, all she currently still had on bar the sapphires and diamonds he'd given her.

He succeeded in getting his hands on her lush, naked curves. Her skin, soft, smooth, silken, acted like an aphrodisiac, one he most certainly did not need. Clenching his jaw against the resultant throbbing ache, he rolled to his back, wrestling her atop him long enough to rip the distracting chemise away.

As he flung it aside, she slipped from his arms, scooting down his thighs as she tugged his trousers to his knees. On a curse, he shifted his legs and finished the business for her, pushing his trousers to the end of the bed, but before he could roll again and put her beneath him, she slapped her palms to his chest, leaned her full weight on her braced arms, and gasped, "No!"

No? He stared up at her. The necklace and earrings fractured the light, glittering about her throat, dangling from her earlobes, marks of his ownership. He wanted to claim her, ravish her. "No" didn't, to his mind, fit anywhere in their current situation.

She wanted him; he wanted her.

He could easily have tipped her and put her on her back.

Reining in the raging urgency that insisted he do exactly that made him ache, but something in the searing blue of her eyes held him immobile. "What?" he managed to rasp.

"This is about me thanking you."

"You can do that best by—"

"How do you know?" Her voice was a breathy thread, desire pulsing in every word. She licked her lips; the sight nearly made him groan. "How do you know what is best if you don't know what I want to do? To you."

He'd been aching before; now he was in agony. "Mary—"

"This is our wedding night, and the boon I ask of you is for you to lie back and let me give to you . . ." She held his gaze, then her lips faintly curved. "Exactly what you wish to give to me."

He knew he should refuse, but . . . looking into her eyes, he was passingly sure that she'd already realized that he was constitutionally incapable of refusing her anything she'd set her heart on . . . and just that thought—that she had set her heart on this—made him haul in a huge breath, then nod. "All right—but only because it's tonight."

She smiled as if she saw straight through that lie, but then she slid her hands up over his shoulders, letting herself down fully atop him. Sliding sinuously up to bring her head above his, she paused to look into his eyes, then bent her head and kissed him.

Like a houri. Like a woman whose life held only one aim—to please and pleasure him.

He had no real notion of where she'd learned to do as she did, but he suspected that she'd learned from him, then extrapolated.

Each caress, every wet lash of her tongue, every subtle but deliberate pressure of her hands and drift of her fingers was laced with a potent mix of innocence and concupiscence.

He had no real idea how long the excruciatingly exquisite intimate torture lasted, for how many heart-pounding, senses-stealing minutes she practiced her magic, only knew that by the time he finally broke, when, biting back a curse, he released the powerful suction of her mouth, drew his iron-hard erection from that hot, wet haven and hauled her up to straddle him, he was long past thinking.

She was no better, but with the sudden gripping of her knees about his waist, an almost violent tossing of her tumbling curls, and the sharp bite of her nails sinking into his forearms, she made it perfectly clear she wasn't yet ready to give up the reins.

Quite the opposite. Before he had time to do more than drag in a breath, to fight against the tension and fill his chest, she positioned herself and sank down, slowly, inch by inch impaling herself on his aching shaft, enclosing that oh-so-sensitive part of him in scalding glory—stealing his breath. Stealing his wits and every last ounce of his will.

By the time she pressed fully down, enveloping him to the hilt, he was lost.

Then she rode him and shattered him utterly.

Rising and falling, her lids low, the light from the lamps occasionally glinting in the intense blue of her eyes, with her hands spread on his chest, arms braced, she gave herself over to her driving ambition.

To the elemental driving rhythm.

To the primitive pleasure, lashing him with desire, his and hers, wracking him with passion, theirs, combined.

He and all he was answered her call, unable to hold back, to resist the surging frenzy. To resist the compulsion to merge with her, to join and fuse and lose all identity in the unrelenting drive to be one.

He surrendered, let go of all restraint and joined her in the wild ride, racing, hearts thundering, through the raging glory. Then she tightened, tightened, stiffened upon him.

Fingers pressing unforgivingly into her hips, he held her down, thrust up, and they flew.

Together they reached for the sensual sun; stretching, straining, together they touched, and ecstasy blinded them.

Overwhelmed them and wracked them until their senses broke apart—then bliss rolled in, heady and heavy, and drew them down into a sea of golden satiation, of pleasure given, and taken, as one.

She was all he had ever wanted—and more.

So much more.

Slumped on his back, Mary curled at his side, the sheets tugged over their cooling limbs, Ryder finally found some measure of mental clarity—enough, at least, to wonder what the hell had happened . . . and to finally admit that his vision of how his marriage would work had been comprehensively revised.

At no time had he ever imagined . . . anything reaching this deep.

He'd never before met any woman who had the ability to do more than evoke his affection, the mild and rather patriarchal impulse to ensure she was safe and well fed. Fondness was as deep as he'd ever got with any female.

But when it came to Mary . . . what he felt for her, with her, was something else. Something he hadn't foreseen, and wasn't at all sure he welcomed.

Yes, he'd caught glimpses over the past week or so, ever since she had come to his bed, but he'd assumed that with the familiarity of repeated engagements, the feeling would grow less. Less intense, less gripping.

Instead, with each successive interlude that unexpected, unprecedented link had only grown more powerful.

He knew exactly why he'd chosen her, why he'd looked her way in the first place. He'd wanted a lady who would bring him all the things he'd missed in his life—a strong sense of family, of familial devotion and loyalty—who inherently understood the importance of those qualities, and who otherwise fitted his notion of what his wife should be like.

Mary had fitted his bill perfectly—perhaps so perfectly he should have been suspicious, but he'd always been in control of his life and Fate had always smiled on him, so he hadn't seen any reason to be wary.

Not at first.

And even when wariness had raised its head, when his instincts for self-preservation had stirred, he'd been so cocksure, so arrogantly certain he—the greatest lover in the ton with a thousand and more nights of passion under his belt—would never fall victim to any affliction of the heart that he'd ignored them.

He should have remembered that Fate was a female, should have paid attention to the warnings of his fellows that she was prone to turning fickle.

But it was too late now. Far too late to change anything.

Fate had handed him all he'd ever wanted in a wife—and her price was now due and would have to be paid.

Exactly *how* he paid . . . that, perhaps, was the one aspect of the situation still within his control.

Mary, she to whom he was now inextricably linked in a way far more visceral than he'd planned, was manipulative. He knew, because he was, too.

If he allowed her to glimpse the hold she now had over him . . .

That wasn't an attractive proposition, not to a nobleman accustomed to complete and absolute control.

Accustomed to being in control of himself most of all.

No—he would have to find ways to deal with all he felt without allowing his affliction to show.

Eyes closed, body relaxed, he was still vaguely puzzling over how to achieve that when Mary stirred, then wriggled onto her other side, curling deeper under the covers, facing away from him.

He considered, and decided that wisdom dictated that he strive to maintain at least the appearance of mere fondness and nothing more between them—he should therefore remain as he was, on his back, leaving an inch or so of air between them.

A full minute passed.

Then he mentally sighed, unclenched his jaw, shifted onto his side, and, placing one arm over her, curled his body around hers. Now able to relax, he did, and over the space of two heartbeats fell asleep.

Drifting in clouds of slumber, Mary registered Ryder's warmth, felt the weight of his arm around her. She wasn't so asleep she couldn't smile at the thought that wafted through her mind.

Possessive protective, thy name is Ryder Cavanaugh.

What do you mean, you'd rather I didn't go outside?" Mary stared down the length of the breakfast table—and decided that tomorrow she would have Forsythe set her place on Ryder's left; from this distance she couldn't see well enough to read the expression in his eyes.

The expression on his face—a twist of his lips, the faint arch of one brow—told her little as, after one fleeting glance at her face, at her incredulous expression, he returned his attention to his plate. "Exactly that. This being your first day here, I'm sure you'll have plenty to do getting acquainted with the house and how it runs—I know Mrs. Pritchard is holding herself ready to give you an extended tour—so remaining indoors isn't likely to lead to boredom, and . . ." He paused, considered the slice of roast beef on his fork, then stated, still without looking at her, "I would prefer that you remain inside today."

And I am your husband and you will obey. He hadn't said the words, but Mary heard them loud and clear. Although her lips had set in a line, she mentally gaped. What had happened to the man—nobleman, admittedly—who had shared the reins so wonderfully last night? And this morning, too, if it came to that. Mere hours ago, he'd been well on the way to being the husband she intended him to be, and yet there he sat, giving an excellent imitation of the most dictatorial of tyrants.

Imitation? Or reality?

Eyes narrowed, she studied him and wasn't entirely convinced either way. Regardless, she obviously had to take him in hand, had to react and refashion this, but, given he was what he was, and more, that he knew what she was, what was the best way to achieve her desired end? It took her a moment to find the right question. "Why?" When he glanced up at her, she again cursed the distance, but she thought she saw fleeting . . . was it *panic*? . . . in his eyes. Emboldened, she reached for her teacup. "I'm sure you have a reason for such a peculiar prohibition." Taking a sip from her cup, she met his gaze over its rim. "So what has occasioned your . . . request?"

He blinked; his expression appeared studiously blank. Then he said, "Rats."

"Rats?" She lowered her cup and stared. "In this house?"

He grimaced and looked down. "One was found inside this morning." He glanced toward the windows. "We brought the cats in and the house has been completely searched and there are no more inside, and we have men checking the terraces and gardens."

That explained the odd activity she'd sensed in the house and had glimpsed through the windows as she'd made her way downstairs. She'd wondered why so many men were beating the bushes, but really . . . she shrugged and sipped again, then admitted, "I'm not all that frightened of rats."

"You aren't?" He looked faintly nonplussed.

She shook her head. "They're small and they always run away. Not that I would like to think they were inside the house, however, so I am glad the staff reacted so quickly and decisively. But if your edict against me going outdoors was occasioned by imagining I might faint on encountering some poor little rat—"

"They're not little." He shook his head. "Big. Big as the cats. And they're rabid—they won't run away. They'll fly at you and might bite you." He drew in a short breath and looked away. Waved. "Well, you can see why I can't have you exposing yourself to that."

Dumbfounded, Mary stared. After a long moment, she confirmed, "Rabid rats—big as cats?"

Raising his coffee mug, avoiding her eyes, Ryder nodded and prayed she'd swallow the tale. "Exactly. We should be clear of them by tomorrow, or perhaps the day after."

After what they'd discovered that morning, there was no chance he would permit her out of his sight, or out of the close care of his most trusted staff. The panic that was riding him simply wouldn't allow it; it was all he could do not to lock her in his arms and snarl and snap at any who came close. He could barely think, let alone formulate any rational response; the idea that, willful and headstrong as she was, she might not accept his decree and stay safely indoors where he and his staff could keep her safe . . . every time the notion wafted through his brain, he panicked all over again.

And that panic shook him to his core, as if he'd been solidly knocked off his foundations.

Never in his life had he panicked like this; he had no idea how to manage it—how to rein in his out-of-control reactions, how to calm himself enough to think . . . the instant he thought of her, let alone saw her, instincts he'd never known he possessed overwhelmed him and took charge. He was so tense that despite his best efforts his jaw felt like it would crack, and he'd already bent one fork out of shape. And right at this moment, his sanity hinged on Mary believing—or at least accepting the tale—that this sleepy little corner of the English countryside was overrun by rabid rats. As big as cats.

She'd been staring at him, studying him; he watched her from beneath his lashes and nearly sighed with relief when she gently nodded. "As you say, I'll be occupied for the entire morning with Mrs. Pritchard and the staff. I suspect it will be afternoon before I'm free. However"—she waited until he raised his head, then trapped his eyes with hers— "if I could suggest a compromise, perhaps you could then accompany me on a stroll through the rose garden. I would like to see it from ground level, and if you're with me—and perhaps we can take your head gardener as well—then I'm sure between the two of you, you'll be able to protect me from any lingering rats."

Given he felt so much like a drowning man, he recognized the olive branch, grabbed for it and nodded. "That sounds reasonable."

She smiled easily enough, but there was a quality in her expression that suggested her acquiescence was more strategy than surrender.

He didn't care; if she'd agreed to wait for him before venturing outside, she wouldn't be inclined to venture forth by herself—and that, at present, was his number one concern.

Mary spent the day operating, or so it seemed, on two levels. On one, she played the part of Ryder's new marchioness, accompanying Forsythe and Mrs. Pritchard on a comprehensive tour of the great house, which, at Mary's insistence, had included all the staff quarters as well as the attics and the roof. She'd been somewhat relieved to discover that, despite not having any devoted lady in charge, possibly not for decades, the house had been suitably modernized throughout, the facilities brought up to scratch, and the staff quarters remodeled in line with progressive ideals.

When she'd inquired as to what impetus had driven the changes, Forsythe had informed her, "That's largely his lordship's doing, ma'am. He leans toward the progressive side in most things."

She'd salted the observation away, making a mental note to inquire more closely as to Ryder's political aspirations.

Over luncheon, taken with Ryder in the family dining room, she'd peppered him with questions designed to draw out his approach to the estate, what he hoped to achieve in the immediate future and what his long-term plans were. After an initial hesitation—that strangely fraught tension she'd detected at breakfast had still been there—he'd consented to answer; as her questions had continued, he'd relaxed and his revelations had flowed freely.

She hadn't made the mistake of referring to his attitude regarding her venturing out of doors other than, as they quit the dining room, to remind him of his promise to accompany her for a stroll in the rose garden later. He'd nodded and had told her to come and fetch him when she was ready; he would be in the library.

Content enough, she'd spent the next two hours consulting with Mrs. Pritchard in her new sitting room upstairs. While Mary's organizing of how they would jointly manage the household had gone well, the housekeeper had seemed a touch distracted.

Finally free, Mary had made her way downstairs to the library. Ryder had promptly left his correspondence and they'd gone out to the rose garden. The stroll had been pleasant, entirely unmarred by any rodents, rabid or otherwise; she hadn't even sighted a cat.

Detecting, once again, that oddly fragile tension, as if it were something Ryder held on a short and not all that strong leash, she'd forborne from teasing him and instead had enjoyed the roses and his company.

She'd been in a pleasantly mollified mood when they'd returned to the house and the library, and she'd curled up with a book to keep him silent company. He'd studied her for a moment, then had gone back to his desk and his letters. She'd half expected some attempt to send her elsewhere, but instead he'd seemed content to have her there; every time his attention had lifted from his letters, she'd felt the fleeting touch of his gaze.

It was only when she was dressing for dinner and Aggie, assuming Mary had known all along, blurted out the facts that Mary finally learned the truth of what had caused the odd change in Ryder's behavior, what had given rise to his extraordinary decree. What had been behind the staff's somewhat strained reactions.

The full truth about the rabid rats.

Aggie, sensing her erupting temper, grew nervous; Mary instantly reassured her, although she didn't explain. Didn't admit her until-then ignorance.

That was an issue to be discussed with he who had caused it—Ryder.

Her immediate impulse was to leap to her feet, rage down the stairs, and have it out with him then and there, but . . . she drew in a breath, sat still, and allowed Aggie to continue pinning her curls, reminding herself that she was a married lady now, and married ladies needed to be much cleverer than unmarried ladies, especially when it came to dealing with their spouses.

Rather than go against them—which only results in im-mediately meeting the solid and instinctive wall of their resistance—I have found it pays to find a way to work with them. Once you make it clear you are entirely willing to find a way to solve whatever issue they have—that you are content to work alongside them rather than oppose them—the poor dears are usually so grateful they'll happily share the reins, and then one can steer the applecart in a more amenable direction.

The instant she'd heard those words, she'd recognized their significance and the likelihood that they would, one day, be relevant to her. She'd committed the advice to memory, the words spoken by Minerva, Duchess of Wolverstone, on the subject of dealing with dictatorially inclined noblemen of the ilk of her husband, Royce.

There was, in Mary's eyes, no better or more applicable authority with respect to her current situation.

So . . . she sat and let Aggie fuss, and concentrated on dampening her temper and considering ways to learn what she needed to know to reclaim her share of the reins, namely what about the situation had most exercised her new husband.

She didn't rush down to the drawing room the instant she was ready but took her time, using the moments as she walked to the stairs and slowly descended to reinforce her control over her temper and remind herself of her goal.

Reaching the front hall, she raised her head and glided toward the drawing room. A footman leapt to open the door for her; with a regal inclination of her head, she walked into the room.

Ryder was standing by the fireplace, one arm propped on the mantelpiece; his gaze had locked on her the instant she'd appeared.

He'd been waiting for her.

Drawing in a breath, instinctively raising her head a notch higher, her eyes locking with his, Mary walked toward him.

Even before she drew near, Ryder knew she knew. And accepted that he had no choice but to do what he'd realized he must.

He didn't wait for her to halt but raised a hand to shoulder height, palm toward her, a suing for peace. "Mea culpa. I'm sorry."

She halted. Regarded him steadily; he couldn't read her expression, which made him uneasy.

Then she faintly arched a brow. "For what?"

He held her gaze and didn't fall for that; she'd heard the details from someone. "I should have told you straightaway—as soon as I heard."

Her fine brows rose higher. "And?"

And . . . lips thinning, he stated, "I should have discussed it with you, and then decided how to deal with the situation."

She looked faintly intrigued. "Why didn't you?"

"Because . . ." He filled his chest and it almost hurt. "I wanted your first day here, as my wife, to be . . . perfect. I wanted you to feel welcome here, and to view this place and its people with all—every last soupçon of—your usual wide-eyed eagerness."

Her gaze grew cynical, but the line of her lips softened. "I might be wide-eyed, and eager, too, but I'm not blind."

"No. I know." Eyes still locked with hers, he drew in a deeper breath; all in all, this had gone better than he'd hoped. "So." He let the word lie, an invitation for her to accept and use as she chose.

She considered him for a moment longer, then gave a fractional nod. "So what have you learned?"

His instincts bade him seize the question and run, but . . . he couldn't quite believe he was getting off that easily. "That's it? You're not going to rail at me?"

She didn't look away; a heartbeat passed, then she lightly shrugged. "As you've realized your shortcomings on your own, railing would be superfluous and would only waste time. And my temper." She tipped her head. "So, to repeat, what have you learned?"

He had, apparently, saved himself from the worst, but . . . he grimaced. "Absolutely nothing."

She frowned, then turned and sat on the nearer end of the chaise. She was wearing a blue-and-black striped evening gown, with a cameo on a blue velvet band about her neck; she looked fresh and vivid, the gown perfect for a quiet country dinner alone with her husband. With him.

Looking up at him, she stated, "All I've heard is that there was an adder found in my bed this morning. I'm sure you've been trying to learn how it got there."

He fought not to let his expression grow too grim. "We're surrounded by woods and forests, and there are adders out there, but we've never had one in the gardens, much less the house. When the tweeny went into your bedroom this morning to check the fireplace, she noticed movement under the coverlet and had the sense to summon Forsythe. He and the gardeners caught and removed the snake, but . . . to say that everyone's mystified as to how it got there, on the first floor and between your sheets, would be an understatement."

She blinked, for a long moment simply stared up at him, then he saw her breasts rise as she drew in a deep, then deeper, breath. "Someone put it there." She sounded as disbelieving as he'd felt.

"Yes, *but*." Pushing away from the mantelpiece, he moved past her. "As far as it's humanly possible to be certain, I do not believe it was any of the staff."

Sitting on the sofa alongside her, he met her eyes as she shifted to face him. "Literally everyone who serves in this house, even in the gardens and stables, belongs to one of the estate families. When it comes to loyalty, you know what that means as well as I. According to Forsythe and Mrs. Pritchard, and Filmore, the head stableman, and Dukes, the head gardener, everyone's been in alt over our marriage, and eager and excited over meeting you. Not a word has been spoken against you—and yes, I asked them to check, and they did. Nothing. Everyone in the household has been shocked by the news."

He hesitated, then went on, "More to the point, because yesterday was yesterday and everyone was determined to make sure everything was perfect, the maids and footmen were up and down the stairs, constantly in and out of our rooms. Your bed wasn't made up until about four o'clock, and your maid, Aggie, was in the dressing room next door more or less from the moment she arrived in the early afternoon to when the staff were summoned to line up outside to greet you."

Mary blinked, then caught his gaze. "That's when it was done—when everyone was lined up outside. It was the one time anyone wishing to do such a thing could be absolutely certain there was no one inside the house—that they could get in and out without anyone seeing them."

He frowned. "But—"

Reaching out, Mary gripped his hand. "Have you checked to see if any stranger was seen in the neighborhood?"

His frown deepened. "No." Turning his hand, he closed his fingers around hers. "We've only just finished checking about the house, making sure everyone here was accounted for."

She nodded; a sense of sudden urgency gripped her as another explanation surfaced in her mind. Looking into Ryder's eyes, gripping his hand more tightly, she asked, "Could this possibly be what Barnaby warned us about—that the same miscreant who tried to have you killed in London wants you dead, and this is his next attempt?"

He looked into her eyes, but then, lips setting, shook his head. "If that were so, don't you think they would have put the adder in my bed?"

"Why? It was our wedding night. They would have assumed you'd sleep in—or at least first come to—*my* bed, wouldn't they?"

"That's"—he grimaced—"possible, I suppose . . ." Then he frowned and shook his head again. "No—that won't wash. If we'd followed tradition, then you would have already been in the bed when I arrived to claim my conjugal rights."

"Perhaps he put the snake right at the end of the bed and assumed my feet wouldn't reach—which, in fact, they wouldn't. Yours, on the other hand, would."

"I still think the notion's fanciful."

Mary didn't, but she wasn't going to argue, not until she'd had time to properly think. And plan.

Ryder glanced toward the door. "Forsythe will be here to summon us to dinner at any moment." Looking back at her, he met her eyes. "So now you know the situation in as much detail as I do, how do you suggest we react?" He tipped his head toward the door. "Toward the staff. They'll be watching and waiting to see."

She held his gaze, then said, "I've been trained to believe that loyal staff are our strongest allies. From what you've said, from all I've observed myself, I see no reason to suspect any of them, even of any degree of complicity."

He nodded, plainly relieved. "I concur."

"Well, then." She looked toward the double doors as footsteps sounded immediately beyond them. "I suggest that, at least for now, we pass this off as some sort of freak accident."

He hesitated, then inclined his head.

Rising, he drew her to her feet and together they turned to face Forsythe as he set the doors wide and, with regal assurance, informed them that dinner was served.

After allowing Ryder to seat her at the foot of the table, then retreat to his own grand carver at the opposite end, Mary made several comments, to which Ryder appropriately replied, establishing their considered view of the matter of the adder, with the unvoiced understanding that Forsythe and the two footmen would convey their words to the rest of the staff.

Once that was done, neither she nor Ryder referred to the matter again, although she was perfectly certain it remained in the forefront of their thoughts. Nevertheless, they strove to entertain each other with talk of myriad other subjects and succeeded well enough.

After dinner, they repaired to the library; Ryder didn't ask her preference, but she decided she approved of him guiding her into his den apparently without conscious thought. Settling into the armchair she'd selected as hers, she picked up her book and tried to escape into the history of gardening.

Ryder tidied his desk, then went to join her. Sinking into the armchair opposite hers, he emulated her, at least as far as opening a book and attempting to read. He suspected she succeeded better than he; he was still coming to grips with his day. With the events, and the emotions they'd provoked.

This morning . . . had certainly been eye-opening. He'd had no idea he could feel such panic, to the extent that he'd been unable to think and so had acted in ways his more rational side—once it had been able to break through—had immediately recognized as unwise.

Most especially if he wished to conceal just how deeply he felt about his wife.

He hadn't known he *could* care to the point of panicking to that degree. Now he knew, and that was almost more frightening.

As for her suggestion that the adder might have been intended for him . . . he couldn't make up his mind if he should be relieved that she might not have been the intended victim, or horrified that, as Barnaby had foreseen, she had nearly become an incidental casualty of some madman's attempt to kill him.

At the thought, his emotions threatened to geyser again; determinedly he pushed it away. No sense torturing himself with what-ifs and maybes. More pertinently, he had her reaction on learning the news to assimilate. To wonder at. He knew he hadn't gauged her temper wrongly; she should have come at him like a brigantine with all guns brought to bear. Instead, she'd behaved . . . much more reasonably than he had.

Either she was far more placid and mild-tempered than he'd thought, or . . . she'd understood why he'd behaved as he had.

Given he wasn't sure he fully understood that, the thought left him feeling more exposed, and more uncertain, than he'd ever felt in his life.

The clock on the mantelpiece ticked on, then she stifled a yawn, closed her book, and laid it aside. "I'm for bed." She rose.

He came to his feet as if pulled by strings. "I'll come up, too."

She arched a brow, a slow, sirenlike smile curving her lips. "I'd hoped you would. If you don't mind, in the circumstances I'd rather share your bed than slide into mine."

Quelling a shiver, he waved her to the door. "I wouldn't have it any other way."

Side by side they walked up the stairs and around to their rooms; he let her lead the way into the sitting room, then straight on into his room.

Following her in, he closed the door, then reached out, caught her hand, and drew her to him, into his arms as he stepped deeper into the room.

A quick glance confirmed that two lamps had been lit, the curtains drawn against the deepening night. The bed had been turned down, and even though he hadn't ordered it, he felt confident the room and the bed itself had been thoroughly searched. His staff had been deeply shocked and, indeed, affronted; they wouldn't allow a repetition of what, in their hearts, they saw as an attack on him and them, on the House of Cavanaugh that they served, and Mary was now, in their eyes as well as his, a vital and valued part of the family.

Fastening his hands about her waist, he looked down at her face, studied the mystery of her violet-blue eyes. He took a moment to savor the lithe strength of her, the supple steel beneath his hands, before saying, "Thank you for understanding and forgiving my atrocious behavior today." He faintly arched a brow. "You do forgive me, don't you?"

Mary smiled up at him. "Of course."

When he didn't seem convinced, she laughed. "I'm a Cynster—I know how men like you behave."

And why. She omitted those two words, but that *why* was what most interested her, what commanded her attention. It might very well be everything she sought, the bedrock on which they might build their future life.

Far from being disheartened by today, she now had solid hope.

And, as always, she wanted to press on. Smiling, unable to hide her expectation, she raised her hands to his nape. "Let's put today behind us and go on from here. From where we are now, in this room, in this moment."

She could see the wariness that crept into his eyes, that of a wild predator who scents not a trap but a hidden binding. But if she was right, the binding lay within him, and was one that, ultimately, he would willingly bear.

Now, however, she suspected he wouldn't see it—or if he did, would do his best to ignore it.

Sure enough, after that momentary hesitation, he nodded.

Agreed and bent his head as she stretched up.

Their lips met, touched, brushed, then fused. She had no idea why it was so different every time, yet thus it seemed. And this time was all about reassurance.

About exploring anew, connecting anew. Revisiting past experiences, but with a more acute understanding, one born of the day, of the emotions provoked and unleashed, then reined back.

Until now. Now, when they could be unchained and allowed to run, when they could be given free rein to infuse and direct, to seek expression through the physical act he and she both sought to harness, to bend to their wills.

As before, neither succeeded. That force that came to be when they joined, that together they seemed to create and bring to life, inevitably overcame them.

Overwhelmed them.

This time it transformed into a firestorm of passion, of heated touches, possessive caresses, his and hers, and a burning need to satisfy the hunger that had taken root and grown within them both, ravenous and demanding.

Commanding.

At the last they bent, bowed, and surrendered, and let the flames take them and fuse them, consume and reforge them, before flinging them, limp and ragged, into the cooling sea of satiation to drift to the distant shore . . . where bliss waited, heavy and soothing, and rolled over them.

Echoes of ecstasy still tingled through their flesh as, wrecked and helpless, they disengaged only to draw the covers up before slumping back into each other's arms.

Together, where they needed to be.

Chapter Thirteen

Life was good. Over the following days, Mary felt increasingly pleased, as she found the position of Ryder's marchioness not just to her liking but fitting her like a glove.

The incident of the adder remained unresolved, yet as several days passed and nothing further occurred to mar the moments as she settled into her new home, the incident largely faded from their collective consciousness.

Enough for Mary to decide that it was time Ryder took her for a ride about the estate. Seated beside him at the breakfast table, she made her request, before he could reply adding, "As I mentioned last night, I think we should invite all the estate families and workers to a picnic later in the summer, and before we do I'd like to get a better idea of the estate and all those who live on it." She glanced at his face. "And you are unarguably the best source of information on that subject." She arched her brows. "So when can we go?"

Accustomed by now to her manipulative ploys—her last question presumed he'd agreed—Ryder looked at her and considered her request, yet her picnic was precisely the sort of event he would like to see instituted, the sort of major estate annual function Raventhorne currently lacked and that he'd hoped his wife would attend to. And, after all, he would be with her. He nodded. "All right." Seeing triumph light her face, he raised his cup to hide his amused grin. "When are you free?"

She'd noticed his amusement and blinked her big blue eyes at him. "Whenever you are."

The challenge in the words ensured they met in her sitting room immediately they'd changed into their riding clothes. He wasn't surprised to discover her riding habit was in a shade of mid-blue, but the frogging over her breasts, the jacket's tight waist, and the draped and flowing skirt fixed his attention; he followed her out of the door and was halfway around the gallery before his gaze rose and he noticed the bobbing feather in the tiny cap anchored atop her curls.

She strode along at her usual forceful pace and the feather bobbed, and he found himself grinning foolishly.

He showed her the fastest way out of the house to the stables. He'd sent word ahead, and their horses were saddled and waiting; his raking gray hunter, Julius, and the nimble-footed bay mare she'd had sent from London were both shifting restlessly, eager for a run, their hooves clacking on the cobbles of the stable yard.

Ryder cast his eyes assessingly over the mare, then lifted Mary to her saddle. He watched as she settled and accepted the reins from the groom. "I take it she's from Demon's stables?"

"Yes." She looped the reins through her gloved fingers with casual expertise. "He provides all the family's horses."

"I've heard he's careful about matching horses to riders."

Clearly recognizing the question behind his statement, she smiled and nodded. "Indeed—he refuses to let us ride any beast we can't control." Leaning forward, she smoothed a palm over the mare's glossy neck. Arched a brow as she met his eyes. "So we all learn to control the animals we ride."

He held her gaze for a finite moment, trying to decide whether the double entendre was deliberate or not, then snorted and turned away.

Accepting the reins of his big gelding, he swung up to the saddle. The instant he'd settled, Mary flicked him a glance and led the way out of the stable yard.

He drew level in the forecourt, and with a nod directed her across a gentle grassy slope. "How are you with fences and hedges?"

She'd been assessing the gray's points; raising her gaze to Ryder's eyes, she arched a haughty brow. "Lucinda and I can take anything you and that brute can."

Having noted how steady, how assured in the saddle she rode, he suspected that was no idle boast, but rather than rise to her lure, he nodded and said, "Very well. We'll see."

She softly humphed but fluidly followed him as he led the way over the first fence and into the field beyond. They cantered through the fields and paddocks of the home farm, but both horses remained restless, wanting to run.

As they left the fields and turned toward the woods, taking a well-worn bridle path, he called, "Let's give them a chance to get rid of their fidgets—there's a long glade just ahead."

"Lovely! Lead on."

He did; without exchanging so much as a glance, the instant they saw the glade ahead both dropped their reins, let their horses stretch their legs, and side by side raced into a flat gallop.

Both horses flew. The gray was stronger, but the mare was sleek and had plenty of power. Ryder found himself grinning delightedly as neck and neck they thundered down the glade.

Leaning low over the mare's back, Mary laughed, the rush of their passage whipping away the sound. Her heart pounded in time with Lucinda's hooves as they stayed with Ryder's gray, matching horse and rider inch for inch; the moment filled her with glorious joy.

Lucinda's stride broke.

Mary was too experienced a rider not to react immediately; drawing evenly back on the reins, she straightened, adjusting her weight to help draw the horse from their headlong rush.

Beneath her, Lucinda slowed, but also shifted, half twisting, muscles bunching and twitching as if she wanted to buck. Alarmed—Lucinda never behaved badly—Mary clung to calm, knowing that was the surest way to keep Lucinda calm, too. Focusing fully on the mare, she reined the horse in, slowed her—and the instant she safely could, unlooped her leg from the pommel, drew her foot from the stirrup, and dropped to the grass.

Clutching the reins tightly, she waited until the mare came to a quivering halt, then, puzzled, careful not to startle the horse, she went to Lucinda's head and stroked her long nose. "What is it?"

Noticing her sudden absence, Ryder had wrestled his gray into a turn and now halted a few paces away. "What happened?"

Frowning, Mary shook her head. "I don't know." She gestured with one hand. "But just look at her. She's shivering. It's as if she's distressed."

Ryder cursed. Glancing over her shoulder, she saw him dismount. After tying his reins to a convenient branch, he strode across to her.

Hazel eyes hard, he surveyed the mare, circling to her other side.

Mary continued to stroke Lucinda's nose and croon; the mare seemed to be calming, but still her hide flickered and her breathing wasn't steady. "Can you see anything?"

"No." After a moment, Ryder asked, "Tell me exactly what happened—what made you halt?"

"She broke stride—I worried she might have put a hoof wrong, partly down a rabbit hole or something of the sort. It wasn't a big jerk, more like a hop, but . . ." Closing her eyes, she thought back. "I think it was one of her rear hooves that had just struck when it happened."

Ryder humphed. "Hold her steady. I'll check her legs and hooves."

He did, but there was nothing—no soreness, no damage, no stone in a hoof—to account for a sudden change in the mare's gait. And although she'd calmed considerably, the mare was still twitchy.

Standing back, hands on hips, beyond puzzled, he said, "Walk her. Let's see if we can pinpoint what's bothering her."

Mary dutifully walked the mare—who paced without any obvious restriction, long brown legs shifting fluidly, exactly as they should, each movement as assured as it should be . . . except that, after a few steps, the mare shifted and twisted and her hide rippled.

"It's nothing to do with her legs." Mystified, but now certain of that, he walked to the mare; halting opposite Mary, he met her eyes. "It seems to be something to do with your saddle."

Mary blinked, then looked at the saddle. "It's my usual saddle—the one I always use on her."

"Regardless, let's get it off her and see what that does."

He circled the mare. When he tugged on the buckle securing the girth, the horse snorted and sidestepped away.

"Oh." Mary drew the mare back. "I see what you mean. Perhaps something broke and is sticking out underneath."

She held the mare steady; more carefully, Ryder released the girth. With the saddle finally loose, he lifted it free—and they saw the problem.

"Gorse." Disgusted, Mary picked up the spiky branchlet, went to toss it away, but then stopped. Going up on her toes, she peered at the spot where the prickles had marred the bay's glossy hide. She frowned. "How the devil did it get there?"

Ryder looked and had to agree. "It couldn't have slipped in there—not that far under—while you were in the saddle."

"Or even before—the saddle fits too well." Mary smoothed her gloved hand over the spot, and the mare shivered, almost shuddering with relief. "Well, regardless, that seems to have been the problem."

"That part of the problem, perhaps." Ryder tried not to sound too grim. "But as to how it got there . . ."

Mary met his eyes. After a moment said, "It can't have been there when they saddled her—she wasn't bothered when I mounted her. But at the same time, I can't see how a piece of gorse that size could possibly have worked its way under the saddle while we were riding."

"Agreed." He followed the thought to the only conclusion. "It had to have been there when she was saddled, but somehow not pricking her." Turning to where he'd set down the saddle, he turned it over and crouched to examine it. Still holding the mare's reins, Mary came to the other side and leaned down.

"There." She pointed to a fold in the saddle's leather underside. "There's a tiny leaflet in the groove—see?"

He looked where she was pointing. Pulling off his gloves, he examined the fold . . . "It's a seam. It's been unpicked and opened to make a pocket of sorts."

Slowly raising his head, he looked at Mary.

She met his eyes, read his expression, and blew out a breath. "So—not an accident."

Rather than risk her riding the mare, Ryder took Mary up before him on Julius and they rode back to the stable yard with the mare, loosely saddled, following on lengthened reins.

Their unexpected reappearance in such fashion created an immediate stir; Filmore and two grooms—the same two who had saddled the horses earlier—were there to greet them as they clattered in.

"What happened?" Filmore asked.

"A slight problem." Ryder's clenched jaw and clipped tone gave that "slight" the lie. Swinging down to the cobbles, he lifted Mary down. Filmore was already examining the mare, trying to find something wrong. "It's the saddle," Ryder said. "Take it off and I'll show you."

The older groom, Benson, complied, setting the saddle on the mounting block. Ryder turned it over and showed Filmore and the others the opened seam in the underside. "There was gorse—a nice sturdy twig of it—tucked inside." He glanced at the grooms. "No fault of yours—I doubt anyone would have noticed it. But, of course, the further we rode, the gorse worked loose—especially when we galloped. Once it had, the mare started to react." He glanced at Mary, felt his jaw tighten. "Luckily, the marchioness is an experienced rider and halted the mare without accident."

All three men looked aghast.

As aghast as Ryder still felt; if Mary hadn't reacted as quickly as she had . . . and how many riders, especially female riders, were as well schooled as she was?

Then Filmore's expression abruptly cleared; a second later, his face darkened. "So *that's* what the bastards were about!" Registering Mary's presence, Filmore ducked his head. "Begging your pardon, m'lady."

"No, no." Mary waved aside the apology. "What bastards?"

Filmore glanced at Ryder. "The tack room door was open two mornings ago—and it shouldn't have been. I know I'd locked it the night before. But the lock wasn't broken, and when we checked, nothing had been stolen—nothing at all seemed even out of place." Disgusted, he waved at the saddle. "They—whoever they were—must have come to do this. To slit that seam and stuff in some gorse. It's an old trick for causing problems during horse races."

Well, quite clearly it wouldn't have been anyone here." Mary led the way into the library, heading for the chairs before the hearth. "There would have been no reason for any of the staff to have to break into the tack room at night. They could have slipped in during the day—there would be plenty of opportunities."

"I can't see that that's any comfort." Ryder followed her in and shut the door.

"Can't you?" Tossing her crop and gloves on a side table, she sat in what had become her chair. "Well, perhaps not comfort, but it does tell us that whoever Filmore's bastards are, they didn't want to risk being seen. So they're not from the household but are people the staff would recognize."

Ryder met her determinedly confident gaze, then sat in the chair opposite. "That—as you well know—is not the critical point. Who did it is one thing, but why is another, and a much more troubling question."

He wasn't entirely surprised to hear her sigh.

"I have no enemies that I know of, and no reason to believe anyone bears me sufficient ill will to wish me harm." She held up her hands. "Perhaps someone is trying to frighten me, but I can't imagine why."

"Frighten you." He managed to keep his tone even. "A bite from an adder at this time of year could well be fatal, especially for someone your size. A fall from the back of a spirited horse, especially at a gallop, could easily have broken your neck. If you imagine—"

"Actually." Capturing his gaze, she frowned, paused, but before he could resume his tirade, went on, "Has it occurred to you that one reason someone might stage such accidents is to disrupt, if not end, our marriage?"

The words sent a chill through him. It took a moment to rein in his instinctive reaction; once he had, he asked, his tone level, "What, exactly, do you mean?" He'd seen it, too, but hadn't wanted to think of it; now he needed to know what she thought, how she saw it.

"I mean that it's really too coincidental that first someone sends two thugs to kill you in London, and then when they fail, and you and I marry, someone then targets me—first with an adder in what should have been my wedding bed, and you have to admit when considered in that light that's something of a statement, and when that didn't work, then with a trick that should have seen me thrown from my horse the first time we went out riding—almost certainly alone." She held his gaze unwaveringly. "What are the odds that those three incidents aren't connected? And if they are, then who—what sort of person—might strike first at you, but then once you wed, strike instead at your wife?"

Several seconds passed in silence, then he fractionally inclined his head. "The most likely culprit would be some gentleman who imagined I had stolen his wife."

"We thought it was Fitzhugh, but as that seems not to be the case, who else might it be?"

He studied her eyes; unwavering self-certainty, an assurance of who she was, and also who he was, remained steady and strong in her cornflower-blue gaze. She wasn't rattled; she was focused and, if he judged correctly, just a tad irritated. Not with him but with whoever had had the temerity to disturb her definition of how their life should be.

Be that as it may, he was far beyond disturbed; it was taking fully half his mind to hold back, lock down the clawing need to savage whoever had dared attempt to harm her, to take her from him. And most of the rest of his mental capacity was absorbed with formulating plans to ensure beyond all possibility that she remained safe. That she remained with him; he couldn't view the prospect of losing her with any degree of calm.

With what faculties he could spare, he racked his brain for the answer to her question. It was the right question, and there ought to be an answer, but . . . finally, he shook his head. "I honestly don't know. I accept that such a man is most likely behind the incidents, but I don't know—can't guess—who he might be."

She wrinkled her nose. "Well, you didn't know about Fitzhugh, either—that he might have had cause to imagine you'd stolen his wife. It's possible there's some other gentleman who, like Fitzhugh, has been fed a tale by his wife, perhaps to conceal a dalliance with some other rake."

After a moment, he confessed, "I'm starting to feel that I'm reaping the ill rewards of my previous life—and you've been involved because of me."

She didn't smile too easily and brush aside his statement; instead, she held his gaze for a long moment—long enough to make him wonder just how much of his mind she could read—then she smiled wryly in agreement, rose, and, before he could join her on her feet, with a swish of her heavy skirts, she dropped into his lap.

Placing a hand on his cheek, she angled his face to hers, met his eyes, and simply said, "Don't worry. Together, we can overcome anything." Holding his gaze, she confidently stated, "Together, we'll work this out."

Y ou can't leave the house." Halting beside her chair half an hour later, he shut his lips and braced for her arguments.

Mary looked up at him, then arched her brows and looked back at her book. "I don't want to go out at the moment."

When he continued to stare down at her—not daring to believe—she glanced briefly up at him. "I told you we'd work this out."

I thought you'd agreed not to go outside?" Sudden panic churned in his gut.

"That was yesterday. Today—well, there's no need to go far from the house. Just the rose garden will do." Mary looped her arm in his. "You can come to make sure I'm safe. The walk will do you good—you're far too tense."

H e was starting to believe that Fate had, indeed, arranged their match. Mary wasn't just more than he'd expected, she was more than he deserved.

Together, we'll work this out. He'd assumed she'd meant

that they'd pool their mental resources in investigating who
was behind the attacks, not that they would, together, work
on the ways, the precautions, the plans, all the elements of
her security necessary to allow him to cope with all he felt.

So he could sleep alongside her and not fear the morning.

He wasn't about to—had no spare space in his mind
to—examine what he felt, if it was rational or even logical,
much less define what the so powerful, so dominant, and so
utterly demanding emotion that had taken root in his heart
and guts actually was, not while she was under any degree
of threat.

And to his everlasting gratitude she understood, at least
enough to comprehend that his conversion to martinet, to
dictator and tyrant, wasn't something he could control,
wasn't the way he actually wished to act but was instead the
result of something he was quite simply helpless to coun-
teract.

Given his temper and personality, and hers, if she hadn't
understood . . . in the days that followed their ill-fated ride,
he constantly gave thanks that she could.

If anyone had told him that he would, one day, be grateful
that his wife could see into his soul, he would have laughed
himself into a stupor.

He wasn't laughing on the morning she'd determined as
the time for her to once again venture beyond the grounds.

Since the disaster of that first ride, she'd remained within
the protective cordon he, with the grimly determined assistance of the staff, had fashioned. For the first day, she'd
remained inside the house; yesterday, she'd convinced him
to walk with her in the gardens. Later, during luncheon,
she'd broached the subject of riding again, but when he'd
voiced his continuing antipathy to allowing her back in her
saddle, she'd regarded him shrewdly, then had nodded and
acquiesced—and insisted he allow her to drive herself in the
gig on a visit to the nearby village.

Having earlier informed her that the men he'd sent to scour

the neighborhood for any sighting of strangers had reported that none had been seen, and more, that none were lingering in the vicinity, he'd lost the ability to cite lurking would-be villains as a threat. Not that that had stopped him from arguing, vehemently, but for once she wouldn't be moved—and given she had thus far been so accommodating . . .

Unable to assemble sufficient ammunition to quash her notion outright, he'd fallen back on the tactic of agreeing *subject to* her demonstrating her expertise with the reins sufficient to pass his standards.

She'd smiled and agreed.

How could he have known she had at some point inveigled Simon to teach her to drive?

After she'd tooled the gig about the drive with every evidence of not just capability but enjoyment, he hadn't been able to deny her the outing.

So that morning, after they'd breakfasted and she'd finished her daily meeting with Mrs. Pritchard, they walked out to the forecourt where the gig stood waiting, a well-conditioned roan, a nice, solid stepper with an exceedingly even temper, between the shafts.

The gig was small, light; it couldn't carry them both, and given his weight, he wouldn't have used it himself, even alone. He helped Mary up to the seat, then turned to where Benson held Julius's reins. Swinging up to the saddle, he picked up the reins, then looked at Mary—met her brilliant smile.

She pointed with her whip. "Onward."

In more ways than one. Gritting his teeth, he set Julius to trotting along the verge, keeping pace with the gig as Mary tooled it sedately out along the back drive.

The village of Axford lay less than two miles distant and was more directly reached via the rear drive and the country lane beyond. While Ryder had a curricle and a phaeton in the stables, either of which would have served for him to drive her to the village, neither was well suited to the country lanes, and he would have had to handle the ribbons—and trying to protect a female while managing a pair of highly strung horses was, in his estimation, a less favorable arrangement than him mounted on Julius, acting as guard, a pistol in his saddle holster and a short sword in a saddle scabbard.

In addition, from Julius's back he could see much further.

His own pastures stretched for some way, the well-graded drive gently wending through them.

Mary held the roan to a steady, entirely unexciting pace. At least she was out in the fresh air, and despite his heightened watchfulness and the tension that inevitably still gripped him, Ryder was with her, riding alongside—and the day was, in her eyes, fine and destined to improve.

She was, she felt, very successfully making lemons into lemonade. She was pleased if not delighted with the outcome of her plan, the results thus far of her adherence to Minerva's edict on how to deal with an overly protective nobleman. Indeed, she rather thought she could now write her own advice on how to tame such a nobleman—agree with him, work with him, to find solutions to his problems . . . and gently turn the applecart in a more amenable direction.

Yesterday she'd written to Minerva to thank her sincerely for her long-ago advice and tell her that it was bearing fruit even as she wrote. Ryder might still be wary—she occasionally glimpsed that in his hazel eyes—but he was increasingly learning to ask for her views, to incorporate or defer to her suggestions, her version of how they might best get along together.

A little way ahead, a lane ran across the end of the drive. Ryder angled Julius closer to the gig. "I'll jump the hedge over there"—with a nod he indicated a spot a little way along the lane—"and wait for you."

"All right." With a breezy smile, she twirled her whip in salute.

As Mary slowed even more for the turn, Ryder swung

Julius for the hedge, tapped his heels to the gray's flanks, and gloried in the surge of power as the big gelding accelerated across the open ground, then soared, clearing the hedge with ease to come down in the lane beyond.

Reining Julius in, wheeling, Ryder checked the lane—the real reason he'd come ahead. There was no one in sight; relaxing, he drew Julius to a restless halt and looked back along the lane to the opening of the drive.

Just as the roan turned neatly out into the lane, Ryder noticed some dark twiglike things scattered across the surface of the lane between him and the gig. "What the devil?"

His disbelieving brain told him what the things were just as Mary saw them, too, and reacted. She hauled on the reins, not just to stop the roan but to turn the horse aside—toward the ditch. The roan fought the sudden redirection, but Mary insisted and the horse responded . . . but not fast enough; the roan stepped on one of the objects—and screamed.

The horse half reared, kicking out with one foreleg, sending the gig wildly slewing.

Dropping the reins, Mary leapt from the gig.

The roan staggered and went down, half rolling, half sliding into the ditch; dragged behind, the gig overturned, smashing as it tipped into the ditch, too.

Ryder was already galloping madly back, cursing, panicking.

Reining Julius in before he hit the wide swath of caltrops, too, Ryder flung himself from the saddle. As he raced the last few yards, his heart in his throat, his eyes locked on Mary lying facedown on the far bank of the ditch, he saw her move. Then she pushed back on her arms, blew her hair—tumbling loose—from her face, and started to get up.

Leaping the ditch, he raced past the roan—now lying mostly in the ditch with one foreleg extended, but no longer in such panic; jumping over the smashed gig, Ryder stooped, swooped, and wrapped Mary in his arms, held her tightly to him.

For a long moment, he stood with his face buried in her curls, breathing in the scent of her, feeling her body lithe and warm against him. He was shaking, inside at least; he thought she was, too.

Eventually freeing a hand, she stroked the side of his face. "I'm all right." There was none of her usual brightness in her tone.

Barely daring to believe she'd escaped unharmed, he raised his head and eased his hold enough to look into her face; her expression was sober but showed no hint of pain. "Nothing hurt at all—no bruises or sprains?"

"No—that's why I jumped. I could see the grass was thick over here, and once the horse reared, I knew I wouldn't be able to manage well enough to do anything more."

Quick thinking; her wits and her abilities had saved her again.

Looking at the destruction of the gig, she grimaced and patted his arm. "We have to see to the horse."

They approached the roan with due caution, but the caltrop embedded in its left front hoof appeared to be the only damage. Once Ryder removed that, then freed the horse from the wreckage of the gig, between them they urged the roan back on his feet, then carefully checked him over, but other than favoring his wounded hoof, the horse seemed otherwise unharmed.

"If you hadn't had the sense to pull to the side, ditch or no, it would have been much worse." Handing the reins to Mary, Ryder said, "Hold him while I get rid of those damned things."

Absentmindedly stroking the roan's nose, Mary watched as Ryder reached into the wreckage of the gig, retrieved her empty basket, and proceeded to fill it with the strange twisted metal spikes that had been strewn in a wide band across the lane.

After gathering them all, Ryder caught Julius's reins and walked back to her. Halting before her, he lifted one of the metal things from the basket, turning it in his fingers so they both could see. It was about the size of his fist, composed of three long nails twisted about each other.

Mary frowned. "What is it?"

"It's a caltrop. They were invented to disrupt cavalry charges. This one's not cavalry-grade—it's a crude fashioning, but effective nevertheless." Ryder set it on his palm. "It's constructed so it sits on the heads, so the spikes stick up."

Mary shook her head. "How horrible. Just think of the pain caused to the poor horses."

"Hmm." Ryder thought more of the pain that might have been caused to her. He glanced at the broken gig, the wooden struts smashed, one wheel caved in, the seat in two pieces, then he raised his gaze to Mary's eyes. "Let's turn the roan into the nearest field inside the grounds, then we'll ride back on Julius."

She nodded. "Filmore's going to have a fit when he sees us riding back in, both on Julius again."

Filmore wasn't the only one about to have a fit, but his first concern was to get her back within the safety of the abbey.

Later that night, when they lay side by side and watched moonbeams drift across the ceiling of his room, still floating on the flushed tide of aftermath, he murmured, "Perhaps we should go back to London."

"No." Mary's answer was immediate. "I am not letting some blackguard force me out of my new home."

She lay wrapped in his arms. He tightened them slightly. "I was thinking more in terms of protecting you."

"I can't see how . . ." A second passed, then she amended, "Well yes, I can, but if you're entertaining the notion of leaving me in London in the care of my family, then coming back here alone to discover who's behind this, possibly by tempting them to make another attempt on your life . . ."

Pausing, she drew in a breath, then concluded, "Put simply, you will need to think again."

Turning in his arms, through the shadows Mary studied his face; from the tension in the big body pressed against hers, she knew she'd guessed his intentions aright. "I'm not quitting your side. We're married, and in case you've forgotten, I vowed 'to have and to hold from this day forward, for better, for worse, for richer for poorer, in sickness and in health, to love and to cherish until death do us part.' There's nothing in that about leaving you to face unknown foes alone."

Ryder heard the belligerence in her tone. "I haven't forgotten." He noticed she'd omitted the "obey" from her vows, but . . . he sighed. Admitted, "Keeping you safe is . . . critically important to me."

She nodded. "And in the exact same way, keeping you hale and whole is vital to me. So we'll simply have to accept that neither of us is going to back away from this—in fact, we should probably view it as a challenge."

"A challenge." His instincts flickered warily, but he had to ask, "How so?"

"Well, once we've learned to manage our way through this, we'll know how to manage through anything that might come."

Given what he was going through . . . she might well be right. The situation was starting to feel like a baptism by fire.

When he said nothing, she wriggled higher to look into his face, to in the poor light study his eyes. "Trust me," she said. "I'm right. You'll see. We'll come through this stronger—more sure of ourselves together. I'm viewing this as a learning experience—and if you stop to think, you'll realize you're inclined to use it in the same way."

He'd already realized that; as usual, she held the positive up like temptation. There was no real reply he wished to make, so he grunted, drew her down into his arms, and planted a kiss on her curls. "We'll see."

After due discussion, Mary agreed to remain within the estate grounds over the following days.

The first two were enlivened by a succession of bride-visits from the surrounding gentry; the ladies had held off for the customary seven days, but now that Mary and Ryder had lived at the abbey as man and wife for a full week, the carriages rolled up the drive and the ladies, and some of their husbands, too, called to make her acquaintance.

Caught up in the whirl of navigating the shoals of county allegiances and social rank, less dangerous than those among the haut ton, perhaps, but nevertheless present, Mary almost forgot the incidents that had marred her first week as Ryder's wife. The visits from their neighbors gave her and Ryder plenty to talk about, to discuss, and in her case to probe and learn; the days, evenings, and nights passed in exactly the sort of pleasant whirl she considered their due.

The following morning saw the last of what Ryder expected in the way of bride-visits, a visitation from Lady Hamberly; the nearest representative of the grande dame set, her ladyship stayed for just over half an hour and appeared to approve of all she saw.

Standing at Ryder's side on the front porch as they waved her ladyship away, Mary murmured, "What will you wager she spends the entire afternoon writing missives to her peers around the country?"

"That," Ryder said, casting her a jaundiced look as they turned inside, "is no wager at all—it's a sure thing."

Laughing, Mary looped her arm in his and they headed back to the library.

As the possessor of a massive estate and also a significant fortune, Ryder had a near endless stream of correspondence to deal with; Mary sat in the chair and read her book, and in between, when he paused to check on her—to give her at least a little of his time—she grasped the chance to question him about his various smaller estates scattered the length and breadth of the land.

Later in the afternoon, deciding it was time to establish a place of her own, somewhere comfortable where she could retire when he was out or she didn't feel like sitting in the library, she went on a solo tour of the house, going into the various reception rooms on the ground floor, sitting in this chair and that, but none felt right.

In the end, she tried her sitting room upstairs—and discovered that suited her perfectly. There was something about the way the light flooded in from the windows flanking the writing desk. An armchair sat in the corner to the left of the writing desk and simply beckoned.

Sinking into the chair, she looked back down the room; she hadn't immediately chosen this room because it was so distant from the rest of the reception rooms, yet it felt so uniquely hers, thanks in large part to Ryder's decorating. He'd envisaged the place as a sort of temple for her, and it felt like she belonged.

Smiling, she relaxed; turning her head, she admired the views, then wondered if she should go downstairs and retrieve her book.

She was debating doing so when her eye fell on her wicker embroidery box. She hadn't done any embroidering for some time, but Aggie had left the box alongside the armchair, which, indeed, offered the best light for the purpose. Smiling, deciding that it probably was time she got back to the cushion cover she'd started, she leaned down, flipped open the lid, and reached in—

A scorpion skittered about, turning toward her hand, tail arching high.

On a scream, she pulled back her hand just as the scorpion struck.

Leaping to her feet, with the toe of her shoe she flipped the lid of the box closed.

Her heart in her throat, she stared at the box, unable—

unwilling—to shift her gaze in case the scorpion might somehow push the lid up and escape.

Footsteps thundered down the corridor, then the door crashed open and Ryder was there, wrapping her protectively in his arms, one hand cradling her head. "What is it?" He scanned the room as two footmen, followed by Forsythe, all looking alarmed and pugnacious, rushed into the room. "Where?"

Still shaking, Mary pulled out of Ryder's hold enough to point at her embroidery box. "Scorpion. In there."

"Scorpion?" Not scorn but puzzlement.

Mary nodded, gulped, then said, "I'm not frightened of rodents, but I hate creepy crawlies, and there's definitely a scorpion in there, a red one. It was on top of everything and it tried to sting me."

Ryder cursed; jaw clenching, he set Mary gently aside, then crossed to the box, bent, and, clamping the lid shut, picked it up.

"Be careful." Despite her fear, Mary hovered. "It's already aroused and you don't have gloves on."

Ryder didn't reply. He carried the box to the door, then, with Mary hurrying alongside and the footmen and Forsythe following, he marched through the house, down the stairs, and, after waiting for Forsythe to open the front door, out onto the porch. There, he bent and set down the box. He glanced at Mary. "Stay well back."

She nodded uncertainly but, for once obedient, hovered in the open doorway. Forsythe obligingly stationed himself in front of her, a little to one side so she could view the proceedings.

Satisfied, Ryder glanced up at the footmen, who had come to stand to either side of him. "Ready?"

When both grimly nodded, he used the toe of his boot to flip the lid of the box open. Sure enough, a scorpion, a remarkably brightly colored specimen, skittered on top of the folded linens inside. When the scorpion, somewhat wisely, showed no inclination to climb out, Ryder circled to the other side of the box, bent, and, grasping the rear side and bottom of the box, partially upended it, shaking it as he did.

Several pieces of embroidery fell out—along with the scorpion. Clicking and skittering, the beast shot out to Ryder's right.

He crushed it under his boot.

Leaving the footmen to examine the remains—they'd never seen a scorpion before—he looked into the box. No further sounds came from it; carefully lifting aside each piece of cloth, each skein of silk, he searched it thoroughly. Finding nothing, he bent, picked up the two pieces of embroidery that had fallen out, shook them vigorously, then tucked them back in the box. Finally closing the box, he carried it to Mary and handed it to her. "All clear."

She accepted the box, nodded. "Thank you." She looked up, and he could still see the shock in her face.

He put an arm around her shoulders, tucked her against him. "Forsythe?"

"Aye, my lord—we'll do a sweep of the room and all your apartments. In fact, I rather think we'll do the whole wing."

Ryder nodded. "Do." He turned Mary, unresisting, inside. "Come and sit with me in the library."

Some brandy would do them both good.

Half an hour later, Mary had progressed from shock to outright anger. "This has got to stop!"

"I couldn't agree more." Sprawled in the armchair opposite hers, Ryder sipped his second glass of brandy. The first he'd downed in a single gulp; Mary was still nursing hers.

After a moment, she said, "I've never seen a scorpion before, only in books."

"I have." He paused, then added, "I've a friend whose house lies outside Rye. He sees them occasionally, but they're quite different—larger and dark brown. They're not poisonous, although I've heard the sting is painful."

"Hmm. That one was red."

"I noticed."

After a long moment, Mary drew in a breath, then said, "I've been wondering if we've leapt to the wrong conclusion."

Ryder's gaze shifted to fix on her. "How so?"

"We assumed that whoever tried to have you killed in London is also behind these incidents aimed at me, but when you look at what's happened here—an adder in my bed, gorse under my saddle, caltrops in the road when I went out driving, and now the scorpion—while each of those incidents might have been fatal, the chances of them being so aren't all that high." She met his gaze. "Against that, getting stabbed almost in your heart is far more likely to be lethal."

He frowned. After a moment said, "I can't argue, but I'm not sure I follow where you're leading."

"What if the incidents here weren't intended to do me harm so much as send me scurrying off, and potentially disrupting our marriage?"

His frown darkened. "That's possible, I suppose."

"It does bear considering, and also casts the incidents here in a somewhat less fraught light."

Ryder humphed.

Mary watched him sip his brandy and hoped he was imbibing her obliquely reassuring words as completely. The principal reason for her increasing ire at whoever was behind the recent incidents was that the outcome of said incidents was feeding and stoking and insistently escalating Ryder's protectiveness. He'd several times verged on the dictatorial and was becoming less and less pliable with every successive incident—and really, who could blame him?

Said incidents were prodding at a spot that—if all was as she hoped—would be terribly sensitive.

In fact, that he was reacting as he was was proof that what

she'd hoped from the first would evolve between them was developing exactly as she wished. Yet she knew from experience with the males in her family just how entrenched such overprotective feelings in men like him could grow to be, and he was, indeed, a classic example of that type of male.

"I suggest," she said before he could suggest something else, "that I remain within the house or the immediate grounds for the next few days, and with everyone on alert, let's see what comes. With luck, we might catch whoever it is next time they try to creep inside."

Ryder grunted, but he didn't disagree, and she was content enough with that.

"Meanwhile," she continued, "perhaps we can consult with Barnaby and Penelope, and also widen our search for someone in the ton who might wish you ill."

"Hmm." Ryder drained his glass, then rose. "I'll draft a letter to Adair now." He glanced down at her. "I trust you'll want to add a note to Penelope?"

She nodded. "Yes—you write, and I'll add it at the end." After she'd read what he'd written.

While he crossed to the desk, she viewed her current strategy; keeping them both busy doing whatever they could to identify whoever was behind the spate of attacks while simultaneously doing everything she could to avoid further incidents seemed indubitably wise.

He and she had come so far; she was not of a mind to allow some villain to pull apart all they'd achieved.

So she's still alive?"

"Yes. Caught sight of her this morning strolling on the terrace."

"This isn't good enough. You told me you could manage it."

"I can, easily enough, but you insisted it had to look like an accident. There's only so many ways that can possibly be done, and in every case—as she and his lordship have proved—there's always a chance death won't be the result."

"Damn him! He's always had the devil's own luck, and now she, it seems, is just as favored."

"That may be so, but if you want my advice, if you truly want them removed, you're going to have to allow us to try something more direct and definite. Something certain of working, once and for all."

A long silence ensued, then, "What do you have in mind?"

Chapter Fourteen

A week passed in untrammeled peace.

"Finally." Strolling into the gallery on the way to the drawing room prior to dinner, Mary paused to draw in a deep breath, then let it out on a happy sigh. She listened; letting her senses expand, she detected the expected scurrying of footmen in the dining room and Forsythe's majestic tread. Everything seemed calm, nothing out of place.

Ryder would already be waiting in the drawing room; they'd fallen into the habit of starting the exchange of their day's activities there, then continuing through dinner, before retiring to the library, where she would read and he would finish any outstanding business or correspondence before joining her, either in reading or heading up the stairs to his bed.

Expectation welling, she started down the stairs.

They'd been at the abbey for nearly three weeks and at last the regulated serenity she considered the norm for any well-run noble house had been established and now prevailed. Running such a household was all but second nature to her; she'd been bred to fill such a position, and it accorded well with her personality. She liked to run things and have them run well—and the abbey household was hers.

Its master was hers, too, although in a significantly different sense.

Initially, she'd viewed the attacks on her as an unmitigated negative, but over the last fortnight her attitude had changed. She now considered not the attacks but the demands they had forced on her and Ryder to quite possibly have been the making of them as a couple.

She couldn't imagine any situation that could have so rapidly compelled them to deal with the most fraught aspects of love. The nuances and outcomes of his feelings for her, and hers for him.

Over the last weeks, she'd learned a lot, and not all of it about him.

He'd been learning, too, and his deeper understanding now colored every interaction between them.

Stepping off the last stair, lips curving, she headed for the drawing room. Regally inclining her head to the footman who opened the door, she sailed through—and saw Ryder waiting as he usually was, one foot propped on the brass hearth surround, one arm resting on the mantelpiece.

Even in the country, he was always impeccably dressed; she smiled at the confirmation of her mental image of him as a lion of the ton. He'd been riding about the estate over the past days, and strands in his hair had lightened, brightened, the tawny contrast more pronounced; the sight still made her palms itch even though she now knew very well what his mane felt like. Heaven knew she'd clutched it often enough.

He'd smiled at the sight of her; still smiling, he straightened as she neared.

There was a light in his eyes, a softening in the sharp hazel as they met hers that touched her in ways that had nothing to do with the sensual, and everything to do with the connection they now shared. The villain behind the attacks had hurried them down the path, but they'd been willing and, to her mind, were almost there.

Reaching for her hand, Ryder carried it to his lips and brushed a light kiss to the backs of her fingers. Smiling into her eyes, he retained her hand, his fingers idly stroking hers. "Did Mrs. Hubert bore you with talk of the church bazaar?"

"Yes, and no. She's very opinionated, but then so am I." Mary smiled back, a touch more intently. "But as she's accustomed to being in charge, I decided that I would simply be the figurehead, which is really all she wanted. I have enough on my plate with the household here, and I do want to push ahead with my idea for an estate picnic."

Standing hand in hand, they discussed that prospect for the few minutes before Forsythe appeared to summon them to dine.

As she allowed Ryder to lead her into the family dining room and seat her, Mary registered that all the staff, too, seemed to be smiling more these days.

The meal passed in their customary vein—an exchange of the wider issues they'd encountered through the day. Today it was gypsies, and the locals' distrust of the travelers who had set up on Axford common, then they embarked on a political discussion sparked by a controversy each had noted in that day's news sheets. As always, the back-and-forth exchanges were entertaining, stimulating. Without the slightest effort, they filled the time and took the last subject with them to the library.

Walking alongside Mary and listening to her opinion on the latest development in gas lighting, Ryder was once again amazed—by himself, by her; never had he imagined interacting with his wife in such a way. Prior to deciding on Mary, he hadn't had any clear view of that female, but if he'd stopped to think . . . he'd never have dreamt of a lady with whom he discussed such matters, let alone one whose opinions he'd learned to seriously consider, and to which he now gave weight. More weight than those of anyone else he knew.

They entered the library on the conclusion of her argument.

"I agree." He followed her to her chair, paused while she sat, then when she looked up at him, brows rising, he nodded. "We should bear it in mind when next the question arises—most likely with the London house."

She smiled and reached for her book. He trailed his fingertips lightly across her shoulder and continued to his desk.

He still had several letters to deal with, but they were mundane matters requiring little thought.

While he wrote, his mind, largely disengaged, drifted to more appealing vistas. Such as Mary and him, and the connection—the true partnership—evolving between them.

He didn't know how it had happened—hadn't even known that it could—but somehow, through the events that had brought them together, through the dramas and demands of the last weeks, they'd reached for and found a togetherness, a direct, deeply personal link that connected them each to the other. A connection that could manifest in a look, a private smile, a kiss brushed over her fingers, or the pressure of his hand about hers. In the trailing of his fingertips over her shoulder.

The other side of that link showed in her openness, in the eagerness for his company she allowed to shine so clearly, in the softer light in her cornflower-blue eyes whenever she looked at him.

He hadn't expected any of it. He hadn't anticipated any emotional connection because he hadn't known he possessed the potential for such feelings. Now he knew—now she'd proved it beyond doubt—he . . . wanted it.

More, his instincts urged him to seize it, to secure it and the promise it held. In that connection, through it, lay the surest, most certain route to all he'd ever wanted—of his marriage, of his life.

He'd always listened to his instincts, and in this, his instincts knew. They were unshakably, unwaveringly sure.

They'd fixed on Mary from the start and were now even more fixated, more devoted and possessively locked on her. She was the foundation stone for his future; for him, all that was to come would be built around her.

Which made the letter he'd received from Barnaby Adair unsettling.

He hadn't shown it to Mary; the letter had been written for him alone, Barnaby's words had made that plain. Barnaby had argued that, despite the apparent cessation of attacks on Mary, despite the possibility that those incidents had never been intended as anything more than nasty attempts to scare her and disrupt their marriage, in Barnaby's and Stokes's experienced view the less favorable possibility that the attacks on them both were all part of one strategy remained. And if that were so, then the chances were good the perpetrator wouldn't stop, although he might well pause to regroup and redeploy.

Stay on guard. That had been Barnaby and Stokes's warning, clearly spelled out in words impossible to misconstrue.

Further compounding the uncertainties, despite considerable investigation by all the Cynsters, as well as those gentlemen connected by marriage like Jeremy Carling, Breckenridge, Meredith, and the others, all of whom Ryder knew, no one had been able to unearth any clue as to any gentleman wanting him dead.

Ryder's own investigation into who had hired the two thugs he'd killed in the alley had returned no further result; that trail was now beyond cold.

As Barnaby had stated in his closing remark, that left them facing an unknown threat, one that could strike from any direction at any time.

Not a situation designed to soothe his inner beast, but . . . finishing the last of his letters, he glanced down the room at Mary's bent head, and—again—gave thanks for her understanding, and her intelligence. She continued to accept the need to remain within the house and the surrounding gardens without so much as a quibble, much less a complaint.

Scrawling his title across the corner of the envelopes, he tossed them on a salver for Forsythe to collect and dispatch, then rose and headed for his wife.

She looked up as he neared.

He smiled and held out his hands. Laying aside her book, she put her hands in his and allowed him to draw her to her feet.

Still holding her hands, he looked down at her. "Barnaby sends his regards—and warns that we should remain on guard."

She tipped her head, studying his eyes, his face. "Luckily, at the moment, there's no reason I need to venture further afield."

"You're content to remain within the house and grounds?"

She nodded. "For the moment." Sliding her hands from his and taking his arm, she turned to the door. "Anyone who wishes to consult with me can come and visit me here. And I've discovered that peace becomes me."

He chuckled and let her steer him out of the room, through the front hall, and up the stairs to their rooms, but the suggestion of uncertainty, that for today they had this, but that tomorrow it might be threatened, lingered.

He followed her into what used to be his bedroom but now showed signs of her occupation—a silk robe neatly laid over a chair, a brush on the lower of the tallboys, along with a shallow dish she used to set her pins and jewelry in. Collier and Aggie had come to some sort of agreement and now seemed to share territorial rights, over this room, at least.

With a happy little sigh, Mary went straight to the tallboy and started unpinning her hair.

Ryder pulled the pin from his cravat and started unraveling it. His cravat was the one item of his clothing Mary had most difficulty divesting him of; the intricate knots he favored defeated her and had on occasion sent her into fits of frustrated impatience, much to his amusement.

Tonight, however, he wasn't in the mood to test her temper. He was impatient and eager enough on his own.

He wasn't sure why, but the compulsive thud was already there, a slow, steady pounding through his veins. An outcome of that lingering uncertainty, perhaps. He didn't question it but followed her across the room; his cravat finally loose, he reached for her.

Her hair tumbling down about her face and shoulders, Mary turned into his arms; hands splaying over his chest, fingers instinctively lightly gripping, she looked into his face and arched her brows. Sometimes they played games, but most often they opted for the direct and dramatic, their needs simple and complementary. Tonight . . . in the hardness of his hazel eyes, from the steely tension in the arm about her waist, she sensed there was something more he wanted, something he thought of to suggest, but, after an instant's hesitation, he rejected all words and lowered his head, and she offered up her lips, his to claim.

He claimed them, and more. From that first touch of his lips, the first commanding kiss, she knew that tonight would be no simple repetition of anything that had gone before. Of anything they'd done before.

After his initial conquering foray, he supped and enticed, and she followed, into a long-drawn exchange of heated delight, of assured and unhurried savoring, not he of her or her of him but of them both relishing the moment, the confident presaging of the deeper, more enthralling intimacy to come.

From there, the engagement spun out; for once he openly brought to bear all his vaunted expertise and laid it at the feet of not her but what had grown between them. He deployed his undeniable prowess in its name, in its service.

She knew; she could taste that intent in his kiss, reveled in the passionate devotion that infused not just the melding of their mouths but every touch, every caress, every pressure.

Their clothes fell, shed by hands now well-accustomed to the ritual, to the worship of flesh and naked skin as it was bared to the night air, to the gilding of moonlight.

To the touch of a lover's hands.

To the caress of fingertips that, as the primitive beat rose, trembled.

He drew her fully against him, her delicate frame and silken skin flush against his powerfully muscled, hair-dusted body, and they paused, both caught in the sensual succulence of the instant, enraptured.

The feel of him all around her, his heat, the hardness of his flesh, the tension investing his heavy muscles, the hot, rigid column pressed against her belly, all impinged and drove her on.

Her hands sweeping up over his shoulders, she sank her fingers into his hair and deepened the kiss even further.

Wantonly met his challenge and, shifting sinuously against him, issued her own.

She'd been right; there was more for them both in this deeper engagement as blindly they breached some level beyond and intensity abruptly flared, their senses expanding dizzyingly until the physical merged with passion, with feeling and driving need, was subsumed by that all-consuming desire and became a conduit, a means of pure expression—of honest, unscreened, irrefutable communication.

Breaking the kiss, he swept her up in his arms and carried her to the bed.

As he laid her down, then joined her, she opened her senses to everything he said. Not in words but with his actions, both the caresses he swept over her quivering flesh, with the web of delight he wove to snare her awareness and hold it captive to the pleasure, the joy, the passion—and the overwhelming, near suffocating eruption of their desire.

She felt it as a pressure in her chest, a swelling, welling, geysering need to give, to open her heart and share, to let that unrelenting build of emotion out. To give it to him, share it with him. Openly.

To let it free.

Her hands tangling in the soft mane of his hair, as she bucked and writhed as his tongue licked and probed and his lips caressed, lightly tugged, and he tasted, eyes closed, breathing ragged, she searched for the way.

He raised his head a heartbeat from the point where it would have been too late, and rose over her.

And she reached for him. Raked her hands down his chest, and felt him shudder.

She found him, rigid and burning, and guided him to her entrance.

He pressed in, then, on a harsh groan, thrust fully home.

He hung over her, head hanging, the muscles in his braced arms quivering with the strain of control, of holding still as she adjusted to the deep penetration, to the solid intrusion, the glorious filling.

Even in extremis, her lips curved.

After the last weeks, she no longer needed that moment but nevertheless gloried in it. Took it and, tonight, used it to reach up, draw his head down to hers, meet his lips with hers, arch her body to his, and join with him.

Wholly and completely and with no reservation.

None.

No screen, no holding back.

She felt her heart open, let it happen, didn't try to hold anything back. She'd already given him her hand, pledged her future, surrendered her body; now she gave him the last tiny part of her she hadn't yet bestowed, the small careful piece of her heart she'd held back in case he never fully gave to her.

It was time. She sensed that in every driving thrust, in every synchronous beat of their thundering hearts. Time to risk giving her all. Time to believe in all they could be, to commit herself wholly, irrevocably, in her entirety to that, to being that, to becoming that, to sharing it all with him.

Ryder was long past thinking. Feeling had taken over and now drove him relentlessly, mercilessly on, whipping him toward a surrender he'd never thought to make, to an acknowledgment, a bending of the knee, he'd never even dreamt he might come to.

Nothing had prepared him for this, yet everything that was in him wanted it.

Roared for it.

He thrust into her body deeper and harder, and felt her rise to him, their bodies effortlessly coming together, not just in the physical sense, consumed by the friction and the heat, the slickness and the sensual glory, but driven and determined, reckless and abandoned, merging in a far more fundamental way.

On some deeper level, on some higher plane.

Giving and taking, receiving and lavishing, striving to achieve that last ultimate degree of togetherness.

Racing, urgent and intent, for the cataclysm that would bind them forever.

Sunk so deeply in the pleasure of her body, and of her openly shared pleasure in his, though his senses were reeling that fact shone clearly, glowing in his mind with crystal clarity.

This was what it meant to be as one.

To truly reach the pinnacle of togetherness. Of closeness.

Of shattering physical intimacy driven and overwhelmed by emotion.

This was what it meant to love.

To lay aside all reservation, to give without limitation.

To lose one's heart.

No—to willingly give it into another's keeping, to become dependent and possessive, to accept that as the price for them doing the same in return.

This was their moment, and similar as they were, they'd reached it together.

Unlocked each other's doors, led each other to the brink.

This was the ultimate linking.

And in that fraction of an instant of lucidity as they raced, gasping and clinging, up the final peak, he recognized it as that, as an irrevocable step that once taken could never be undone—and still he wanted it.

It would link him to her, but also her to him.

And that was worth any price.

With the last gasp of his desperation, he reached for it, that ultimate gift of him to her and her to him, closed a mental fist about it and held on as, in a firestorm of passion, sensation and emotion collided and they burned.

In the furnace of their joint passion, in the conflagration of their shared love.

Acknowledged, embraced, it consumed them, transmuted them, welded and reforged them.

Made them new, made them whole. Made them more.

As the last shudders of completion racked him, as the last of her contractions faded, he slumped upon her, too wrung out to move, too exhausted and overwhelmed to think.

Even much later, when he lifted from her, slumped alongside her and gathered her into his arms, all he could manage by way of thought was that he was never going to let her go.

He couldn't. She was his everything.

After the passion of the night and their underlying new reality, Ryder had anticipated some degree of awkwardness between them, certainly a degree of wariness from him if not from her, but instead, when they'd woken they'd looked at each other. Looked into each other's eyes—and seen—and they'd both smiled.

He'd rolled over and they'd made love, and their day had sailed on, idyllic and untroubled, from there.

The clock on the library mantelpiece chimed five times. As he tidied away the last of his calculations on the coming season's crops, his mind continued to explore his new state. An unlooked-for, unexpected, unanticipated state—one of such contentment and promise that it constituted a very real vulnerability.

He was surprised at himself that he'd accepted it, that vulnerability, so readily, so easily, yet even now, while in full possession of his wits, had he the decision to make again, he would make it in the same way.

There were, indeed, some things worth the price. That were worth any price.

Putting off that acceptance, delaying this contented joy because of the threat hovering over them . . . neither he nor Mary was the type to play safe, much less to allow some villainous knave to rule them via fear.

No. Whatever came, they would handle it. And, if anything, courtesy of the night, they were even stronger now.

His mind shifting to the pleasures of the evening to come, he shut his desk drawer, then heard a crisp tap at the door. "Come."

Forsythe entered, a faintly puzzled frown on his face. In one hand he held a salver on which rested several letters, the afternoon mail; offering the salver, Forsythe said, "My lord, Aggie, her ladyship's maid, is looking for her ladyship but can't seem to find her. Do you have any idea where her ladyship might be?"

Accepting the letters, Ryder frowned. "She said she was going to do some embroidery, but"—he glanced at the window, at the sunshine outside—"she might have gone for a stroll." Pushing back his chair, he stood. "She won't have gone far. Has Aggie checked the rose garden?"

Aggie had. She'd also checked the terraces and the immediate surrounds of the house, as well as their rooms upstairs.

The maid wrung her hands. "She's usually about, m'lord, and she likes me to check round about now over what gown she wants to wear to dinner."

It took the footmen fifteen minutes to quarter the rest of the house.

Meanwhile, Ryder sent for Dukes, the head gardener, who immediately went out to consult with his far-flung crew.

"Her ladyship is definitely not within the house, my lord."

Forsythe looked like Ryder felt—unwilling to panic yet, but starting to feel the first nibblings of fear. "Send to the stables. She won't have gone riding, but perhaps she walked down to see her horse."

At this time of day, that was a long shot, and so it proved.

"We haven't seen her ladyship at all today, my lord," Filmore reported.

Dukes strode rapidly back in, an unusual enough action from the normally lugubrious gardener to fix all attention on him. He nodded to Ryder. "One of my lads saw her ladyship walking in the shrubbery, my lord. He was working there. She smiled, spoke a pleasant word, then turned back to the house. Far as he knows, she returned to the east terrace, but this was some time ago, hours at least, and from where he was, he couldn't see if she actually did come all the way to the house or turned off to somewhere else."

A chill unlike any he'd ever experienced was seeping into Ryder's chest. He glanced at Forsythe, Filmore, then back at Dukes. "I want every able-bodied man—assemble them in the forecourt. We need to mount a search."

"Yes, my lord." Forsythe looked grim.

"At once." Filmore saluted and headed for the door.

Dukes didn't reply, just grimly nodded and followed Filmore. Forsythe sent a footman scurrying but remained to help Ryder set out maps of the estate and surrounding areas.

Somewhat to Ryder's surprise, Aggie stopped wringing her hands and, jaw firming, whirled and rushed from the room.

In the end, it wasn't only the men who assembled in the forecourt but all the younger women on the staff as well, recruited by Aggie, and with the approval of Mrs. Pritchard all ready to do their bit to find their missing mistress.

That gave Ryder some leeway; dispatching the women in pairs to search every inch of the grounds left him with enough men to send riders to the nearby farms as well as organize comprehensive sweeps through the surrounding woods and fields.

Even though this was Wiltshire, as calm and gentle a county as any in England, it was nevertheless possible that some accident had befallen Mary, even if she hadn't ventured into the woods.

That was what he was hoping, what they were all thinking. A fall, a twisted ankle—anything of that sort would be preferable to the alternative.

That something more heinous had befallen her.

It was full light when they started the search, but within the first hour, the sun started to dip, and the shadows cast by the trees lengthened. But light enough remained and the search continued, with each group reporting back to the house as they finished their allotted area, only to have Ryder send them out to another as yet unsearched locale.

Raventhorne was a large estate; covering it was going to take time. Ultimately even Forsythe, born and bred on abbey lands, left to add his number to the searchers.

Dusk was insidiously closing in when a tap on the library door had Ryder lifting his head—only to have his leaping heart crash as Mrs. Pritchard looked in. "Yes?" He tried not to sound too harsh.

"My lord, I've Dixon's lad here, from Axford, and I think you need to hear what he has to say."

Frowning, Ryder straightened from the maps he'd been poring over. "Dixon?"

"The fishmonger." Mrs. Pritchard stepped across the threshold and beckoned someone in.

Ryder tried to blank his expression—the best he could do in the circumstances—as a boy peeked around the door, then immediately ducked his head. Ryder struggled to find an unthreatening tone. "Dixon, the younger, is it?"

The boy ducked his head again. "Aye, m'lord." He glanced up at Mrs. Pritchard, who waved him on toward the desk.

Clearly unsure, the boy advanced three steps, then halted. Ryder looked at Mrs. Pritchard.

"Davy here brought our delivery just now and happened to mention delivering to the Dower House yesterday."

"The Dower House." Instantly, Ryder focused on the boy. "Who was in residence—who was there? Do you know?"

The boy shook his head. "Don't know who. Didn't see

anyone but Cook and her two girls, but I can tell you what was ordered?"

When Ryder nodded encouragingly, the boy rattled off a list of fishes. Ryder had no way of interpreting the significance; he looked to Mrs. Pritchard for translation.

Her expression severe, his housekeeper obliged. "The turbot, my lord, wouldn't be for the staff, nor yet the sturgeon."

"I'll say!" Davy Dixon snorted. "Top of the slate, they are."

For an instant, Ryder's mind reeled with the wild possibility whipping through it, but then he shook aside the fanciful notion and refocused on Davy Dixon. "Thank you. Mrs. Pritchard, I'm sure we should reward such a useful report."

Mrs. Pritchard nodded. "Come along, Davy. There's some cake and a shilling with your name on it in the kitchen."

Steering the boy out, Mrs. Pritchard closed the door. Ryder stood staring at the panels for several moments, then he glanced at the maps, then at the deepening dusk outside, debated for a second longer, then headed for the door and the stairs.

Mrs. Pritchard was waiting in the front hall when he came quickly down, having thrown on his riding clothes and hauled on his boots. "You're riding over there?"

Pulling on his gloves, he nodded. "At the very least, I should ask if anyone there has seen anything of her ladyship. If they haven't . . . when Forsythe returns, tell him to take over organizing the searchers, and that I'll work my way through the Dower House woods. We haven't sent anyone over that way yet, and if I'm there anyway, I might as well check."

Mrs. Pritchard grimaced. "I would say you should stay here and let someone else go, but there's no one left but myself and Cook."

"No point." Ryder turned to the corridor that was the fastest way to the stables. "If my stepmother's in residence, as it seems she is, I'm the only one here to whom she'll consent to grant an audience."

Mrs. Pritchard humphed and watched him go. He felt the concern in her gaze as he headed down the corridor, striding increasingly swiftly as, despite all rational arguments, premonition took hold.

Chapter Fifteen

Lavinia wouldn't have dared." He muttered the words as he rode into the band of woodland that formed the eastern border of the home farm fields. There were no lanes through the woods, only the bridle path along which he was riding.

The trees there grew thickly, old stands of oak and beech shading the path and shrouding the woods in deep shadow.

The Dower House was as old as the original part of the abbey and had been one of the original ecclesiastical buildings attached to the holy house. His paternal grandmother had been living at the Dower House when he'd been born, but she'd died soon after, and subsequently the house had been lived in only by caretakers, until he'd effectively banished Lavinia there.

As none of the locals wished to work in her household, she'd been forced to seek staff from further afield. Consequently, unlike what generally occurred in the country, especially in a well-populated county like Wiltshire, the household at the Dower House had little contact and less connection with the staffs of the surrounding houses. More, although Lavinia insisted on living in the country for a decent part of the year, even while she'd reigned at the abbey, she had never put herself out to court the local gentry, had largely shunned them and their entertainments as beneath her, so she now had little truck with their neighbors.

Which meant the household at the Dower House was isolated, and something of an unknown world.

Ryder rode steadily on, Julius's hoofbeats an echo of his own heartbeat.

His reaction to Mary's disappearance had hardened with each passing hour. Each minute she was not by his side, within his protection, where she was supposed to be, strengthened his instinctive reaction. And increased his suspicion that she'd been abducted; nothing else could explain her continued absence. The unknown enemy who had first tried to kill him, then had shifted their sights to her, had taken her.

Whoever it was, they would pay.

Sometime over the past hours, the instincts he normally kept well leashed had come to the fore and now largely ruled him. When it came to Mary, to anyone threatening any danger, much less harm, to her, he wasn't inclined to be anywhere near civilized.

Instinct and intellect were now wholly focused on one goal: On getting her back, safe within his keeping.

The thought that Lavinia might be the one responsible for Mary's disappearance and all the rest . . . until now he'd dismissed the notion out of hand. Lavinia was a personal irritant, vindictive, vituperative, but essentially ineffectual; he hadn't believed it at all likely that she would actually *act* in any concerted way. She never had. Ranting was one thing, making plans and setting them in train quite another.

Lavinia had always been a ranter, not a doer.

If she'd acted, then something had changed.

And as if signaling such a change . . . until now, whenever she'd taken up residence at the Dower House, she had sent a haughty note to the abbey, informing those on the estate that she was in the neighborhood. Often the carriages of her London friends would bowl up the abbey drive and have to be redirected out and around to the separate entrance to the Dower House drive.

This time Lavinia hadn't sent a note.

Some might say that was because his marriage had put her nose even further out of joint, yet he would have thought she would have wanted Mary, and him, too, to know she was there, also a marchioness, and therefore a competitor in the neighborhood status stakes. That sounded more like the Lavinia he knew.

There was no competition—not between his wife and his self-absorbed stepmother—but Lavinia wouldn't see it like that, which begged the question of why she hadn't sent a note.

Mrs. Pritchard knew of the antipathy between him and Lavinia, as, indeed, did most of his staff. None of them had fared well under, much less liked, Lavinia, which was why they all viewed him as a savior of sorts.

So on learning that Lavinia had taken up residence at the Dower House, but this time secretly, Mrs. Pritchard had been quick to leap to the conclusion he was still resisting.

He simply couldn't imagine Lavinia actively—and nearly successfully—arranging his murder. Of plotting and planning to have Mary abducted.

Glimpsing the steep roofs of the Dower House through the trees, he slowed Julius to a trot, then a walk. No need to advertise his arrival, not until he'd had a look around.

The bridle path joined the gravel drive fifty yards from the forecourt before the front porch. The Dower House had little by way of gardens, the woods crowding close on three sides. It was a very quiet, private place.

Registering that quietness, indeed, the pervasive silence, he reined to a halt just inside the path, within the shadows of overarching branches, and studied the house.

It appeared . . . not uninhabited but temporarily deserted, as if everyone had gone out for the day.

Leaving the front door ajar.

The sight filled him with cold dread.

All the thoughts he'd been avoiding consciously thinking spilled through his mind. Lavinia had the wherewithal to hire thugs to kill him—and to hire men to hire them, and so forth. She knew which routes he used when walking home in town. Here, in the country, despite the lack of friendship between the staffs at the abbey and the Dower House, Lavinia's stableman or grooms would know where the abbey tack room was, would have been able to identify which saddle was Mary's, the only newish sidesaddle there, and could easily have watched from the woods and seen him assessing her driving the gig and guessed which road they would take to Axford . . .

The scorpion he couldn't immediately explain, but as for the adder, Lavinia's staff would have known when the abbey staff would be gathered on the front steps greeting Mary, and would have known which bedroom would be hers, and how to reach it quickly and leave again via the servants' stairs.

He sat on Julius's back and considered that half-open door. It was clearly an invitation of sorts—which spoke to the caliber of the men behind this.

Unsophisticated, but effective.

They were currently watching him from somewhere in the woods on the other side of the drive.

He could feel their gazes, but he knew those woods. Chasing anyone through them was a fool's errand, and he didn't doubt there would be more than one of them; few men would be so foolish as to come against him unarmed, one on one.

Despite the difficulty his rational mind was having casting Lavinia—petty and spiteful with all the acuity of a turnip—in the role of arch-villainess, his instincts had no such problem but at that moment considered the point irrelevant; they were solely focused on how to rescue Mary.

That she was somewhere in the Dower House he didn't doubt; that was the message of that half-open door. But he hadn't come armed, and as far as he knew there weren't any helpful crossed swords on any of the Dower House walls.

Holding back the impulse, the emotional imperative to gallop up, rush inside, and find her—to wrap her in his arms and reassure his oh-so-exposed heart that she was unharmed, that she was all right—wasn't easy, but if he just rushed ahead . . . this wasn't a situation he'd expected, much less foreseen, and he fully intended them both to survive.

How else could he exact his vengeance?

Even more pertinently, he wasn't about to surrender all he and Mary had so recently claimed.

Pushing aside all emotion, he filled his chest and forced his mind to cool logic. It was unlikely they, whoever they were, would hurt Mary, not yet. It was his life Lavinia had targeted; she might have tried to scare Mary away, but at this moment his wife was . . . bait. No need to harm her yet, and every reason not to; a live lure always worked best.

Weighing up the possibilities, balancing them against his options, took time he forced himself to take, but eventually he dismounted. Shortening Julius's reins, he wove them into one stirrup strap. Julius would wait for him untethered, but if anyone else approached and tried to grab him, the big gelding wouldn't have it, and ultimately would return to the abbey stables.

It was the best he could do by way of a message should something go awry. More awry.

Not allowing himself to think further than that, he walked out into the drive, paused to look up at the old house, at the many-paned leaded windows, at the cool gray stone. His gaze came to rest on the half-open door; focusing on the dark section of shadowed hall beyond, he strode forward.

At his touch, the door opened further. The hall beyond lay in cool darkness. Not a sound reached his ears, not a scrape or a scuff, not any hint of human life.

He walked into the drawing room. It was unoccupied, as were the other reception rooms, all on the ground floor. He kept his ears peeled as he did the rounds, but the silence continued, heavy and unbroken.

Slowly, senses wide, he climbed the stairs. The bedrooms showed signs of occupation. In the largest, he found scent bottles and powders on the dressing table, and the gowns in the armoire confirmed all belonged to Lavinia; he recognized her style. In a bedroom further down the corridor, he discovered brushes, combs, and male attire. The particular designs of the coats and waistcoats, and the floppy silk scarves instead of cravats, told him who was also currently residing at the house.

Potherby. With icy calm, Ryder considered the fact. He'd known about Potherby for as long as he could recall knowing Lavinia; she and Potherby had been childhood friends, but despite the conclusion many leapt to, Ryder didn't believe Potherby had been—or, indeed, was—Lavinia's lover. There was something in the way Potherby looked at Lavinia, an expression more consistent with his being that childhood friend. But could Potherby be involved in the attacks on Ryder and Mary?

The man certainly had the intelligence Lavinia lacked, but . . . Ryder had always considered Potherby, despite his allegiance to Lavinia, to be a decent sort.

Then again, he'd never imagined Lavinia would turn her hand to murder.

Leaving the question of Potherby for later, Ryder quit that room. He paused in the corridor, listening. The house was so eerily silent that he didn't doubt there was no one else—no other breathing being—on that floor. His senses, flaring wide, detected no hint of Mary. But there was an attic.

Walking to the end of the corridor, he opened the narrow door that gave onto the attic stairs. They rose into relative darkness, but slivers of faint twilight showed here and there between the roof slates; once his eyes adjusted, he would be able to see well enough.

Slowly, step by step, he went up the stairs.

Had he been in his opponents' shoes, this was where he would have staged an ambush; emerging up a stairwell so narrow that he had to angle his shoulders to pass, he was at a very real disadvantage . . . but no. Even before his head cleared the level of the attic floor, he knew there was no one waiting to cosh him, to shoot him. And no Mary, either.

People, alive and awake, were simply never that still.

After one quick glance, he went back down the narrow stairs, senses alert as he emerged into the first-floor corridor, but no one had sneaked up while he'd been above.

Striding more quickly, he headed back to the main stairs. Going rapidly down, he reviewed again his certainty that Mary was somewhere there, that she was hidden somewhere in the Dower House. Despite all the evidence thus far, he remained convinced she was there; why else the open door? Why else the complete absence of staff?

Pushing through the green baize-covered door at the rear of the front hall, he went down a short corridor, past a small butler's pantry, then down three shallow steps to the kitchen. Like the house above, it was devoid of life, but utensils were lined up on the cook's table, selected plates and cutlery were stacked on a sideboard, along with folded napkins, and a tea tray was set ready on a bench by the stove.

The staff were still living there but had been sent out for the day . . . or perhaps for several days. A glance through the windows confirmed it was growing steadily darker outside, but as it was just past midsummer, full dark was still hours away.

Walking further into the kitchen, he looked around—and saw the basement door had also been left ajar.

He considered the sight, then noticed several lanterns ready and waiting on a nearby shelf. Picking up one, he saw there was a mark where another, currently absent, normally sat. Hunting up tinder, he lit the lamp; after adjusting the wick, he pushed the door to the basement wider. It was the only place within the house he'd yet to search, and while there was a smallish stables, with rooms for coachman and groom above, to hide Mary somewhere secure, somewhere they could trap him as he came for her . . .

With his senses still confirming no one else had come past the green baize door, that no enemy was yet creeping up close behind him, he stepped onto the landing at the top of the basement steps and shone the lantern into the darkness.

The beam played over bins of apples, potatoes, and onions, barrels of various stuffs, shelves of dry goods in boxes and sacks, and lots of glass jars, but the shelves inhibited his view of the further reaches of the room.

He couldn't see anyone, see any evidence that Mary was there, still could not sense her presence.

Yet, once again, why had the door been left ajar?

Stepping back into the kitchen, he looked at the shallow steps from the front of the house, glanced across at the kitchen door. His would-be attackers could come from either direction, but they hadn't dared show themselves yet.

A moment's consideration was all it took to convince him that, if they had any choice, they wouldn't appear until he'd found Mary; that was when he would be at his most vulnerable, with her to protect and his attention divided.

They might not know he was unarmed, but few men carried pistols or swords these days, and not when searching for missing ladies on their own damned estates.

His gaze fell on the utensils lined up on the cook's table. Setting the lamp down, he swiftly searched. No knives. Not there or anywhere else; he went through the drawers and cupboards, but there wasn't a single decent knife left. His would-be attackers might be unsophisticated; they weren't stupid.

He found a few other items he could use.

One of the fire irons did a nice job of breaking the bolt off the basement door. A long spatula wedged under the lower edge of the door made it difficult to shift; setting that aside, he continued his hunt.

The poker might come in handy. Hefting it, he dropped a set of metal skewers into his pocket, cast a last glance at the other utensils he'd uncovered.

As well as the knives, his opponents had removed all long, pointy implements, like the long-handled forks he was sure should have been there. As an afterthought, he tucked four ordinary forks into another pocket, then finally turned to the basement door.

They had to be watching him from outside, from the cover of the nearby woods. The kitchen faced west; the last of the fading light was probably sufficient to illuminate the room enough for them to follow his movements. So they would know he had the poker.

And from the fading glow of the lantern he carried they would know that he'd finally gone down the basement steps.

Reaching the bottom, he moved quickly, playing the lantern beam to either side as he strode down the aisle between the high shelves. There was an open area at the far end of the room. It was completely bare, but there the floor was wood, not stone, and the fine dust on the boards, drifting from bags of grain stacked along the back wall, showed evidence of footprints and the swishing of a woman's skirts.

The marks circled a square trapdoor set in the floor.

He'd never been into the basement before, didn't remember—had never heard—what lay beneath the trapdoor.

A heavy iron ring was set into the surface. Setting the lantern on the floor, he bent and hauled the trap—literally as well as figuratively, he feared—open. The door was heavy, weighted by a metal frame and bracing. Leaving it tilted back on its hinges, he crouched beside the opening and looked down, into a largely featureless void. Picking up the lantern, he directed the beam down, revealing a stone floor, not flagged but rough-hewn, more than ten feet below. There were no steps, not even a ladder.

The chamber was empty. He angled his head and the lantern, bent lower and peered, but all he saw was empty space leading to blank walls, also cut directly into the stone. The hole might have been part of a long-ago rock quarry, later built over. A tunnel, large enough for him to walk down, led off in one direction. He glanced briefly at it, his gaze passing over and on, but then he looked back. After a moment, he cursed and turned the lantern away—and yes, there was light, distant and faint, seeping out through that tunnel.

He hesitated, then with nothing to lose, called, "Mary?"

Instantly, distantly, he heard the drum of heels on stone. Even more faintly, he heard muffled sounds. She was there!

"Wait—I'm coming."

The words unleashed a positive torrent of muffled protest; she wanted to warn him not to come down, that it was a trap.

He already knew that. Accepted it. He was still going down.

Even before he'd walked through the front door, he'd realized that leaving her there and returning to the abbey for help was not an option; if he did, when he returned with his men, she wouldn't be there anymore. She was the bait to lure him to his doom; Lavinia and her henchmen now knew they had that right, that that would work, so they would keep her until he did as they wished and stepped into their trap. Putting it off would only prolong the drama and risk Mary's health, and most likely shift the venue from which he had to rescue her to somewhere even less advantageous to him.

Yet if he dropped through the trapdoor—easy enough—there was no way he could see of getting back up. And if there was no other way out of what appeared to be a long-unused cellar . . .

He paused, thought again, but still could see no option. Even if he attempted to wait them out, they would come for him eventually—long before anyone from the abbey came looking for him—and he was unarmed. He doubted they were.

All he had to work with was his wits and his strength. Together, they would have to suffice.

And Mary was down there, alone, tied and gagged.

He hunted through the basement and found what he'd

imagined had to be there somewhere—a rope. Tying one end to the iron ring, he threaded the rope through the gap beside the big hinges on the door and let the length fall; it reached nearly to the cellar floor.

He thought for a moment, then hauled the free end of the rope up, tied it around the handle of his lantern, then lowered the lantern down into the cellar.

Glancing back at the basement door, now barely visible, he hesitated, then stalked back toward the steps, along the way gathering as many of the glass jars as he could carry and two empty metal pails.

Pausing at the bottom of the steps, he set the jars and pails down, then went up, into the kitchen, and lit three more lamps. He played the beams around, warning the wary watchers that he was still in the kitchen and hadn't yet dropped down into their trap.

Then he left the lanterns before the basement door, their beams shining outward so there was no easy way for his would-be attackers to know if he was in the basement or lower by the amount of light. After that he quickly shut the basement door and wedged it closed with the spatula, then he went down and arranged the glass jars across the steps and set the metal pails strategically—his makeshift alarm— then without further thought, he ran to the trapdoor, kicked the poker through the hole, sat on the edge, grasped the sides, and swung himself down.

And let go.

The instant his boots hit the stone floor, he caught up the poker and ran full tilt down the tunnel. It was wide enough for two men abreast, and curved away from the house for a good twenty yards. Ahead he saw an old stone wall; a lamp sat at the base of the wall, shining back down the tunnel— the light set to lure him. He erupted into the roomlike space before it, another rough-hewn chamber about four yards across, and running for five or so yards on either side.

A muffled wailing rose from his left. Whirling, he saw

Mary seated on a chair at that end of the chamber. She was lashed to the chair, a black cloth hood over her head.

Why the latter should make him so furious, he wasn't sure—but had they asked if she was frightened of the dark first? Striding across, dropping the poker, he grasped the offending hood and gently eased it off.

Furious blue eyes met his. Through the gag fastened over her lips, she growled at him.

Despite his prevailing grimness, he grinned. "Good evening, Mary."

Her eyes spat sparks, then she twisted her head to the side. He obediently went to work on the gag. "I know it's a trap. I've done what I could to try to get us out of it, but they left me no option"—the knot loosened—"other than to come down after you." She jerked her head and the gag fell.

"There's always a choice!" Mary moistened her lips, shocked by the hoarseness of her voice.

"Indeed." Ryder met her eyes as he shifted to start on the knots holding her to the chair. "And I've made mine."

What could she say? She growled low in her throat and waited, more than impatient, urgent and concerned and *frightened*—for him more than her—as he worked at her bonds. "They'll come back—there's three of them. Three largish men. Where are we?"

"The Dower House. You haven't been here before."

She glanced around, tried to glimpse his face. "Where your stepmother lives?"

"Yes." His tone was flat and hard.

The ropes fell and she rose, stumbled, but he caught her. Steadied her. "We have to hurry."

"Yes—please let's."

He bent and picked up a poker, then with her hand locked in his, they ran as fast as she was able toward the opening to the passageway he must have come down. She hadn't seen anything of her prison before; she'd been hooded when they'd carried her down.

They turned into the passage—and glass crashed, smashed, and metal clanged, the sounds coming from somewhere above.

Ryder swore, swept her up in his arms, and charged down the passage.

More curses exploded over their heads. Pounding feet thundered on floorboards.

They burst into another chamber at the end of the passage—just in time to see a rope that had been dangling from a hole high above, along with the lantern swinging wildly from its end, fall with a small crash and a slithering thump to the floor.

Holding her in his arms, Ryder stared up at the hole, then calmly stated, "You bastards will die."

There was enough icy certainty in his tone to make Mary shiver.

Silence greeted his pronouncement, then she heard a click.

Ryder swore and whirled back into the passage.

Sound exploded behind them; rock shattered and shards flew.

With her clutched in his arms, his body curled over hers, Ryder halted, leaning against the passage wall out of sight of the men above.

Rough laughter fell, echoing in the chamber. "Aint us who's slated to die, me fine lord. Just you and your missus, too."

A percussive thud followed hard on the words.

Ryder didn't need to look to know they'd shut the trapdoor.

Mary wriggled. He straightened and released her legs, allowing her to swing them down and stand, but he kept one arm around her. With her leaning into him and him holding onto her, they leaned back against the tunnel wall and took stock.

The men were still moving around above; Ryder and Mary heard muffled words, then a few seconds later shuffling footsteps, then a solid thump.

The first was followed by others, increasingly muffled.

Mary frowned. "What's that?"

Ryder realized. Letting his head fall back against the rock wall, he closed his eyes and swore. "Damn!" He listened again, then sighed. "I saw bags of grain or flour by one wall. They've shifted the bags over the trapdoor."

"Why? It's not as if we were about to climb up and push it open."

"No, but the bags will hide the trapdoor." Opening his eyes, he looked down at her.

She frowned back. "But surely those working here will know it's there."

He grimaced. "Possibly, but"—he glanced at the empty chambers to either side—"this place is clearly not used for anything, and as I didn't know it existed, it's possible few others do."

He could see her working it out, then she met his eyes. "Does anyone at the abbey know you came here?"

"Yes, but I didn't know you were here. We'd only just learned Lavinia was in residence and I came to check if anyone here had seen you. I didn't imagine that you'd been trapped here—I said that after asking here I'd scout through the woods."

"So if you don't return, no one will raise the alarm?"

"Probably not until morning." He pulled a face. "And even then, there's no reason for anyone to believe I'm here. I left Julius loose—he'll find his way back to the stables, but there's nothing to say we parted company here, rather than in the depths of the woods."

For a long moment, they stood in silence, drawing strength from each other, from simply having the other there, then Mary pulled out of his arms and he let her go.

"Well, in that case"—she marched out into the chamber— "we may as well take this lantern and search to see if there's another way out."

Her dogged optimism struck him as bittersweet; he seriously doubted there was another exit. Why seal them down here if there was?

He watched while she retrieved the fallen lantern; it had only dropped a few inches and was undamaged. Straightening, she played the lantern beam over the walls. Still carrying the poker, he joined her; together they checked the roughly round chamber, but it was nothing more than a pit cut directly out of the rock, with only the tunnel leading out of it. Walking back down the tunnel, scanning the solid walls as they went, they emerged into the rectangular space at the other end.

Slowly pirouetting, Mary surveyed the chamber. The passageway entered midway down one long side. The floor, ceiling, and three walls were solid, roughly hewn stone, but the side facing the passage was an old wall of large stone blocks. The chair she'd been tied to sat to the left of the passage entrance, facing down the room; to the right of the passage, at the other end of the rectangular space, stood a table, a jug of water, and two glasses on a tray sitting atop the scarred surface.

Ryder had also noticed the table. He walked to it.

She followed more slowly, trying to remember when the tray had been placed there—before or after . . . "How long have I been down here?"

Reaching for the jug, Ryder glanced at her. "When did they take you?"

"Not that long after luncheon. I went for a stroll in the gardens. I'd left the shrubbery and decided to take a quick look at the kitchen garden. I was walking along the rhododendron walk when they sprang through the bushes and grabbed me. One caught my arms, another gagged me, the other pulled the hood over my head, and that was it. They tied my hands, my ankles, and carried me off like a sack of potatoes."

"So two o'clock or just after, and"—pulling out his fob watch, he checked—"it's now after eight."

"Six hours." She grimaced. "It felt much longer." She watched him pour water into both glasses, wondering at what was bothering her, a nebulous niggle at the back of her brain.

Ryder handed her one glass. She took it, watched him raise the other to his lips—

"*No!*" She shoved his hand, the one with the glass, down and away. Then she stared at the glass in her hand. "Why is this here?"

Ryder frowned, then his face cleared and he looked at the glass he held. "Poison?"

She glanced back at the chair. "They tie me up, hooded and gagged. Then"—she glanced at the passage—"they shoot at us." Turning back, she looked at the jug. "But they leave water and two glasses?" Lips firming, she set her glass down.

Ryder stared at the water jug, then with one violent swipe, he swept it off the table. Tray, glasses, and all went flying; the jug and the glasses shattered on the stone.

Closing his eyes, he drew in a deep breath, drew his temper back, in, under his control. He felt Mary grip his arm, grimaced. "Sorry."

"Don't be. I thought of doing exactly that but could never have managed quite the same effect."

The dry comment startled a laugh out of him. Opening his eyes, he looked at her, met her gaze and her inquiring look, but simply shook his head.

She glanced around the room, then considered the wall. "Perhaps there's a hidden door."

Picking up the other lantern, he joined her in examining the stonework, but there was no obvious doorway, no suggestion of a concealed exit. Stepping back, he shook his head. "It looks like a retaining wall—they must have had to build it to hold back the earth on that side."

Mary pulled a face and extended her inspection to the other walls, but as in the first chamber, they were solid rock.

Finally halting, she blew out a breath. "Well, having settled that question in the negative, I suppose we may as well sit down and think, and decide what else we can do."

He walked to the section of the retaining wall level with the chair. "Come, sit." He waved her to the chair, then slid down the wall to sit with his back against it, his long legs bent. Resting his hands on his thighs, he watched as, after considering him for an instant, she came to join him. Eschewing the chair, she settled on the stone floor beside him. Closing her hands about his upper arm, she leaned her head against his shoulder.

He hesitated, then tipped his head to rest his cheek against her hair. Softly said, "They can't simply leave us here. At some point, other staff will come into the basement, and if we yell, they'll hear us. So our captors have to finish us off, most likely tonight." He paused, then simply said, "They're going to come for us, and there's not a damned thing I can do to stop them."

"They haven't killed us yet." Mary's tone was fierce. "And you know what they say—where there's life, there's hope." After a moment, she added, "And trying to poison us—you, really, as I'm hardly any threat—tells us they don't want to take the risk of facing you. At least not a healthy, alive, and enraged you."

He snorted and glanced at the opening to the tunnel. "I could stop them if they came unarmed, but if they come with pistols . . ."

A long moment passed, then, her voice softer, smaller, she said, "They will come with pistols, won't they?"

He sighed. "If I were them, I'd bring two pistols each, just to make sure."

Silence fell as they absorbed the situation and faced the reality of the most likely outcome. There was no way out, and nowhere to hide, to take cover. Nowhere they could stage an ambush and hope to win.

Facing death was a chilling prospect; he wasn't surprised

to feel her shiver. Raising his arm, he curved it over her shoulders; urging her closer against his side, he pressed a kiss to her hair.

She settled. After a moment asked, "Why are they waiting—do you know?"

He was grateful they were, but he followed her thought . . . "Lavinia. She isn't here. There's no one at all upstairs, except whoever shot at us and shut the trapdoor—presumably the three who seized you."

Shifting her head, she stared into his face. "*She's* behind this?"

His expression grim, he let his head fall back. "I think she must be. Her things are upstairs, and only she could have ordered her staff away for the day—and the evening, too. And I can definitely see her wanting to gloat to my face." He paused, then added, "It could also be that, this time, she wants to make sure I am, indeed, killed, and don't somehow escape."

"So where is she?"

Equally puzzled, he shook his head. "I can't see her patiently waiting in some tavern to be summoned."

After a moment, Mary said, "Actually, if I were her and planning our deaths, I'd make sure I was nowhere near the abbey and had lots of people to vouch for that." She looked at Ryder. "Consider the time—I'd wager she went off to some luncheon or other, and then stayed on for some dinner or ball, all at a good distance from here."

He grimaced. "That sounds too well planned for Lavinia, but Potherby is staying here, too—his things are upstairs— and while I have no idea if he's involved, what you suggest might have been Lavinia's best way of ensuring Potherby wasn't here, either."

Mary snuggled closer. "Regardless of whether Potherby knows of her scheme or not, his being with her the whole time ensures she has an alibi for both our disappearances—or so it will seem."

Ryder nodded. "If that's what she's doing, then it'll probably be several hours before they come for us."

Thinking of what might happen when they did . . .

Silence fell, stretched, then, closing his hand about one of Mary's, he murmured, "It's me they—she—wants."

"Actually, I don't think that's true—well, not anymore. You heard what that blackguard said. 'You and your missus, too.' They can't let me live—quite aside from bringing down the wrath of God and the Cynsters on their heads, from Lavinia's perspective, there's the rather pertinent matter of your heir."

"What?" Startled, he looked at Mary's head, then ducked his own to look into her face.

Meeting his eyes, she shrugged. "I might be pregnant already—who knows? And no, I can't be sure, but neither can she."

He fell silent. After several long moments, he asked, "You truly believe she's intent on killing me—and you, and any unborn child of ours—so Rand will inherit?"

Mary nodded decisively. "You told me she always expected Randolph would inherit, and while there seemed a chance Fate or you would bring that about without any effort from her, she was content to wait, but now . . ." Breaking off, Mary frowned. "Why now? Why after all these years did she finally decide it was time to act? It wasn't our marriage— that came after the attempt on your life . . . oh! Of course." Mary met his eyes. "Randolph."

He shook his head. "Rand won't have had anything to do with this."

She held his gaze. "Are you sure?"

"Yes. Rand and I—and Kit, and Stacie, and Godfrey— we're close in a way that's difficult to define. Trust me— none of them would have had anything to do with this, with harming me and you. As for Rand wanting to inherit—he doesn't. The attendant responsibility scares him." Lips twisting, he admitted, "That was one of the reasons I knew

Rand wasn't the right man for you but I was. Even as a sickly child, I always knew Raventhorne would one day be mine—I always expected to shoulder the burden someday. But Rand . . . he would do it if it was thrust upon him, but he's counting on you and me to ensure he never has to."

Searching his eyes, reading his unshakeable conviction, Mary nodded. "All right, but Randolph's still at the heart of this, whether he means to be or not. Does Lavinia know how he feels about the marquessate, and even if she does, will she care?"

"No, she won't." Ryder paused, then went on, "Lavinia sees her children—all of them, still—solely as an extension of herself. To her, they have no other purpose in life other than being her children. While my father tried to intercede, to have more influence in their lives, Lavinia fought him tooth and nail, until he more or less gave up. He had me, and he and I were close. He was allowed to have little relationship with the others."

She nodded again. "So regardless of Randolph's wishes, Lavinia is intent on him inheriting the title, and if that's the case . . ." Narrowing her eyes thoughtfully on Ryder, she asked, "How old were you when you inherited?"

"I was twenty-four when my father died . . ." He paused, then, his voice strengthening, continued, "But by the time everything was sorted out, I was twenty-five and inherited in my own right, without any guardianship." He met her eyes, curtly nodded. "That's it. Rand's age is what's brought this on."

"Exactly. You inheriting from your father showed Lavinia how the process worked, and what the earliest age at which Randolph could cleanly inherit from you was—so she waited until the time was right. Am I correct in thinking that if you died now, by the time matters were sorted out, Randolph would be twenty-five?"

"Yes." Ryder's jaw clenched. "So she's been waiting all this time, and then, when Rand was the right age, she arranged to have me killed—and damned near succeeded."

"Oh, great heavens!" With her free hand, Mary gripped his arm. "*That's* why she called at your house that morning. It was after eleven and she still hadn't received word of your death, so she came to your house to see what was going on—"

"Bringing the ton's two greatest gossipmongers with her to help spread the word—she must have thought my people were suppressing news of my death." Ryder paused, then added, "I wish I'd known at the time so I could have better appreciated her reaction when she saw me so very much alive."

Mary shivered. "You weren't so alive—you were pale and weak and propped up with pillows!" Then she gave a short laugh, the sound cynically ironic. "It's just occurred to me." She looked at him. "The last thing Lavinia would have wanted at that point was for you to marry and father an heir. But if she hadn't sent those men to kill you, would we have married, do you think?"

"Yes, we would have, although perhaps not so quickly." When she arched a brow, he smiled gently and tightened his hold on her hand. "I'd already made up my mind it was you I wanted as my marchioness, and I wouldn't have given up."

She tipped her head, studied his eyes. "Why? I always wondered why you were so sure, so focused—because you were, virtually from the moment we ran into each other at Henrietta and James's engagement ball."

His smile deepened. "I wasn't certain when we met there—I was afterward."

"Good God—what did I say?"

"It wasn't what you said so much as what you did."

"Ah." She nodded. "I remember. The challenge. I didn't swoon at your feet."

He grunted. "You've never swooned in your life."

"True, but confess—it was that, wasn't it?"

"No. It wasn't." He hesitated but felt compelled to admit, "That was part of it, I suppose, but it was more that I couldn't control you, that you were unpredictable, and that fascinated me." Death was coming; there was no reason not to tell her the rest. He drew breath and went on, "But that wasn't the reason I thought to look your way in the first place—why I deliberately sought you out at the ball."

Her gaze turned arrested, intrigued. "Why, then?"

"In a word, family." He focused on their linked hands. "The Cavanaughs . . . I told you my half siblings and I are close, that we share a difficult to describe bond. That bond grew out of our common lack of anything like normal mothering. My mother died when I was three, and even though the others had Lavinia, I've described how she views them, how she's always treated them. They're little more than animated dolls to her. Our bond grew out of not having a normal family, not having the hub, the lynchpin a mother normally provides. Not having a mother to care for us was one thing all five of us shared. And as I was the oldest by six and more years, the others looked to me. We held together and cared for each other as best we could. My father did what he could, but with Lavinia constantly in his way, he didn't get far. After he died, I helped Rand, and later Kit, get out from under Lavinia's paw, but Stacie and Godfrey are still trapped, and I won't . . ." He tipped his head. "Wouldn't have been able to free them until they turned twenty-five."

He paused, then, his gaze on their twined fingers, went on, "But the pertinent point is that since my grandparents' generation, the Cavanaughs haven't functioned as a family. I wanted to . . . make that better, to put it right, but I don't, myself, know the ways. I haven't experienced them. I saw other families in the ton—like the Cynsters, and some others—that are so . . . strong. That's the only word I have for it—that structure where each branch supports the others to the extent that the entire tree is damned near invincible."

Raising his head, he met her eyes. "I wanted that for the Cavanaughs, and there you were, the last Cynster girl unwed . . . and then you refused to swoon at my feet and our fates were sealed."

Her eyes had narrowed slightly; her lips parted, but before she could speak, he held up a staying hand. "And yes, knowing that Cynsters only marry for love, I freely admit that I was perfectly prepared to cold-bloodedly pretend to fall in love with you if that was what it took to win you as my marchioness, to be the mother of my children and the matriarch of the Cavanaughs . . ." Eyes locking with hers, he drew in a massive breath, let it out with, "But then I discovered I didn't need to pretend."

Lost in the deepening cornflower-blue of her eyes, he raised her hand, pressed a kiss to her knuckles, then turned her hand and brushed a caress to her wrist while uncurling her fingers; lowering his head, eyes still locked with hers, he pressed an even more lingering kiss to her palm. And soft and low stated, "I discovered that, somewhere along the way, I'd fallen in love with you."

She blinked rapidly, then rather mistily smiled. "Yes, I know. And if you don't know that I love you as much as you love me, you haven't been paying attention."

He grinned, then let the expression turn rueful. "So I didn't need to confess?"

Her smile deepened. "Don't misunderstand—hearing you say the words is wonderful, and I used to think that was the pinnacle of my desire. But over the last weeks, I've realized that seeing the emotion, the sentiment, in action, feeling it and experiencing it every day in myriad little ways, is simply so much more. Feeling love, experiencing being loved, is priceless—it's all I could ever want, and all I'll ever ask of you, that you continue to love me as you already do."

No longer smiling, he murmured, "That's one thing you don't need to ask—you've possessed my heart for weeks. It will be yours forever."

They were both aware of time running out, of this possibly being the last private exchange they would ever share. Neither mentioned loving until death did them part; death hovered too close to bear.

Still, she found a soft smile. "Well, now that you've given me the words, you won't need to confess again. I know how it is for noblemen like you—the violence it does to your feelings."

He let his brows rise, after a moment said, "Strangely, I think *not* saying the words, not owning to loving you and trying instead to deny the feeling . . . the violence that would do would far outstrip any effect of admitting to said feeling." He met her gaze. "Admitting to love."

She laughed softly—and even he heard the effort she was making, trying to be brave. Ducking her head, she pressed into his arms. He closed them around her; the temperature underground was cool, and they'd both started losing heat.

Time ticked inexorably by.

And suddenly, sitting there in their underground prison with her warm and vital and so much his, so perfectly complementary, in his arms, full realization of what he'd succeeded in seizing—what together they'd succeeded in creating—and now stood on the brink of losing, welled up and overflowed.

She'd brought him all he'd ever wanted, and more. Combined, their potential was beyond his wildest dreams. But their successes would go for naught; their potential would never be fulfilled.

Regret and helplessness, bitterness and sorrow, swamped him.

He couldn't remember the last time he'd cried, but tears welled, and he bent his head. Laid his cheek against her hair. Moistened his lips and said, his voice low, rough, "My only regret will be that we didn't have a chance to grow old together—to have our children, and laugh and cry and challenge each other." His voice broke and he stopped.

She clutched him more tightly; he felt her gulp, felt her breath hitch, sensed the tightness in her chest that matched the constriction of his own.

He sighed and let his head sag lower. "I'm sorry."

She lifted her head, raised her hands and framed his face. "No! This is not your fault. It's *hers*." Fierce and indomitable, she looked into his eyes. Her fingertips found his tears and brushed them away with no flicker in her gaze to show she'd even registered. She searched his eyes. "You—" She froze.

Then, very slowly, she drew one hand from his cheek and stared at her fingertips.

The look on her face brought him instantly alert. "What?" He glanced at the tunnel mouth, but there was no sound from there. He looked back at her and saw an expression of dawning wonder break across her face.

"There's a breeze." Pushing out of his arms, she sat up and held her hand to the wall between them, turning her palm and fingers around an inch from the surface. "I can feel it on my damp skin."

Scrambling to her feet, she faced the wall. "It's coming from around here."

Getting up, he joined her. Had to ask, "Are you sure?"

The look she cast him told him not to be stupid. "Lick a finger—you should be able to feel it, too." She was moving her hand, dampened with his tears, along the seam between two rows of stone blocks. "There!" Excitement rang in her voice. Stepping close to the wall, she squinted at the mortar, then turned to him, urgency and more in her eyes. "There's a crack—and I can feel cool air on my face." She stepped back and waved him forward. "Try it."

He licked a finger, held it near the spot. And felt nothing. Inwardly sighing, he started to turn—a definite waft of air passed across his dampened skin. Hardly daring to breathe, he focused on the spot and saw the fracture in the mortar.

Stepping back, he studied the wall, then glanced over his shoulder. Looking down at the floor, he saw what from any other position was far less obvious—a slight trough worn in the stone. "Damn—the tunnel diverts, but goes on." Following the line of the trough, he turned to the wall. "It goes on, but—"

"It's been blocked up." Mary rushed to pick up the poker. "If we can shift the stones, we might be able to escape."

He took the poker from her, then remembered. "Here." He fished in his pockets, pulled out the skewers from one, the forks from another. "Use these, and let's try to loosen just this one stone."

They fell to with a combined will born of inner strength and stubborn determination. She scraped along one side, he on the other. Between the forks and the skewers, they cleared the joints to a depth of four inches. The block was still stuck, but pressing both hands and throwing his weight onto it, he sensed it was only just holding.

"Step away." He waved her back, then, holding the poker by the haft, he rammed the blunt end of the handle onto a corner of the block, then repeated the exercise down one side, then along the next, around the edge of the stone.

Mary glanced back at the tunnel. "How long do you think we have?"

"I checked a few minutes ago. It's heading toward eleven o'clock." He bashed at the stone and felt it jar. "We'll know when they're coming—they'll have to shift those sacks. But if I was Lavinia, I wouldn't get back here until midnight at least. Assuming Claude Potherby isn't a party to this—and the more I consider it, the more I doubt he would be—then returning any earlier would risk raising his suspicions."

"True." Impatient, she jigged. "Is it moving?"

"Not yet." He struck twice more with the poker, then handed it to her. "Now, let's see."

Settling his feet on the floor, he flattened his palms on the stone, braced his arms, his back, then drew in a massive breath, held it, and shoved.

The block shifted half an inch.

Mary softly cheered, literally danced.

He dragged in another breath, braced, and pushed again—this time leaning further, longer . . .

With Mary calling encouragement, he repeated the process three more times before the stone finally gave, yielding to the pressure, scraping slowly back, then with a last *scritch* the block suddenly fell, toppling back and down. They heard it thud on the ground beyond the wall.

Drawing his arms out of the hole, he stepped back as Mary rushed up with one of the lanterns. She played the light through the hole. "It *is* a passage! Thank God!" Then, "Ugh—cobwebs!"

He laughed. When she sent him a narrow-eyed look, he waved at the hole. "Freedom beckons and you're worried about cobwebs?"

"No—I'm worried about what *makes* cobwebs. I told you I hate creepy crawlies, and spiders definitely qualify."

"Somehow, I think you'll bear it." He examined the stone blocks above and below the hole they'd made. "We need these two blocks out, then I think I'll be able to fit through."

They set to work again. Conscious of the minutes ticking by, once they'd pushed the second block through he tried to insist that she squeeze through and work from the other side—from where, if their would-be killers came for them, she could still run off and escape—but she refused point-blank. "Spiders, remember. I'll need you by my side to bear with them."

One glance at her face, at the stubborn set of her lips and chin, warned him further argument would be a waste of breath. And they didn't have time to waste, either.

Luckily, the third block came away more easily, gravity helping it fall from its moorings.

"All right." Mary looked around. "What do we take?"

"The poker." He hefted it. "And both lanterns."

She picked up both lanterns; they'd turned one very low to conserve the oil.

Taking the brighter lantern, he leaned into the gap and used its light to scan the tunnel beyond. "No spiders." And the tunnel walls and ceiling looked solid and stable, safe enough. Reaching as far as he could, he set the lantern down on the tunnel floor, then drew back and offered Mary his hand. He saw her debate urging him to go first, but she was starting to get nervous over the passing time; so was he. Gripping his hand, she gathered her skirts in the other and clambered through the opening.

Releasing her, he cast a last glance around their prison, so nearly, he suspected, their tomb, then he handed the second lantern and the poker through to her and, with much angling of his shoulders and a curse or two, climbed though.

They set out immediately, needing no urging to put distance between them and the cellar. Neither spoke for a good ten minutes, then Mary, walking at Ryder's side, her fingers clutching his left sleeve, whispered, "Do you know where we're going?"

"No, but the area is riddled with cave systems."

After a moment, she murmured, "Aren't there stories about people getting lost in such labyrinths and never being seen again?"

"Yes, but we're not in just any tunnel. This one's man-made—or rather it most likely started out as part of a natural system, but it's been widened and worked on." He nodded at the walls. "You can see the marks of chisels and picks."

She looked and felt some of the fear that had wormed its way into her recede. "So . . . if this tunnel's been worked on by people, then presumably it leads somewhere."

"That's my theory. And the air is moving, which means there's an opening to outside somewhere."

They hurried on as fast as they could, that tantalizing waft of air in their faces the ultimate promise of survival. They came to branches, the opening to other passages, but those were natural, the floors and walls untouched by human tools. It was easy enough to stay on their path, one that, as far as Mary could tell, led them steadily away from the Dower House and its secret cellar.

Eventually, she whispered, "Do you have any idea in which direction we're going?"

"It's not easy to tell underground, but I think we're heading toward Axford, which means the abbey is some way to our right."

As the words left Ryder's lips, the lantern beam he was playing ahead of them was suddenly swallowed by black. They both slowed; swinging the lantern beam in a wider arc, he realized they'd come to a cavern.

Stepping inside, they halted. He played the light up and could just discern the ceiling. The cavern was wide enough that only the section the lantern beam lit remained visible, but as he swept the beam across the floor, Mary gripped his arm. "There." She pointed to their left.

He shone the lantern that way and saw what she had. A large stone block, roughly rectangular, higher than his waist and wider than he was tall . . . "It's an altar." As they neared, that became clearer. A glint of metal on the cavern wall had him lifting the lantern beam.

"A crucifix."

Crude, rusty, but recognizable.

Mary glanced around. "This was a church. A secret chapel."

He nodded. "Protestants or Catholics—could have been either."

"Mary's reign or Elizabeth's. They came here to worship in secret."

With his back to the altar, Ryder played the lantern beam slowly around the cavern. There were five entrances. He thought, then said, "It was the Protestants in Mary's reign."

"How can you be sure?"

"Because the Cavanaughs, and most of the families around here, were never Catholic, or at least, not truly." He pointed to the entrance now to their left, almost opposite the passage from which they'd come. "So that way will lead to Axford, the village. And that"—he pointed to the next tunnel mouth—"makes that The Oaks. And that one's Kitchener Hall, and that leaves that"—he pointed to the tunnel almost directly opposite the altar—"as the way to the abbey."

Mary glanced at him. "Are you sure?"

"No." Through the dimness, he met her eyes. "But we need to keep moving, and as long as we stick to a worked-on tunnel with air on our faces, we should come out somewhere."

Glancing back at the tunnel from the Dower House, she nodded. "Let's go."

They did. The tunnel they hoped led to the abbey had been cut wider and the floor evened out; they made good time. They'd been striding along for perhaps half a mile when Mary tugged his sleeve. "What's the time?"

He glanced at her, decided a pause wouldn't hurt. Handing the fully lit lantern to her, he pulled out his watch, held its face in the beam. "Not quite midnight." Tucking the watch back, he retook the lantern and they walked on.

The tunnel slowly climbed, then they came to a spot where it narrowed severely, leaving just enough space for a man to fit through. There appeared to be a wider space beyond, and past that . . . came the soft swoosh and splash of falling water.

Ryder stared through the gap; he tried angling the lantern beam through, but the light reflected back—from a curtain of falling water. "I don't believe it."

Peering past his shoulder, Mary asked, "Where is it?"

"I think we're behind the waterfall in the grotto above the abbey lake." He stood back and waved her through. "Trust me, there won't be any spiders. Not with all that water about."

Mary handed him her lantern, then stepped into the crevice and edged through. "Just as long as I don't get soaked."

She emerged onto a narrow rock ledge that curved to her left around the waterfall.

"Here—take the lanterns."

She turned and took the lanterns as Ryder handed them through, followed by the poker.

Then, with difficulty and several curses, he squeezed

through the opening and they were both standing in the spray from the waterfall—one she'd thus far seen only from the mouth of the grotto.

Instead of clambering on and making her way out, she set down her burdens, looked up at Ryder, then smiled, stretched up, wrapped her arms about his neck and kissed him—ferociously.

He closed his arms around her and kissed her back— equally passionate, even more possessive—but then he drew back and set her on her feet. "We're not safe yet. It's a good half mile to the house."

Once out of the grotto, damp but not soaked, they doused the lanterns. Ryder knew every inch of his gardens, and the moon shed enough light for them to see their way.

Carrying one lantern and the poker in one hand, his other hand closed firmly about Mary's, Ryder strode along as rapidly as her shorter legs would allow. He'd given thanks several times that she was no delicate miss, no weak, wilting female; she'd kept up without complaint through the tunnels and continued to walk swiftly by his side.

Ahead of them, the abbey was ablaze. Light shone from the long library windows, and flares had been planted in the forecourt. There was activity in the stable yard but, Ryder was relieved to note, no carriage drawn up before the front steps. "Just pray that Forsythe hasn't reached the point of sending for the magistrate, Lord Hughes, yet. If at all possible, I want to handle this myself."

Mary glanced at him. "You're the Lord Marshal for the area, aren't you?"

He nodded. "But as I'm the one who's disappeared . . ."

"Yes, well, you're back now, and ready to resume control."

He smiled, but as they strode on and he thought further, he sobered. "I'm trying to think of what evidence we have that it was Lavinia behind this—the men who abducted you are the best and very likely only witnesses." He met Mary's eyes as she looked at him. "Did you get a look at any of the three when they grabbed you?"

"No."

He grimaced and looked ahead.

"But I smelled them."

He looked at her. "Smelled?"

"Horses—all three of them. It's not a smell I would mistake. And one gave orders to the others—I'll know him by his voice, too." Mary glanced at him. "How many men work in the Dower House stables?"

Slowly, he grinned. "Lavinia has a favorite groom, and there are two stable hands, I believe."

"Well, then." Mary quickened her pace. "I suspect we know who our three miscreants are."

"Hmm . . . that may be, but I understand the groom, Snickert, is devoted to Lavinia—she'll doubtless claim he acted on his own, and he might not give her up."

"Perhaps, but do you think all three will hang for her?"

He inclined his head. "Probably not." They reached the terrace and went up the steps, heading around the house to the front door. "I suggest we calm the troops, then tidy ourselves, and then, despite the hour, I believe we should pay Lavinia a visit."

Glancing at Mary, he saw a smile—a particularly ferocious one—curve her lips. "Yes. Let's."

They turned the corner.

And walked into consternation.

Chapter Sixteen

$\mathcal{T}$he pandemonium that erupted when they walked calmly into the midst of their panicking household took mere minutes to calm.

Ryder was astonished—and abjectly grateful he had Mary by his side; despite having been his marchioness for only three weeks, she'd established her position and developed a certain no-nonsense tone his staff patently found reassuring. She stemmed their fussing and the inevitable avalanche of questions with a minimum of declarative sentences. Subsequently, unimpeded by her bedraggled state, she marched across the tiles issuing crisp orders right and left, and like a well-conditioned team, the household responded to her hands on their reins; in short order he and she were in their respective bathing chambers, supplied with hot water and fresh clothes, brushes, towels, and scented soaps.

Fifteen minutes later, restored to their customary sartorial elegance, side by side they descended the main stairs, crossed the front hall, and went out through the doors Forsythe held open. Their carriage stood waiting, with Ridges on the box, Filmore beside him, and two burly grooms, one already up behind, the other holding open the carriage door.

Behind them, other than Forsythe, the great house was once again devoid of males. Before he'd followed Mary upstairs, Ryder had dispatched every man, other than the four who would travel with them, to form a cordon around the Dower House. He'd put Dukes in charge; the man knew every inch of the estate, including the Dower House woods. Ryder's orders had been for every man to keep silent and out of sight, and to allow any who wished to enter to do so unchallenged, but to ensure that no one left.

Handing Mary into the carriage, he followed. The footman shut the door, then swung up behind as Ridges set the horses in motion.

"What's the time?" Mary had seen Ryder check his watch just before they reached the carriage.

"Twenty minutes after midnight. We'll be there in less than five minutes."

"So she might or might not have returned yet."

Ryder had settled beside her, his hand wrapped around one of hers; her shoulder rocked against his arm as the carriage turned out of the abbey drive. "I asked Dukes to scout the house and see what he could learn of who was there, and in particular where Lavinia's groom—Snickert—and the other two stable hands were."

"Hmm . . . correct me if I'm wrong, but we assume Potherby will return with Lavinia, and we don't actually know his standing in this."

"No, we don't." Ryder gently squeezed her hand. "We'll have to play it by ear and watch how he reacts."

The carriage slowed, turned, then rolled slowly forward.

A soft owl-call sounded just ahead, and the horses were drawn to a halt.

Ryder let down the window as Dukes appeared.

The head gardener saluted. "Her ladyship hasn't returned yet, my lord. The Dower House staff are here, but it seems they've only just got in. They're all in the kitchen having a late supper. We've been listening from outside the window. Seems her ladyship insisted they all go off to see the circus in Marlborough—all except Snickert and the two stable hands. None of the rest of the staff knows what those three have been doing—there've been questions aplenty—but all three are there now, standing about the kitchen and looking right smug. Did hear the cook complaining that the bolt on the basement door had been broken—Snickert told her not to worry about it, but he and his two mates are sticking close by that door."

Ryder thought, then nodded. "Here's what I want done."

Three minutes later, their carriage drew up before the Dower House front steps. Ryder handed Mary down. Head high, gowned in an elegant carriage dress, she walked beside him up the steps to the front door. A small lamp high on the wall was still burning, shedding a pool of light immediately before the door but leaving the space to either side in deep shadow.

Halting in the light, Ryder nodded at Dukes. Leading the six men who were melting back into the dimness on either side of the door, Dukes pulled a dangling chain, and in the distance they heard a bell jangle.

Dukes joined his men, indiscernible in the gloom.

A minute passed, then they heard the measured tread of a butler's footsteps approaching, then the latch was lifted and the door swung open.

The middle-aged butler who stood in the doorway, a lanky footman hovering behind him, blinked in surprise. "My lord?"

"Good evening, Caldicott." Sweeping Mary forward, Ryder ushered her in.

Caldicott fell back, uncertain. "My lord?" Then Caldicott saw the seven large men crowding the doorway behind them. "What . . . ? My lord!" Caldicott's eyes went wide and he looked back at Ryder. "Her ladyship—"

"Is, I understand, not presently here." Ryder caught and held Caldicott's gaze. "You know who owns this house, and who in reality pays the wages of all those who work here."

Caldicott hesitated, then carefully nodded. "Indeed, my lord."

"That being so, speaking as the ultimate employer of all the staff here, this is what I want you to do."

Five minutes later, the household was secure. The Dower House staff were confined in the kitchen, with two of the abbey footmen standing guard inside the door leading to the kitchens and another blocking the back door. Snickert and his two helpers, reportedly belligerently mutinous, were sitting atop the stacked sacks of grain in the basement, watched over by Dukes and three of the abbey men, all armed. The abbey coach had been driven into the stable yard, out of sight of the front of the house; Ridges and Filmore were in charge in the stable yard, waiting for Lavinia's carriage to roll in.

Satisfied, Ryder led Mary into the unlighted drawing room and shut the door. Through the gloom, he met her eyes. "Now we wait."

She nodded, looked around, then crossed to a chaise and sat. "Why didn't you want Snickert and the other two to see or hear us? Or to in any way learn that we've escaped their trap?"

Ryder had had Dukes take charge of securing Snickert, giving orders for the abbey staff to behave as if they had no idea where he and Mary were. He paused by a table to light the lamp atop it. "Because while Snickert and his cronies think they hold the winning card—that you and I are still trapped below them—they'll be much easier to manage. Snickert, at least, will believe to the last that Lavinia will be grateful enough to get them out of any potential difficulty . . . and, in truth, if you and I were still missing, no amount of suspicion of foul deeds befalling us would get the abbey staff or even the authorities anywhere."

He'd also sworn Caldicott and the footman who had come to the door to secrecy regarding his and Mary's presence, then had allowed them to rejoin the others in the kitchen. That neither Caldicott nor the rest of the staff had any idea what had been going on had been transparent enough; Dukes had reported that they were puzzled and confused, but willing enough to wait in the kitchen and allow whatever game their betters were engaged in to play out elsewhere.

The wick of the lamp caught and Ryder turned the flame low. Replacing the lamp glass, he glanced at the window. Mary had realized and was already on her feet. Crossing to the wide bay window, she hauled one long heavy curtain halfway across, then went to the other side and started to draw its mate, but then paused. Screened by the curtain, she stared out through the narrow gap remaining. "There's a carriage—a curricle, I think—coming up the drive. Whoever's driving it, they're in a furious rush."

Frowning, Ryder circled to peer over her head. Using the curtain as a screen as she was, he looked out.

Glancing up, Mary saw his frown deepen. "Who is it?"

His expression grew grimmer. "Rand." His hand clenched on the edge of the curtain, then he met her eyes. "I still don't believe he had anything to do with this."

She let her lips curve. "Nor do I."

Ryder studied her eyes, read her confidence in his judgment, then, glancing up as, gravel crunching, Rand angled his lathered horses into the forecourt, he drew the curtain fully closed. "Wait here. I'll go and let him in."

By the time Ryder reached the front door and swung it open, Rand was striding up the steps.

He checked his pace at the sight of Ryder in the doorway.

Even in the poor light, Ryder could tell Rand's face was unnaturally pale, his features drawn—and clearly saw those features transform, saw them light up with relief and unrestrained joy as Rand took in the sight of him.

"You're all right!" Quickening his pace, Rand crossed the porch.

Ryder gestured. "As you see—but come in."

As Rand stepped past him, Ryder saw the shadowy figures of his men drift in to take the curricle around the house. Shutting the door, he turned to find Rand looking him up and down.

A puzzled frown forming on his face, Rand met Ryder's eyes. "You're not even injured."

"No. Not in the least." Ryder waved him into the drawing room and Rand instinctively obeyed, but as Ryder followed him in and shut the door, he could see the questions forming in Rand's mind.

Seeing Mary, Rand halted, then moved forward, holding out his hands. "Mary."

"Randolph." She gave him her hands and Rand bussed her proffered cheek.

But as he drew back, he looked even more confused. He glanced at Ryder. "Clearly, you're both well."

Ryder arched a brow. "Why did you think we weren't? And why are you here?"

"For one and the same reason." His frown deepening, Rand reached into his pocket and drew out a note. He handed it to Ryder, then glanced from him to Mary. "And if it comes to that, what are you two doing here? Where's Mama?"

Smoothing out the note, Ryder scanned its few lines, then offered the single sheet to Mary. "As it transpires, it appears we're all here as part of the same game."

Taking the note, Mary read it aloud. " 'Randolph, dearest. Come urgently, darling—something's gone terribly wrong at the abbey. Come to the Dower House first, and I'll explain.' " Raising her head, Mary looked at Ryder. "When did she write this?"

At Ryder's inquiring look, Rand shrugged. "It was delivered by courier. I got it at nine o'clock and left as soon as I could."

"So assuming she didn't dispatch it from here," Ryder said, "but from somewhere closer to London, then the latest she could have written this was about six o'clock."

Lips tightening, Mary nodded her agreement.

Rand looked from one to the other. "What's going on?" A thread of weary wariness wound through his voice. He sighed. "What's Mama done now, and where is she?"

"At a guess, she's been out since early afternoon, possibly even earlier. As for what she's done . . . I believe it would be best if you hear that from her."

Rand studied Ryder's face, then nodded. "All right."

The three of them turned to the sofa and chairs but halted. All raised their heads, listening. Mary met Ryder's eyes. "Another carriage."

"Also racketing along." Ryder went to look through the curtains, Rand at his shoulder.

"That's Kit's curricle," Rand said.

"And he's got Stacie and Godfrey with him." Ryder glanced at Rand. "She must have sent notes to all of you."

Rand nodded. "I'll let them in."

He went out, and Ryder returned to stand beside Mary. Rand had left the drawing room door open. They heard Kit yell, "What's happened?"

"Nothing, apparently," Rand replied. "Ryder and Mary are here—come inside."

Stacie reached Rand first. "My God! Are they really all right? That's all I could think that Mama's note meant."

The next instant Stacie rushed into the drawing room, saw Ryder and Mary, and all but flew across the room to hug first Ryder, then Mary. "Thank God you're all right!"

Then Godfrey and Kit came in, followed by Rand, who closed the door. Hugs and transparently genuine exclamations of relief came first, then the questions.

Having had time to think, Ryder held to his tack of refusing to answer the latter, other than to assure his half siblings that he and Mary were indeed as hale and whole as they appeared. Standing with his back to the fireplace, he kept his hands clasped behind his back; he'd torn several nails while wrestling with the stone blocks, and that was the sort of thing Stacie might notice.

Although puzzled, the four accepted his edict readily enough, all so relieved by his continuing health that they were willing to humor him. Seizing on that, he said, "When your mother arrives . . . it would be best you hear what she has to say without any input from Mary or me." He glanced at Mary, now seated on the sofa. "In fact, it would be best if you gave no indication that we were here and simply asked her your questions." Looking down the room, he tipped his head at the oriental screen used in deepest winter to block the draft from the door; it was presently standing half folded in the corner and would be half concealed by the opened door. "When Lavinia comes in, Mary and I will stand behind the screen and"—he glanced at the others—"I would greatly appreciate it if you could all summon sufficient histrionic ability to convincingly pretend that you haven't seen us and have no idea where we are."

The others exchanged glances; none knew better the fraught nature of the relationship between Ryder and their mother, and all were intelligent enough to guess that some critical point had been reached, if not passed. But as they looked back at him, Ryder saw in their faces that each was willing to do as he'd asked. That each of them trusted him, even in this.

After a moment's hesitation, Rand asked, "Is this really necessary?"

Ryder knew Rand posed the question in the sense of sparing them, not Lavinia. Meeting Rand's eyes, he nodded. "Yes. I believe it is." If he'd had difficulty accepting that Lavinia was a would-be murderess, one who had attempted to have him and Mary killed, how much more difficult would accepting that truth be for her own children? "As I said, you need to hear the explanation for all this directly from her."

Lips thinning, Rand inclined his head. "Then, yes, of course we'll do as you ask."

The others all nodded their agreement.

Kit rose and went to the screen. He widened it, angling it to create a larger space behind it.

Ryder went to help him, but as he reached Kit, they all heard the rattle of carriage wheels—this time not racing but rolling sedately along. "That will most likely be Lavinia." Ryder glanced at Mary; she rose and crossed to his side.

Kit finished resetting the screen. "That should do."

Ryder took Mary's hand and looked across the room at Rand.

Rand nodded. "Get out of sight, and I'll go and let her in." He glanced at his siblings—Kit going to sit alongside Stacie on the sofa, with Godfrey on his feet by the hearth. "Ready?"

They all nodded; Ryder drew Mary to the screen, let her slip into the space behind it, then followed.

He looked over the top of the screen, nodded to the other three, then crouched down; he was too tall to stand. The gap between the screen's panels allowed him to see the area before the fireplace well enough. One hand resting on his shoulder, Mary remained upright and peered out, too.

They heard voices in the hall, Lavinia exclaiming, and Rand greeting her, then Potherby. The front door shut, then Lavinia swept into the room. She was dressed for a ball in a cream-and-red striped gown, a fringed red silk shawl draped about her shoulders.

Seeing her younger children gathered before the fireplace, she flung her arms wide. "My dears! I didn't expect any of you until tomorrow, but really, it's just as well. *Such* a disaster! Such a dreadful, *dreadful* thing!"

Kit had risen at her entrance. "What dreadful thing, Mama?"

"Why, whatever has happened to Ryder and his Mary, of course—they've disappeared! Everyone at the abbey is no doubt searching high and low, but it seems they've vanished." Dropping her evening gloves and reticule on the table, Lavinia advanced on the three, patently expecting to be hugged and kissed. Kit, Stacie, and Godfrey obliged; if she noticed their uneasiness, Lavinia gave no sign.

Rand, who had followed Claude Potherby in and shut the door, hung back at that end of the room; for his part,

Potherby was staring at Lavinia, a puzzled expression on his face. Rand saw it. He looked at Lavinia. "What do you think has happened to Ryder and Mary, Mama?"

Lavinia spread her hands. "How on earth should I know, dearest? Perhaps he took her out driving in one of those ridiculous phaetons of his and overturned, and they've both broken their necks."

"And you don't think Filmore or the abbey grooms would know?" Godfrey, pale, shook his head. "You know that can't be right."

Lavinia flung up her hands. "Well, I'm sure I don't know, but I can't see that it matters. Perhaps they went walking and robbers set on them, or they fell down a mine shaft, or off a cliff, or . . . or . . . whatever! The important point is that they're gone!"

"When did you hear of their disappearance, Lavinia?"

The quiet question from Claude Potherby brought Lavinia up short. Swinging to face him, she frowned, opened her mouth, then closed it and blinked.

Her children all looked at her, watching as, features blanking, she patently tried to work out her best answer.

Looking increasingly ill, Potherby moistened his lips, then, speaking as much to the others as reminding Lavinia, said, "I've been staying here for the past two days. We left here this morning at about eleven o'clock to drive to Marlborough to have luncheon there, then drove on to Quilley House later, to have dinner and attend the Hunt Ball. We left a trifle early and drove straight back." A silent moment passed, then Potherby looked at Rand. "This is the first I've heard of Raventhorne's disappearance."

Lavinia drew herself up; her face mottling, a sure sign of erupting temper, she looked down her nose at her childhood friend. "I have no idea what you're hinting at, Claude, but whatever it is, it's neither here nor there. You may take yourself off—I don't need you!" With a dismissive wave, she shifted her attention to Rand. "The critical thing—which it appears I have to spell out for you all—is that as something, *whatever it is,* has happened to Ryder and Mary, then regardless of whatever it is, it's up to *you,* Randolph, to take charge at the abbey—it's too great an estate to be left rudderless, without a master, even for a day!

"Of course, it would have been better if you'd married already—better still if you'd married Mary as I'd intended—but that's all water under the bridge—"

"What?—*wait*!" Rand had paled. "What do you mean, you intended me to marry Mary?"

Lavinia looked at him as if he were being unbelievably obtuse. "Why, that I arranged to steer her in your direction, of course. Why do you think she came swanning around?"

Behind the screen, Ryder slanted a glance at Mary's face, unsurprised to see that her lips were a thin line and her eyes had narrowed to shards.

Petulantly, Lavinia went on, "But then Ryder stepped in and stole her away, and you did nothing to stop him, you foolish boy, but in retrospect she turned out to be more hoity and difficult than I'd foreseen, so perhaps that was for the best. I'm sure I'll be able to find some nice, complaisant young lady for you once you've been installed as the Marquess of Raventhorne, but that's for later. Now . . ." Swinging around and pointing dramatically toward the abbey, Lavinia declared, "You must do what your father would have wished you to do—you have to get over there and step into Ryder's shoes and do what must be done!"

Rand held her gaze for a long moment, then his chest swelled as he drew in a breath—and shook his head. "No, Mama—I won't be stepping into Ryder's shoes, not now, and most likely not ever."

Lavinia's jaw dropped, then temper surged through her. Her eyes flared, all but incandescent with rage. Fists clenching, she closed her eyes, tipped back her head, and all but screamed, *"Don't be so stupid*! If he's gone, then you're the marquess—and trust me." Lowering her head, refocusing on

Rand, she gritted through clenched teeth, "He is *gone,* most definitely gone this time, and—"

"Actually, Lavinia"—smoothly rising, Ryder stepped out from behind the screen—"I haven't gone anywhere." He drew Mary out to stand alongside him. "And neither has my wife."

The furious choler abruptly drained from Lavinia's face. Her eyes rounded; utter disbelief was stamped across her features. "*No!*" The word was all breathless denial. She hauled in a breath. "That is . . ." She clutched her chest. "What I mean is . . ."

Ryder arched his brows. "How did we get away from your henchmen?"

Lavinia jerked as if he'd struck her. She took a step back. Glancing at Rand, then Potherby, she waved her hands, fingers spread as if to ward off the implication. "I don't know what you're talking about."

"You don't?" Ryder considered her, then coolly suggested, "Why don't we go down to the basement and see what Snickert and your stable hands have to say?"

Lavinia would have backed further, but Kit was there. He reached for her arm, but she jerked away. "No!" She looked at Kit, then at Godfrey beside him, then looked down the room at Rand. "Why are you listening to him? You always listen to him." She stamped her foot. "I'm your mother! You will do as I say—you will *not* allow him to speak to me like that."

No one said anything.

Lavinia glanced at Potherby.

His expression like stone, he met her gaze for only a fleeting instant, then turned to Ryder, met his eyes, and half bowed. "With your permission, my lord, I will leave. This is, I believe, a family matter, and not one I, I do assure you, have any role in, nor wish to have any role in."

Ryder considered, then nodded. "As you say." He hesitated, then held out his hand. "I know you've been a staunch friend to her over the years, but sometimes being a friend is not enough."

Lips a tight line, Potherby inclined his head. "Clearly." He shook Ryder's hand, then looked at Rand and nodded. "Cavanaugh." He glanced at the others, inclined his head. At the very last, he looked at Lavinia. Head rising, Potherby drew in a tight breath, then evenly stated, "Good-bye, Lavinia." With that, he turned and walked out of the room.

The door shut with a soft click behind him.

Lavinia stared at the panels. After a moment, she shifted her gaze to Ryder and drew herself up, poker-stiff. "I don't know what you're about, what aspersions you're seeking to cast—"

"No aspersions, Lavinia. Rest assured, all I'm seeking is to establish the facts." Ryder paused, then went on, "And to my way of thinking, the facts will be most clearly revealed by hearing what your men presently in the basement have to say."

"By all means." Lavinia waved at the door. "Go down to the basement if you think it will help you. I'll remain here."

Before she could sit, Kit caught her arm. "No, Mama— you have to come, too."

At a look from Kit, Godfrey, white-faced but as determined as the others, took Lavinia's other arm. Between them, the brothers turned her to the door.

"No!" Lavinia tried to struggle, but they held her fast. She all but wailed, "I don't want to go down to the basement."

"Hush, Mama—how undignified." Coming up beside Kit, Stacie reached across and lightly gripped her mother's hand. "There's no sense in fighting this—we're all resolved—and you won't want the staff to see and gossip, you know you won't."

That argument succeeded where most others would have failed; Lavinia ceased struggling.

Ryder added, "You can't seriously imagine any harm will come to you in your own basement with your children all around you."

His even tone had the desired effect; Lavinia once again pulled herself up, drew in a huge breath, then raised her head. "Very well. As you are all so intent on this, let's go down and see what we'll see."

Ryder and Mary led the way out. Rand and Stacie followed, with Lavinia, Kit, and Godfrey, the brothers unobtrusively holding Lavinia between them, bringing up the rear.

In the kitchen, Ryder paused before the basement door to tell Dukes to pass the word that Potherby, his valet, and his coachman and groom were to be allowed to leave, and that the rest of the staff were free to go to their beds, then their small procession descended the steps into the basement.

Two of the abbey gardeners were standing guard at the bottom of the steps. Ryder caught their eyes. "Go up and wait with Dukes."

The pair nodded, hung back until the others had descended, then went up and pulled the door shut.

One lantern had been left by the steps; several others lit the area where Snickert and his companions sat lounging on the sacks concealing the trapdoor. Noting the continuing smugness on the three men's faces, their relaxed postures, Mary realized that, with no light falling on her and Ryder as they walked down the aisle between the high shelves, the men hadn't yet realized that it was the prisoners they thought trapped beneath them who were approaching.

Sure enough, the instant she and Ryder moved into the circle of light at that end of the room, all smugness fell from the men's expressions; their faces blanked, then, eyes widening, they tensed.

One—she assumed he was Snickert—snarled; features abruptly contorting, he launched himself at Ryder.

Releasing Ryder's arm, Mary stepped smartly back.

As Ryder stepped forward and smashed his fist—powered by his considerable temper—into Snickert's face.

Something crunched. Snickert staggered back, then,

blood welling from his nose, sprawled on his back on the floor.

"You *beast*!"

Mary turned to see Lavinia break free from Kit and Godfrey; startled by Snickert's attack, both brothers had loosened their grips.

But Lavinia didn't try to flee; she rushed forward, pushing past Stacie, then ducking around Mary to fly to Snickert's side.

Astonished, they all stared at her as she crouched beside Snickert, bending over him, apparently raising his head.

Snickert moaned—then *shrieked*. His legs jerked, stiffened, then fell lax.

Utter shock held them all immobile for a heartbeat, then Ryder cursed. Swooping, he clamped Lavinia's wrists, one in each of his hands, and hauled her bodily up. "Damn you," he ground out. "What have you done?"

"Oh, God!" Randolph had rushed forward, too. Now he stared in horror at something clutched in Lavinia's left hand. Something that glinted, then dripped.

Mary discovered she'd slapped a hand over her lips. Through her fingers, she said, "It's her shawl pin."

Lavinia's shawl was now trailing, a tide of crimson silk, along the floor.

Randolph crouched beside Snickert. A second later, in a tone of stunned disbelief, he said, "She stabbed him through the eye. He's dead."

Ryder's grip tightened about Lavinia's wrists.

She seemed not to notice. She was panting, looking down at Snickert, at Randolph crouching there. "I had to kill him—you see that, don't you?"

Slowly turning, Randolph looked up at her. "No, I don't. Why?" Face contorting in something close to pain, he thrust a hand toward Snickert's still form. "You just *murdered* him! My God, what do you think can excuse that?"

Lavinia tried to go to Randolph; Ryder held her back. Ignoring that, as if she could convince Randolph, she hurried to say, "He was the only one who knew. Now he's gone"— she lifted one shoulder a fraction—"there's nothing to be done. Nothing anyone can prove, so everything's all right."

"All right?" Randolph's expression lay well beyond incredulous. "How can you imagine this will ever be *all right*?" Condemnation, absolute and unwavering, was etched in his features.

Still panting, Lavinia studied his face, then her eyes narrowed. Without warning, she tipped back her head and screeched, "I did it for you!" Pulling against Ryder's hold, she repeated the words, all but spitting them at Randolph. When all he did was stare at her, horror in every line of his face, she shrieked at him, "*For you!*"

Mary saw the words hit Randolph, saw his face set, his expression lock, but her attention immediately shifted to Ryder. Ryder, who protected everyone in his care, and in this case . . .

She saw the violence that rolled through him, the wave that turned his muscles to iron, saw the stark reality in his face as, eyes closing, he fought against the urge . . . he could so very easily kill Lavinia.

Drawing breath, Mary walked up behind him, put her hand to his back, and gently rubbed. "Ryder."

Ryder shuddered. She didn't have to say or do anything more. The contact, her voice, his name, was enough. Nevertheless, it took effort, and several seconds, to pull back from the brink. Slowly filling his lungs, he opened his eyes. He still held Lavinia by her wrists. As he looked at Rand, his half brother rose, turning away from his mother, patently unable to look upon her anymore; walking toward the basement wall, he halted, staring at it. Ryder found his voice. "Kit—please."

He didn't have to ask twice. Kit, the most pragmatic and solidly practical of Ryder's half brothers, came forward. Kit gestured to the two stable hands, who had witnessed the entire incident and remained frozen in shock atop the pile of sacks. "You two—off. Stand over there." Kit pointed to the side of the basement, a little way from Rand.

The two men jerked to awareness, then scrambled to obey.

Kit turned to Lavinia; not a trace of emotion showed in his face or colored his voice as he said, "Madam." As Ryder eased his hold on her wrists, Kit indicated the sacks. "Please sit."

Wrenching her wrists free, Lavinia rubbed them. Narrowing, her gaze traveled over Kit, then shifted to Godfrey and Stacie. Ryder glanced back; the younger two stood shoulder to shoulder, blocking the way out of the basement. Under their mother's scrutiny, they remained unmoving, unresponsive.

Finally, Lavinia turned, walked to the pile of sacks, swung about, and sat.

Only then did she look at Ryder, but Ryder was no longer interested in her.

To spare his half siblings, he needed to bring this entire tale to as neat an end as possible. Fixing his gaze on the two stable hands, he said, "As I'm sure you know, I'm the Lord Marshal of this area. That means I can hand you over to the authorities—it also means I can act as the authority."

"We saw her." The older of the pair nodded at Lavinia. "Plain as day saw her stab Snickert right in the eye with that pin of hers. Killed him, she did. In cold blood an' all."

"Yes, I know," Ryder replied. "But that's not what I need you to tell me. Both of you helped Snickert abduct my wife from the grounds of our home yesterday afternoon."

The man who'd spoken looked at Mary. "She can't've known it were us—none of us was ever in her sight, and Snickert was the only one who spoke."

"Indeed." Ryder inwardly shook his head. "But as you've just confirmed, you were there. Don't waste time trying to deny it. Abducting a marchioness, incarcerating her, shooting at us—"

"That were Snickert."

"Regardless, by helping him, you are guilty of the crime, too. For doing those three things alone, you are headed for the gallows. However"—Ryder held up a finger—"if you co-operate, given that I am the Lord Marshal and it was me and my wife you sought to harm, I will agree to convert your sentence from hanging to transportation." He paused, then went on, "But that will only occur if you tell me all I want to know."

The stable hands exchanged a long glance, then they looked at Ryder. Resignation seeping into his expression, the older man asked, "What do you want to know?"

"I want you to tell me, and all those here, everything you know, everything that Snickert told you, about his plans to murder me and my wife."

The man pursed his lips in thought, then said, "Don't know much about what happened in Lunnon, but he did say as how he'd hired this bent lawyer who knew some navvies weren't too particular—"

The story came tumbling out, more or less whole. La-vinia's initial plan to murder Ryder, subsequently expanded after his and Mary's marriage to include Mary, too.

"He said as she said"—the stableman nodded toward Lavinia—"that now you was married, she needed your missus bumped off first, because if we bumped you off first, you might already have knocked her up, and as her family's right powerful, they'd have swept her up and off and no one would have been able to touch her and your babe, and for some reason that weren't any good, either. You and your get—she wanted you wiped from the earth."

Rand shot a glance at Lavinia that was close to hate.

"So then—"

The stablemen continued, detailing how Snickert had got into the abbey, first to plant the adder, then the scorpion, by using a secret tunnel that led from the Dower House priest hole, hidden behind the mantelpiece in the dining room, to the chapel on the first floor of the abbey.

Ryder turned to his half siblings. "What tunnel?"

They all blinked at him. "Didn't you know?" Godfrey asked.

When Ryder shook his head, Kit humphed. "I suppose we all just assumed you did."

Turning back to the stablemen, Ryder gestured for them to continue. With a prompt here and there from Mary, and a question from Rand, they confirmed the entirety of Snickert's actions on Lavinia's behalf, ending with them using Mary to bait their trap for him, and then locking him and Mary in the cellar beneath the basement.

"Snickert thought the poisoned water was a nice touch, and apparently her ladyship agreed. We thought when her ladyship came home, we'd be opening up the door under the sacks there and finding your dead bodies laid out all neat and nice." The stableman looked at him with a certain shrewd acceptance. "Weren't to be, though, was it? Told Snickert it were never a good thing to cross swords with a nob."

Ryder met his gaze. "You should have listened to your own advice."

The older man inclined his head. "Aye, so I should." He straightened. "So, what now?"

"Now I'm going to hand you over to my men. They'll take you to the abbey—there's a holding cell there. You'll be placed in it until I can summon the constables to take you away."

"Wait." Rand walked to Lavinia and halted directly in front of her. He looked into her face. "Do you deny any of what they've said?"

She looked flatly back at him, then sneered. "Of course not." She glanced at Ryder with naked hate. "I'm just sorry I couldn't find more competent staff."

Rand studied her for a moment more, then turned and faced Ryder. "Kit and I will take her upstairs and lock her in her room."

Ryder nodded. "The rest of us will wait in the drawing

room." Without looking at Lavinia, he reached for Mary. "We'll need to discuss what to do."

Twining her arm with his, Mary walked beside him out of the basement, collecting Stacie and Godfrey as they went, leaving Rand and Kit to deal with their mother.

Now very definitely a murderess.

Tea was the universal remedy.

At Mary's suggestion, Caldicott, who had remained on duty, brought in a tray. In addition to two teapots, he'd set out some pound cake on a plate.

Watching Godfrey crumble a slice rather than eat it, Mary said, "You must be starving."

Godfrey looked down at the mound of crumbs, sighed. "I am—but I don't think I'll be able to eat anything in this house again."

Stacie shivered. "Let alone in Chapel Street."

Mary glanced at Ryder, then reached out to close her hand around one of Stacie's. "Don't worry about that. You'll be staying with us, of course." She looked across at Godfrey. "Both of you."

The looks of relief combined with real gratitude that passed over their faces were heart-wrenching.

The door opened and Randolph, followed by Kit, walked in.

Mary held up the teapot, a question in her eyes. Randolph caught his breath, then saw the glass of brandy in Ryder's hand. "Ah—no, thank you." He turned to see Kit already at the sideboard pouring two glasses. "That speaks more to my need."

Once Randolph and Kit, glasses of brandy in hand, had settled in two armchairs, Ryder glanced around the circle, then said, "So what do we do?"

"It has to be incarceration," Randolph declared. "The only question is where."

Kit nodded and leaned forward, cradling his glass between his hands. "It can't be here, for obvious reasons, nor yet on any of the family estates—too hard to keep it secret. Yet where else is possible, and—more to the point—I'm not sure I would trust anyone except us not to be drawn in by her . . . well, her ways."

Grimly, Godfrey nodded. "She doesn't look like a woman who would pull out her scarf pin and stab a man through the eye."

Stacie didn't say anything, just hugged herself tighter.

Ryder sat back. "I'll support whatever decision you make, as long as it will keep me and mine safe from her and her plotting."

"That goes without saying." Randolph looked into his glass, swirling the liquid. "I understand now why you insisted we had to hear it from her." Abruptly, he drained the glass; lowering it, he admitted, "If you'd told me that—even if I'd heard it from those men without her sitting there, listening and not reacting, and then not denying it—I honestly don't think I would truly have believed—"

A scream cut off his words. They all looked up in time to see a shape fall past the windows.

"Oh, *no!*" Hands to her face, Stacie shot to her feet.

Everyone else did, too. Mary held Stacie back, let the men rush ahead, Randolph and Kit in the lead, Godfrey close behind. Pausing in the doorway, Ryder glanced back and saw Mary following more slowly with Stacie; he met her eyes, briefly nodded, then went ahead.

By the time Mary and Stacie reached the front steps, Randolph and Kit had covered their mother's body with their coats.

Mary was grateful; she'd had more than enough shocks for one day, and she knew Stacie was at the end of her reserves. She and her brothers had had to face more in a few hours than anyone ever should have to endure.

Ryder came to Stacie's other side and helped her down the steps.

The three of them drew nearer but halted when Stacie's faltering feet did not seem to want to go further.

Her brothers saw her standing there, trembling in Mary's arms, Ryder's arm around her shoulders, and one by one they left their mother's body and joined them—the living.

Mary and Ryder surrendered Stacie into Kit's arms.

Randolph came to stand beside Ryder, his face a mask of shock. "Did she jump, do you think, or did she fall while trying to escape?"

Ryder hesitated, then said, "I can't imagine her even contemplating suicide, can you?"

One after another, they shook their heads.

"In that case," Ryder said, "as we're all agreed, I can declare her death an accident."

"She would have wanted that—it will gain her some sympathy. It was always about her." Randolph glanced back at the shrouded body lying on the gravel. "It was *always* all about her."

Mary let a moment of silence pass, then briskly stated, "Very well. Now that's been decided, let's go back inside. We have orders to give, and then all of you are coming home with us to the abbey."

She'd used her marchioness's voice and was entirely unsurprised that no one argued.

𝔇awn was painting its first pale streaks across the eastern sky when Ryder followed Mary into their bedroom.

Mary heaved a gigantic sigh. "Finally, it's over."

They'd spent the last hours sorting everyone and everything out as well as they could. Rand, Kit, Stacie, and Godfrey had been gathered in by the abbey staff, led by Mary herself. As Ryder's half siblings often visited, they had their own rooms; wrung out, they'd retired as soon as their quarters had been made ready. "I just hope," he said, "that the others can sleep."

"Hmm." Mary glanced at him. "Do you foresee any difficulties with the two stable hands over Snickert's death?"

He shook his head. "Lavinia, through Snickert, had offered them a small fortune to help him do away with us—they know how close to the gallows they stand." He hesitated, then admitted, "If Lavinia hadn't died, then Snickert's death would pose more of a problem, but as she has, and the stable hands know that, then . . ." He exhaled. "I think—hope—that this will blow over without anything that might damage the others socially coming out."

"How much detail do you need to give of the manner of Lavinia's death?"

"Officially, not much—just that she died of an accident. Death through misadventure, which is true enough. Given the staff at the Dower House rallied around, and will deal with the body and the undertakers tomorrow—no, today—other than organizing the funeral itself, there's very little more that needs to be done to set this matter to rest."

"To lay Lavinia to rest, and free her children."

"That, too." Looping an arm about Mary's waist, Ryder drew her with him to the window.

They stood there, leaning against each other, watching the dawn break across the sky.

Eventually, Mary stirred. "A new dawn—a new beginning."

Ryder glanced at her. "Not just for us, but for the other four, too—for the Cavanaughs."

Meeting his gaze, Mary smiled. "For the Cavanaughs." Catching both his hands in hers, she backed toward the bed, towing him, unresisting, with her.

"Continuing in that vein"—halting beside the bed and releasing his hands, Mary pressed close, stretched up, wound her arms about his neck and looked deep into his hazel eyes—"I believe we should fall into this bed, and do what we can to make certain of the next generation."

Ryder's lips slowly curved, then he laughed, swept her up

in his arms, set his lips to hers, kissed her—and tipped them both onto the bed.

They bounced.

Mary shrieked, then laughed.

Then fell to as they wrestled each other out of their clothes, as they paused, both caught by the lancing sensual jolt as skin met naked skin, only to be filled with piercing pleasure as hands caressed and stroked, lovingly, worshipfully tracing now familiar curves, reclaiming, possessing anew—familiar yet never before so poignant.

Their eyes met—and in the blue, in the hazel, dwelled the same knowledge of comprehension and capitulation, the rock-solid certainty of what, through the tumult of the night's events, they'd embraced, shared, and owned to.

Openly. Directly. Without guile.

Without any screens to shield them from each other they came together on a shared gasp, in a moment of shining clarity caught their breaths, then she drew his lips to hers, and he bent to her, and they let their passion and the power that fueled it rear like a wave—let it roar in and take them, let it sweep them away.

Let desire and need and hunger coalesce into a fire beyond their control.

Let the indescribable joy of being alive—of having cheated death together, of having survived together to come together like this, in wonder and in hope, in commitment and in reverence—flood them.

Sink and submerge them, meld and fuse them until they were one.

In love and in passion. In joy and in ecstasy.

In hope and in surrender.

To all they would be, to all that would come, to all they would create together.

Chapter Seventeen

shes to ashes, dust to dust.

Lavinia's funeral marked the end of a lost era for the Cavanaughs. Ryder was determined that from that point onward, with no Lavinia attempting to create schisms between him and her children, the five of them—with Mary to guide them—would become, or grow into, the sort of family they'd all yearned to be for so long.

It would take time and a degree of learning, but they had time, were more than willing, and had Mary to help them understand when they should be sharing their difficulties. She'd well and truly taken the bit between her teeth and thrown herself into the role of his marchioness, into being the matriarch of the family, both immediate and wider, and had already made it plain that she expected any difficulties of any kind to be made known to them—if not to him, then at the very least to her.

He loved her bossiness; what always amazed him was how she got away with it. Most often he suspected it wasn't that people agreed so much as they surrendered to a patently greater force and gave in. Increasingly quickly. He could see it becoming a habit.

There wasn't a day when something she said or did didn't bring a smile to his face—sometimes a smile he hid, but just as often he shared his amusement with her, just to see her narrow her vivid eyes at him, then humph and turn haughtily away.

Having her beside him through the days following Lavinia's death, helping him to help the others over the hurdles, social and otherwise, had been a huge boon. He honestly wasn't sure how he would have managed without her.

Together, the six of them had tackled the question of mourning. He and Mary had concluded that, for them, a week's full mourning, followed by three weeks of half-mourning, would be appropriate; given the widely recognized antipathy between him and Lavinia, anything more would smack of hypocrisy. They'd encouraged Rand, Kit, Stacie, and Godfrey to make up their own minds; in the end, the four had decided on one month of full mourning, and three of half-mourning, and all those who gathered at Raventhorne for the funeral and wake had nodded and approved.

Following the formal funeral at the nearby church and the brief ceremony of interment, the wake, held at the abbey, was, socially speaking, more in the nature of a new beginning; the neighbors who attended made it plain they were doing so primarily to show their support of him and Mary rather than to acknowledge Lavinia's passing other than it being the end of the past. Everyone clearly looked to him and Mary for a new direction, and to his everlasting gratitude, his marchioness was up to the challenge.

She swept regally through the crowd, dispensing grace and calm and a species of reassurance that was uniquely hers. Those who hadn't met her before quickly thawed and smiled; those who had been previously captivated were happy to be so again. Watching her delight and manage, manage and delight, he felt reassured himself, content and more that in being there, in managing his household and, as far as he would allow, determining his life, she was in her true element.

Being his marchioness was where she should be; the position was hers—it was where she belonged.

Where she needed to be, for his sake, and hers, and that of so many others.

Throughout the afternoon, she constantly circled, popping up beside him to lay a hand on his arm, to lean close and ensnare his senses while sharing a shrewd observation or comment, and then she would be off again, sweeping on to oversee and direct.

One who had attended the service, the interment, and the wake was Claude Potherby. In light of what Ryder knew of the man's long-standing devotion to Lavinia, he had sent Potherby a personal note, inviting him to attend. Potherby had come but had remained at the wake only long enough to satisfy social expectations; his role as Lavinia's confidant had been widely known.

Potherby had looked shattered; he'd aged ten years in less than a week. He'd seized a private moment to ask Ryder whether Lavinia had taken her own life. When Ryder had assured him that her death had been an accident, brought about by an attempt to flee justice, Potherby had nodded and quietly reflected, "She wouldn't have chosen it, but this end . . . might well have been for the best." After a moment, he'd added, "For her . . . and for me." Glancing at Ryder, he'd somewhat ambiguously said, "It's time I moved on."

After tendering transparently sincere wishes for Ryder's, Mary's, and the Cavanaugh family's future, Potherby had departed.

Thinking back to that conversation, Ryder had to agree with Potherby's direction; it was, indeed, a day for counting blessings, and then moving on.

Apropos of which, looking over the sea of heads crowding the abbey's drawing room, he felt as if he was, at last, setting out unencumbered on the path he'd promised his father he would take. For the Cavanaughs, his time would be one of rebuilding. And, glancing around, he no longer lacked for guidance in how best to accomplish all he wished.

Devil and Honoria, as well as Lord Arthur and Lady

Louise, had come from London to represent the Cynsters. Mary had blinked at him when he'd asked if the rest of her immediate family would attend—as if the answer was so obvious the question hadn't needed to be asked.

As, apparently, it hadn't; all her closest family were there—from Simon and Portia, and Henrietta and James, to Amanda and Martin, and Amelia and Luc.

Somewhat to Ryder's surprise, Helena, Dowager Duchess of St. Ives, the elder matriarch of the Cynster clan, and her bosom-bow, Therese, Lady Osbaldestone, had arrived with Devil and Honoria. Lady Osbaldestone had shrewdly looked him up and down, then told him being Mary's husband suited him, and that he would do. Bad enough, but mere minutes later, Helena had patted his cheek, told him he was a good boy, and that all would be well—he would see.

His instincts had all but jibbered.

Later, when he'd mentioned the exchange to Mary, clearly seeking reassurance, she'd told him Helena was widely regarded as perspicacious in the highest degree, and that he should be grateful she hadn't been more explicit.

Apparently, his instincts had been right.

Yet in terms of family, appreciating the strength and innate power the Cynsters possessed—what the result of successive generations who had stood together had generated—and knowing that the main line of the Cavanaughs had been reduced to him and his half siblings, the route to the future, the future he wanted to create, was clear.

The clocks throughout the house had just chimed three times when Mary swanned up, twined her arm with his, and turned him toward the door. "It's time to go out to the porch and wave people off."

Closing his hand over hers on his sleeve, he was only too happy to obey.

Naturally everyone followed their lead.

Despite the somber reason for the gathering, people departed with smiles and waves. Within half an hour, the bulk of the guests had left, and Ryder allowed Mary to lead him back inside to the library, where those staying overnight had retreated.

Mary paused in the front hall to confer with Forsythe and Mrs. Pritchard, who'd been waiting for her instructions. Footmen and maids were already in the drawing room, setting the big room to rights. After commending the staff on their performance, she confirmed the arrangements for dinner. "As I suspected, we'll be fourteen at table."

"Indeed, ma'am," Forsythe said. "In the formal dining room, then."

Mary hesitated, but then nodded. "Yes—it will be an excellent opportunity to open up that room."

With a nod of dismissal, she turned back to Ryder, waiting patiently by her side. Tucking her hand into the crook of his arm, she said, "It went well, don't you think?"

Resuming their progress toward the library, he closed his hand, warm and strong, over hers. "Exceedingly well. An end on the one hand, a beginning on the other."

"Exactly." She wasn't surprised he'd seen it as she had.

"So who is staying—you said fourteen?"

"Yes. Devil and Honoria took Helena and Lady Osbaldestone back to town, so it's only my parents and brother and sisters and their spouses, and your half siblings."

"Good." When she glanced up and met his eyes, a question in hers, he explained, "We need to discuss arrangements for Stacie and Godfrey in particular, and I would value your parents'—and your siblings'—thoughts."

Drawing her hand from his arm as he opened the library door, she grinned. "Don't worry. You won't even need to ask—they'll offer their opinions regardless."

From Ryder's point of view, that would be another blessing for which to be grateful.

They joined the others on the sofas and chairs, and after a brief review of the day, Mary turned the conversation to the question of where Stacie and Godfrey would now reside.

"You're all welcome here at any time, of course, but what do you wish to do in London?"

Rand had his lodgings. "But sadly I have no extra rooms."

Neither did Kit. "Moreover, I need to find a new place."

Ryder looked at him and Godfrey. "You can return to live at Raventhorne House if you wish—it's more than big enough, and Mary and I will only be there during the Season and for a few weeks in autumn."

Kit and Godfrey exchanged glances, then Kit looked back at Ryder. "Perhaps we can try that, at least to begin with, then see how we fare?" He smiled at Mary. "Mary might find us too bothersome, or wish us out of your hair come spring and the Season, but for now . . . the two of us moving back to Raventhorne House might serve."

Tapping one finger on the chair arm, Ryder said, "Next point—the Chapel Street house. It's owned by the estate. Do you wish it retained, or should it be sold?"

Despite Lavinia's children all promptly declaring they wanted nothing to do with that house, the discussion was lengthy, weighing up the various options such as hiring the place, balancing the long-term costs of staffing and upkeep against the value to the estate, but, ultimately, selling the property was the unanimous verdict. Ryder was grateful for the knowledgeable inputs from Lord Arthur, Louise, and the twins and their husbands. He inclined his head. "That's settled then. I'll send word to Montague."

"Excellent." Mary turned to Stacie. "That leaves us with Stacie to organize." She smiled encouragingly at Ryder's half sister. "As I mentioned, you will always be welcome here, but as Ryder said, at least until the Season next year, aside from the weeks of the autumn session, he and I will most likely remain in the country. However, I imagine you would prefer to be in town for more weeks than that."

Stacie grimaced. "Well, to begin with, I need to go back and pack, especially if the Chapel Street house is to be sold. And although that might take only a week or so, I do have several weddings of friends to attend, and other invitations I had already accepted . . ." She paused, then in a smaller voice said, "I could cry off—"

"If I might make a suggestion?" Smiling, Louise waited for Ryder as well as Mary to incline their heads, then she looked at Stacie. "If you would like it, you're welcome to stay with us in Upper Brook Street. Now Mary and Henrietta are both gone, as well as the others"—Louise waved at Amanda, Amelia, and Simon—"there's just Arthur and me, so we've more than enough room, and in general I would be attending all the events you've been invited to—I would be happy to act as your chaperon, at least until the autumn session when Mary returns to town." Louise looked at her youngest daughter, and a slow, anticipatory smile curved her lips. "And then, perhaps, we might all go about together until Mary learns the ropes of how to be a chaperon—not a role she's previously been called on to perform."

The rest of Mary's family laughed; a slew of comments, observations, and stories ensued, many pointed, all amusing, and all thoroughly good-natured in a family-teasing kind of way.

Ryder listened to the happy ribbing, saw Mary's eyes sparkle as she capped one of Luc's comments with a quip of her own—saw his half siblings watching, noting, taking it in, with a longing that mirrored his own, a wish to understand, experience, and be a part of just such an interaction.

This was the other side of family—the warmth, the support, the detailed understanding and unconditional acceptance of who and what each member was, what they could contribute, their traits and foibles, their strengths and passions, and the abiding affection and inclusiveness that embraced each individual and forged them into such a powerful whole.

Family—strength, warmth, support—power.

After being reassured several times by multiple people that she would not in the least be in anyone's way, Stacie accepted Louise's proposal. Older head and younger bent together to plan.

As a group, they spent the rest of the day and the early evening together, chatting amiably, discovering common interests and pursuing them, eventually devolving into two groups, the ladies settling in the library chairs to swap tales of fashion and scandal, while the gentlemen took themselves off to the billiard room, there to engage in an impromptu tournament, Cavanaughs versus Cynsters and connections.

Neither side won.

Dinner, even held in the grand and gracious setting of the formal dining room, wasn't, in that company, allowed to be anything but a relaxed affair, a fitting end to the last hours of unwinding. After passing the port and brandy, the gentlemen rejoined the ladies in the drawing room; by the time everyone trooped up the stairs an hour and a half later, the dark strain of the earlier part of the day had been wiped away, and every last one of them, Ryder would have sworn, was focused ahead.

Looking forward to the next day, and the next, and to all that their lives would bring.

Mary paused in the gallery at the head of the main stairs to bid her family—both sides of it—a good night, and to ensure they all remembered where their rooms were. After seeing everyone off down the right corridors, she smiled, turned, and found Ryder waiting.

As she'd known he would be.

Slipping her hand into his, she strolled by his side down the corridor to their apartments. Her heart felt buoyant; she felt like swinging their linked hands and skipping along, but now she was a marchioness that, sadly, would not accord with her dignity.

But she could smile. Ryder held the door to the sitting room open; she flashed a beaming smile at him as she stepped inside—and, catching his hand as she passed, she towed him to the left—to her bedroom. The room he'd had decorated so superbly for her, but which they'd yet to use.

Collecting the lighted candelabra from the sideboard as they passed, he followed readily enough, as, indeed, he had all day, but when she halted and swung to face him, he looked into her eyes, arched a brow. "Are you sure you want to sleep here?"

"Yes." She held his gaze. "This morning we buried the past, this afternoon we drew a line under it, and this evening we've started on our future. It's fitting that we use this room tonight—the first night on our new journey."

Briefly, he searched her eyes, enough to see her decision, her commitment, then nodded. His lips lightly curved. "As ever, your wish is my command."

She laughed and turned away to pull the pins from her hair.

Setting the candelabra down, Ryder watched for a moment, then shrugged off his coat. Trying to decide where in this room he would leave it, he followed the thought further . . . "I just hope we don't cause consternation tomorrow morning when Collier and Aggie look for us and find us apparently gone."

"They'll realize, I'm sure. No one would dream that you and I would run away." She presented him with her back. "Help me with these laces."

Tossing his coat on the end of the bed, he obliged, then, leaving her to strip away her gown, he retrieved his coat and walked down the room to lay it over a chair. After stripping off his waistcoat, he set his fingers to his cravat. He'd just finished unraveling the long band when a rustle had him glancing around—in time to see a nicely naked Mary slip under the sheets.

His smile was all appreciation, not just for the brief sight but in anticipation of what he would shortly find waiting for him in the bed. The lovely bed he'd had created just for her.

They'd been married for only three weeks, yet already they were behaving like a long-married couple. He'd wondered about her unvoiced but clear preference for, most often, undressing separately, each stripping their own clothes off, until he'd realized she liked watching him disrobe. Until he'd realized that she hurried to get her own clothes off so she could lie back in the bed and watch him strip—exactly as she was doing now.

Even if she tried to undress him, if he got his hands on her first, she didn't get to see this—him revealing himself to her. And in oh-so-many ways.

He didn't hurry but took his time drawing the cravat away and letting it fall on his waistcoat and coat, then unbuttoning his cuffs before starting on the long placket of buttons closing his shirt.

Beneath the covers, she shifted.

Glancing down to hide his grin, he remembered something he'd been dying to ask. Perhaps tonight was the right time, now the right moment. Stripping off his shirt, he raised his head and looked at her—saw her gaze wasn't on his face. "I wondered . . ." He waited until, reluctantly, her gaze, followed by her attention, rose to his face before continuing, "If there was anything you wanted to tell me? To share with me?"

She held his gaze for a moment, then, openly coy, arched a brow. "What sort of thing?"

He didn't immediately reply but slipped off his shoes, sat and stripped off his stockings, then stood; refocusing on her, he prowled slowly to the bed, unfastening the buttons at his waist as he did.

Reaching the bed, he knelt on it, continued his prowling, crawling advance until he was poised on hands and knees over her, all but nose to nose. "I can count, you know."

Although her eyes remained locked with his, her body stirred, eager, impatient, restless and reckless. Her hands tensed, but she kept them where they were, her arms draped over the pillows above her head, while she debated.

Then she made up her mind and, slowly lifting her arms, wound them about his neck, clasped her hands at his nape, used the leverage to evocatively settle herself beneath him, and smiled.

Cornflower blue glory met his gaze. "Yes," she murmured and, stretching up, she touched her lips to his chin. "I believe I'm pregnant." She pressed her lips to his briefly, then drew back to whisper, the words a wash of sensation over his lips, "With your heir."

She kissed him again—and he kissed her back, the sudden surge of emotion catching them both.

Then she pulled away again, lay back, lips lightly swollen, eyes darkening with desire, and imperiously waved down his body—at his trousers. As he shifted to strip them off his long legs, she said, "Of course, it could well be a girl."

"I don't care." Naked, he lifted the covers and slid beneath—and found her, all silken skin and firm curves, waiting to draw him into her arms. Coming over her, propping himself on his elbows above her, he looked into her eyes, saw her faintly skeptical expression, and smiled. Kissed the tip of her nose. "I truly don't care—girl or boy, they'll be the first new bud on our family tree."

She smiled, then laughed, then she pulled him down to her and their lips and desires met, fused, merged.

And joyously, with open hearts, with minds attuned and souls committed, they gave themselves over to what waited for them—to the power, the passion, and the solid, abiding love that now anchored them.

Their future was clear, the journey defined; as they loved and laughed, they had one goal, one aim, one desire to which they devoted themselves. To which they renewed their commitment with each gasp, with each frantic, desperate clutch of their hands, with each heady, hungry beat of their hearts.

Neither needed any longer to even think of that desire, to shape it with words. It was forged within them and branded on their souls.

They would create a family of their own.

They would fill their house with their children, and work

to draw in and encourage their siblings, to build the network of uncles, aunts, and cousins to form the branches and twigs of a healthy family tree.

They would reinvigorate and revitalize and reestablish the Cavanaughs.

Soaring on cataclysmic sensation, they raced, then flew, then tumbled from the peak, spiraling through ecstasy, riding the surging tide.

Hands locked, fingers entwined, in that moment when their hearts beat as one, they breathed in and, from beneath heavy lids, met each other's eyes.

They would do all that, and then take it further.

Into the future.

Breaths mingling, they held tight to the moment, to the promise in each other's gazes, then their lips touched, brushed, in a wordless vow. Together they had so much strength, so much passion. So much they could bring to, could devote to, the task.

Family. Forever.

There was no greater, no more satisfying goal.

Epilogue

August, 1837
Somersham Place, Cambridgeshire

The Cynsters gathered that summer, as they had for the past seventeen years, to celebrate the bounties the year had brought. The weddings, the connections, the children—as always especially the latter. To welcome, to give thanks for, to appreciate all the blessings being such a large, well-anchored, and fruitful family had wrought.

Honoria, Duchess of St. Ives, hostess and chief instigator of the gathering, stood on the porch of the sprawling mansion that was her home and surveyed the sea of heads dotting the lawns with deep satisfaction. "For the first time in a very long time—since the triple wedding, I think, and that was in '29—every last one of us is here."

Standing beside Honoria, Patience Cynster smiled. "You can thank Henrietta, and even more, Mary, for that. Their timing really was impeccable. With two weddings to attend in such quick succession, and then the death of the king, and Victoria's ascension, all those who traveled from a distance for the weddings had no chance even to ponder going home before the timing made it too tempting to remain for this event."

"Indeed." Catriona strolled along the porch to join them, Phyllida and Alathea ambling beside her. "As one of the second furthest-flung party, while I hadn't planned on being away for so long, I'm grateful Mary and her Ryder kept us here. If they hadn't, we would have been in the Vale again before we heard of the king's illness, and then on his death Richard would have wanted to come south again to assess the political situation."

Flick, who had paused to lean over the balustrade and admonish one of her sons, caught up; joining the others in looking over the crowd, she sighed contentedly. "It's growing bigger every year—who would have thought, in that first summer in 1820, that we would, all together, create such a large and robust brood."

Honoria snorted. "I'm quite sure our husbands, were they standing here, would claim all honors and declare the sight only right and appropriate, their due and nothing more."

The others laughed.

"Where are they, incidentally?" Like the others, Catriona had instinctively searched for the particular Cynster head that inevitably drew her eye.

"I saw them heading for the stables." Resignation colored Flick's tone. "Demon insisted on riding his latest acquisition over, and, of course, the others all have to look and salivate, and ask when any offspring might be available."

The other ladies all smiled, their shared understanding of their husbands' foibles etched in their expressions. For several minutes, they stood and watched in silence, proud matrons regarding their growing children, while viewing the antics of those even younger with an indulgent eye.

"I have to say"—Phyllida leaned one hip against the balustrade—"that while I'm quite looking forward to getting my brood home to Devon again, I wouldn't have wanted to miss this year's gathering." She glanced at the others. "It feels very much as if it's the end of an era, with a new one hovering, but not quite here yet."

"Hmm." Alathea was looking at a group of youngsters playing knucklebones at the bottom of the steps. "Gabriel heard that the palace is saying the coronation won't be until the middle of next year, so we'll have a little time before the new eventuates."

"Socially and politically." One fine brow arching, Honoria regarded the others. "And possibly on the family front as well."

Patience nodded. "It *is* the end of a generation, isn't it? Mary was the youngest yet unwed."

"True," Catriona said. "But while it will be ten or more years before the next round of weddings, the births will continue, and those we must celebrate as we always have."

"As we always will," Alathea affirmed. "Monarchs, politicians, and even social habits will wax and wane, but family goes on."

"This one at least," Honoria stated. "And given it's up to us—and the other ladies—to steer it on, I have no doubt whatever that we'll manage it."

They all laughed, but underneath their amusement, all were resolved, and all understood that. When it came to family—this family—they would stand together, manage together. Go forward into the future, whatever it held, together.

As if setting out on that next phase of their journey, in a loose group they trailed down the steps and spread out among the throng.

The last to step down from the porch steps, Honoria, smiling, watched the others as they strolled into the crowd, locating and keeping watch over their bountiful broods. Every union represented there that day had proved fruitful, as the significant number of the next generation milling across the lawns and spilling into various areas of the extensive gardens testified.

Crossing to where her mother-in-law, Helena, considered the elder matriarch of the clan, sat on a bench, one of the newest additions—Portia and Simon's Persephone—cradled on her lap, Honoria felt her smile grow wider. The tiny tot, only months old, was gurgling and waving her tiny fists in the air.

Helena looked up as Honoria approached, met her eyes, smiled her lovely smile, then directed her green gaze round about. "How many are there—do you know?"

Honoria chuckled. "I counted. We've reached seventy-nine, if you can believe it."

Therese, Lady Osbaldestone, who had gone for a short walk, returned in time to hear those words. Sinking down on the other end of the bench, she protested, "But you Cynsters can't take credit for all of those—you've the Carmarthen pair here, plus the Kirkpatricks—let alone the Anstruther-Wetherbys, the Ashfords, the Tallents, the Morwellans, the Caxtons, not to mention the Adairs."

"True." Honoria turned to look over the crowd. "But they are all connected in one way or another, and . . . well, that's how it works, isn't it? The friendships our children form at gatherings like this will stand them in good stead all their lives."

Both Lady Osbaldestone and Helena nodded decisively.

"You have it exactly right," Helena said. "This is how it happens, and you and all the others are to be commended for bringing the Cynsters to this." She paused, then, unusually wistfully, murmured, "I wish Sebastian had lived to see this—he would have been so proud."

Lady Osbaldestone humphed. "Aye, well—it wouldn't have been the same, and might not have happened at all if he'd lived. Sylvester would have been St. Earith, which is not the same as St. Ives, and none of the rest of it might have happened as it did, and . . . well, you take my meaning. Fate has her own ways of taking, then giving, and while she took him, she gave you this. I suspect Sebastian would see that as fitting."

Helena softly laughed. "Oh, yes—you're right in that. He

would definitely see this as what should be—an appropriate legacy."

Leaving the two grandes dames pointing out and swapping comments on various members of the younger set, Honoria moved on, like any good hostess keeping her finger on the pulse of her widely dispersed guests.

Helena's grandson Sebastian, her husband's namesake and Honoria's elder son, better known as the Marquess of St. Earith, was the most senior of the next generation; eighteen years old and bidding fair to becoming even more lethally handsome than his father, he was standing with a group comprised of the other seventeen- and sixteen-year-old males—budding gentlemen all. Michael, Sebastian's brother, was there, as were Christopher and Gregory, Vane and Patience's older sons, Marcus, Richard and Catriona's eldest son, Justin, Gabriel and Alathea's older son, and Aidan, Lucifer and Phyllida's eldest son. They were, Honoria suspected, swapping tales she'd rather not hear.

Males, she was well aware, changed little with the generations.

Luckily, someone had persuaded the fifteen-, fourteen-, and thirteen-year-old lads that overseeing the younger boys playing a spirited game of cricket would be much more fun than listening to their elders fill their heads with adolescent dreams. Nicholas, Demon and Flick's older son, Evan, Lucifer and Phyllida's middle son, Julius, Gyles and Francesca's older son, and Gavin and Bryce, Dominic and Angelica's wards were actively engaged in the rowdy game presently being waged between two teams formed with the assembled nine-, ten-, and eleven-year old males, of which there were eleven.

Flick, the most tomboyish of the matrons—and the one who had a passing understanding of the rules of the boys' game—had been keeping a watchful eye over the group; she ambled up to stand alongside Honoria.

Registering the names, the faces, the ages, Honoria

grinned. "Twenty-six was a good year for males—we added eight to the score that year."

Flick frowned. "There were no girls, were there?"

"Not that year, but we had five the next, and the year after we added two girls, but no boys at all."

"Hmm . . . well, if you're wondering where our young ladies are"—Flick tipped her guinea-gold head toward the walled garden—"I believe they're swapping secrets in amongst the roses."

Honoria smiled. "Predictable, I suppose. Did you see who went that way?"

"Only Lucilla, my Prudence, and Antonia. As for the rest, your daughter appears to have taken on your mantle—the last I saw she had the others, at least all the girls beyond the stage of rushing about madly playing tag, sitting in a circle on the grass beyond the oaks."

Honoria arched her brows. "Knowing Louisa, I suspect I'd better check that they're all still there and haven't decided to embark on some adventure or quest."

Laughing, Flick nodded and they parted, Flick to continue ambling beneath the trees, pausing to chat with the other ladies while watching over the boys, while Honoria, also pausing to chat here and there, circled the gathering.

She passed close enough to the entrance to the rose garden to glimpse the three young ladies seated on the bench at the far end of the central path. Lucilla's red hair, highlighted by the sun, burned flame bright. Prudence, Demon and Flick's fair-haired older daughter, was on Lucilla's right, while Antonia, Gyles and Francesca's oldest child, dark-haired and vivid, sat on Lucilla's left. Lucilla was seventeen, the other two sixteen. The three made a striking picture. Honoria noted it, noted the expressive way they were talking, hands gesticulating; smiling, she left them undisturbed.

By the time she reached the line of oaks bordering the far side of the lawn, more than twenty minutes had passed; she was therefore somewhat relieved to see the bevy of girls still seated on the grass, their dresses a spectrum of pastel hues making them look like so many blooms scattered upon the sward.

Honoria counted, verifying that all twelve girls aged between nine and fourteen years old were there. Although they were sitting in a circle, there was no doubt who was their leader—her own daughter, Louisa, at fourteen already well on her way to becoming her father's worst nightmare.

Louisa was a female version of Devil in oh-so-many ways. Shrewdly intelligent, quick-witted, and very accomplished in managing people, their daughter's pale green eyes were eerily similar to Devil's and Helena's, but the mind behind was, in Honoria's estimation, even more willful, more stubborn.

Honoria wasn't entirely looking forward to managing Devil through the coming years.

But, as usual, watching her daughter made her lips twitch, made maternal pride well and overflow in quite a different way to when she viewed Sebastian or Michael.

Turning away, Honoria quit the shadows under the oaks and moved back into the main body of the crowd assembled on the wide south lawn.

She paused to chat to Francesca and Priscilla, joining them in admiring Jordan, Dillon and Priscilla's new baby, born mere weeks before and currently lovingly cradled in Priscilla's arms, then passing on to spend a few minutes with Sarah and Charlie, similarly admiring their young Celia, almost old enough to sit up in her father's proud arms. The men had started strolling back from the stables to rejoin the gathering, gradually finding their way back to their wives.

The eleven eight- to six-year-olds, boys and girls both, were engaged in a rambunctious game of tag, weaving in and about their elders, all of whom kept a wary eye on the darting figures flashing past like fish in a stream. The activity had become something of a tradition; quite how the participants managed never to come to grief was a mystery that, despite the years, Honoria had not yet solved.

Those younger still, five years old or less, were by general consensus relegated to the firm hands of their nursemaids. The maids had clustered on one corner of the lawn, using perambulators, baskets, and satchels to hem in their charges. There were blocks, rings, and a variety of other toys scattered on the grass while toddlers staggered drunkenly and younger ones crawled and they all yelled and laughed.

Deeming that group safe, Honoria did nothing more than cast a glance over the bright heads. Including those currently in their parents' arms, there were twenty-five, a number to make any matriarch puffed up.

Smiling, she moved on through the crowd, then noticed two men standing alone, plainly having failed to find their wives among the once again thickening throng. James Glossup and Ryder Cavanaugh looked faintly lost, but then Luc and Martin strolled up, and an instant later, Portia, having left little Persephone in her grandmother's care, joined the group, and, no doubt, explained.

About the one who wasn't there. And that Amanda, Amelia, Simon, Henrietta, and Mary unfailingly slipped away from the gathering every year to spend a few quiet minutes at Tolly's grave.

Just them, the siblings; none of them had been married when Tolly had died.

Honoria paused, remembering—hearing again the echo of the shot that, for her, too, reverberated down the years. That shot had taken Tolly's life and had brought her and Devil together. All but forced them together. It had been the start . . . in some ways, of it all.

Glancing around, she saw all those gathered, acknowledged the number, the strength, the depths of the connections, and, as she had in years past, she raised a mental toast to Tolly. In part, this—all they had become—was because of him. Because of his sacrifice.

Family in all its aspects—the heartache and the pain, as well as the joy, the warmth, and the wonder.

After a moment of quiet reflection, Honoria rediscovered her smile and walked on.

Ten minutes later, Mary materialized at Ryder's side. When he arched a brow at her, she twined her arm with his, lightly squeezed. "I'll tell you later."

He smiled gently. "No need." He tipped his head to where Portia stood, Simon having just joined her, while next to Mary, Henrietta had returned to James's side. "Portia explained."

Mary smiled a touch mistily, then drew in a breath and turned to the others.

As if by agreement, they slid back into their previous occupation, chatting about family and family happenings. Henrietta and James's bridal trip, from which they had only just returned, provided an easy start.

"Italy was simply marvelous!" Henrietta assured them.

"Lots of old ruins, all of which she perforce had to see." James grinned. "Mind you, some of the statues were arresting."

The others laughed, then a shrieking wail cut through the conversations and Portia, alerted, looked around. "Oh, good heavens!" She poked Simon's shoulder. "Go and rescue poor Milly from your son. He'll quiet if you carry him about."

"*My* son?" But Simon was already turning to the circle of nursemaids. "Why is he always my son when he's being difficult?"

"Well, he didn't get 'difficult' from me, so who else would be responsible?" Portia prodded him on his way, waved to the others, and followed.

Leaving the other four staring after them, watching . . . after an instant, each couple drew their gazes away and exchanged a private glance, then Henrietta turned to Mary just as Mary turned to her.

"We're expecting . . ."

They'd spoken in unison. Both blinked, then identical smiles bloomed, lighting their faces.

Henrietta whooped and hugged Mary.

Who jigged and hugged her tightly back. "When?"

"March! And you?"

"Sometime in March, too!"

James and Ryder, both beaming fit to crack their faces, shook hands and clapped each other on the shoulder. "We haven't told anyone else yet," Ryder confessed.

"Neither have we," James confirmed. He glanced at the crowd all around, then arched a brow at Ryder. "We thought we might wait a few months."

"Sound notion," Ryder said. "We thought the same."

The men stood shoulder to shoulder and, with proud expressions stamped on their faces, watched their wives, heads together now, chattering nonstop. Then James said, "It takes a little getting used to, the notion of having a child in your life."

"It does." Ryder nodded. "But I can't think of a more . . . glorious expectation."

"True." James drew in a half-laughing breath. "It's a scarifying prospect, but so damned wonderful."

Later, when they'd parted from Henrietta and James, each couple swearing to keep the other's secret, and were once again ambling idly through the crowd, Ryder glanced at Mary, strolling by his side, her arm twined with his. "Would you like to go on a wedding trip, too?"

She considered, then looked up and, smiling, shook her head. "There's a lot I want to get settled, at the abbey, on your other estates, and in the London house, too—all before March. I'd rather devote myself to that, and to all the rest we have on our plate, than swan around to places unknown. Sometime, perhaps, when our children are grown . . ." Brows rising, she added, "I really ought to suggest that to Mama. Once we go up to town and Stacie is settled with us, there's no reason Mama and Papa can't travel and see more of the world."

Ryder's lips twitched. "The only event I would consider less likely than your father agreeing to leave England when you and Henrietta, or Portia, or even the twins might decide to be increasing is for your mother to agree to such a trip."

Mary grimaced. "There is that."

A moment later, she drew him to the edge of the lawn. "I've been thinking that, quite aside from the estate picnic—which, by the way, I've decided should coincide with the harvest—as head of the Cavanaugh family, we really ought to host an event similar to this. Not just for your half siblings, but for the connections, too. As is done here." She glanced up at him. "It helps—"

"To bind people together," he supplied. "To give them common cause."

"To underscore the common cause." Mary nodded, then arched her brows. "So can we?"

Ryder smiled and started them strolling again. "Organize away, wife, with my blessing."

"Excellent!" Beaming with anticipatory delight, Mary walked on.

Fifteen minutes later, she and Henrietta met again at the tea trolley. Once supplied with full cups by Webster, they retreated to the shade of an oak to sip.

They were sharing quiet comments on their expectations of the coming months when Lucilla walked past.

Mary frowned. "Lucilla!" When Lucilla turned, Mary beckoned.

As Lucilla drew near, Henrietta, too, frowned. She glanced at Mary. "You handed on the necklace, didn't you? At your engagement ball?"

"Yes. Of course." Mary looked at Lucilla. "Why aren't you wearing it?"

Lucilla arched her brows but answered readily, "Because my time is not yet, and . . ." A faint frown disturbed the fine line of her brows. "The place, apparently, is not here."

Refocusing on Mary and Henrietta, she grimaced slightly and shrugged. "You know how it is. I don't know the details—I just know I have to wait."

Someone called Lucilla's name; she looked, then, with a small wave, left the two sisters and forged into the crowd.

Mary snorted and took another sip of tea. "Better her than me."

Henrietta laughed. "Indubitably."

Tea consumed, the sisters returned their cups to Sligo, then with a fond kiss on each other's cheeks, they parted, turning to follow their own paths, each returning to walk by the side of the hero into whose arms The Lady had steered them.

Across the crowd, Lucilla joined her twin; it had been Marcus who had hailed her. His was one voice, one call, she would always hear, would always answer, no matter the distractions, no matter the distance. Meeting his eyes, dark blue like their father's, she arched a brow. "What is it?"

With a tip of his dark head, he drew her to the side of the lawn. Originally his hair had been as red as hers, but while hers had held its color, his had progressively darkened, almost to black. "We—me and the others—wondered if you and the other girls might like to join us for a stroll around the lake."

"Why?" The obvious question.

Marcus flicked a glance at the crowd of their elders. "Sebastian suggested—and all of us agree—that perhaps we should make plans for Christmas. He and the others would like to celebrate this Christmas in the Vale—we haven't had everyone up for an age. You know the elders will need persuading, but we thought, if you and the other girls agreed, we might talk it through—discuss strategy, as it were."

Lucilla considered the prospect and found it to her liking. She nodded. "All right." She turned to look over the crowd. "I'll go and find Prudence and Antonia. We'll meet you and the others at the summerhouse—we can set out from there."

Marcus shifted. "You might want to winkle out some of the others, too—Therese and Juliet, at least—and, of course, if we want to succeed—"

"We'll need Louisa." Lucilla nodded more definitely. "I'll find her first, and she can round up the others."

With no further words—despite the years, they still understood each other instinctively—the twins parted, Lucilla fixing her sights on Louisa while Marcus retreated to summon his peers.

Five minutes later, Devil found his wife by the porch steps, her gaze fixed on the group of youngsters gathering before the summerhouse. Dipping his head, he murmured in her ear, "What's that about, do you know?"

She gave a deliciously distracted shiver but after a second replied, "I'm not sure, but, given our three are there, and Louisa is at the heart of it, I'm sure we'll hear soon enough."

They watched as the group formed up, then started strolling, heading toward the lake.

Closing his hand about one of Honoria's, Devil said, "They're growing up. In another year, Sebastian will be down from Oxford, then a year later, Michael will join him, along with Christopher, and probably Marcus, too."

Honoria glanced up at Devil's harsh-featured face, a warrior's face that had changed little with the years. Thought of her sons, especially the elder, who shared such similar features with his sire. "Have you given any thought as to how to keep Sebastian occupied for that first year—when he hasn't got the others around him?"

"Filling his time will be easy enough—there's a great deal he has yet to learn about managing the dukedom." Devil glanced down and met her eyes. "And what it takes to manage a ducal family."

Honoria smiled. "He won't have to do that—his wife will. And until he marries, Louisa will always be there, just itching to take the reins."

"True, but he needs to appreciate what it is they do." Devil held her gaze. "What it is you, and the other ladies, too, bring to the family."

Seeing that appreciation writ large in his eyes, Honoria

discovered she couldn't speak, that emotion had, for just a few seconds, closed her throat.

No doubt sensing that—and that she wouldn't approve if he discombobulated her for too long—Devil's lips curved and he looked ahead.

Released, she drew breath, then fell in beside him as, twining her arm with his, he led her back into the crowd.

They wended their way around their guests, their family, their close friends, exchanging comments and, often, looking ahead, prognosticating on the future.

Momentarily distracted by the sight of a laughing line of younger children dancing through the crowd, they were standing at the edge of the gathering, not far from the toddlers and infants in the nursemaid's crèche, within sight of the cricket match on the side lawn, and the group of girls now making daisy-chains nearby, when the older children returned from their walk.

Both Devil and Honoria noticed, looked.

Took in the confident strides, the energy, the inherent power.

Devil smiled, every inch the proud patriarch. "That's our future—the future of this house, the next generation."

"It is." Honoria raised her head. "And they're healthy and strong, and know the value of kinship and friendship, and . . ."

When she said nothing more, Devil tipped his head to look into her face. "And what?"

A heartbeat passed, then, lips curving, Honoria took his arm; turning him, she cast him a measuring glance. "And they're planning."

Predictably, he frowned and looked back at the group. "That's good?"

She patted his arm, waited until he looked back at her to say, "It means they're looking ahead—that they're facing forward and seeking to shape their own futures. And, yes, that is, indeed, how it should be. How they need to be."

Faintly disgruntled, he allowed her to steer him back into the crowd, but then murmured, "And what will our role in that future be?"

Facing forward, confident herself, Honoria smiled gently and murmured back, "Our role is to keep the foundation rock-solid, steady and sure, and otherwise . . . learn to let them go."

She knew that the latter would find little favor with him and his peers. It would go against their ingrained instincts, but that was, indeed, the next battle they would face.

Eventually, however, the Duke of St. Ives drew in a deep breath and asked, "So by your estimation, all is well?"

And, still smiling, his duchess replied, "In my estimation, everything is exactly as it should be in our family's world."

Read on for an excerpt of

Where the Heart Leads

The first volume in
The Casebook of Barnaby Adair
By No. 1 New York Times bestselling author
Stephanie Laurens
Available now from Piatkus

The second and third volumes of
The Casebook of Barnaby Adair
will be released in 2014

November 1835
London

"Thank you, Mostyn." Slumped at ease in an armchair before the fire in the parlor of his fashionable lodgings in Jermyn Street, Barnaby Adair, third son of the Earl of Cothelstone, lifted the crystal tumbler from the salver his man offered. "I won't need anything further."

"Very good, sir. I'll wish you a good night." The epitome of his calling, Mostyn bowed and silently withdrew.

Straining his ears, Barnaby heard the door shut. He smiled, sipped. Mostyn had been foisted on him by his mother when he'd first come up to town in the fond hope that the man would instil some degree of tractability into a son who, as she frequently declared, was ungovernable. Yet despite Mostyn's rigid adherence to the mores of class distinction and his belief in the deference due to the son of an earl, master and man had quickly reached an accommodation. Barnaby could no longer imagine being in London without the succor Mostyn provided, largely, as with the glass of fine brandy in his hand, without prompting.

Over the years, Mostyn had mellowed. Or perhaps both of them had. Regardless, theirs was now a very comfortable household.

Stretching his long legs toward the hearth, crossing his ankles, sinking his chin on his cravat, Barnaby studied the polished toes of his boots, bathed in the light of the crackling flames. All *should* have been well in his world, but. . . .

He was comfortable yet . . . restless.

At peace—no, *wrapped* in blessed peace—yet dissatisfied.

It wasn't as if the last months hadn't been successful. After more than nine months of careful sleuthing he'd exposed a cadre of young gentlemen, all from ton families, who, not content with using dens of inquity had thought it a lark to run them. He'd delivered enough proof to charge and convict them despite their station. It had been a difficult, long-drawn and arduous case; its successful conclusion had earned him grateful accolades from the peers who oversaw London's Metropolitan Police Force.

On hearing the news his mother would no doubt have primmed her lips, perhaps evinced an acid wish that he would develop as much interest in fox-hunting as in villain-hunting, but she wouldn't—couldn't—say more, not with his father being one of the aforementioned peers.

In any modern society, justice needed to be seen to be served even-handedly, without fear or favor, despite those among the ton who refused to believe that Parliament's laws applied to them. The Prime Minister himself had been moved to compliment him over this latest triumph.

Raising his glass, Barnaby sipped. The success had been sweet, yet had left him strangely hollow. Unfulfilled in some unexpected way. Certainly he'd anticipated feeling happier, rather than empty and peculiarly rudderless, aimlessly drifting now he no longer had a case to absorb him, to challenge his ingenuity and fill his time.

Perhaps his mood was simply a reflection of the season— the closing phases of another year, the time when cold fogs descended and polite society fled to the warmth of ancestral hearths, there to prepare for the coming festive season and the attendant revels. For him this time of year had always been difficult—difficult to find any viable excuse to avoid his mother's artfully engineered social gatherings.

She'd married both his elder brothers and his sister, Melissa, far too easily; in him, she'd met her Waterloo, yet she continued more doggedly and indefatigably than Napoleon. She was determined to see him, the last of her brood, suitably wed, and was fully prepared to bring to bear whatever weapons were necessary to achieve that goal.

Despite being at loose ends, he didn't want to deliver himself up at the Cothelstone Castle gates, a candidate for his mother's matrimonial machinations. What if it snowed and he couldn't escape?

Unfortunately, even villains tended to hibernate over winter.

A sharp *rat-a-tat-tat* shattered the comfortable silence.

Glancing at the parlor door, Barnaby realized he'd heard a carriage on the cobbles. The rattle of wheels had ceased outside his residence. He listened as Mostyn's measured tread passed the parlor on the way to the front door. Who could be calling at such an hour—a quick glance at the mantelpiece clock confirmed it was after eleven—and on such a night? Beyond the heavily curtained windows the night was bleak, a dense chill fog wreathing the streets, swallowing houses and converting familiar streetscapes into ghostly gothic realms.

No one would venture out on such a night without good reason.

Voices, muted, reached him. It appeared Mostyn was engaged in dissuading whoever was attempting to disrupt his master's peace.

Abruptly the voices fell silent.

A moment later the door opened and Mostyn entered, carefully closing the door behind him. One glance at Mostyn's tight lips and studiously blank expression informed Barnaby that Mostyn did not approve of whomever had called. Even more interesting was the transparent implication that Mostyn had been routed—efficiently and comprehensively—in his attempt to deny the visitor.

"A . . . lady to see you, sir. A Miss—"

"Penelope Ashford."

The crisp, determined tones had both Barnaby and Mostyn looking to the door—which now stood open, swung wide to admit a lady in a dark, severe yet fashionable pelisse. A sable-lined muff dangled from one wrist and her hands were encased in fur-edged leather gloves.

Lustrous mahogany hair, pulled into a knot at the back of her head, gleamed as she crossed the room with a grace and self-confidence that screamed her station even more than her delicate, quintessentially aristocratic features. Features that were animated by so much determination, so much sheer will, that the force of her personality seemed to roll like a wave before her.

Mostyn stepped back as she neared.

His eyes never leaving her, Barnaby unhurriedly uncrossed his legs and rose. "Miss Ashford."

An exceptional pair of dark brown eyes framed by finely wrought gold-rimmed spectacles fixed on his face. "Mr. Adair. We met nearly two years ago, at Morwellan Park in the ballroom at Charlie and Sarah's wedding." Halting two paces away, she studied him, as if estimating the quality of his memory. "We spoke briefly if you recall."

She didn't offer her hand. Barnaby looked down into her uptilted face—her head barely cleared his shoulder—and found he remembered her surprisingly well. "You asked if I was the one who investigates crimes."

She smiled—brilliantly. "Yes. That's right."

Barnaby blinked; he felt a trifle winded. He could, he realized, recall how, all those months ago, her small fingers had felt in his. They'd merely shaken hands, yet he could remember it perfectly; even now, his fingers tingled with tactile memory.

She'd obviously made an impression on him even if he

hadn't been so aware of it at the time. At the time he'd been focused on another case, and had been more intent on deflecting her interest than on her.

Since he'd last seen her, she'd grown. Not taller. Indeed, he wasn't sure she'd gained inches anywhere; she was as neatly rounded as his memory painted her. Yet she'd gained in stature, in self-assurance and confidence; although he doubted she'd ever been lacking in the latter, she was now the sort of lady any fool would recognize as a natural force of nature, to be crossed at one's peril.

Little wonder she'd rolled up Mostyn.

Her smile had faded. She'd been examining him openly; in most others he would have termed it brazenly, but she seemed to be evaluating him intellectually rather than physically.

Rosy lips, distractingly lush, firmed, as if she'd made some decision.

Curious, he tilted his head. "To what do I owe this visit?"

This highly irregular, not to say potentially scandalous visit. She was a gently bred lady of marriageable age, calling on a single gentleman who was in no way related very late at night. Alone. Entirely unchaperoned.

He should protest and send her away. Mostyn certainly thought so.

Her fine dark eyes met his. Squarely, without the slightest hint of guile or trepidation. "I want you to help me solve a crime."

He held her gaze.

She returned the favor.

A pregnant moment passed, then he gestured elegantly to the other armchair. "Please sit. Perhaps you'd like some refreshment?"

Her smile—it transformed her face from vividly attractive to stunning—flashed as she moved to the chair facing his. "Thank you, but no. I require nothing but your time." She waved Mostyn away. "You may go."

Mostyn stiffened. He cast an outraged glance at Barnaby.

Battling a grin, Barnaby endorsed the order with a nod. Mostyn didn't like it, but departed, bowing himself out, but leaving the door ajar. Barnaby noted it, but said nothing. Mostyn knew he was hunted, often quite inventively, by young ladies; he clearly believed Miss Ashford might be such a schemer. Barnaby knew better. Penelope Ashford might scheme with the best of them, but marriage would not be her goal.

While she arranged her muff on her lap, he sank back into his armchair and studied her anew.

She was the most unusual young lady he'd ever encountered.

He'd decided that even before she said, "Mr. Adair, I need your help to find four missing boys, and stop any more being kidnapped."

Penelope raised her eyes and locked them on Barnaby Adair's face. And tried her damnedest not to see. When she'd determined to call on him, she hadn't imagined he— his appearance—would have the slightest effect on her. Why would she? No man had ever made her feel breathless, so why should he? It was distinctly annoying.

Golden hair clustering in wavy curls about a well-shaped head, strong, aquiline features and cerulean blue eyes that held a piercing intelligence were doubtless interesting enough, yet quite aside from his features there was something about him, about his presence, that was playing on her nerves in a disconcerting way.

Why he should affect her at all was a mystery. He was tall, with a long-limbed, rangy build, yet he was no taller than her brother Luc, and while his shoulders were broad, they were no broader than her brother-in-law Simon's. And he was certainly not prettier than either Luc or Simon, although he could easily hold his own in the handsome stakes; she'd heard Barnaby Adair described as an Adonis and had to concede the point.

All of which was entirely by the by and she had no clue why she was even noticing.

She focused instead on the numerous questions she could see forming behind his blue eyes. "The reason I am here, and not a host of outraged parents, is because the boys in question are paupers and foundlings."

He frowned.

Stripping off her gloves, she grimaced lightly. "I'd better start at the beginning."

He nodded. "That would probably facilitate matters—namely my understanding—significantly."

She laid her gloves on top of her muff. She wasn't sure she appreciated his tone, but decided to ignore it. "I don't know if you're aware of it, but my sister Portia—she's now married to Simon Cynster—three other ladies of the ton, and I, established the Foundling House opposite the Foundling Hospital in Bloomsbury. That was back in '30. The House has been in operation ever since, taking in foundlings, mostly from the East End, and training them as maids, footmen, and more recently in various trades."

"You were asking Sarah about her orphanage's training programs when we last met."

"Indeed." She hadn't known he'd overheard that. "My older sister Anne, now Anne Carmarthen, is also involved, but since their marriages, with their own households to run, both Anne and lately Portia have had to curtail the time they spend at the Foundling House. The other three ladies likewise have many calls on their time. Consequently, at present I am in charge of overseeing the day-to-day administration of the place. It's in that capacity that I'm here tonight."

Folding her hands over her gloves, she met his eyes, held his steady gaze. "The normal procedure is for children to be formally placed in the care of the Foundling House by the authorities, or by their last surviving guardian.

"The latter is quite common. What usually occurs is that a dying relative, recognizing that their ward will soon be alone in the world, contacts us and we visit and make arrangements. The child usually stays with their guardian until the last, then, on the guardian's death, we're informed, usually by helpful neighbors, and we return and fetch the orphan and take him or her to the Foundling House."

He nodded, signifying all to that point was clear.

Drawing breath, she went on, feeling her lungs tighten, her diction growing crisp as anger resurged, "Over the last month, on four separate occasions we've arrived to fetch away a boy, only to discover some man has been before us. He told the neighbors he was a local official, but there is no central authority that collects orphans. If there were, we'd know."

Adair's blue gaze had grown razor-sharp. "Is it always the same man?"

"From all I've heard, it could be. But equally, it might not be."

She waited while he mulled over that. She bit her tongue, forced herself to sit still and not fidget, and instead watch the concentration in his face.

Her inclination was to forge ahead, to demand he act and tell him how. She was used to directing, to taking charge and ordering all as she deemed fit. She was usually right in her thinking, and generally people were a great deal better off if they simply did as she said. But . . . she needed Barnaby Adair's help, and instinct was warning her, stridently, to tread carefully. To guide rather than push.

To persuade rather than dictate.

His gaze had grown distant, but now abruptly refocused on her face. "You take boys and girls. Is it only boys who've gone missing?"

"Yes." She nodded for emphasis. "We've accepted more girls than boys in recent months, but it's only boys this man has taken."

A moment passed. "He's taken four—tell me about each. Start from the first—everything you know, every detail, no matter how apparently inconsequential."

Barnaby watched as she delved into her memory; her dark gaze turned inward, her features smoothed, losing some of their characteristic vitality.

She drew breath; her gaze fixed on the fire as if she were reading from the flames. "The first was from Chicksand Street in Spitalfields, off Brick Lane north of the White-chapel Road. He was eight years old, or so his uncle told us. He, the uncle, was dying, and . . ."

Barnaby listened as she, not entirely to his surprise, did precisely as he'd requested and recited the details of each occurrence, chapter and verse. Other than an occasional minor query, he didn't have to prod her or her memory.

He was accustomed to dealing with ladies of the ton, to interrogating young ladies whose minds skittered and wandered around subjects, and flitted and danced around facts, so that it took the wisdom of Solomon and the patience of Job to gain any understanding of what they actually knew.

Penelope Ashford was a different breed. He'd heard that she was something of a firebrand, one who paid scant attention to social restraints if said restraints stood in her way. He'd heard her described as too intelligent for her own good, and direct and forthright to a fault, that combination of traits being popularly held to account for her unmarried state.

As she was remarkably attractive in an unusual way—not pretty or beautiful but so vividly alive she effortlessly drew men's eyes—as well as being extremely well-connected, the daughter of a viscount, and with her brother Luc, the current title holder, eminently wealthy and able to dower her more than appropriately, that popular judgment might well be correct. Yet her sister Portia had recently married Simon Cynster, and while Portia might perhaps be more subtle in her dealings, Barnaby recalled that the Cynster ladies, judges he trusted in such matters, saw little difference between Portia and Penelope beyond Penelope's directness.

And, if he was remembering aright, her utterly implacable will.

From what little he'd seen of the sisters, he, too, would have said that Portia would bend, or at least agree to negotiate, far earlier than Penelope.

"And just as with the others, when we went to Herb Lane to fetch Dick this morning, he was gone. He'd been collected by this mystery man at seven o'clock, barely after dawn."

Her story concluded, she shifted her dark, compelling eyes from the flames to his face.

Barnaby held her gaze for a moment, then slowly nodded. "So somehow these people—let's assume it's one group collecting these boys—"

"I can't see it being more than one group. We've never had this happen before, and now four instances in less than a month, and all with the same modus operandi." Brows raised, she met his eyes.

Somewhat tersely, he nodded. "Precisely. As I was saying, these people, whoever they are, seem to know of your potential charges—"

"Before you suggest that they might be learning of the boys through someone at the Foundling House, let me assure you that's highly unlikely. If you knew the people involved, you'd understand why I'm so sure of that. And indeed, although I've come to you with our four cases, there's nothing to say other newly orphaned boys in the East End aren't also disappearing. Most orphans aren't brought to our attention. There may be many more vanishing, but who is there who would sound any alarm?"

Barnaby stared at her while the scenario she was describing took shape in his mind.

"I had hoped," she said, the light glinting off her spectacles as she glanced down and smoothed her gloves, "that you might agree to look into this latest disappearance, seeing as Dick was whisked away only this morning. I do realize that you generally investigate crimes involving the ton, but I wondered, as it is November and most of us have upped stakes for the country, whether you might have time to consider our problem." Looking up, she met his gaze; there was nothing remotely diffident in her eyes. "I could, of course, pursue the matter myself—"

Barnaby only just stopped himself from reacting.

"But I thought enlisting someone with more experience in such matters might lead to a more rapid resolution."

Penelope held his gaze and hoped he was as quick-witted as he was purported to be. Then again, in her experience, it rarely hurt to be blunt. "To be perfectly clear, Mr. Adair, I am here seeking aid in pursuing our lost charges, rather than merely wishing to inform someone of their disappearance and thereafter wash my hands of them. I fully intend to search for Dick and the other three boys until I find them. Not being a simpleton, I would prefer to have beside me someone with experience of crime and the necessary investigative methods. Moreover, while through our work we naturally have contacts in the East End, few if any of those move among the criminal elements, so my ability to gain information in that arena is limited."

Halting, she searched his face. His expression gave little away; his broad brow, straight brown brows, the strong, well-delineated cheekbones, the rather austere lines of cheek and jaw, remained set and unrevealing.

She spread her hands. "I've described our situation—will you help us?"

To her irritation, he didn't immediately reply. Didn't leap in, goaded to action by the notion of her tramping through the East End by herself.

He didn't, however, refuse. For a long moment, he studied her, his expression unreadable—long enough for her to wonder if he'd seen through her ploy—then he shifted, resettling his shoulders against the chair, and gestured to her in invitation. "How do you imagine our investigation would proceed?"

She hid her smile. "I thought, if you were free, you might visit the Foundling House tomorrow, to get some idea of the way we work and the type of children we take in. Then . . ."

Barnaby listened while she outlined an eminently rational strategy that would expose him to the basic facts, enough to ascertain where an investigation might lead, and consequently how best to proceed.

Watching the sensible, logical words fall from her ruby lips—still lush and ripe, still distracting—only confirmed that Penelope Ashford was dangerous. Every bit as dangerous as her reputation suggested, possibly more.

In his case undoubtedly more, given his fascination with her lips.

In addition, she was offering him something no other young lady had ever thought to wave before his nose.

A case. Just when he was in dire need of one.

"Once we've talked to the neighbors who saw Dick taken away, I'm hoping you'll be able to suggest some way forward from there."

Her lips stopped moving. He raised his gaze to her eyes. "Indeed." He hesitated; it was patently obvious that she had every intention of playing an active role in the ensuing investigation. Given he knew her family, he was unquestionably honor-bound to dissuade her from such a reckless endeavor, yet equally unquestionably any suggestion she retreat to the hearth and leave him to chase the villains would meet with stiff opposition. He inclined his head. "As it happens I'm free tomorrow. Perhaps I could meet you at the Foundling House in the morning?"

He'd steer her out of the investigation after he had all the facts, after he'd learned everything she knew about this strange business.

She smiled brilliantly, once again disrupting his thoughts.

"Excellent!" Penelope gathered her gloves and muff, and stood. She'd gained what she wanted; it was time to leave. Before he could say anything she didn't want to hear. Best not to get into any argument now. Not yet.

He rose and waved her to the door. She led the way, pulling on her gloves. He had the loveliest hands she'd ever seen on a man, long-fingered, elegant and utterly distracting. She'd remembered them from before, which was why she hadn't offered to shake his hand.

He walked beside her across his front hall. "Is your carriage outside?"

"Yes." Halting before the front door, she glanced up at him. "It's waiting outside the house next door."

His lips twitched. "I see." His man was hovering; he waved him back and reached for the doorknob. "I'll walk you to it."

She inclined her head. When he opened the door, she walked out onto the narrow front porch. Her nerves flickered as he joined her; large and rather overpoweringly male, he escorted her down the three steps to the pavement, then along to where her brother's town carriage stood, the coachman patient and resigned on the box.

Adair reached for the carriage door, opened it and offered his hand. Holding her breath, she gave him her fingers—and tried hard not to register the sensation of her slender digits being engulfed by his much larger ones, tried not to notice the warmth of his firm clasp as he helped her up into the carriage.

And failed.

She didn't—couldn't—breathe until he released her hand. She sank onto the leather seat, managed a smile and a nod. "Thank you, Mr. Adair. I'll see you tomorrow morning."

Through the enveloping gloom he studied her, then he raised his hand in salute, stepped back and closed the door.

The coachman jigged his reins and the carriage jerked forward, then settled to a steady roll. With a sigh, Penelope sat back, and smiled into the darkness. Satisfied, and a trifle smug. She'd recruited Barnaby Adair to her cause, and despite her unprecedented attack of sensibility had managed the encounter without revealing her affliction.

All in all, her night had been a success.

Barnaby stood in the street, in the wreathing fog, and watched the carriage roll away. Once the rattle of its wheels had faded, he grinned and turned back to this door.

Climbing his front steps, he realized his mood had lifted. His earlier despondency had vanished, replaced with a keen anticipation for what the morrow would bring.

And for that he had Penelope Ashford to thank.

Not only had she brought him a case, one outside his normal arena and therefore likely to challenge him and expand his knowledge, but even more importantly that case was one not even his mother would disapprove of him pursuing.

Mentally composing the letter he would pen to his parent first thing the next morning, he entered his house whistling beneath his breath, and let Mostyn bolt the door behind him.

Do you love historical fiction?

Want the chance to hear news about your favourite authors (and the chance to win free books)?

Mary Balogh
Charlotte Betts
Jessica Blair
Frances Brody
Gaelen Foley
Elizabeth Hoyt
Eloisa James
Lisa Kleypas
Stephanie Laurens
Claire Lorrimer
Sarah MacLean
Amanda Quick
Julia Quinn

Then visit the Piatkus website and blog
www.piatkus.co.uk | www.piatkusbooks.net

And follow us on Facebook and Twitter
www.facebook.com/piatkusfiction | www.twitter.com/piatkusbooks

piatkus